TRAILER PARK PRINCE

TRAILER PARK PRINCE

Andre L. Bradley

"I don't believe an accident of birth makes people sisters or brothers. It makes them siblings, gives them mutuality of parentage. Sisterhood and brotherhood is a condition people have to work at."
Maya Angelou

"Equality is the soul of liberty; there is, in fact, no liberty without it."
Frances Wright

<u>PART ONE</u>

TO PRETEND SPRINGTIME IN SUMMER

CHAPTER ONE
NOAN

IT WAS THE LIGHT THAT CAUGHT MY ATTENTION, not the smell of smoke sneaking through the open window, like last time, nor the heat the time before that. The effect was the same: Uncle Tobin, my twin brother Jormon, and I stood in our pajamas, staring out the window at a wooden cross burning in front of our trailer. Attached to it was a straw effigy of a person already catching fire around its legs and midsection, and though the shoddy craftsmanship didn't offer any fine details, I knew it represented one of us. A Kaydan. An outsider. Yeah, we looked like them in almost every way, but they always managed to remind us we didn't belong here. It was the third occurrence in as many weeks, and I imagined the folks around town—the human folks—hadn't seen anything, heard anything, or would even want to discuss the incident. That's how it always went.

Uncle whispered a few words, and the fire dissipated. He whispered a few more and the charred construction dissolved into nothing, all that remained was a circle of blackened grass where the cross once stood.

"It's starting again," Jormon said.

"Did it ever end?" I asked. He shrugged.

"If they keep this up, there won't be any trees left by the end of summer," Uncle said. His attempt to lighten the mood fell flat, but I appreciated the effort. A thought flashed to mind that we should burn the whole of Gordonia Park and every other pine tree in

Georgia, down to the last splinter. But without any wood to make crosses, the only thing left to set on fire would be us.

I looked at the surrounding mobile homes to see which of our neighbors would rush over to check on us and which ones would be delighted by our misfortune from behind their tacky curtains. All Kaydans. All cowards if you asked me.

"Is Nana Lura okay?" I asked.

"They threw a brick through her window last time and she slept through that," Jormon said. "I'm sure she's fine. Besides, she's supposed to be the one making sure *we* are okay."

"Go check on her. Just in case," Uncle said.

"In case of what? She died in her sleep?"

"In case she's awake and waiting for one of you to check on her," Uncle said in a sterner tone.

"Noan, go check on her," Jormon said.

"You're the oldest. You go," I told him, at which point he mocked me with childish imitation. I wouldn't have gotten so annoyed if he were bad at it, but his imitations were extremely accurate. Always close enough to be unmistakably me but distorted enough so that everyone found it hilarious.

"How about you both go?" Uncle said. "On your way, cut out all the bickering. Princes don't bicker, not even spoiled ones like yourselves. When you're done, grab your shoes and come with me outside. You're both seventeen now. It's time I teach you how to dissipate fire."

We peeked in on Nana Lura, still in bed with the covers pulled over her. No sooner had we opened the door, she raised a hand in the air and waved us off.

Minutes later, Jormon, Uncle, and I trod in silence beneath the waning crescent moon until the gravel trail gave way to freshly mowed grass just at the edge of the woods. Even this far from the trailer, hints of the recent cross burning were carried in the soft breeze.

Jormon, more comfortable with his body than I had ever been, removed his ratty shirt and fashioned it around his head like a bandana, tucking his dark hair beneath the dingy folds of fabric. His lean body glistened in the moonlight as sweat formed over the peaks and dents of his muscled, brown torso and illuminated his *sheriaan*—the copper-colored lines that spiraled from our hands toward our shoulders. They were the solitary feature that differentiated Kaydans from humans. He cracked his knuckles and rolled his head one way and then the other, then bent over to stretch his hamstrings as if he was gearing up to run away from the task to come.

Ten years later and this is where we are, I thought.

It wasn't supposed to happen the way it did. None of it. Like most escape parties, ours was supposed to be small: my parents, Uncle Tobin, Nana Lura, Jormon, and me, Noan Ladoan. The Red Cloaks had tracked us to the last safe spot my parents knew and, after months of hiding, nowhere on our planet was safe. Our arrival was to be clandestine: one portal connecting our home planet Kayda to Earth, small enough for the six of us to squeeze through, and open briefly enough not to arouse curiosities on either end. Earth was supposed to be a haven, light-years from Kayda, a place where being born a twin was not punishable by death, where our parents could be just our parents and not our abettors, and where we could exist in a world far from the long reach of the Red Cloaks. But, like most great plans, it didn't work out. Instead of a sneaky side-door exit, we got a sky-splitting, mega-sized rift. It turned our 'under-the-radar' move into a full-blown spectacle, with thousands of Kaydans spilling through. Earth was supposed to be this great hideout, but it didn't exactly roll out the welcome mat in the way we'd hoped.

First, the military came and, within six months, over fifty thousand Kaydans died in battle. We learned the hard way that our supernatural powers hardly compare to that of an M-16 assault rifle. A *mustedi*, a master in their use of powers, can get shot in the back of the head as easily as anyone else.

After the war ended, the Riders in His Holy Name formed as the premier hate group founded on the principle that Kaydans were an abomination in God's eye. They hunted us like dogs for two years and the government had but one thing to say about it. "Murder only applies to people, and Kaydans aren't people."

Now, there was this crap. Being an out and proud Rider fell out of popularity years ago, but being a midnight bigot never went out of style. Apparently, neither did burning crosses. If there was anything to loath about spending weekends and summers with Uncle in Lyons, Georgia, it was this. Not our staying in Gray Flats trailer park, but the hatred we couldn't seem to escape, even in our own home.

Uncle whispered something and a soft green glow sheened along the intertwining loops of his *sheriaan,* just above his left wrist. The light danced and jigged along the beautiful patterns until it moved from his wrist and poured into his open palm, and when it died out, a leatherbound book rested in its place. The book fell open to just the right page, and Uncle read aloud a passage about fire and energy transference. I shook away all thoughts of the past and focused on the lesson. He conjured a cross of his own and set it on fire. He looked at Jormon and me. I whispered a few words, and the fire dissipated. I whispered a few more and the charred construction dissolved into nothing, and all that remained was a circle of blackened grass.

A soft knock on my bedroom door woke me up. It was still dark outside. I'd only been asleep for an hour, maybe. My heartbeat quickened at the thought that something else had happened. Was it another cross? Did something happen to one of the neighbors?

The knocking grew louder, and when I didn't respond, the caller entered without an invitation.

It was Jormon. "Dad's here," he whispered. "He's arguing with Uncle Tobin about something."

"About what?" Jormon gave a look that told me my guess was as good as any. If Father had come all the way down from his perch in Washington, D.C., it was serious. Maybe serious enough for him to snatch us back to the nation's capital. As much as I hated enduring the stares and whispers of the trailer park locals, I hated living under my father's keen eye even more. I wouldn't go back, not so soon. It was barely July. My stomach sank, and I hoped this was about something else.

We left my room, tiptoeing down the hall like escaping convicts, and made for the parlor. The door was open, and a voice shot toward us as loud as a cannon. We froze in place. We'd get more information skulking outside the doorway than walking in on the conversation.

"This will only make things worse," Uncle yelled at my father, King Rosh. "I agree with you, we cannot stagnate, not in these times. However, this form of progress comes too soon. Integration with humans? Are you serious? People are going to get killed." They weren't talking about taking us back to D.C., but Jormon was right. What they were discussing sounded serious.

We inched closer to the parlor.

"We've been here for what? Ten years, now? This hardly comes too soon," my father boomed back at him. "Integration is the only way. As long as they see us as separate, they'll never see us as equal."

"Why involve the twins in this?" Uncle said. "Most days, I barely want to be out there with humans, and you want to put the boys in the thick of it? Your own sons, Rosh. Be serious."

"I am being serious. You stay down here in Gray Flats with the rest of our people. You don't see what I see in D.C. There's talk."

"About what?"

"War."

Uncle scoffed. "Oh, please. No idiot would want that again."

"You must not know idiots. Let me tell you, the candidate running for the American presidency is a piece of work, and if he gets his way, I give us a year before we're back at war."

"Which is why we should go back," Uncle shouted, and I knew what he meant. Go back to Kayda. Go back to our home planet. Go back to where we belong. It was a sentiment a lot of folks shared, but most of them were humans. I'd never heard Uncle talk like that before.

"No! I made that clear a long time ago."

"You never explained why. You asked me to protect the *miftah*, and I did. You asked me to leave your side and stay here with our people, and I did. I didn't need to know why back then, but I need to know now."

"Because I am your king, and I say we stay," my father shouted.

I'd never heard them argue like this. I turned to Jormon. His eyes raised as open as mine, and he bit at the side of his lip. "What's a *miftah*?" he mouthed.

"It's the thing that created the portal that brought us here," I said just as quietly.

Ice sloshed against a glass. Of course, Father was drinking. Bourbon, I bet.

"Let them go to the Academy. Jormon will set a great example there, and it's what Noan always wanted."

Ice sloshed again as Father took another sip. "It's what you always wanted for him."

"What's that supposed to mean?"

Another sip. "I'm his father, not you."

"Then you should act like it."

Silence. My heart leaped into my throat, and I had to swallow it down. I couldn't breathe. If my father and uncle fought, we would never be able to visit Uncle again. Father would punish him by keeping us away, which would be more of a punishment for me than for anyone. Jormon enjoyed living in Father's shadow. Father was different with him. Jormon was the Crown Prince who could do no wrong. When Father saw me, it was as if he was staring at every regret he ever had.

I had to stop this before it went any further. I started down the hall, and Jormon's strong arm flew across my chest. He shook his head, warning me not to interfere.

"That didn't come out as I intended," Uncle said. "I only meant that you should listen to them more. Take a break from being their king and just be their dad. Noan needs this. Jormon does, too."

"Jormon will do as I say," Father said, elevating his voice slightly.

"It won't make him happy."

"Who cares about happiness?"

That could've easily been the family motto. Even after feeling protected, we were never allowed to feel happy. Under Father, it was all duty. Study this government or get to know that group of people, all done in the name of being representatives of Kaydans on Earth. Under Uncle, it was all education. Study this *sahdr* or read this ancient text. We were probably better for their teachings, but it didn't make us happy.

Father continued. "A few months ago, I saw Jormon chatting it up with the neighbor boy, some human kid about his age. Dev was his name. Or maybe Dave." A pause stretched out as long as train smoke. "I didn't like what I saw, and if you think that's me being a king and not a father, so be it."

That took an unexpected turn. As I wondered which neighbor boy Father could be talking about and how long he's been keeping this observation to himself, a firm hand landed on my shoulder. I turned and was face-to-face with Nana Lura.

"This conversation was not meant for you," she said, and a sudden force wrapped around me and squeezed. I looked over at Jormon just as the force hoisted us from the ground, spinning us until we were shoulder to shoulder, our elbows knocking sharply against each other. Propelled by her power, we stumbled toward the room where my father and uncle awaited. I tried to free my arms, but it was useless.

"Nana Lura, is that you? We're in here," Uncle called. We were shoved through the door, suspended a foot above the floor.

Busted.

Nana Lura released us from her telekinetic hold, and we landed softly on our feet. I rubbed my shoulders where her grasp was strongest, then my elbow, which hurt just as bad.

Our faces were flushed with embarrassment from being caught eavesdropping, but we acted with as much dignity as we could.

"May *Heemrah* guide you far, my king," Jormon greeted in *Maerinish*, moving his palm from his chest toward our father, sending forward brilliant specks the color of midnight blue as he extended his energy to our father. I did the same, sending specks in nocturnal purple hues.

"May *Zereq* shine you home, my princes," he returned, sending specks of jade and ash from his chest that intertwined with our particles before fading into nothing. Through the connection, I felt his anger and irritation, and I know he sensed my apprehension.

Nana Lura entered the room but gave no obeisance to my father or uncle. "They were nosing about in the hall. I don't know for how long." Nana Lura was my mother's caregiver when she was a little girl and had been ours, too. She spoke too loudly on account of her failing hearing, and Father, who never liked her, dismissed her with a curt wave of the hand. She walked away as quietly as she had when she snuck up on us.

"Dad, what's going on?" Jormon asked.

"It's nothing. Your uncle and I were disagreeing."

"You were yelling," I dared say.

"We were talking about the future," Uncle said.

Father finished the last of his drink, ice and all. "No more talking riddles, Tobin. Here's the truth as plain as I can put it: Integration will happen, and starting this fall, both of you will start school here in Georgia."

It was the closest I'd ever been to getting punched in the gut, and it hurt as much as the real thing. "Father, you can't be serious.

All I want is to go to the Academy. It's *all* I ever wanted. You know that." I'd never spoken to my father this way.

Father waved me off as easily as if I were any other Kaydan and not his son. "Calm down, Noan. You'll still get to study *sahdr* under you uncle, don't you worry about your precious dream of becoming a *mustedi*."

"It's not about that," I said. "Well, it's about…It's about more than that."

"Don't keep us all in suspense, Prince Noan. Tell us what more it's about."

"It's about…" I wouldn't dare say the rest. It was about needing to be free. I'd spent every waking moment of my life in shadow, and whether it was the shadows of our shared past or my brother's shadow, it was all equally dark. I needed to be away from it all. Jormon was never meant to go to the Academy. He had a shadow of his own to follow. Going to the Academy meant being free of him, my twin, the perfect reflection who shows me just how much I'll never measure up.

"We're waiting," Father said. Everyone stared at me in anticipation.

"Never mind," I said.

"You see? The poor kid doesn't know what he wants," Father said, and continued discussing how the transition to adolescent mediocrity would work.

I couldn't hear him, though. I couldn't breathe. My heart sank into my stomach, and I didn't know whether I was going to crap my pants or puke on the floor. In just a few words, the future I'd imagined for myself, the future where I'm no longer the shadow child, was ripped from the realm of possibility and replaced with a new one. It played out in my head as clearly as if I'd already lived it. In this new future, I would forever be tied to my brother, the lovable prince who could do no wrong. I wouldn't be a great *mustedi*, capable of protecting my people. I would be my brother's shadow. I would be my father's whipping post. I would be my uncle's thing to pity.

My esophagus flexed, and a bitter acidity rose to the back of my throat, filled my mouth, and erupted onto the carpet.

"You never loved me." The words were out of me before I knew I said them, thickening the air along with the stench of vomit. How long had I been waiting to say them? My whole life? Since I learned what a shadow child was and that I was one of them? Since internalizing it was all my fault. Everything. Our entire race living like refugees, stuffed into a trailer park no bigger than a football field. Jormon is respected for being the crown prince, and I'm his stupid twin, the one who should never have been born.

My thoughts spiraled, and my mouth moved. I was saying words, but I couldn't hear them. Blood rushed to my head and my ears rang, and all around me, the world thudded. I yelled my every thought, but all I took in was the twisting and distorting of the surrounding faces. Father's lips danced and puckered, flinging spit with every other word. Uncle's head nodded from side to side as he waved his arms in front of his chest. "No," all the motion seemed to say. "You've gone too far." Jormon positioned himself between my father and me, arms extended to stop my father from getting too close. What was I saying? What could I say to make my father even angrier than I was?

CHAPTER TWO
JORMON

IT WAS THE LIGHT THAT WOKE ME UP, NOT THE sound of the birds or the smell of food climbing the stairs and barging through my door. The effect was the same: a somber me, lying in bed thinking of the heavy revelations Dad shared last night and feeling sick about it. I could live with not going to the Academy. What I couldn't stomach was that Dad, after seeing me speak with Dav Shah one time, suspected I was gay and wanted to change that. How closely had he been watching me?

After Dad left last night, I snuck in three glasses of whiskey, came to my room, and let the evening's highlights run through my head on a loop until they all blurred into one overwhelming message. No, to the Academy. Yes, to high school. No, to being gay. Yes, to being unhappy for the rest of my life.

Noan wouldn't want to be alone in his feelings after last night. This I knew. I fixed us two cups of coffee before easing my way into his room, using the time to forget about my own problems and focus on my little twin brother. He was still in bed. Daylight poured through his window and reflected off the white bed sheets.

He sensed he was not alone, and when he rolled over, I saw his eyes were still red.

"When did you come in?" he asked, his voice raspy.

"Just now. Here," I handed him a mug. "It's coffee, so don't go crazy with it."

He took a sip and clutched the mug to his chest. "Thanks. Was I awful last night?"

"You've had better moments. Dad won't hold any of it against you." That was a lie, but telling the truth would do no good.

"What did I say? Everything after Nana Lura threw us into the lion's den is a blur."

"You said—" I wanted to imitate his words exactly, but he wouldn't find the humor in it. "You told Dad you hated him, and you know he hates you, too. You called Uncle Tobin weak and said he should stand up to Dad. Oh, and when Dad said we have to live in Gray Flats to go to school here, you said, and I quote, 'I hate this fucking place. I hate all of you. You all should have let me die back on Kayda.' End quote."

"Really?" His face sank, and he rolled his eyes until they closed. "I don't know why I said that. I actually like it here. It's better than the alternative, I mean."

"Yeah, I thought it was pretty dramatic, too. But hey, you're playing the angsty high school teen role perfectly. Speaking of which, I'm super confused now. I thought you'd be over the moon—literally—for the chance to live with Uncle Tobin and get away from Dad. Yet, last night, you were being a little b—"

"Don't call me that."

"I was gonna say 'bitch.' You were being a little—"

"I know what you were gonna say, and I said don't call me that." Noan glared at me, and I raised my hands in surrender.

"I don't get it. Couldn't this still be part of your master plan? To earn your way into the Academy, prove you're *mustedi* material? Okay, so this isn't the straight path you envisioned, but it's still a path. Dad will have to respect you for this, and our people will, too."

He shook his head, his expression a mixture of anger and heartbreak.

"Noan," I said. I didn't know how to be supportive, but I hoped my soft tone was enough to convey my sympathy.

"They're scared of me. They really think if I get powerful enough, I'll do something to destroy them all. What am I supposed to do with that?" He shook his head slowly, as though he was playing my side of the conversation in his head without me. "He blames me, you know. Even if Uncle didn't say it last night, I know in my gut that Father blames me."

"We were just kids. No one can blame you for being born."

Noan rolled his eyes at me.

"Can I speak a hard truth?" I hoped he'd say no or make some annoying comment about last night, but he waved me on. "You had to know, even a little, that people can't stand you. I mean, you feel it, right? We're twins in a society where twins can't exist. You'd be naive to think everyone was okay with all of this."

"I know. I guess I thought I could change all that by going to the Academy."

"You think you have to prove yourself to these people, but you don't. As long as you know you're good, that's all that matters."

It was his turn to be dismissive. "Can we leave? I don't want to be here when Father gets back from his precious press conference." He took another sip of coffee.

"Sure. Let's go somewhere." I finished up my coffee and placed the mug on Noan's nightstand. "Maybe we can go shopping for furniture to put in your sad ass room. Look at this nightstand. It's hideous." It wasn't, really, but I hoped the insult would help shift the gears of this conversation.

"I have everything I need, thanks," he said, and he meant it. Noan had never valued possessions. When we first moved into the trailer, before Uncle Tobin transfigured the inside space, there were only two bedrooms. Noan and I shared a room that was barely big enough for a double bed, a dresser, and a nightstand. After the transfiguration, Noan kept the furniture from the original room, even though his new space was over three times the size. He would covet a book all day, as evident by the piles of them stacked against the wall but offer him a bookshelf and he'd look at you like you offered him a fart in a bag.

"Okay. Let's go somewhere else. You choose. But please don't say the library. I've read all the fiction, and I've had enough facts for one day."

"There's only so many places we're allowed to go in this town—the library, the diner… that about sums it up."

"Which is why integration is going to be so amazing!" I said with false cheer. I ripped the sheets off his lap before he could protest.

"We can go to Issek's. I could use another candle for my nightstand, maybe one that sings as it burns. I could use a song today."

"I can sing for you. What do you want to hear?" I started a version of *When We Were Young*, and Noan slid his hand across his throat.

"Stop, please. I can still taste the puke in my mouth from last night. I'm not trying to get sick again." He stood to get dressed, and a large hole in the side of his red underwear caught my eye.

"I'll get you a candle and a pack of underwear. Holes in your drawers? Really, Noan? You're a prince. Do better."

From inside his closet, he flung the worn underwear at me. *Helaqi*, I thought, and the underwear halted midair inches in front of my face. "If these dirty-ass drawers would've hit me in the face, Noan, I swear!" I flung them back in his direction, not caring if they landed in the laundry basket or not.

He came out of the closet with clothes just as raggedy. "I'm ready."

"Cool. Now, promise not to be mad at me for not being as upset as you."

"A candle won't make me forget you didn't have my back."

"I'm sorry. Noan, look at me. I'm really sorry. I mean it. I will never do anything like that again. I'll always have your back. I promise."

We left the house within the hour. Smells of breakfast drifted in sweet and savory ribbons from a nearby trailer—maple ham and burnt toast. The sun was still on its ascent, and its warm rays cut through the leaves of the surrounding pine trees, glinting wherever they found the morning dew.

As we were leaving Gray Flats, we passed a beat-up delivery van pulling in, driving slowly in search of a trailer. There were probably a hundred in total, each positioned to form an untidy grid, navigable along a network of gravel trails that branched off from a central driveway. It was established as an emergency housing village for Kaydans, but it remained empty until our family moved into one of the units. Now Gray Flats was like Little Kayda, our home away from home, a kingdom far, far away where we could be ourselves. All the tenants were Kaydan. There was something to be said about living among your own. We didn't get that living in D.C. with Dad, so maybe moving here for the school year wouldn't be so bad.

The walk into town took less than an hour. It was a direct line from Gray Flats to downtown Lyons, three miles distance traveled by a lone, two-lane road. Both sides were lined with neglected grass that grew past my bare calves, and further away from the road on either side were commercial pine forests.

Lyons had grown over the years, but not by much. Most of the citizens were local, but there was a growing contingent of people from all over the world who moved to the area after what the locals called "The Intrusion." Despite the increasing population, little was done to improve the city's commercial services, at least not in Lyons itself.

"Explain to me again why you don't fly?" Noan asked. He brushed at his legs to remove the blackish seeds left behind by the Bahia grass, but his legs were wet with morning dew, and he only smeared the seeds across his shins. "We could've been to town and back already."

"It's awkward. I never know what to do with my arms, so they just sort of dangle at my side." It was only partly true. In reality, flying gave me terrible motion sickness. Uncle Tobin said it's because I'm too inefficient with my energy usage, but I never understood what that had to do with anything. Noan rose a few feet above the ground and floated ahead so that I had to trot to keep up.

"Did you ever wonder what life was like for me back on Kayda?" he asked.

I wasn't expecting the question. I hesitated just long enough for him to pick up speed. "We were kids. Looking back on it now, I see it wasn't right that you had to be locked away all those years." Between the heat, humidity, and hangover, I was panting trying to keep up. "Could you come back down? Or slow down, at least. I wasn't expecting to get a workout this morning."

"Why aren't you more upset about this whole high school business?" Noan said, still not slowing down. "Doesn't this derail your fast track to being Daddy's Little Helper?"

The truth was simple: I didn't want to be around Dad for a while, not if he was trying to find me a girlfriend. I couldn't tell Noan that. I didn't fully trust him not to use it against me to gain Dad's favor. "It's a bummer, but I'd rather be wherever you are. You know that."

A large, silver bus blew past faster than the speed limit, and the rush of warm air that trailed it threw Noan off balance. He staggered in the air like an unstrung marionette before falling to his knees.

"Are you okay?" I caught up to him and helped him to his feet.

"I'm fine. I don't like hovering low anyhow."

"Good. For a second there, I thought you might have hurt your pride."

"My pride is all good here." He paused for only a second, and I saw the words coming before he formed his lips. "Speaking of pride, do you want to talk about what Father said last night?"

"Nope. Not at all."

Is it why you told me telepathy was off-limits a few years ago? You didn't want me to learn something about you?

The sudden intrusion of my brother's voice in my head startled me.

16

"Telepathy and mind magic is forbidden," I said.

So is being a twin, yet here we are.

I didn't want you jumping in my head while I was rubbing one out. And vice versa, I guess. Trust me, I was doing you a favor, I said.

Gross. Now that you mention it, I don't want to know what goes on in your head or in your bedroom.

Even a prince goes through puberty. We can't stay kids forever.

Were we ever kids? We learned how to defend against a mortar attack before we learned how to ride a bicycle. Some childhood.

We walked the rest of the way in silence until we got to Tastee Freeze, a squalid diner in the heart of downtown known for its two-for-one breakfast sandwiches before eight o'clock and its half-priced ice cream sundaes between three and five in the afternoon. Mayola McCall was inside working, and from what I could tell, she was alone. I was about to tap on the glass and wave when Noan grabbed my hand. "Ouch! What was that for?"

"If she sees me, she'll ask me to help her pick and shell peas. I don't want to tell her no, but I don't feel like working in her field all day either."

"Some hard work might be exactly what you need. What we both need. Let's go for it."

Noan laughed. "You? Hard work? You don't even know what hard work feels like."

"My guess is it feels a lot like this conversation with you. Boring, tedious, and seems never to end?"

"Oh, shut it. You wouldn't know what to do if you didn't have me to talk to."

We carried on without stopping, though the smell of bacon frying wrapped around me and tugged at me like a leash. Usually, coffee was enough to stave off my appetite at least until noon, but my hungover body was telling me to eat. "Can we eat?" I whined. He walked on like he didn't hear me. "Don't be a jerk, Noan. I'm starving."

"Let's do my thing first, then yours, yeah? Isn't that why we're out in town?"

"Fine." It was almost a pout, but it wasn't.

Three police vehicles slowly passed us as we neared the next block, each occupant turning to see if they'd spotted it right: two males, tall, dark hair, tattoos up their forearms, definitely Kaydans, possibly criminals. One officer parked his vehicle at the intersection and radioed something to dispatch, and before we passed Village Pizza the buzzing of a drone crept down from over the low-roofed building line.

Instinctively, I used exaggerated motions to make it clear my hands were at my side—not in my pockets or concealing anything— and that I was not a threat. Noan did the same.

"Are the drones getting faster, or am I imagining that?" Noan asked.

In another few minutes, we were on the far side of downtown at the Blue Marquee, a former theater space that had been converted into a thrift shop. We waited at a distance as an older gentleman grabbed the door by its handle, pulled it open, and walked through. Once the door had closed again, we approached the storefront. I reached for a spot on the door near the middle hinge opposite the handle and grabbed an unseen doorknob. With a twist and a push, the door should have swung inwards not into the Blue Marquee, but into Issek's Mystical *Mitjer,* the local bazaar for Kaydan merchants. But it was locked.

"This is odd," Noan said. "Issek's is never closed."

The officer down the street eyed us as we fidgeted with the invisible handle, and a drone flew closer. Its underbelly lights were still white. Praise be for small blessings.

"Maybe we should leave," Noan suggested. Just as he said it, the door squeaked open and Issek's daughter, Calinea, greeted us with a dead smile.

"Hello, Prince Jormon. And Noan."

Noan's jaw tightened almost imperceptibly as he registered the slight, but he remained tacit.

"What's with the locked door?" I moved my head to look past her into the dimly lit store, and she stepped out and closed the door behind her. "Is that Hargi Stolt I saw talking to your dad?"

"No. Maybe." She cleared her throat and tugged at the hem of her yellow shirt, seemingly realizing she was lying to a prince. "Daddy's having a meeting. The store is closed today."

"I'm sure he wouldn't mind if we stopped in. I can pass along greetings from the king." I waited to see what she would say to that, but she stood there as though her mouth had suddenly broken. "Are you going to move out of the way, or what?"

"Your Highness, my father is tending to a private matter that must be handled, um, privately." She struggled to find the proper way to tell us to fuck off, but it was a point that needed no articulation.

"Is the matter so private his king shouldn't know about it?" I asked. I moved to open the door, and she leaned her weight against my arm until it hurt me to keep my grip on the knob. "Does he know I'm out here wanting to get in?"

"He does, Prince Jormon."

"But he doesn't care." Issek would know the slight would get back to Dad. He must not care about that, either. What could they be up to that's so important and secretive as to keep me out? My first instinct was to kick the door down, run inside and knock all the shit off the shelves. How dare she block me from coming in like I was a door-to-door insurance salesman.

Calinea flicked her eyes upwards at the drone as it lost elevation and banked eastward to get a better view of our exchange. "I'll let Daddy know that you both called. I'm so sorry about this, but it really is a family matter."

"Jormon, I think we should go." Noan placed a hand on my shoulder, and I realized I'd been glaring at Calinea. "Calinea, seeing you today has been as awful as it always is."

"I don't know what to say to that, Noan."

"Prince Noan," he corrected.

"Yes. That." She released the hem of her shirt and plastered on an unconvincing smile. "It was nice seeing you, too."

She stood in the doorway as vigilant as the drone hovering above her head as we left.

"Can you believe what just happened?" I asked. "Let me rephrase that: did you see what just happened? I can't believe it! Issek has some nerve to keep us out."

"And Calinea."

"Especially her. She has no clout. Yeah, she was doing what her dad wanted, but—hey, where are you going?"

Noan spun around abruptly and doubled back towards Issek's. "I want to go around the block the other way. I don't want to pass by Officer Shoot 'Em Up. I'm not in the mood for more shenanigans."

"I bet we could take him. I feel like punching someone so hard right now. Ugh!"

It was a joke, of course. A run-in with the police was the fastest way for a Kaydan to die around Lyons.

"You're calm for what just happened," I said. "You seemed more offended by Dad last night than Calinea just now."

"I'm mad, but I can't show people I'm mad."

"What's that supposed to mean?"

He shook his head in exasperation. "If you don't know, then you're an idiot."

"Don't call me that. I might not punch a girl in the face, but I will punch you."

We walked a couple of blocks away from the patrol car and turned down the narrow alley that ran behind Farmers' Furniture and the bus station. As we neared the connecting street, the sounds of a heated conversation caught our attention.

Not again, I thought.

"Give it back! Please! I just want my stuff, and I'll be on my way."

"You left it on the street, copper. That means it's free for the taking."

Noan inched ahead of me and stopped at the edge of the building. He peered around the corner.

What is it? I asked, opting for telepathy over being overheard by whatever asshole lurked around the corner. *What do you see?*

Three guys are picking on another guy. They're going through his bag, it looks like.

Do you recognize any of them?

Noan rolled his eyes. *How would I recognize any of them? From one of the books I read? I never go anywhere.*

I shoved him gently. *I figured you might recognize them from their shitty personalities. Birds of a feather and all of that.*

He peeked again. *They're all in their teens, I think. Some assholes giving this redhead a hard time.*

It's none of our business. Let's go back the other way. I grabbed his arm to pull him back into the alley.

Hold on. I think the one being picked on is Kaydan. I can't tell from here, but they called him 'copper.'

Copper, the racist pejorative meant to put us down.

"The sign said 'No Bags Allowed,' so I left my bag out here," said a stammering voice. "I was following the rules, now please give it back so I can leave."

"The sign also says 'No Coppers,' Mr. I Can Read So Goddamn Good. If you want, we can get the police and have them sort it out."

I peeked around the corner in time to catch them high-fiving one another. It was dumb and adolescent. Something from a movie about how to be an asshole. The one looking like he led the pack wore a cut-off shirt, backward ball cap, khaki shorts, and sandals. The other two wore much of the same. They were bullies, but cartoonishly so. Regardless, the other kid needed help.

Did you hear what he just said? We have to help him. If the police come, the guy is done.

What should we do? Noan asked.

I don't know. You're the one with all the answers.

And you're usually the one telling me to mind my own business.

Fine. Don't mind your own business. But do something. Anything to get him out of there. But be quick about it. You'll only get in trouble if you hurt a human. Just…just try not to hurt anybody.

What if I can't help it?

If you think you're gonna hurt somebody, don't, I said, unsure myself about whatever that meant.

We stepped out of hiding. Halfway down the block stood four guys, all of whom looked about our age. The one with his back against the wall was tall and muscular, perhaps strong enough to take on one of the guys, but not all three. His hair was fire spun into silk. I'd never seen anything so brilliant. Freckles coated his face, and even though he tried to seem brave, his eyebrows—not quite furrowed—gave away his fear.

"Hey!" Noan shouted. "You have something that belongs to our friend, and he asked you to give it back." I would've led with something better, but it got their attention. Their heads whipped in our direction. The leader held a dingy, green backpack that had been unzipped, and some of its contents were piled around his feet.

"Looks like the Copper Calvary has arrived, boys," he said to his buddies, and they thought that was so damn funny. "If your friend wants his bag back, he can take it from me."

Noan, if he tries to get it back, it won't end well for him. Or for us, either. Do something now!

Noan held out his hand and whispered, *"Elaqina."*

As if drawn by a magnet, the backpack yanked towards Noan. The guy was taken by surprise. He clenched the strap instinctively, but the bag was already in motion. He was snatched along with it and dragged across the ground until he finally let go. The bag flew to Noan, followed by the stuff that had been removed. Noan shouted, "Hey, kid! What are you waiting for? Run!"

He ran towards us, jumping over the sleeveless asshole along the way. We were already running. The newcomer fell into pace beside us. His breaths synchronized with ours, and a silent pact of survival formed between us with each pound of our sneakers against the pavement. The guy on the ground let out a barrage of curses as he got up. I looked over my shoulder. All three of them were chasing after us.

We dashed past the alley and crossed the empty parking lot in front of Village Pizza. If a drone caught what was happening, it would be over for us.

"Now we have to hide," I panted. We'd been running for less than a minute, but already I was winded. The heat and humidity made running twice as hard. I stole a glance over my shoulder. The three guys weren't far behind. Barefoot, they sprinted across the street and were nearly at the grassy divide before the parking lot when one of them shouted something into the air.

He was trying to get us killed. Maybe not on purpose, but it's what would happen if a drone caught us in a low-speed chase.

"Hey kid, can you fly?" I shouted.

"No," he said between breaths. "Sorry."

"We can't outrun them. And if a drone sees us—"

As though we had summoned it ourselves, a buzzing sounded low above the adjacent row of buildings. *Fuck fuck fuck fuck fuck. What have I gotten us into?*

We rounded another corner. The drone hadn't seen us, but the guys were right on our tails. "Turn into May May's!" I shouted.

"Huh?"

"Aunt May May's. Tastee Freeze. That's the back of the building right there!" In the blur of red brick sidings, Tastee Freeze's dirty beige facade stood out, damn near called out, as a safe space.

"I have a better idea," Noan said. "Brace yourselves."

I felt my waist cinch as though a giant was hugging me, then my feet left the ground. Noan was in the air, dragging us behind him with a telekinetic link.

"Whoa!" said the redhead. I was as shocked as he was. I closed my eyes to keep my head from spinning, but that was worse than looking at the town blurring beneath me.

Instead of heading straight down the road, Noan took us into the woods where neither the drone nor the thugs could easily follow us. We dodged between trunks and branches until we reached the outer fence of Gray Flats. The grip around my torso loosened, and I fell the short distance onto the overgrown grass below.

Gurgling sounds erupted from somewhere beside me, and when I turned, the redhead was hunched over on his knees vomiting. He stopped, then started again. That could've easily been me.

Do I rub his back or something? Noan asked, seemingly unphased by what just happened.

I got it. This guy was not having a good day.

I walked over and placed my hand on his back between his shoulders. It was damp and sticky, but I resisted the urge to retract my arm.

"If that's how flying feels, I don't want anything to do with it," he said, then started puking again. "Where's my bag?"

"Here," Noan walked it over to him and introduced himself, then pointed to me. "This is my brother, Jormon."

He wiped the edges of his mouth with the back of his hand. "I'm Dirk Wilkes."

"Dirk? That name doesn't sound Kaydan," said Noan.

"Yet it's the only one I got." He stood and took his bag from Noan.

"Everybody knows not to go near the bus stop. Where are you from?"

"I'm from Kayda, I reckon. By way of Alabama." Dirk unfastened his watch and slid it up his arm to reveal a thin *sheria.* "I just got into town a bit ago. I went inside the station to ask for directions, but the guy behind the counter turned me away."

"Where were you looking to go?"

"Gray Flats. Can y'all help me find it?"

"It depends. What do you want with it?" Noan asked. His tone wasn't harsh, but the question was enough to put a defensive look on Dirk's face.

Dirk hoisted his bag over his shoulder and tightened his hands around the straps. "Answers, I reckon."

'I reckon,' he says. He reckons. His words poured from his lips as thick as cane syrup, and as sweetly, too. I was a fly attracted to the sweetness and caught up in the stickiness of it all.

Noan nudged me, and I pretended to think about something other than Dirk's voice.

"Uh, you have grass on the side of your face. May I?" With the back of my hand, I brushed the specks of dirt and grass from his cheek and ear. "Dirk, you say? Are you sure I don't know you from somewhere? The last arrival memorial? Or the Galije Festival? Or maybe the Xan Ball?"

"The only 'ball' I know is football. I ain't that fancy, and I ain't never been outside of Alabama until this week."

"How old are you?" Noan asked Dirk, then to me he said, *I'm not buying this guy's story.*

"I turned seventeen last month."

He's seventeen and barely knows he's Kaydan? Jormon, we should leave this guy here. Everything about this guy says he's trouble.

The drone will know we were coming to Gray Flats. We need to get inside before more arrive.

Maybe it was foolish of me to offer help, but I did it anyway. "I think we can help you, but first, can you tell us what you want with Gray Flats?"

Dirk's grip on his bag tightened even more. "I heard it's where all the Kaydans live. I came here to find it."

"Are you in trouble? Are you running away from something?"

"Look, guys, I don't mean to be rude, especially after what you did for me back there. My story is as long as the road I took to get here, and I don't much care to tell it right now."

I pointed over Dirk's shoulder at the row of trailers. Something in his face shifted upon seeing them. Hope and relief, was it?

"We can take you to my uncle. He'll know what to do."

We can't bring him home, said Noan. *It's not proper. Not if Father is back.*

It's the right thing to do, isn't it?

The right thing to do isn't always the right thing to do. I hurt a guy back there trying to do the right thing. A human. I say we dump this kid right here and let him figure out the rest on his own.

Since when are you okay watching Kaydans struggle?

I just helped him, and it's probably going to cost me. Noan leaned against a tree with his head tilted up at the cloudless sky.

Are you nervous? I asked. *I can't tell with you anymore.*

I'm fine. A little tired is all.

Okay. But what about him? Are we doing this?

Whatever. "Jormon is right," Noan said to Dirk. "Uncle Tobin will know what to do. Are you well enough to walk?"

We entered the back side of the trailer park and walked the gravel trails until we made it home. The sun was higher now, and the dry grass cracked as it bent under our shoes when we stepped into the front yard. As we neared the front door, Nana Lura stepped out to meet us. Her eyes were narrowed and focused right on me. Dad must be home already. And we were in trouble.

"When did he get home?" I asked.

"Less than a minute ago."

"Where is he?"

"In the study."

"Is Uncle with him?" Noan asked.

"Enough questions. Go. Now."

Oh, shit.

"Dirk, this is Nana Lura, our—"

"Grandmother," I interjected. "On our mother's side." I could not tell this guy I still had a babysitter. I was a prince for crying out loud.

Noan looked askance at me, "Yes. Grandmother," he said slowly, drawing out his suspicion. "Nana Lura, this is Dirk. He's new in town and needs help. Could you tend to him while we visit with Father?" He could've just as easily been ordering breakfast. His tone was even and direct, not at all reflecting how shit was about to hit the fan.

She walked off briskly, leaving a confused Dirk to follow in her wake. "Dirk, we'll find you later," I said. Despite what trouble I might be in at the moment, I could hardly think about that when my mind was flooded with thoughts of Dirk's smile, or how his skin felt when I brushed the grass away. In all my life, I had never felt this smitten about anyone, especially so quickly.

It was a feeling I shouldn't have—couldn't have—if I wanted to be king someday.

Dirk scurried after Nana Lura, and I felt suddenly exposed, as though Noan could pick up on this new feeling washing over me. He said, "Why would you want to see that guy again? So far, he's been nothing but trouble."

I didn't believe that at all, but I wasn't going to argue with Noan. He was insightful on a good day when his guard was down, and everything was honky dory. He would read me to filth for being reckless. Besides, weren't we all on the run at some point? Instead, I asked, *Could Dad know what happened at the bus stop?*

If he does, I'm in big trouble.

You were only doing what I asked. I won't let anything happen to you.

He looked at me like he believed me, and I hoped like hell I wouldn't let him down.

CHAPTER THREE
DIRK

"LHENIVA," SHE SAID.

"'Scuse me, ma'am?" Miss Lura had walked me to a nearby trailer and dropped me off with a shaved-headed black woman in her late thirties.

"My name, kid. You don't strike me as stupid, so please try to keep up." She opened the screen door until it pressed against the porch's outer wall. "Come on in. It's too hot outside to be lallygagging."

Lallygagging? My God, she was my grandma. No one uses words like that outside of Alabama, or so I thought. I pondered where she'd learned English, but I wasn't fool enough to ask.

I stepped through the trailer door into a room much bigger than it should've been. I'm not sure if it was the cold air, the stench of menthol, or the disorienting size of the room, but I puked again. I apologized, but Lheniva kept on walking. "No worries, kid. You can clean it up later."

We descended a long stairwell that shouldn't exist until we reached a hallway with perpendicular offshoots. The hall extended farther than I could see, and I had to close my eyes to settle my stomach. My first thought was it reminded me of a prison catwalk, each hall lined end to end with doors like so many cells. As we got further along, the hall unexpectedly twisted and bent, I saw it as an ant bed, a series of thoroughfares of uneven lengths and tricky elevations.

"What is this place?"

"This is my home, dear. Well, not so much a home as it is a refuge. An orphanage or an asylum, or whatever you want to call it. It started as a home for foundlings after the Hunts ended, and we established ourselves here. So many children were without parents. Over time, this place has been many things to many people."

"It doesn't look this big from the outside. How is that possible?"

She looked at me askance, as if I was asking questions I should already know the answers to. "It's our powers. I'll let someone else explain the details. I notice you don't have an accent. Do you speak *Maerinish*?"

"No, ma'am."

"Droviin? Or any of the other languages of Kayda?"

"No, ma'am. It's a long story."

"Hmph. Tell it to someone else. It'll get back to me eventually. Everything does." She chuckled, then added, "I say it as a joke, but I mean it as a warning, too. Don't deceive us, kid. I will find out, and I will do you harm. Do you understand? We've been through too much to have to deal with deceivers."

I was tall for my age, but she was even taller. As she stared down at me in my pitiful state, all I could do was nod.

"Good."

We walked some more.

"How many people live here?"

"About ninety, but you'll likely never run into most of them. To maintain order, each wing holds everything you'll need: bedrooms, kitchens, bathrooms, and so forth. You shouldn't need to visit any other wing, nor should you look for need. Most folks here have had a rough go of it and like to keep to themselves."

Just as I wondered if I'd made the right choice leaving home, we turned down a corridor and stopped at the fourth door on the left. Lheniva tapped on the door with the back of her knuckles. "Are you decent?"

"Am I ever?" came a deep voice from the other side. The door opened, and a tall, dark-haired guy appeared. From the patchy placement of his facial hair, he looked like he couldn't have been more than sixteen or seventeen.

"Taavi, meet your new roommate, Dirk. He has a lot to learn, you'll come to know."

"And you're trusting me to show him the ropes? How sweet." He beamed with playful delight, and I couldn't tell whether he was sincere or if this was part of some banter between him and Lheniva.

"It's the blind leading the blind, but I'm sure you can manage. I wish I could say more, but I have an old biddy waiting for me outside. Check in with me this evening and I can give you further guidance."

"Wait, where is he supposed to sleep?" he called as she hurried down the hall.

"For now, you two can share your bed."

"Miss Lheniva, you can't be serious. I'm too tall for that bed as it is."

"Make it work, Taavi." She disappeared around the corner, leaving me alone with the brown-eyed giant.

"You don't have to share your bed, man. I'm fine sleeping on the floor." I stepped past Taavi into the saddest room I'd ever seen. It was a runaway's room if there were ever such a thing. The bed had no headboard. The walls were made of pale, yellow bricks, and the only decoration was a mirror hung too high for me to see more than the top of my head. There weren't any family photos or movie posters. No dry-erase board listing off the week's chores. No hanging shelves topped with knickknacks. Nothing in the room pointed to a hobby except for a small stack of books in the corner. The carpet was old and musty, and as I paced around, dust lifted from the floor and hung in the beam of sunlight shining through the lone window.

"How is there sunlight coming through that window? I must've walked down twenty steps to get here."

"The glass has been manipulated to show what's outside. If you watch long enough, you'll catch Sandi Nash throwing scraps out her back door for her cats to eat. Be careful walking through her piece of yard. The grass is always greasy, and you're liable to fall."

"This is amazing."

"Calm down, New Guy. It's actually substandard, but maybe you don't come from much, either. The space is pretty limited in Gray Flats. Most of the trailers are stretched out enough to house a few families. This one takes the cake, though. It's not as fancy as the Royal trailer—it's just a row or so over from this one. Do you know what a *sahdr* is?" I shook my head. "A *sahdr is* what humans often call a 'spell.' Anyway, their trailer's been touched by a badass *sahdr* that transforms the space into something fancy, like a manor or something like that. On the outside, it's just your run-of-the-mill trailer, same as every other one around here. But inside? Bro, that's a whole different story. And the ceiling has been manipulated to show a Kaydan sky. The whole time I was there, it looked purple because of the clashing of light from the red and blue suns. Do you know about the suns of Kayda?"

I shook my head. I didn't know anything about Kayda, and even hearing about spells and manipulations intimidated me. Taavi mentioned something about Hee-ma-roar and some other name, but it all went over my head.

"Wow, you do have a lot to learn. Set your bag down and we'll take the tour."

He reached for my bag, and I clenched my fist tightly around the working strap. The bag and I had been through a lot since last night, and though I assumed I could trust Taavi, I didn't want to take any chances.

"Mind if I shower first?" My clothes had dried from falling in dumpster juice the previous night, but the rancid odor of trash radiated from dried stains in my pants.

If he noticed my apprehension, he paid it no mind. "Dude, that's you smelling like that? I thought it was me! I just finished an overnight shift in the Factory, and I usually reek afterward. Gotta make them coins, though." He lifted his arm and sniffed at his armpit, then shrugged at however he found his stench. "The bathroom is at the end of the hall. I'm gonna get a quick nap in, so knock loud in case I don't hear you."

The shower was warm but unenjoyable. The water pressure was weak, black mildew lined the tub, and I kept feeling as though somebody would walk in on me. Still, it was the first shower I'd had since leaving Alabama earlier in the week, and I savored it as long as I could.

I banged on the door as instructed, and Taavi opened it in short order. "Enjoyed the shower?" He was in the middle of putting on a t-shirt so worn his skin was visible along the chest and shoulders.

"I did." I tucked my backpack underneath the foot of the bed. "So, this is life here? A bed, a desk, a wardrobe, and a window?"

"Yessir, this is where the tragic happens. If you want to watch TV, there's a common room on the first floor. You won't be able to hear whatever's on, though. The old folks sit around talking about the 'good ol' days' back on Kayda and it drowns out the tv completely. There's a small study on the first floor, too. You'll be better off spending your time there. There are lots of books to teach you the basics of matter manipulation—*sahdriin,* as we call it. There are a few advanced books, too, but you won't be there for a while."

I had too many questions and too much catching up to do. I was embarrassed about not knowing who I was and excited for finally being able to discover the truth about myself.

He tossed me a book from the stack in the corner. I flipped through a few pages. "Am I supposed to be able to read this?"

"A Kaydan that doesn't know *Maerinish* is about as useful as a bible in a whorehouse. Come on, I'll take you on the tour and try to teach you some things along the way. Lesson one," he said as we left the room. "Always lock your shit up. This isn't a prison, but we live by prison rules. Most folks around here didn't grow up with much, so if they don't know you, they won't mind stealing from you."

He held his hand close to the door, and red and blue specks left his palm and marched around the doorframe forming a seal, then jetted into the keyhole. "I just programmed this door to respond to my energy pattern. We can program it to respond to yours, too. Go ahead, hold out your arm."

I held my hand near the door, but nothing happened. "I'm sorry. I don't know what I'm supposed to do."

He grabbed my wrist in his massive hand. "Wow, you're a babe!"

"Huh?" I retracted my hand, but he didn't let go.

"Your *sheriaan* are a few inches long." He traced his finger over the copper lines that barely made it halfway around my wrist. "These markings are the *sheriaan* of the Kaydan people and indicate who we are as a *mustedi*. It sounds so cool when I say that, right?"

"Uh, right." His touch made me uneasy, so I pulled my arm back and stuck my hands in my pockets. He didn't mean anything by it, but given what I'd gone through, I wanted to keep to myself. "I don't know how to ask this without sounding stupid, but what's a *mustedi*?"

He squinted his eyes, likely taken aback by my ignorance, then smiled. "It just hit me: I'm the Aladdin to your Jasmine."

"No, you're not."

"Bro, I'm totally showing you the world. All I need is a magic carpet and a talking monkey."

"Can you just answer the question? Please?" My older sister used to do that to me, hold knowledge over me and make me feel dumb for not knowing. Momma would yell at her, usually from the kitchen where she would sit and read magazines, and eventually my sister would share what it was she knew. But Momma wasn't there. I was on my own.

"I'm just trying to keep things light, Bro," Taavi said. "No offense." He walked around tidying up the nearly empty room, all the while explaining that not everyone on Kayda has powers, and those who do wield them differently. "*Mustediin* are the most respected. They're 'knowledgeable and disciplined,' whatever the hell that means."

"What else are there besides *mustediin*?"

"The *suhrat* get their power from nature. Oh, and from spirits, too, I think. Humans might call them 'witches' if I had to think of an equivalent. They are the least respected class of people, and before you start judging me for saying that, know that I don't make the rules, nor do I judge anyone. In fact, my best friend is half *suhrat*."

I wasn't going to touch that one. "Can we go back to the *sheriaan*? What do they mean?"

"We all begin the same; no one is good, no one is evil. The choices that we make in life shape our character. Similarly, the choices we make as *mustediin* shape and color our *sheriaan*. From the looks of yours, you're pretty basic."

"That's not insulting at all." I fought the urge to roll my eyes and say something nasty about his raggedy clothes.

"They'll grow as you learn more, Baby's Breath. We can start with how to bring out your energy. If you've never done it before, it helps if you close your eyes and take deep breaths."

I closed my eyes and inhaled. "I feel stupid doing this."

"You look stupid, too, but it's okay. It'll work. Trust me on this. Now, imagine there's a pot of water boiling inside you, and that your body is the lid. That pot is gonna boil over and make a mess unless you take the lid off. You feel it?"

All I felt was him staring at me. My sinuses twitched from the dust in the air, and my skin tingled from the newness of it all, but otherwise, nothing. I opened my eyes. "Sorry, man. It's not working."

"Keep trying."

It was the most unhelpful advice ever, but I closed my eyes again. This time, instead of water in the pot, I thought about the conversation I had with my momma the night before I ran away. She was so calm and resolute and determined to keep her secrets.

Secrets about me. I got so angry. I'd never been so angry, even after the time that thing happened at church.

"It's working!" Taavi shouted. "Now, instead of taking the lid all the way off, just crack it a bit."

My skin itched all over, like worms crawling through my veins. I squirmed and shrugged and arched my back. I needed this to end. If only I could just…

The itching stopped.

I opened my eyes and found myself surrounded by gold and silver dots that fell around me like the dying embers of fireworks. "I did it! Taavi, I did it."

"Right on, man."

He showed me how to focus the energy, and together we added my signature to the door. "Now you can come and go whenever you want."

"Awesome." I inspected my copper tattoos. "My lines, they didn't grow at all. You said they'd get longer once I know more."

"They will; just be patient. Haven't you ever lifted weights? You look like you have. You know, your muscles don't grow during your workout. You must've used your powers before for them to show at all. It'll happen just like it did then."

I pulled my hands close to my chest and rubbed at both wrists. I didn't want to think about what happened back then. That's why I ran away in the first place.

We walked, and Taavi explained things. Each wing in the first sub-level housed its own grouping of people. Taavi and I were Pita Wing, nicknamed "Pain Wing" because the tenants were pains in everyone's ass. We were the youth. The unruly. The uncontrollable. The ones without discipline. The ones without parents.

"How did you lose your folks?" I asked. It might not have been appropriate, but he answered anyway like he probably had to do a hundred times before.

"My parents were servants to the Azalas—some rich family back in Maerin. They were at work and I was home with my gran when the sky broke open. The rip took us both. I was six at the time and knew as much about being a *mustedi* as you do now. My gran saved me during the fall. She saved me but couldn't save herself."

"You must've been scared."

"I remember crying, but I don't remember how I felt at the time. Shocked, maybe? It was so long ago."

We walked down another set of stairs at the far side of the hallway.

"What about you? How'd you get separated from the pack?"

I shrugged. "I'm not sure. I thought I was human until a few weeks ago when I used my powers for the first time. I had no clue what I was doing or how it happened, but it changed everything. After that, I couldn't stay in Alabama anymore." That's all I cared to say, and I was glad he didn't pry. It embarrassed me that I didn't know I was Kaydan, and I had zero memory of ever having been there, ever having come through the rift, or ever really suffering like the rest of them. It was as though I went through life, passing myself off as something I wasn't.

The stairs led to a balcony overlooking a warehouse floor of some kind. The back of the room contained row after row of boxes stacked on shelves. It reminded me of the first time I went to Ikea and learned I had to grab all the big stuff on my own at the end of the maze. Near the front of the room were a dozen individual stations staffed by adults sorting through little black rocks.

"What is this place?"

"This is the Factory. There's no fancy name for it other than that. It used to be in the basement of the trailer on the left just as you enter Gray Flats, but humans threw an explosive through the window. It didn't detonate, but it scared everyone enough to want to move it deeper in the Flats. Same with the Academy. That used to be in the trailer near the back fence, but now the Academy is pretty much next door."

Lord, what have I gotten myself into? I wasn't happy at home, but no one was trying to bomb my house.

"Anyway," Taavi continued, "working here is how we make our living. You know those nifty little stones that humans use to make them fly or give them telekinesis?"

"Yeah, I've heard of them." They were never allowed in our house. Momma would've had a fit.

"Those stones don't make themselves. Everyone here pitches in and makes them. You'll be on shift soon enough."

"Ah. Do we get paid?" Not that I knew how to make the stones, but having money would be nice.

"Not much. Mostly room and board."

"Are the hours long?"

"Depends on how fast you make your quota."

"I think they call this a sweatshop."

"Oh yeah, you'll sweat. It's not that bad, though. It's how we do our part for our people. We make products, someone sells them, the money gets pooled, and our bills get paid. That's all I know. If you want to make some real money, you can create your own stuff and sell it at Issek's—that's the store in town where they sell Kaydan shit. It's like a bazaar, only most people are selling pretty much the same thing. Not me, though."

"What makes your stuff so different?"

"Um, people actually want to buy it. I've invented a few nifty little things that have sold pretty well. I haven't made enough to get rich, but I've saved a pretty penny."

He showed me where the kitchen and dining halls were located upstairs, then we walked to the study and found me a book on basic *Maerinish*. "You'll need to know the language before you'll be any good at *sahdriin*. I can teach you some things to help you get by, but that book is gonna be your best friend."

"Thanks." I flipped through the pages. Many pictures and directional markings illustrated how letters are drawn and connected to one another. Back in my old school, I did pretty well in Spanish, but this new language looked a bit more complicated. "Speaking of friends, two guys helped me out of a jam at the bus station. I was hauled off so fast that I didn't really get to thank them. Maybe you know who they are. Noan and Jormon, they said, but I didn't catch their last name. They live a couple of trailers up from here."

"Whoa! Are you freaking kidding me? You've been here for five whole minutes and you've already met Prince Jormon and Prince Noan. That's great."

"Princes? As in royal? As in their dad is the king?"

"It's a long story, but yes. To all of that. Prince Jormon is the crown prince and his brother Noan—Prince Noan—is the reason we're all stranded on this planet."

"What's the story there?"

"It's not my story to tell, bro. Sorry." I hated being called 'bro,' but it didn't feel right to bring it up.

"The crown prince just saved my life, then I puked on his shoes."

"You what!"

"It's not my story to tell," I joked, hoping to get one over on him. "Speaking of puke, I got a mess to clean up in the foyer. Can you show me how to get back there?"

"Don't worry about the mess. I'll clean it up for you. You should head back to the room and get started reading."

"Sure," I said. If only I could remember the way.

CHAPTER FOUR
NOAN

THE STUDY WAS A SIMPLE ROOM: A DESK YOU HAD TO stand up to use, and books along every space of every wall, twenty feet up to the ceiling. I spent most of my time in Gray Flats in Uncle's study, stepping through the doorway always felt like coming home. This time, Father was there. It still felt like coming home, if your house was smack in the middle of a minefield. Every word I said could trigger a trap. Every eye roll could set off an explosion.

He was talking to Uncle with his back towards the door, but he turned and beamed the phoniest smile the moment we entered. "My boys! My beautiful boys. Come greet your father!"

He extended both arms, and waves of jade and ash particles arced towards us. Jormon was too eager to return the embrace. His blues locked themselves in and he basked in Father's light.

I knew I had to join, but I was afraid of what I'd feel when I did. I smiled at my father and extended my energy, and when it met Father's, warmth and love washed over me. I also felt…hope? *What in the hell is going on?* Did he forgive me for being a complete ass last night?

Father said, "I wished we'd had a better visit last night, but there's no changing that. Tobin was just catching me up on what you've been up to. He said you've mastered Trohol's *Techniques for Manipulating Kinetic Energy* and can put out fire now."

"I came really close, but Noan did it on his first try," Jormon said.

"Is that right?" Father asked, and I immediately blushed.

"It was nothing, really," I said.

"It wasn't 'nothing,' Noan. It was hard, and you did it."

"Jormon, don't contradict your brother," Father said. "If he says it's nothing, I'm sure it's nothing. After all, he tends to be right about most things."

I hardly had time to process the verbal assault before he moved on to the next thing.

"Did you catch the press conference this morning?"

"No, sir," I said. "We were out in town."

"Oh? Doing what, might I ask?"

"Uhhh," I started.

"Never mind—I brought you both something back from my recent travels to Jerusalem. It's not the same as it once was, if you can imagine. Still, members of the Israeli Delegation to the Council for Interspecies Affairs invited the Spirit Matron and me to visit the Temple Mount for some business." He paused as if he expected us to guess what he and the Spirit Matron were invited there to do. Broker a Middle East peace treaty? Resurrect Jesus Christ? The Spirit Matron dealt with the dead all the time, but Jesus was *dead* dead, if he ever really existed to begin with.

"While I was there, I tried this delicious thing called halva, and I just knew you boys would love it."

A gift-wrapped box materialized in his hand from wherever it had been stashed away. "I would have given it to you last night, but of course 'last night' happened. Anyway, enjoy."

What's going on here? I projected to Jormon. One second, Father was being a jerk, and the next, he's handing out treats. Mix that with the feeling I got when he greeted me, and I'd swear my father was psychotic.

Shut up, Noan. "Thank you, Dad."

Father smiled. Was it possible he didn't know about the attack at the bus station? It just happened, but Father prided himself on how he always knew everything the moment it occurred.

"Now that we're all here, it's time to talk business. There are a lot of significant things that will soon happen, and it's too bad you didn't see the joint press conference with me and the American President, Serena Sunwarden. The Integration Initiative is going to take America by storm, and there are so many broad-sweeping changes that will take effect by the end of this week!"

He was almost giddy with excitement, and it made me question if I was being overly pessimistic about the whole thing. It didn't erase the sting of not going to the Academy, but it gave me something else to think about instead.

"To start," Father continued, "no legal establishment that sells goods or provides services can deny the patronage of a Kaydan individual."

"What does that mean for us?" Jormon asked, clearly a softball question to garner favor.

"It means that we can eat at any restaurant we want, not just the select few here near Gray Flats. You'd think being king comes with unique privileges, but you'd be surprised how often I'm turned away from places in D.C."

"Really?" I asked. We never left the house when we were in D.C., except to sit in the yard to study when we grew tired of being indoors. I'd always assumed Father had the run of the town, being the highest-ranking Kaydan and representative of our people on Earth. He wasn't some mere plenipotentiary, for *Zereq*'s sake. He was our king, and he was out there being treated the way I often was here in Gray Flats. "What do you do when it happens?"

"I behave as an ideal representative of Kayda should, and as I expect you both to do. I smile, thank the host for their time, and I respectfully leave. You see, we can't afford to make a scene and return their nastiness with nastiness of our own, not if we expect to get anywhere. That goes for any Kaydan, not just the two of you."

Off to the side, Uncle nodded his head in agreement.

What about school, I wanted to ask, but Father was on a roll, and I didn't dare interrupt him.

He continued, "The Initiative also means that merchants who sell Kaydan *sabejaan* must buy it from us at fair market value, which will be the economic boost we need and deserve. It'll also open up Issek's Mystical *Mitjer* for public patronage, which will improve the entrepreneurial endeavors of any Kaydan making and selling *sabejaan* of their own creation. Isn't that great?"

"Yes, Dad. That's wonderful news. I'm sure our people will be elated to learn this," Jormon said.

Kiss ass.

Shut it, Noan!

"There's more. Equal work for equal pay, fair access to housing… Things we never dreamed are now possible."

"All thanks to you, Dad."

"You're too kind, Son," Father said, and Jormon blushed.

Consciously, I tucked my unease away and smiled. I wanted to be where Jormon was. I wanted to be comfortable in my father's company. To say something nice to him and have him react with kindness. It was a new feeling, a new desire. Something I didn't even know I wanted until that moment.

I bit into a piece of halva and delighted in the cardamom and pistachio richness. It was as delicious as Father said. I took another piece, then another.

Father rolled from one topic to the next, but the conversation always returned to integration. "Boys, your uncle and I were discussing a dinner party in celebration of the progress we've made. My residence will be the perfect place to host it. We can consider it your debut as well. You boys will be the hosts as much as I."

"That's a brilliant idea," I volunteered. "All of it."

"You think so?" Father asked. He was still smiling, but his eyes narrowed on me, and there was no joy in them. He looked the way you would as you watched your chess opponent make the one move that was sure to put him in checkmate. "Tell me, if you think it's all so brilliant, why are you doing everything in your power to subvert it?"

"Pardon me?" I finished chewing the halva and sat up straight, legs shoulder width apart, feet flat on the floor.

"The incident at the bus stop an hour ago. That was you, wasn't it? The one who dragged that little shit across the sidewalk with your summoning *sahdr*?"

I opened my mouth, and my words clogged my throat until I couldn't breathe. He knew. Of course, he did.

"Were it a different time, I'd dismiss your actions as a display of youthful exuberance. He's a bully, and I don't like bullies. Brett's his name. Brett Brantley. Bully Brett." He kept repeating the sobriquets to himself as he stood and paced in front of us. "Brett's father, Clint, is also a bully, and as it happens, he's a member of the Council for Interspecies Affairs. He tried so hard to derail this Integration Initiative, and where he failed to turn the vote, you're out in the streets trying to help him succeed. Attacking a human? What were you thinking?"

I didn't want to open my mouth, afraid I'd choke again. I looked over at Jormon, who could've easily passed for a Roman bust. His skin was as gray and pallid as the statue he was pretending to be.

"I cannot let this go unpunished. You understand that, don't you?"

I didn't let him repeat the question. "Yes, Father. I understand." I understood that he hadn't changed, not one bit. He was still the meanest person I knew.

Just like the box of halva, another item materialized in his hands. At first, I thought it was a snake coiled tightly around itself. It was silver with thick, ornate scales. Father held one end and let the other fall to the floor. That's when I saw it for what it was: a whip, thin as a razor at the tip and completely covered in dull, rusty thorns up to the handle.

I'd seen something like it before in one of Uncle's books. It was a *rhualka*. A spirit leech used in burial rituals to separate the spirit from the body.

All color drained from my face. My father was going to kill me. We had come this far only for him to do what the Red Cloaks said he should've done the day I was born. To do what the U.S. Army didn't, and what the Riders couldn't. After hating me for so long, he was going to straight up kill me.

"Rosh, we didn't discuss this," Uncle said, swooping in on Father and grabbing him by the forearm. "It was a youthful indiscretion. No one was seriously injured."

Father scowled and shook his arm free. "Tobin, am I going to have to speak to you again?"

"No, my king. You are not." Uncle took a step back, then another, until he was nearly out of view. His eyes stayed trained on me, yet his face lost all warmth, and his stoic (if not stern) countenance projected his disapproval of what had just happened and what was about to. To me, it was another act of betrayal.

Jormon, usually the last one to pick up on things, said, "Dad, that's a tool of the Spirit Matron. A *rhualka,* it's called. She uses it on the dead to extract the spirit from the body before putting it to rest. Do you intend to—" He didn't finish. He couldn't. Who could imagine something so vile happening?

My father laughed. Chuckled, rather, as if Jormon had told a dumb joke. "It has another purpose as well, one that we discovered many, many years ago. But you're right. While applied to the dead, the *rhualka* drains the body's spirit and returns it to nature. It's how we give back to Kayda for all that the Great Dragon has given to us. When applied to the living, however, it has a much more practical purpose."

In a flash, Father swung the *rhualka* and its razor laden edge struck me in the center of my chest.

All around me screams echoed, and I wasn't sure if they were coming from me, or if it was merely blood rushing to my head. My flesh ripped open and purple waves wailed as they shot out of the wound. I screamed in pain as I fell to my knees.

"On the living, it drains a Kaydan's essence. It leeches away their powers for a duration. They were all the rage for years in Maerin, back before the Spirit Matrons discovered they were being used in disciplinary practices and confiscated them all. But they couldn't confiscate this one. This one is mine."

I ran my fingers through the tear in my shirt. My skin was back intact, and the only reminder it had struck me was the strong throb where the wound once was.

"My boys. My beautiful boys. Both of your actions deserve punishment. It pains me to be the one to dole it out. Truly, it does. Noan, because you used your powers to hurt a human, you will be drained of them for one week. Does that seem fair to you?"

What could I say? Kiss my ass. I didn't do anything wrong. "Yes, Father."

"And Jormon, because Noan acted under your direction, your punishment will be to administer the lashes. A leader must learn firsthand the consequences of his decisions, don't you agree?"

Jormon struggled to find the words. He'd spent his life following Father blindly. Now, he was seeing him for the first time as I'd always seen him. Jormon knew saying yes would mean he'd be standing across from me, beating my ass. Taking the life from me. From the panic strapped across his face, I could tell he was determining what it would mean if he refused Father.

"What? No. I can't," Jormon said, backing away from Father. "I won't. I won't hurt Noan like that. He's my brother. How could you ask that of me?"

"Would you rather it be reversed?"

"No," he blurted out.

"What do you think Noan would say if I asked him the same thing? Do you think he'd switch places and leech you instead? Should we ask?"

Jormon stood with his hands behind his back like a kid caught stealing from the cookie jar. Father turned so quickly I hardly caught the movement. This time, Jormon clutched at his chest as dark specks seeped from between his fingers like so much smoke. Screams echoed yet again. Jormon's screams.

"When you've stopped screaming, ask your brother how he feels about switching places," Father said.

Just do it, Jormon. I'll be fine. Our eyes met, and we looked at each other in a way we hadn't since we were little boys and bombs were falling all around us. The premature swelling of tears in our eyes as we wondered if we would survive this thing, or the next.

I can't. I promised I wouldn't let you get hurt.

Let it be a lesson in promises. I'll be fine. I'm tougher than you. I'm used to suffering.

Then let me do the suffering this time. I'm tougher than you think I am.

I know you're tough. You're going to have to be to do what comes next. Now hurry.

I looked for Uncle, but in the commotion, he'd left the room. Disappeared. As much as Uncle loved us, he was the king's subject as much as he was his brother. He'd let the whipping happen to us as though we were anyone one else not the Princes of Maerin.

Jormon took the *rhualka* by the thick end, and his muscles flexed under the weight.

"How do I do this?" His voice was shallow, and his eyes had already begun to fill with tears.

"Stop crying. Do it like you mean it. The harder you swing it, the fewer lashes it will take."

"How will I know when it's over?" His voice trembled as every word fell out of bubbling lips.

"Swing until I tell you to stop."

I closed my eyes and listened to the whip scratch across the wooden floor. Jormon swung it high overhead, and a melodic aria filled the room. It was the most beautiful song I'd ever heard. It must've been three voices, maybe four, harmonizing across low and high octaves. It was impossibly elegant. It was enchanting. All I wanted in that moment was for the music to take me. Then the music transformed into a deafening scream, and my chest filled with pain as the *rhualka's* pointed edge bit into my rib.

And then it sang again. And again. And again.

CHAPTER FIVE
DIRK

"DUDE, WAKE UP."

A hand rocked my shoulder, and I cracked my eyes a little. Threads of moonlight streamed through the window, lighting Taavi's face and chest as he sat up in bed next to me.

"Wake up, man. You pissed the bed."

I reached a hand beneath the sheets. The front of my shorts were warm and wet. So was the mattress.

Heat rushed over me, and I jumped out of the bed and backed against the wall. "I'm so sorry. So, so sorry. I told you I was okay sleeping on the floor. This happens sometimes when I'm in a new place. You should've let me sleep on the floor."

The air laden with the scent of urine lingered in the stillness, and I wanted to be anywhere else. I'd have taken getting stabbed at the Atlanta bus terminal over sitting next to the guy I had just pissed on.

"It's not that serious, bro. Don't be embarrassed. I'm not judging you."

"I appreciate that, but I'm too old for this to happen. It hasn't happened in years. Really."

"Accidents happen. Especially when you're stressed or worried. I bet that's what it is. You're worried about being away from your folks."

I pulled a pair of shorts out of my bag while Taavi stripped the bed and threw the sheets into a pile in the corner. "I'll wash those in the morning."

"Don't worry about it, bro. I can take care of it."

"You don't have to be this nice to me. You don't even know me."

"I've been trying to change that, but you keep dodging my questions. Not to pressure you or anything, but it's time you open up."

"It's been a crazy few weeks. I still haven't wrapped my head around any of it. I feel like if I start talking, I'll just end up crying or punching a wall, or doing something else just as embarrassing."

"More embarrassing than pissing up my leg?"

"Oh, fuck off." *Lord, forgive me.*

"It was a joke." He walked over and wrapped a hand around my shoulder. "Lighten up. This is a safe space."

I forced a smile.

"Wanna hear about the last time I pissed the bed?"

"Sure. Go on." A tit-for-tat would be nice.

He cleared his throat as he gazed out the window. "I was eight years old."

"Eight? You jerk! That's not opening up. That's almost ancient history."

"I'm only getting started. Listen for a sec. I was eight years old, and the Hunts had been going on for about a year. Do you remember the Hunts?"

"I read about it in school, but that's about it."

"There isn't a book out there that can tell you how scary that shit really was. Moving from house to house in the dark of night so that the Riders couldn't keep up with you. Hearing the front door blasted open with a shotgun and watching one or two—sometimes three people—get shot before someone could use the right *sahdr* to stop the Hunter. I got so used to leaving stuff behind I stopped wanting anything. When I saw you rolling in with your backpack, it reminded me a lot of who I used to be. Always on the go. Always looking for the next bed." He grabbed a set of sheets from the bottom drawer. Even in the dim light, I could tell the set didn't match.

"Lheniva was like my momma back then. I was young, and she was the only familiar face everywhere we went. I guess I sort of gravitated to her. One night, we were both hiding out in this old woman's attic. It was kinda nice because I got to sleep on my own mattress. Right before bed, someone banged on the door as loud as thunder. It scared the crap out of me. Heart stopping, pants-shitting loud, you know?

"Anyway, the lady opened the door, ready to tear somebody a new one. It was a group of Riders. Somehow, somewhere, they'd picked up a rumor that the lady was in the business of hiding Kaydans. She didn't take shit from any of them, not for one second. To this day, I have never heard someone get cursed out so bad. She screamed, 'I don't care what y'all do out in the streets, but I run Seven Sixty-five Canady Street' and 'blah, blah, blah…' We heard them run off, even from up in the attic. I was scared they'd come back. I didn't have a chance to use the bathroom before bed, so I laid there that night on the first mattress I'd been on in weeks and pissed myself."

I didn't know what to say, and as by some unspoken agreement, we both knew to avoid catching one another's eye. He told the story like it was a bad thing, and it made me think he'd certainly gone through much worse. As I'd gone all those rough years passing as human, he was living the full Kaydan experience. My skin itched as the awkwardness built up. Without warning, a burst of gold and gray erupted from my chest and swirled aimlessly around the room.

"You're getting pretty good at that."

"Thanks. And thanks for telling me that story. You didn't have to open up like that."

"It was either that story, or the one about the time I shit myself at Dairy Queen. Let me tell you, it was not the best way to find out you're lactose intolerant."

"That. Sounds. Gross."

"Eh, it was nothing." He grabbed some clothes from the wardrobe and walked to the door. "I'm gonna hit the showers and try to get some of your wee off. Care to join me?"

"You're joking, right?"

I spent the next few days with my nose buried deep in my *Maerinish-for-Dummies* book, by the end of which I could read it, write it, and speak it. Granted, I sounded like a kindergartner with a speech impediment—or maybe a Pre-K kid with a lisp—but it was an accomplishment I was proud of. My Spanish was crap, and I dropped French after one semester, but this I would get. I didn't have a choice. I asked Taavi when I'd be good enough to learn spells or whatever it's called that Kaydans can do, and he laughed his goofy laugh and grinned his goofy grin and told me to keep reading. A day or so later, I returned to the room after dinner and found him sitting cross-legged on the floor holding a plastic box.

"Can you read this?" He ran his fingers over the letters written on the lid. I read the words aloud to him in my childlike tone. "Do you understand what you just said?"

I didn't.

"It roughly translates to 'Picking up the Pieces.' It's a matching game for kids." He opened the lid and poured the contents onto the dirty floor: a few dozen marbles in various colors and a stack of cards with patterns drawn on both sides. "The objective of the game is to pick up two matching color marbles using telekinesis and create the pattern on these here cards before your opponent. You're supposed to take turns picking them up, put them in a pattern, yada yada yada. The point is to focus on picking shit up with your mind. Repeat after me: *elaqi*."

I repeated the words again and again until I pronounced them according to Taavi's liking.

"If it makes it easier for you, you can think about this as a spell. You aren't a witch, so never call it a spell. You'll only end up pissing off actual witches, like, the human ones. Let me remind you: spells are their thing. Our thing is how we can connect to the world around us and manipulate it. For example, *elaqi* is a way of manipulating position. Moving things, you know? Telekinesis. Once you understand that, you can make it happen."

"That's all it takes? Understanding? Seems simple enough." I rolled my neck, squared my shoulders, and spoke the words. "*ELAQI!*" Nothing happened. "*ELAQI!*" The marbles didn't roll, they didn't spin, they didn't lift. They sat there like I wasn't talking to them. "*Elaqi. Elaqi?* Taavi, what am I doing wrong?"

"You don't understand what you're doing."

"I thought I did, though. It's just a word. I even said it right, without my Southern accent or anything."

"Think of it like math. If someone tells you that the derivative of x-squared is two-x, the derivative of x-cubed is three-x squared, and asks you the derivative of x to the fourth power, you'd say…?"

I thought about all the math classes I'd slept through and cursed under my breath. "Four-x?" I answered sheepishly.

"Wrong!" he said comically.

"Four-x cubed?"

"Correct, but you came to that answer because you followed the pattern, not because you understood the rules of derivatives."

"Or what a derivative is, for that matter."

"Good point. Knowing and understanding are different things. As you look at the marbles, understand the connection between them and your intentions. Understand how your will is gonna make them move, and that *elaqi* is how you direct your will to the marble."

I tried it again. And again. I inhaled a long, loud stream of dank air, determined to master this before I got so frustrated that I'd jump out the non-window on the wall.

"Keep it up, bro. Once you're able to pick up one marble, move on to trying to pick up the other of the same color."

"Sure." Screw math, and screw this.

Taavi and I were eating bowls of cereal at the kitchen table when a girl skipped in. Her mouth was agape, and her eyes rolled around in giddy anticipation. She spun around on one foot in neat pirouettes until she was close enough to the table to bruise a hip, and just when I thought she was going to float up in the air, she stopped. Her wide grin turned into a toothy smile, and she screamed in delight.

"Dirk, meet Phae," Taavi said.

I placed my hand over my heart in the way Taavi had taught me, and as I brought my energy out to greet her, she spun around again, sending green and pink sparks in the shape of butterflies up into the air.

"What's got you so excited?" Taavi asked.

"Haven't you heard? We've been invited to dine with the royal family! Ahhh! The prince is giving a ball." Her voice was light and sing-songy. She spun again, and some of her butterflies landed in my bowl, flapped around in the milk and disappeared beneath the Lucky Charms.

"Is it a ball, or just brunch?" Taavi asked.

"It doesn't matter. In either case, I will be rocking my finest couture, serving you Cinderella realness all day!"

"Trying to land a prince? I'd hold off on the glass slippers if I were you. I heard you're not his type."

"I'm a poor orphan girl wearing raggedy clothes, I spend most of my day cleaning up after ungrateful idiots like you, and I can talk to birds and rats and shit. Don't kill my vibe; I'm trying to live the full fantasy right now." She twirled and sang a melodic ditty that ended in a high-pitched vibrato.

"I thought you were done trying to be rescued by wealthy men of status."

"Don't forget Calinea. She and I were a thing for a hot minute until her mean, mean daddy found out and busted that wide open. When it comes to rising out of poverty, I don't discriminate on the basis of sex."

"Hmm. While you're chumming it up with the princes, ask them for a new mattress for me, wouldya? Dirk pissed the bed last night."

My eyes snapped up from the dying butterflies and locked square onto Taavi's. He winked. I could've thrown my bowl right at his crooked front teeth.

She must've seen how intently I was staring at Taavi, sizing him up in case we actually did come to blows. She said, "Don't mind Taavi. He tells me everything."

"Did he tell you he shat himself at Dairy Queen?" I asked, happy to throw a small trauma back in his face.

"I was there when it happened. Who do you think bought him the ice cream?" She grabbed a bowl from the upper cabinets and helped herself to some Cheerios. "As I was saying, this ball is going to be epic. I can picture it already. I'm wearing something green. Hunter green, for sure. Or maybe chartreuse. Either way, I'm gonna be a whole snack—Taavi, are you listening to me?"

"I hear you," he said with a jaw full of cereal. "Keep talking."

"Don't act like you're not as excited as I am to spend the evening with the prince. You think I don't know you look forward to the weekends when they deign to come back to the Flats, and that you sneak out every now and again to follow Prince Noan into the woods?"

"What?" A string of milk fell from his lip and he wiped it with the back of his hand. "It's not what you think. I'm not a stalker or anything. I just want to be his friend, seriously. Besides, I only have eyes for you." He drew out the vowel until he sounded like a wolf, then blew a kiss at Phae.

"Ugh. Don't make me throw up. Speaking of which, are you the kid who keeps puking all over the place?"

"The illusion makes me dizzy," I muttered. Something about my excuse made Taavi laugh, but I didn't find anything funny at all.

"Tragic," Phae said. "You'd better get that under control fast. Decorating the royals' walls with your breakfast wouldn't be a good first impression."

"He's already biffed that one," said Taavi. "Made a real impression, too."

"What? How? You've been here five minutes."

"I didn't tell you?" Taavi asked. "They saved his scrawny ass from some punks at the bus stop."

"And?"

"I'll just say that if he pukes in their hallway, they won't be seeing anything new."

"I can't tell if you guys are being jerks, or if you're bringing me in on the joke," I said. Frankly, I wasn't sure how I felt about either scenario. I needed friends, yes, but I wasn't sure I could trust them. Either of them.

All the talk of vomit pushed away my appetite. I poured the rest of my cereal down the sink and fixed myself a glass of water. "You talk about the royals as though they're unapproachable. I ran into them at the bus stop, and they treated me like I was one of them. They live a rock's throw away from here. You never go over to see what they're up to?"

They glanced at one other, and for the first time, the smile left Phae's face. "They're the royals; we're the common folk. If you see them, smile and be polite, but don't engage. Those are the marching orders."

"That seems isolating to me." My sister was ten years older than me, and any time she had friends over, I had to go play by myself in my room. Staying away from everyone drove me crazy, and I came to hate her and her friends. I suddenly felt sorry for the princes.

"That's how it's supposed to be, isn't it? It's how we maintain some semblance of home. If we were back in Maerin, they'd be off on their royal estate behind their tall, royal walls, and we wouldn't see them anyway."

"I see Prince Noan sometimes. From a distance," Taavi said.

"At night, Taavi. When he goes for runs. Because you're a stalker."

"I am not," Taavi said. His voice was calm, but he tightened his grip on his spoon like he thought it would run away.

"Do you really think you have a chance with him? As far as anyone knows, he's never dated anyone."

"Which means he could be playing for my team, if you know what I mean."

I looked at Taavi, then at Phae. I hadn't been around anyone who spoke this openly about sexuality. My thoughts flipped back to my family and what my momma would say if she knew this was the type of people I was hanging with. "The gays," she would call them. My kind of people.

"Your team or not, he's a prince and a snob," Phae said. "He wouldn't stoop so low as to date either of us."

"You don't know that." He shifted in his seat. It was the first time I saw him off balance.

As much as I wanted to see Taavi suffer, I wanted to know more about the twins who saved me. "Taavi said they're the reason we're here. Is it true?"

"A hundred percent," Phae said. "Prince Noan is the shadow child, and folks are still superstitious about it. They say it's because of that we all got stranded here. I call it manifest destiny. It's because of an antiquated tradition that he was forced to hide away in the first place. If they'd've just left it well enough alone, we would all still be in Maerin living the good life. Well, some of us." She winked at Taavi, who in turn rolled his eyes.

"Phae, you should stop there," Taavi said. "Let him make up his own mind without clouding it with the past."

"He's bound to find out soon. It might as well be from someone who doesn't believe a person is defined by the circumstances of their birth." Phae's eyes found a spot on the floor, and she stared at it for what seemed like forever.

"Or defined by the family they're born into," Taavi said. He reached across the table for her hand and brought it to his lips. She must be the friend he mentioned earlier, the one who's part witch. What did he call it? *Suhrat?*

"You're so sweet, but I'm still telling the story." A thick, gray mist formed around us until I could see nothing else. "Three hundred years ago, King Egan had identical twin sons. It was the first time in Maerin history that a king had twins, but otherwise, it was nothing special. King Egan lived a dull and uneventful life, and when he died, the first born of the two, Yelend, inherited the throne. His brother, Leander, wasn't too happy with that."

As she spoke, images animated from within the murky thickness and acted out the story before me.

"Years after the start of King Yelend's rule, the Red Cloaks—I know you've heard of them—started a genocide in a city just north of Maerin. King Yelend, this gentle ass king, refused to intervene. The royal army sat in Maerin for two years doing nothing to stop the massacre. Millions died, and eventually, Leander moved to overthrow his brother and claim the throne.

"For the first time in history, a king was challenged for his throne, and in this case, by none other than his brother. What a bastard, right? Anyway, a battle followed—a brutal battle— and King Yelend lost. Fearing he would later retaliate, Leander killed him instead of doing the honorable thing and sparing his life."

The gray mist turned red as the cloudy silhouette stabbed the other figure.

"People were slow to accept King Leander, but now that he was in power, he wanted the royal army to put an end to the ongoing genocide. The generals refused, then the king did the unthinkable. He used mind manipulation—still one of the forbidden *sahdriin*— and forced them to lead their brigades northward and end the genocide."

Maybe it was in my head, but I could hear the clinging of swords against shields and the whizzing of spells being shot in every direction. The clinging stopped and the animated clouds transformed into a monochromatic cityscape.

"The genocide ended, but the people of Maerin lived in fear of King Leander for many years. The lonely tyrant never took a wife, he never had kids, and he died, missed by no one at all. Afterwards, a member of his Court assumed the throne unchallenged, but from then on, twins were a bad omen, and the second born of any set of twins had to die."

"That sounds excessive," I interjected. And cruel. I pictured a mother holding two babies, both of them crying as she squeezed them too tightly.

"King Rosh thought the same thing," Phae said. The misty figures dissipated into the background and new ones formed. "A few generations pass by and now King Rosh and Queen Aganna come into the picture. The Queen is pregnant and going into labor, meanwhile the king is doing that manly thing where he throws a party while they wait to see if it's a boy. Because that's important, right? Out pops Jormon and everyone is cheering and toasting. As they are celebrating, the doc comes out and taps the king on his shoulders. As it turns out, the queen was still pushing.

"What happened next differs depending on who you ask. Some folks say the king kept partying and left his wife alone with baby Noan. Some folks say Tobin—the king's brother—made up some excuse for the guests to leave. The one thing that is clear: the king didn't kill his son in the way he had expected so many other families to do."

"I heard something different, so take that with a grain of salt," said Taavi. "Or with the whole shaker. No one really knows what happened except the King and his brother, Tobin."

"Is Maerin a primitive place? I mean, there's magic and all, but no ultrasounds? Does everyone ride around on horse and buggy?" I asked.

Phae looked annoyed. "Maerin is traditional, which is not the same as primitive."

"In most places, traditional and primitive are about the same," Taavi said.

"Fellas, I'm doing a thing right now. Hush!" Phae motioned with her hand for us to zip it, and the mist shifted again. "What happened next was awful: They kept baby Noan a secret. They hid him away in a servant's shack in a far corner of the estate with the nanny and paraded Prince Jormon around like an only child. Until one day, when little toddler Noan spots little toddler Jormon playing in the garden with the little toddler Prince of Draelin and comes running out of the shack to play, too. That was the wrong move. The jig was up."

The mist dissipated entirely, and I was left to reckon what happened next. Phae picked at a stain on her blouse, and Taavi's cereal bow had refilled itself. They moved on from the narrative like they'd heard it told a thousand times. Like they'd lived it. But I hadn't. "There has to be more. That doesn't explain how we all got here."

"There's more, but I see what Taavi means when he says not to tell it." She shook her head like she was getting rid of bad memories. "Dirk, it was nice to meet you. Do you swim? The lake is open to Kaydans today."

"Are you sure?" Taavi asked.

"Of course. I'm not trying to get dragged through the lake by some local with an ax to grind. No, Sis. Not before I get to have an audience with the prince. Trust me, it's safe today."

"Famous last words," Taavi said, with a wink and a crooked-toothed smile. "Famous. Last. Words."

CHAPTER SIX
JORMON

"WOULD IT BOTHER YOU IF I CAME IN? IT LOOKS LIKE you're busy." I stood in the doorway of the study, waiting for Uncle Tobin's response. Loose sheets of paper were suspended in the air in front of him, and he walked past each of them, reading them—inspecting them—like a sergeant might do with his soldiers.

In another life, were he not the brother of a king, Uncle Tobin would've been a professor. He certainly had a professor's disposition. He expected Noan and me to be studious, kind, and curious; he held high standards that neither of us could ever live up to, and he knew the answer to everything but would make us look it up ourselves rather than tell us. And, like most professor's, he had a favorite student. News flash: I wasn't it.

"You're never a bother," he said, then quoted something from the ancient texts about a healthy work-life balance. The floating pages shifted this way and that, then tucked themselves neatly under a paperweight on the desk. "I was reviewing some contracts and purchase orders, one of the many tasks that will one day be yours to take over, or to delegate to your brother as King Rosh has done to me."

Not simply Rosh, but King Rosh, he said. The events of the other day still weighed on him, too.

"Contracts for *sabejaan*? Uncle Tobin, does it ever seem unfair to you that we are punished for using our powers against humans, yet we sell them to humans in the form of rocks or rings or necklaces for them to use against us?"

"Fairness is a childish word, one that you, of all people, should never use. We can talk about whether it's right or wrong, but never fair. Fairness implies a foundation of equality, and we are not equal. Is it fair to them we can summon the rain just by thinking about it? Is it fair to us it's illegal for us to summon rain between midnight and six in the morning? These childish considerations help nothing. Consider this, though: our wealth and our worth are directly connected to what we can offer humans. Our powers are our only commodity worth trading here, and if we stopped, we couldn't afford to provide for our own kind. So, then, is it right that we keep doing it, even if it might not be fair?"

I didn't appreciate being challenged. Nor did I care much for being seen as childish.

"What if the government wants them?" I asked. "What if one of those contracts asks instead of rain rocks for farmers, that we sell storm stones to disrupt another nation's agriculture? Or instead of water, fire? Are there limits to how far we will go?"

He looked over at the spot where I stood just days ago, whipping the shit out of my brother. He didn't have to say anything. I was already learning lessons about how far I would go. But avoiding pain is not the same as seeking pleasure. I would never have hurt Noan if the end goal was personal gain, would I?

I shook the thought away as a strange feeling pooled in my gut. It wasn't anger or annoyance, but it bubbled up every time I looked at Uncle Tobin. "You're too hard on me."

"Is that what you think?" His eyes squinted and his lip twisted up a smidge.

"Yes, it's what I think. You challenge me on things when there's no way for me to know the right answer. You say stuff like 'leaders are supposed to know,' but there's no class that teaches you how to be a king. It's like you want me to fail."

As the thought of my latent fallibility set in, the air grew thinner, and my vision blurred. A soft ringing started in the depths of my ear and became so loud I wanted to scream.

I didn't, though. It wouldn't be befitting of a future king.

I shook my head, and it all stopped. My breaths softened and my eyes focused. "Are you hard on me because I'm not Noan? I know he's your favorite."

"I'm hard on both of you. You are my nephews. You're the future of our people. I have to be hard on you both."

I didn't buy it.

"Is this what you came here to ask?"

"Not exactly." I took a deep breath. "I want to talk about Dad. About what happened the other day."

"The leeching, yes. It was rather unfortunate. Your father can be harsh when he wants to make a point. Please, have a seat. *Tharitlath.*" A drop of light dripped from the ceiling, and when it hit the carpet, a plush sofa splashed into existence. It looked like the same *sahdr* Dad used. I wondered who taught whom.

"So you agree it was harsh?" I asked. "Noan locked himself in his room three days ago and I haven't seen him since."

"The punishment was harsh, but perhaps necessary. We must punish our own so that humans don't have to. Would it have been better for King Rosh to turn you both over to the local police?"

"No, not in a million years."

"What would you have done if you had to choose?"

Another question I couldn't answer. Of course, I wouldn't turn my brother over and have him be judged in the corrupt system that governs us outside Gray Flats. But I wouldn't leech his powers, even if the effect was only temporary. I would never choose to do that to family.

"Are you happy here?" I asked. "Sometimes, like right now, I think life would have been better had we stayed on Kayda. I'm not even supposed to be here." I said it without thinking and immediately regretted it. "I didn't mean to say that, Uncle Tobin."

"Yet you said it all the same. From how easily the words came out, I gather you've been wanting to say it for a long time."

"It's true, isn't it? I'm not the sh—"

"Prince Jormon, so help me, if you finish that sentence. We don't refer to your brother in that way. That term was created by ignorant people, and I won't have it under this roof." Uncle Tobin returned to his standing desk and reanimated the contracts. He was such a hypocrite. I'd heard him say about Noan that he was a shadow child. What's worse, he knew full well how we ended up here and the role Noan played in causing it. I couldn't say any of that, though. Dad would surely do me harm if he found out I was so nonchalant with the information he shared in our private talks.

"Uncle Tobin," I said, changing the tone and topic altogether, "can I take Noan something to read from your collection? I think a good book will lift his spirits."

"Take anything you like. The ones at the top might be especially to Noan's liking."

Yeah, I bet they would be.

"You're letting in heat and mosquitos," I said to Noan, slapping at the side of my neck. His window had been open the whole time, but due to nerves or whatever, I didn't notice until something pinched at the skin a few inches below my ear. We were in his room getting ready for the ball. Well, sort of. I was getting ready; Noan was stretched across the bed with a dozen books opened or bookmarked. "Noan? Hello?"

I couldn't tell if he was still upset with me, or if his grunted responses and shoulder shrugs were because he was deep in thought. A week had passed since the leeching, and even after I offered him the book from Uncle Tobin's study, he took it from me and closed the door in my face. I was happy he didn't slam it.

"You should start getting ready soon. Guests are already showing up—the teens, or whatever—and we're supposed to entertain them until Uncle Tobin is ready to transport us to D.C. Noan, are you paying attention? What are you doing, anyway?"

"The book you gave me talked about a scrying *sahdr*. I was testing it out." He walked over to the window and stood with his back to me, staring at something outside. The rusting facades of neighboring trailers? The sun falling behind the tree line? The flock of drones deploying from their base like so many bats in the night?

"Whatever, nerd. Do you think Dirk will be at the ball tonight?" I don't know why I asked. If he had been on my mind, it was only as an afterthought. It's not like I'd seen him in the past week, or even that I wanted to.

Dirk's name was enough to activate Noan. He turned to me long enough to roll his eyes and call Dirk a word I'd never heard him use.

"Noan, don't talk like that. None of what happened was his fault."

"Whatever. Did you hear how he talks? Where'd he say he was from? Ku Klux, Mississippi? He sounds like every country song I never wanted to listen to."

"You're just being mean. I kinda like how he sounds. So rhythmic, you know? Like he's singing."

"You talk like you're smitten," he said. He stepped closer. His eyes squinted as he examined my face.

"I'm not smitten." I tried not to blush but failed.

"You are," Noan said, smiling as though he'd discovered a hidden treasure. "You have a thing for the new guy, even though you know nothing about him. Oh, the scandal. Father would have a fit if he knew. A whole conniption, I bet."

"You're being dramatic again. There's no scandal nor anything for Dad to know. I think a guy is cute. So what?"

"You're setting yourself up for failure, that's what. Father is gonna bust this little thing up like a cheap piñata."

"There's nothing to bust up. I'm just having a private talk with my very private brother, one who is nothing if not discreet."

"What would happen if I told him? Will you whip me again?" He returned to stare at the window.

"You know I didn't want that to happen to you, don't you? You told me yourself to go ahead and do it. I wouldn't have done it otherwise. You know that, right?"

"I'm only trying to make light of the situation. It's over now."

"Are you sure? Can we put it behind us?"

"You said you wouldn't let anything happen to me. I believe you meant it."

But I didn't follow through. Is that what was going unsaid? Should I say it for him, or would that mean admitting that I let him down? Internalizing it in a way that would imprint my failure indelibly in our memories. I didn't want that, and I didn't want him to have it either.

I wanted to say something to remind him I've always loved him and that I always would, but Nana Lura barged in holding two sets of dress uniforms: fitted white robes with black onyx buttons running diagonally from the neck to the left hip, and golden dragons embroidered down the outer seams from the hip to the floor-length finish.

My shirt yanked over my head and my shorts loosened as the button unfastened and the zipper buzzed its descent.

"Nana! Get out!"

She tapped her thumbs together.

"Okay, okay. We're getting ready, now go!" I kicked my shorts off as proof, and once satisfied, she backed out of the room. "Can you believe her? We're not ten years old anymore."

Noan laughed. It was the most natural sound in the world, one that I didn't hear often enough. "Nana wiped our asses as little boys. We will always be ten to her."

We laughed more. We were good again. I was sure of it.

"Stop by my room when you get dressed. I have some shoes and a belt you can wear tonight. I insist."

Back in my room, I looked myself over in the floor-length mirror hanging on the closet door. My hair was perfectly placed, but my skin glistened with a light coat of sweat. I grabbed the t-shirt draping over the back of my desk chair and dabbed my forehead, cheeks, and chin until my skin felt dry and smooth. Damn, I hated being in Georgia, and this would be my life for the foreseeable future: sweat, dirt, and pimples. I balled up the t-shirt and tossed it on the floor, already bracing myself for Nana Lura's disappointment at the state of my room.

All that would have to wait, though, as I had a speech to rehearse for the hundredth time. I closed my eyes and let the words come back to me, words I'd spent the night before memorizing and the morning rehearsing. When failure is not an option, when latent disappointment is an ever-present threat, the only defense is perfection. Perfection, perfection, perfection.

By the time we were both ready, most of the guests had already arrived. The smell of food and the hum of noise reached its crescendo as we came closer to the staircase, and I suddenly felt I needed to make a grand entrance. I'd never made a grand entrance before, so I did my best to seem nonchalant as we inched closer to the topmost stair. It wasn't just to do it, but to do it with aplomb.

Are you nervous? I asked.

What's there to be nervous about? There's a room full of people who've probably been waiting for years to meet you. They're the nervous ones.

Us. They've been waiting to meet us.

I ran the run-of-show through my head once more: welcome speech from me, words from Noan, then turn things over to Uncle Tobin to get us from Grey Flats to our place in D.C. for the celebration. With a gulp and a step, I was out in the open.

The conversation of a room full of adolescents fell off in a wave as they slowly took notice of my arrival. All the guys wore the same white dress uniforms we wore, except theirs were bare up the seams. Their onyx buttons were replaced with opalescent stones, and where our sleeves reached down to the wrists, theirs stopped above the bicep. The girls wore sleeveless evening gowns of various colors with accenting patterns that seemed to move and sway as they shifted their weight from one foot to the other. A guy who I recognized from around the way was midway through devouring a canapé. He wavered between putting the un-chewed part back on a tray hovering past, or stuffing the whole thing in his mouth. He went with the latter and choked. He muffled his coughs and turned his back, farting twice along the way.

The awkwardness was inescapable. At some point, another guest patted him hard on the back and the coughing stopped.

"I had a captivating speech planned, but how could I possibly follow that?" I said. The crowed laughed softly, politely, and the now red-faced choker gave an enthusiastic thumbs up. "On behalf of our father, King Rosh, I want to welcome you into our home. It's no royal palace, but we are proud to be here, and happy you could join us as we celebrate the king's and Council's victory on integration."

Did you have this speech prepared?

Shh. Don't distract me. I never told Noan—not that he was receptive to my company over the past week.

You are so your father's son, Noan said, shaking his head.

I smiled like an idiot, the proper thing to do when receiving applause. "When we arrived ten years ago, we had no way of knowing this day would come. Frankly, we didn't know if the next day would come. For many of us, it didn't. For a while, we considered ourselves lucky to have survived the war, only to endure the Hunts that followed. Then we considered ourselves fortunate to have survived the Hunts, only to live on as second-class citizens. All of that is about to change. Look around the room. Look into the faces of your friends and neighbors. These are the faces of change."

My speech lasted a few more minutes, and by the end, all my nerves were gone. Folks clapped and laughed and spewed their energy where they should, and my tone, I'd say, was even more regal than I could've hoped for. I was doing the prince thing like a pro.

"And you all know my brother, Prince Noan." Energy erupted with the same vigor as it had for me. Either they were over the past, or they were all good fakes. Maybe they were faking with me, too. "Noan, would you like to say a few words?"

Noan, a few paces behind me, put on a fake smile, his lips barely arching upwards. "Not really."

I laughed, giving the crowd the green light to laugh, too. "I was expecting something more magniloquent, but I guess that's my brother for you. If any of you are budding historians, be sure to note this as the shortest speech given by a member of the royal family." More claps. More laughs. More energy. "Ah, and there is my uncle. Uncle Tobin, are we ready to depart?"

"We are, Prince Jormon. If everyone would please follow me."

He led us from inside the cool trailer out into a typical hot, humid evening. The sun was well into its descent, and it was already dark between our trailer and the one in front. Between both trailers, a thin, maroon line glowed in midair. It ran all the way from the ground up to a point just out of arm's reach.

"This is that you've been up to?" Noan whispered to Uncle Tobin, who in turn winked in his direction.

"What is it?" I asked, trying to make out what Noan clearly already knew.

"It's a serpent's gate," answered Noan. "I read all about them in *Thirty-Seven Ways to Get Where You Want to Go*. Unlike portals, serpent's gates can transport you into manipulated spaces, but the creator has to have an understanding—a perfect understanding—of both spaces linked by the gate. Uncle, this is dangerous work."

"We learned a moment ago eating can be dangerous work, Nephew."

We could feel the music from where we waited. Melodic notes of a Kaydan cantata seeped through the serpent's gate and floated in the air as if trapped in a breeze, dancing around us while we waited impatiently to do whatever came next. It beckoned us to enter and be entertained. We were horses, stamping our feet in frustration and anticipation, enticed by the music and chatter on the other side.

The slit peeled apart, and air whooshed past us, bringing with it sweet sounds and even sweeter smells. It peeled further back, and the room opened up to us, unfolded, almost, like a love letter that had been shoved in someone's pocket. First the floor fell until it was under my feet, then walls flew past until they stood erect on every side. One wall was made entirely of glass, outside were the familiar rooftops of D.C., the tip of the Washington Monument barely visible off in the night.

As the room completed itself, astonishment rushed over me. There were people everywhere. I'd never seen so many Kaydans in one place. And if I thought I looked nice, I now saw that we were in rags compared to the elegant gowns, suits, and sparkling jewelry flashing from every corner of the room. From somewhere—maybe everywhere—a voice boomed announcing of our arrival, and the crowed snapped their fingers and let their energies twinkle upwards in applause. It was Drac Trine, the representative for Kaydans on the Council of Interspecies Affairs. He was a short, portly man with a graying head of hair and a matching thick moustache. He stood on a raised platform at the front of the room and waved a pudgy hand as his eyes met mine.

People shifted as Noan and I walked deeper into the crowd. When it fit us, we were supposed to stop and talk to a guest. We circled the room, and I hoped to run into someone I recognized. Conversations were punctuated with laugher, some of which was too loud and too deliberate, solely intended to draw my attention. We made our way until we were back where we started. The slit was gone, and in its place stood the redhead from the other day. Dirk, straight out of Ku Klux, Mississippi.

"I see you've found a crew," I said, pointing my chin at the boy and girl next to him. "Dirk, was it?" Noan threw me an exacerbated look.

"Yes, Sir." I was expecting the twang, but it still hit me in my soft spots.

"It's 'Highness,' not 'Sir,'" Noan said, happy to correct him.

"It's neither," I said. "You've puked on my shoes, Dirk. I think we're past the formalities." His face flashed red enough to hide his freckles. "Who are your friends?"

"I'm Phae," said the eager girl in the emerald dress, as she let loose lime and amaranth sparks into the air. "And this is—"

"I'm Taavi," said her broad-shouldered companion. Navy and crimson burst from his chest and surrounded him, then took the shape of a dragon. The dragon genuflected so low his nose touched the ground, then fell apart and reformed as a bed of dahlias.

"Bamuut. That's my favorite dragon from the Tales of Rush Qatil," I said.

"And dahlias are my favorite flower," Noan added. "This is very thoughtful, Taavi. Thank you. To pull off that display takes talent."

Taavi grinned until his lips parted and his crooked front teeth appeared. "I almost forgot," he said, and reached into a pocket, pulling out two small boxes and giving one each to Noan and me. "It's nothing special, but I thought it was appropriate to bring a gift. You don't have to open it now." He spoke too quickly and stumbled over his words, averting his eyes when I tried to look at him directly.

"Thank you, Taavi."

"It's a Tindex—patent pending on that. I heard you both like to read."

"You heard half-right," I said. "Noan is by far the bigger reader. I say it's because he likes to learn, but really, it's about avoiding spending time with me."

"Jormon is right," Noan said. "He's a real bore. Books are far better company." They laughed politely, and to my surprise, Noan smiled. "What does this Tindex do?"

Taavi blushed as a smile crept across his face. "You hold it up to any book and it indexes everything in it. Then, when you want, you just tell it what you're looking for and the book flips to that page. I thought it would come in handy for school."

"That's clever, Taavi. I'm excited to try it out." Noan tucked the box away in his robe pocket. "What's your surname? Do we know your parents?"

"I'm the son of Jayda Herlehy. She didn't come over with us, unfortunately. And I never knew my dad. I was taken in by Lady Lheniva during the war. She's been looking after me ever since." His quick cadence was replaced by one slow and deliberate, and he looked not at Noan, but at Phae, who nodded in encouragement.

Noan, ever so perceptive, caught on to his embarrassment. "My apologies for not knowing that. I'm afraid I don't get out much, what with the title and the people whispering things when they think I don't hear them."

"Brother, I'm sure our friends here are not those people." They nodded in their own way and looked past each other to avoid catching one another's eyes.

Dirk said, "You both seem like good people to me." The more he talked, the closer he sounded to a country singer. I imagined he sat on porches drinking sweet tea and chewing on toothpicks, a thought that spurred me to giggle. "I mean it. I would've been in real trouble at that bus stop if it weren't for you, Prince Noan, Your Highness. I'm grateful for both of y'all's help. Honest to goodness."

Noan flashed his thanks-but-no-thanks smile, the one he gave me every time I asked him to toss a football with me. Dirk had no idea what Noan's help had cost him. A wave of pain passed through me at the memory.

"Your Highness," called a voice over my shoulder. "Allow me to introduce myself. I am Rughor Stolt, son of Hargi Stolt, the King's Advisor on International Affairs.

"Rughor, I remember from when we used to play together as children," I said. "Your father was the one of the king's advisors back then. We haven't seen you in years. You've certainly grown up." He was taller than I, and his *sheriaan* were almost as long as mine.

"We've been away," he said. "My father was posted in London, and we only returned yesterday."

"Are you sure? We saw Hargi meeting with Issek Hilar in his shop nearly a week ago."

"That's not true, Your Highness," Calinea said, appearing so suddenly her voice startled everyone.

This bitch, Noan said, turning his whole body to avoid looking at her.

Be nice and let me handle this.

Calinea continued, "My daddy was meeting with some overseas buyers. He dropped Mr. Stolt's name and was just conjuring up a likeness to see if they knew him."

Bull. Shit.

I know, but now isn't the time to set her straight. Let it go.

"That's what y'all saw when you came by the shop the other day." She blushed the same shade of pink as her energy. "We must thank the king for the invitation. It's been a long time since we've gathered like this. Has anyone seen anything so fancy?"

It was meant to be rhetorical, but Taavi answered he hadn't. Rughor and Calinea shared a look and laughed. "Of course you haven't," Calinea said. "None of us have." The additional statement was meant to ease the sting of the insult, but there was no recovering. I'd noticed, and more importantly, so had Noan.

"I've never seen anything so nice, either," Noan said. "I always looked forward to when my parents would host *kahdalas* and *hamrillas* and such."

"The debutant balls of Maerin," I added, noticing the puzzled expressions both Taavi and Dirk wore.

"Jormon was too young to go to balls, so he would spend the entire evening with me and Nana Lura. We'd play Dragons and Gusts in the cellar and listen to the music that spilled down the stairs. It was all I had to look forward to when I was hidden away all those years."

Calinea and Rughor both looked like they'd eaten a worm. Noan could kill a mood with the precision of a sniper. Noan reached out unexpectedly and squeezed Taavi's shoulder, thought for a moment, then leaned in and whispered something in his ear. Taavi smiled and reached his hand up to cover his mouth. He leaned over and whispered something back to Noan. It was a private moment playing out in public, causing some among us to shift awkwardly. If Noan meant to make us uncomfortable, he succeeded.

Rughor said, "I used to play Dragons and Gusts when I was little, too."

"That's wonderful—Prince Jormon, we should walk the room a bit." Noan smiled delicately. "Taavi, Phae, Dirk: it was a pleasure meeting you. A real pleasure. Rughor, Calinea."

We hadn't walked two steps before Noan dug into Calinea's lie.

"Issek wasn't meeting some overseas buyers. What could she possibly be hiding?"

"I wouldn't look too much into it," I said.

"If Hargi is meeting with Issek, why is he doing it in secret? And why would they lie about returning from London a week early?"

"We should talk about this later," I said, as an older woman waved at me, and I waved in return.

After working the room and being greeted by the many Kaydans who wanted to get in better with Dad, a chime sounded, tickling my ears and nose with a sweet sound and matching scent. The chiming slowly filled my mouth with the sticky richness of crème anglaise. I swallowed it down and felt surprisingly satisfied. Before I could take in the wonder of it all, Drac's voice boomed. "Ladies and gentlemen, please find your seats. Please, now. Quickly. Adults, to the outer tables with crimson linen. Those under the age of eighteen, please find a seat at the inner tables with white linen."

We made our way to the front of the room and sat at a circular table with ten place settings. For a moment, no one joined us, and I squirmed at the thought of being avoided. I resisted the nagging urge to look around lest I seemed desperate for company. Noan was the only person I needed, and he was here with me.

Drac's voice boomed again, "Thank you, thank you all. And welcome to the Gaddalie Ball." A fluttering of wings drew everyone's eyes upwards as magenta light cascaded down in wavy rays, and I noticed for the first time how high the ceiling was. At the very top through an open skylight, *flanih doves* swooped in and circulated the room, shedding what looked like pinkish pollen that hovered a few feet above everyone's head before vanishing.

"*Flanih doves*," whispered Phae. Her sudden appearance startled me, and I nearly dropped the glass I was holding. "They are great at discerning affection. If they're here, the Matchmaker must be nearby."

She sat to my left, followed by Rughor and Calinea. Dirk, Taavi, and the choking kid from earlier in the evening sat on the other side of Noan. I nearly asked if he could switch seats with me, but the action might offend Phae, who I hardly knew, and draw attention to my move to be nearer to Dirk. A boy and a girl whom I met earlier occupied the remaining two seats.

"The Matchmaker?" I asked. *Noan, what type of party is this? What does any of this have to do with integration?*

"She's here to help with the sorting. And with a few other things, I've been told. See the decorations on the table?" Phae pointed to the table's centerpiece, an array of red and blue dahlias laid flat on the table to form a circle, their stems a perfection of lattice work to lock them all together. Surrounding the arrangement were several black, figurine serpents twined so tightly it looked like one long snake wrapped around itself. A serpent's head poked up every few inches or so. I counted ten in total, one for each person.

"They're called *soulfangs*. You pour your essence into the *soulfang's* mouth, then it reads your energy to see what kind of person you are."

"Pour my essence? That doesn't sound scary at all," Taavi said, reaching hesitantly to tap the serpent ring, losing courage, then removing his hand altogether. Rughor smirked at his cowardice, but Taavi shrugged it off. "What? I didn't want my essence to go in it by accident."

"How's it s'posed to work?" Dirk asked, speaking loudly over the collective hum of chatter.

"Forgive my ignorance," I said, hating to seem ignorant, "but this has never happened before."

"Tonight is two-fold," began Calinea, eager chime in. She was still smiling and blushing, so different from the person who had all but slammed a door in my face a week ago. If she was trying to fall back into good graces, she could save it; I still intended to tell Dad about what happened at Issek's shop.

"Enlighten us," Noan said, not the least bit amused.

"Our population isn't going at the rate it should, so more of us need to…you know?" We got the hint. "And the second purpose has to do with the whole integration business. Tonight, the powers that be will sort us into cohorts. None of the schools could handle an intrusion of a hundred new students—"

"So they're splitting us up, and only a select few will attend the human high school," Noan finished. "How do you know this?"

"I'm not supposed to tell, but I overheard my daddy talking about it the other morning with the Matchmaker. She came to the shop to buy the materials for the centerpieces."

"I think it's a great idea," I said, assuming Dad had a hand in it. "I'd be happy to share this experience with anyone at this table." They all agreed. "I'm kind of excited about going to school. Years back, once things settled after the Hunts, Noan and I read every single Hardy Boys book there is. Then we'd pretend that I was Frank and he was Joe, and we'd go sleuthing around the house solving mysteries. If life as a high school teen is anything like that, I'm all about it."

"You might be disappointed," Dirk said. "The only mystery in my old school was what was in the stew."

74

"You've been to an American school before?" Rughor asked, but before Dirk could answer with his life story, Dad entered from the back of the room and the guests erupted in a spectacular applause. As he passed our table, he kissed Noan and me on the top of the head. I extended my applause and let my energy erupt to form a perfect replica of *Zereq*. I even managed to lighten the blues just so. Dad stopped as the spectacle reached his periphery. He turned and took a step into the glowing sphere and, with eyes closed and chin to the ceiling, basked in *Zereq*'s light.

I didn't know you had it in you, projected Noan as the guests applauded Dad and me alike.

I listened to Dad's speech, but his platitudes were so often interrupted by fantastic displays of light from one ecstatic corner or other, I lost the overall meaning. Still, I raised my glass at the appropriate times and drank when the rest of them did, until finally Dad introduced the Matchmaker.

I'd seen the Matchmaker in less formal situations, and her presentation on this evening was just as plain. She wore a simple blue gown with a matching-colored fascinator in the shape of a *flanih dove*. She didn't float or soar in the cartoonish way I imagined someone in her position would. Instead, she strutted across the dais in high-heeled shoes, waving her gloved arms in wide, arcing motions as she spoke.

"It has been many years since we've all seen each other this way, and I want you all to take a moment to stare into your neighbor's face. Do you recognize them? Have you asked about their families? Do you love them in the way that we all must love each other? Do you care that they survive? Do you wish that they thrive?"

Noan rolled his eyes, and I elbowed him in the ribs. Yes, she was cheesy, and yes, she was borderline preachy, but I didn't want Noan's cynicism to spoil the mood. The Matchmaker droned on about community and the prosperity of our people for what seemed like an hour. Around the room, everyone smiled and drank wine, and summoned hovering trays of hors d'oeurves. I sipped from my glass, hoping it was wine. It was, so I took another sip. Then another.

I was at the bottom of my second glass when the Matchmaker announced the sorting.

"At this time, pour your essence into the mouth of the *soulfang*. Don't be afraid, it won't bite." She laughed without humor. "It will bless you with an aura. Bask in its blessing and look for others who've been blessed in the same way."

I looked around the table and took the lead. Maybe it was the wine. "Are we ready, everyone?"

Everyone but Dirk nodded, and I realized he might need help figuring things out. I should've switched with Noan when I had the chance.

I extended an arm towards the *soulfang*'s mouth and let my energy flow from my hand. Everyone else did this same. For a moment, nothing happened. We stared at the twisted centerpiece, then at each other.

"I guess it's figuring us out," I joked. They laughed nervously, and Dirk slid his chair back from the table as if he were afraid the snake might strike him. Just as he did, the *soulfang* in front of him lunged. It planted its fangs into his wrist, then coiled its black body around his arm.

Before I could react, a *soulfang* bit into my wrist, then Noan's, and into everyone else's. I wanted to scream out of reflex, but the bite didn't hurt. I pressed my thumb around where the serpent's mouth touched my arm, and it felt pleasurable. I touched it again, and a warm amber light rippled up my *sheriaan* and radiated from my skin.

The room's dark ambiance quickly shifted as colors of varying hues and intensities erupted from everyone, reflecting from the white table settings. It was only by coincidence that I looked over at Dirk. He was still staring at his own arm, which was radiating the exact same amber aura as mine. His eyes met mine, and without thinking about it, I smiled at him. He smiled back, which made me smile even bigger.

Despite how many colors there were, it was easy to spot a match. In addition to Dirk, Rughor and a girl I'd met earlier in the evening shared the same color aura, too. Taavi, Calinea, and two others at the table radiated a dark orange that bordered on red.

Noan didn't have a color. The *soulfang* latched onto his wrist, but it struggled to wrap around his arm. Its body tensed and loosened until it went as limp as a worm and fell to the floor.

"I don't know what's happening," Noan said. His voice shook, and panic filled my brother's eyes for the first time since the War. His arm twitched. He grabbed his shoulder to brace it, but it was useless. He rushed from the table and made for a side door. Before he was ten steps away, he let out a banshee's wail, and thick clouds of black smoke erupted from his arm like someone had struck oil. The darkness overtook everything, starting with Noan. It billowed out in thick flows, quickly engulfing our table, then everything else.

"Noan!" I screamed into the darkness, but the smoke absorbed my voice before it reached my own ears. Suddenly blind and deaf, I panicked. The only thing reminding me I existed was the strong beating of my heart. "Noan! Noan!"

CHAPTER SEVEN
NOAN

MY ARM WAS ON FIRE AND I COULDN'T SEE SHIT. A darkness spilled from me so black it clouded everything and so thick it held me in place. I had to leave. If I didn't die on the spot, Father would kill me.

"Uncle!" I shouted. "Please!" Did I lose my voice? "Uncle!" *What the hell is happening?*

I fell to my knees and put my hand over where the *soulfang* bit me, hoping it would plug the hole and stop the darkness from escaping. I needed to get out, even if that meant jumping out the window and landing in D.C. traffic.

Just then, a maroon strip emerged in the darkness and beckoned me to enter. The serpent's gate. *Thank you, Uncle.* I didn't know where it would take me, but anywhere would be better than here.

I crawled to my feet and leaned into the gate's velvety lining. It gave no resistance, and I fell through and landed hard on my shoulder. Shadow continued to leak from my wrist, but it floated upwards into the night air, blocking out the light from the full moon.

I looked around to see if I was somewhere safe. The woods looked familiar, as did the white sand along the path. I was in Gordonia Park, behind Gray Flats.

I lay there feeling like my insides were on fire until my arm stopped leaking. Did it take a minute? Maybe an hour? I was weak and worn, and I must have passed out. One minute I was leaking, and the next minute I was on the ground looking up through pine branches at the evening sky.

I stood slowly and tried to walk away, but my legs buckled, and I leaned against a tree to keep from falling over. Pine sap stuck between my fingers, and I yelled into the night. "Can this night get any worse!" My shouts broke through the nocturnal symphony of bugs chirping and rodents scuttling and faded in the distance.

I tried to ignore the sinking feeling in my gut, the one that pulsed and throbbed and demanded my full attention. I was broken. I was black inside, blacker than an ace of spades. The talk of shadow children was more than just talk, and I was one of them. Pricked and bleeding out my shadow for all the world to see. As I stumbled through the woods alone, my fear turned to anger. Why didn't anyone come with me? Wouldn't they know how scared I was?

A warm breeze blew through the trees, and the leaves brushed together in an uncoordinated clapping, adding percussion to music of the night. A bead of sweat trickled from my armpit down to my waist, tickling my torso and aggravating my mood. I wished I was somewhere cooler. Somewhere where the grass didn't brown if you miss a day of watering, and where the setting of the sun foreshadowed a pleasant evening. Where the katydids chirped for mates, not in complaint of the heat like I imagined they did.

The wind hit a fresh wine stain on my shirt, and the pungent, fruity aroma wafted around my nose and hung there. I must've spilled someone's glass when I stumbled out through the darkness. I removed the shirt and tossed it on the ground, but the smell lingered, reminding me of my fear and humiliation.

I wanted to run, but I wasn't wearing the right shoes. Jormon's shoes were too nice and too new, and too tight. I took them off as well.

I became aware that the borrowed belt gripped desperately around my waist, and as I unfastened it, a rustling came from a nearby bush.

"Who's there?" I sounded so ordinarily human. Not scared or startled, but predictable. Standing in the woods whispering 'who's there' at the slightest noise. No, that's not me. I curled my hand into a fist. *"Nared."* Fire swallowed my hand. I cocked my elbow back, ready to throw flames.

"It's me, Your Highness. Taavi." He released a concentration of energy above his head, casting his face in shades of red and blue. "I figured I should announce myself before you kept stripping."

I exhaled and let the fire dissipate. "What are you doing here? I could've hurt you just now. Where's Prince Jormon?"

"The prince is still at the party. I wanted to make sure you were alright after what just happened. Mr. Tobin said it was okay if I came."

"He sent you alone? Why didn't he come? Or one of the king's guards? What makes you so—" a fatigue slammed into me, dropping me down to one knee, "—goddamn capable?" I shouldn't have been upset with Taavi, but he was the only one here to bear my frustrations. Of course, Uncle couldn't leave the party to tend to me, nor would the guards leave to tend to me when they would be reassuring Father's guests that everything was okay. I was the shadow child. I was meant to be alone.

"Are you alright? It was really quite a scene back there, everyone is really shaken up. I bet you are too, more than anybody."

"I've been through worse. And if people are going to talk about me, at least now they have some gossip worth sharing."

"Being talked about is better than being forgotten." He came closer, and though there was no sadness in his voice, something deep in his eyes told me he spoke from a place of bitter sincerity. "Besides, King Rosh calmed everyone down pretty quickly and turned the focus back on the groupings. They are calling us Cohorts. Isn't that silly?"

It was better than being called a copper, which is what the other students will call us.

He was trying to distract me, and I allowed it. "How do you feel about yours? Forgive me if I didn't see where you landed."

"Only the few who had the same aura as Prince Jormon will go to the public school. I was one of the lucky ones. The rest will either stick around doing factory work, or if they're really talented, maybe they'll go to the Academy."

"Before all this integration mess, I saw myself going to the Academy. I was going to do great things." If I sounded sad, it's because I was. Oh well, ships sailed and all.

"You can still do great things, Your Highness. You don't need the Academy to be great."

"I'm flattered, Taavi. I really am."

"I mean it. I think you're the best of us. The whole world could learn something from you."

Did he really think that? It was true, I could admit with no humility, but I'd never heard anyone acknowledge it. Even Uncle. And how did he know?

"I'm not feeling well. Can you walk me home?"

"Anything you ask, Prince Noan."

I wrapped my arm around his broad shoulders and shifted my weight onto him. He supported me easily, and slowly we covered the dusty trail back to the trailer park.

"Before I forget, King Rosh made an interesting proposal just before the food was served. He put Prince Jormon in charge of training the cohort in *sahdr*. Even though they won't go to the Academy, they'll still get exposed to *mustedi* studies."

I didn't have the strength to laugh. Jormon was the last person alive I'd ever let teach me anything, and now he's to teach them? Were they so bad off that they'd benefit from his tutelage? Instinctively, I looked over to see Taavi's *sheriaan*. They were half as long as mine, and they'd yet to branch off into intricate patterns.

"Prince Jormon will be a great teacher," I said, lying my ass off. "Taavi, this might be too much to ask of you, but I'm suddenly in need of fresh air. Can you fly with me? We don't have to go so high, just over the trees there."

"Of course, Prince Noan." He checked his wristwatch instinctively, but I've flown these skies enough to read the lighting. Curfew hadn't kicked in yet.

Taavi lifted off first, and I used what energy I had to carry some of my weight. We rose slowly. The air lost its humidity, and my breathing eased.

"Whoa! That was super easy," Taavi said. "I feel...powerful!"

"That's great, Superman."

"No, I mean it. It's like I'm having a power surge or something. Do you think what happened back there could've—"

"This is high enough, thank you." The last thing I wanted to hear was that my shadow spilled out of me and made all those hateful people in that room super strong.

I tilted my head so I could see the city. At a glance, the land was a quilt. Perfect square acres of green growth touched perfect squares of brown tillage, which touched various shades of land sprouting various crops. All of this was intersected by brown rivers and reddish, clay roads that weaved around farmland. Two lakes stared up at me like misshapen eyes. The closer eye—the focal point of Gordonia Park—I was familiar with. Uncle took Jormon and me there often before we moved to D.C.

As I took it all in, it occurred to me I might not be here one day. Someone could kill me or shun me for things like what happened tonight, and Jormon would be alone. All the stupid little questions he usually asked me would go unheard, and he'd have to keep his own council as he navigated his existence in this world. I wasn't sure he'd be able to do it, at least not with the world like this.

"Do you think integration will work?" I asked.

"If we make it work."

It was the naive answer of an optimist. It was as though he didn't live in the same world I did, the one where people would rather destroy something they enjoy than to see people they hate enjoy it with them.

"Don't say that because you're talking to me. Kaydans can only do so much. Sure, we can try to make it work from our end, but humans have to meet us in the middle. Oh, don't look that way. If I wanted sad, puppy dog eyes, I'd volunteer at the animal shelter. I didn't say it to challenge your opinion. I want to know what you really think. Forget that I'm the king's son. What would you say if it were—what's her name? Your friend. If it were her asking you."

He erased the tiny hints of dejection from his face and re-squared his shoulders. "If it were Phae asking, I'd tell her the same thing. I believe everyone has the ability to carve a better path for themselves. I'm the child of servants, now I'm keeping the prince company. My mom would be so proud of me if they knew how far I'd come. As a people, if we work at it, we can go so much farther and be so much more."

Ever since I realized there was something called a shadow child, I've been trying not to be that. I spent so much time looking inward at how I am and how I present, glancing only so far out as to observe what people saw in me. I never stopped to see what everyone else was going through. Taavi lost his family, and I now knew it was because of me. Yet there he was, looking towards a brighter future, and all the while I was focusing on feeling like a victim. I owed him to do better. To *be* better. I owed everyone that.

"Can you make me a promise?"

"Anything, Your Highness."

"If you ever catch me living below your expectations, please tell me so."

CHAPTER EIGHT
JORMON

IN THE MONTH THAT FOLLOWED, MURMURS THAT the south would rise again crescendoed until they became a screaming call to arms. The gossip throughout Issek's was that the Riders in His Holy Name had recruited a swell of new, young members, and they pledged to do whatever it took to keep their schools pure. The few humans that lived in Gray Flats moved out, and Kaydans who had grown too afraid to live in their nicer homes in nicer neighborhoods moved in. With only a week left before school began, President Sunwarden's integration initiative wasn't looking too promising.

Kaydans murmured rumors of their own, except their rumblings were about the dangers Noan posed to the community. The blackening at the ball drummed up a swell of old feelings about the inherent evil the second of twins possess. It was all lies, but there's little that can be done about rumors. Instead of focusing on them, I planned daily *mustedi* lessons for our cohort. In the end, it was only five of us: Noan, Dirk, Phae, Taavi, and I.

My first lesson went horribly. Being their prince, teacher, and peer all at the same time was overwhelming, especially when half of them already knew the *sahdr* I was going to demonstrate. After two lessons, I had no choice but to swallow my pride and ask Noan for his help. He'd been distracted, spending his days with Taavi off doing only *Heemrah* knows what, and his nights in Uncle Tobin's study, again doing the mysterious. I was finally able to corner him as he was stepping out of the shower one evening.

"Jormon! Get the hell out!" he yelled.

"Please, Noan. I can't do it alone. Some of them are more advanced than me. We can break them up. I'll teach the ones I can, and you can teach the rest."

It wasn't a simple request. Noan didn't dare show his face in public.

"No, thanks. They don't want to learn anything from me. They think I'm cursed. Especially that Rughor. Taavi told me what he's being going around saying—hand me my towel."

I pulled the towel off the rack and held it tightly. "Ignore Rughor. He's only trying to make friends now that he's back in town."

"Towel, please—Do you think his British accent is real?"

"Focus, Noan. Will you help me? I know you think I'm dumb. I bet you're itching to step in. Don't make me beg." I passed Noan his towel. "Please."

"Fine," he said at last. "But I won't teach them. I'll teach you, and *you* can teach them. I don't want them to know I care."

"Little Brother, I love you so much." I snatched the towel from his hands and kicked his clothes into the hallway before running out.

"Love you, too. Asshole!"

We quickly became the cohort the Matchmaker meant for us to be, which was inevitable. We spent four nights a week together, studying under my demanding tutelage, with Noan training me ahead of the nightly lessons. The last thing I needed was to look stupid in front of people who respected me. Especially Dirk.

We hadn't done anything fun in a while, so it relieved everyone when I announced our lesson the following evening was cancelled. "Uncle Tobin has informed me he will take over tomorrow's lesson, which will be at 7:00am."

"But it's Saturday," Taavi protested.

"Will this cut into your cartoon time?" Noan asked.

"I planned to fly to New York City. I want to stand in line for the lottery to see a Broadway show, and you have to be there super early."

"New York City?" Phae questioned. "I don't believe it."

"Yet, it's true," Taavi bragged.

"You couldn't fly to NYC if you had a cape around your neck and a jet engine strapped to your ass. Where would you get the energy?"

"I've been practicing. It doesn't cost me as much energy as it does you."

"Aren't you afraid of getting shot down like a duck somewhere over the Carolinas? I didn't know a Broadway show was worth that much to you."

"No one is flying anywhere tomorrow," I said. "We'll meet up at the back gate. Considering it's Uncle Tobin leading the way, I suggest you all be there early."

I loitered around the training grounds, waiting on Dirk to pack his raggedy bag. He'd confused the fire and water *sahdriin* and accidentally set Noan's leg on fire. From how badly he performed the rest of the evening, I could tell he never got over the mistake.

"If you want, we can hang around for a bit, just the two of us." My voice was unnaturally high, and even to myself I came off as nervous. I cleared my throat. "I can work with you if you want. Help you get caught up and all."

"It's this stupid language." His eyes got as big as tea saucers, and he froze in place like he'd been caught breaking into someone's window. "I shouldn't have said that in front of you. I'm sorry for being so negative, but it frustrates me to no end. Plus, it's hotter than fish grease out here, and these damn gnats keep breaking my concentration. Every time I think I'm about to get it right, one of 'em flies in my ear and starts buzzing around. I'm just complaining, though. Pay me no mind."

86

"We all have to get this right. I struggle myself, so I know what you're going through. Let's hang back a bit and get in more practice."

"I wish I could, Your Highness, but I have my first shift at the Factory in just a little while. I've been told I've freeloaded long enough."

"The factory?"

"Where we make the, what's the word, *subjoin*?"

"*Sabejaan.*"

"Yeah, those. I can't carve the runes, but I can pump the energy into it. I figured you'd know about the Factory."

"Oh, yeah. I know about it," I lied. "I'm just used to it being referred to by the *Maerinish* word." I began to feel childish and naive. Those contracts in Uncle Tobin's study for thousands of *sabejaan* had to be fulfilled somehow. I assumed the same vendors who sold their stuff as Issek's donated a percentage as some sort of tax. All I could picture now was a smudge-faced Dirk pouring his silver and gold energy into rings and bracelets and charms.

"I can come after my shift. Around midnight?"

It wouldn't look good for me to have a visitor over so late. Nana Lura would be asleep, but somehow, she'd know. She'd tell Uncle Tobin how "unbecoming" my behavior is, then I'd have to hear his mouth move for the next hour.

But Dirk was a friend, was he not? A very handsome, laid-back friend. And I was just a friendly prince who wanted to be laid-back with him. It was one of my duties to see to the well-being of our people. Dirk is one of ours, and I was keen on seeing him be well. "Sure. Midnight is fine."

By the time we'd finished training, it was nearly 2:00 am. The rest of the house was already asleep, nevertheless, I didn't want the evening to end. In a word, I was giddy. Noan wasn't around to hear me butcher instructions on how to do a basic *sahdr helaq*—learning how to lift heavier things using telekinesis—or conjure a *sahdr dura* shield. Regardless of my teaching style, or maybe because of it, Dirk absorbed every word and could perform each task on the third or fourth attempt.

"Are you sure you don't want to stay the night?" I asked. Dirk wiped a trail of sweat from the tips of his sideburns. *Sahdr* was still hard work for him. "We have to be up in a few hours, and I don't mind if you stay. There's a couch in my room you can sleep on if you don't want to sleep with me."

"Oh," Dirk said, and his face reddened.

I realized what I'd said, and my face suddenly felt as if it were on fire. "I mean, if you don't want to share a bed with me, you don't have to. But you can if you want to. But I'm just saying—"

"The couch is fine," Dirk said.

We walked to the room with a cloud of awkwardness floating between us. I wanted to shower, to wash the sweat from my body and heat from my face, but I was afraid I would stumble into inviting Dirk to come shower with me, and I didn't know how I would feel if he said no. Even worse, what if he said yes?

Dirk made himself comfortable on the couch with a sheet and down pillow I brought up from the linen closet. I spent the next hour tossing and turning with the desire to spark conversation. The clean, white sheets clung to my sweaty, dingy skin making it even harder to drift off. Every time I came close to sleep, Dirk would turn on the couch and its springs would squeak, reminding me he was still there. I looked at the clock on my nightstand. It was 3:00 am.

"Can't sleep?" I asked, already knowing the answer. "Where'd the name 'Dirk' come from? Are your parents Norwegian or something?"

"It's a nickname. It's dumb, really. When I was little, I told my momma 'nem I wanted this dirt bike that I saw on TV. Instead of saying 'dirt', I kept calling it a 'dirk bike.' They thought it was hilarious. Most Southern folks take the thing most embarrassing about you and make it your nickname. Mine became Dirk."

"That sounds pretty bad."

"It's actually cute, if you think about it. I have a friend nicknamed Bunny because he stepped in dog crap and hopped all the way home on one foot, and another buddy we call Dirty Junior because his dad, his senior, works for the trash company. All things said, Dirk isn't so bad."

"What's your real name?"

He thought about it longer than he should have. "Dirk is as real a name as the other one. When I stop and think about it, I don't know my given name, the one my real parents called me. If I kept Dirk as my real name, it wouldn't much make a difference, would it?"

I couldn't answer the question. I had no idea what it was like not to know who you are. All my life, I'd been the prince who everyone expected would be king someday. I knew where I came from and where I would end up. A strange sympathy swelled in my chest, and all I wanted to do in that moment was to grab Dirk and hug him tightly. I fought the urge, fearing the same rejection that flooded my mind every time I wanted to get closer to him.

"What name would you give me?" I asked. It wasn't a serious question, but it was enough to pull my mind from the other direction it was heading. I sat up to show I wanted an answer.

He ran his fingers through his hair as he looked up at the clouds passing in front of *Heemrah*. A lone foot hung freely from the bottom of the sheet and dangled over the arm of the couch, and he bounced it restlessly. After minutes of deliberation, he said, "I don't think I should say. I don't want to be unintentionally rude or disrespectful. You're my prince. I'm still trying to wrap my head around that."

"That's just a title. I'm everyone's prince, but I'm not everyone's friend. Wouldn't you say we're friends? I think so." I stopped there, but I wanted to say so much more. That I thought he was a close friend, even though I'd known him less than I'd known anyone else. That I wanted to run my fingers through his hair and see if it was as soft as it looked.

"Did you go to sleep on me?" he asked.

"Huh?" I must've completely zoned out.

"I said your nickname, and you didn't say anything."

"I'm sorry. I-I didn't hear you. Repeat it, please."

"Nope." He chuckled, then laughed out loud.

"You can't laugh and not say anything. You have to tell me."

"I said it once. That's it." He laughed more.

I wanted him to laugh forever.

"Tell me," I insisted.

But he wouldn't tell me, no matter how much I insisted. I threw a pillow at him, and he used a *sahdr* to block it from hitting him in the head. I was so happy that I sat upright.

So did he.

We sat there smiling like two jocks staring at a football. I wanted to say something, to tell him he didn't have to sleep on the couch. That my bed had plenty of room. Instead, I laid back down and pulled the sheets up to my chin.

He tossed and turned, and I turned and tossed. We did that until the sun peaked over the treetops.

PART TWO

TO KNOW AND TO REMEMBER

CHAPTER NINE
NOAN

"BOYS, WAKE UP," UNCLE SHOUTED FROM DOWN THE hall. He rarely ever shouted. "You'll be late for school."

I was already awake. I had been since early morning. I kept thinking about what happened at the ball the other day, afraid it might happen again at school. I still didn't know what caused it. And then there was school itself. I had read a few coming-of-age novels, so I somewhat knew what to expect: sideways glances, direct staring, whispers, the occasional off comment. The quintessence of adolescence.

Jormon was the complete opposite when faced with new situations. When faced with anything, really, so he probably slept like a baby. He quickly took a liking to people, and everyone liked him in return. Granted, he wouldn't be treated like the king-to-be at Toombs County High School, but there was nothing to say that starting his senior year would be any different from how he started anything else. With his luck, he'll get drafted onto the football team and even the locals would treat him like royalty, which I read was a thing in the south.

I showered, dressed, and went to the kitchen to grab something quick to eat.

"Oh look," Jormon said with a grin, "we match." We both wore blue, short-sleeved shirts, dark jeans, matching shoes, and our dark hair fell about in the same manner of disarray. Were it not for the differences in our *sheriaan*, we could be the exact same person.

"Go change," I ordered. "Today is already going to be bad enough, and I don't want to attract needless attention."

"Nope." He grabbed an apple from the fruit bowl and bit into it. "Noan," he began, rotating chewed apple chunks in his jaws, "we are going to make this a great day. Shed the bad attitude, keep the matching get-up, and let's lean into this. We have to set the example, remember?"

"Why are you in such a good mood?" I asked. Jormon strutted around the kitchen like today was any other day. We were about to walk into the lion's den, and he was acting like the goddamn lion. I wish I had his confidence sometimes, but one of us had to be the cautious one.

"You can answer that outside," Uncle interrupted, brushing past us to place his half-empty coffee mug in the sink.

"Is Dad coming to see us off?" Jormon asked. He dusted lint off his shirt collar while he waited for Uncle's calculated response. He knew as well as I did Father wouldn't be here.

"The king has another engagement this morning. Something last minute. He wanted to be here, and he sends his best wishes."

"What's with the outfit?" I asked, pointing at the traditional formal wear. "Are you heading to that same engagement?"

"Outside. Both of you."

Begrudgingly, I started toward the door.

"How are we getting to school? Is the bus stopping by?" I asked.

"We're too cool for a bus," Jormon said. "We should have our own car."

"Neither of you is too cool for anything. Nor do either of you have a driver's license."

"If we had a license, then could we get a car?" Jormon asked.

"I'll do you one better: the Board of Education says it's okay if you fly to school. They've established a landing zone near the parking lot. It's the only designated landing and take-off spot. The Board still prohibits flying on campus."

"Is it safe?" My mind flooded with images of hunters shooting us down like so many ducks.

"Lheniva will travel with you, and escorts from the king's security detail will hover overhead. If anything goes too far south, they'll intervene. Trust me when I say there's no safer way to travel."

"Why can't we use teleport stones? Do we have time to go to Issek's?" Jormon said.

"If you'd learn how to teleport, you wouldn't need a stone," Uncle said plainly.

"So it's an option for the future?"

Uncle exhaled so forcefully I thought he was trying to blow the trailer over. "You two can really work a nerve."

"We love you too, Uncle."

We stepped out into the world as a regular American family, and it felt odd. The new pair of shoes and the outfit picked out just for the occasion. Nana Lura milling about the kitchen cleaning up the breakfast dishes we left on the counter. The backpacks which had been waiting in the hall. Uncle walking out the door with us and closing it behind him like a working dad. None of it was normal.

The oppressive August heat clung to everything, wrapping me in a stifling embrace from the moment my foot hit the ground. The air was dense with the scent of damp pine, intermingling with subtle wafts of magnolia, and somewhere, someone had already started cooking breakfast, sending faint trails of fried pork into the mix. Now outside, the knowledge of the day ahead bore down on me just as heavily as the humid air, filling me with a tangled web of anxiety, anticipation, and uncertainty.

Dirk, Taavi, and Phae were waiting when we turned the corner. Dirk and Taavi had on clothes and shoes I'd never seen them wear before, and Phae's hair seemed newly styled: gathered into thick braids on either side that met and twisted into a swoosh toward the top. Everyone looked their best.

"Lheniva's running late again, but we should still make it on time. Hey Mr. Tobin," Dirk said. "Are you coming with us, too?"

"No, no," Uncle replied. "I have a matter to attend to, but I'll see you later this evening for dinner and you can tell me about your day. Boys, do you have money for lunch and whatever else?"

"Yes, Uncle," I replied, patting my pocket to make sure the ten-dollar bill was still there.

"Good, good. Contact me if you need anything." He waved one last time before vanishing.

"When can I learn how to do that?" asked Dirk.

"When you start making the lesson plans," I said, earning myself a playful punch in the arm from Jormon. Maybe it would be a fun day after all.

The screen door banged shut and Lheniva strutted down the stairs. "Children, you look beautiful." As she approached, her feet left the ground, and she positioned herself in front of us like a drill sergeant examining her platoon. "Tobin probably had the talk with you all about this, but I'm going to repeat it so that it's clear. The five of you need to hear this—especially you, Dirk, since you've gone a lifetime passing for something you're not." She lit a cigarette, took one puff, and stamped it out in the dewy grass. "People are going to look at you differently. They will single you out or make fun of you because you're different. They will provoke you, hoping you'll do something to get yourself in trouble. Whatever happens, you can't let that anger show, do you hear me?"

She didn't wait for our affirmation. "If you get mad and act out, it won't be you that's wild and out of control. It'll be everybody that looks like you. They'll say that people like you can't control themselves and are dangerous to be around. We know it's not true, and I know it's unfair, but that's how it is.

"The best you can do is compose yourselves and show only the best of who we are, okay? Do whatever these teachers ask, and don't give them any reason to think that you're a threat. No sass, no sudden movements, no picking fights, nothing. See those drones out there? They're not out there looking for them. They're looking for you. 'He started it' means nothing.

"And if things seem unfair, come and talk to me or Tobin and let the leadership handle it, okay?" This time she waited for our response, muttered "okays" mixed in with Dirk's "yes ma'am."

She was right, though. Uncle had drilled that into us at an early age. Be careful around law enforcement, and don't make sudden moves. Don't put your hands in your pockets when you're at a store. Things that other people didn't have to worry about. It was easier to just stay in Gray Flats. Out of sight. Out of trouble.

"Shall we go now?" Her smile wasn't enough to put me at ease, but I appreciated the effort.

Without realizing it, we flew in a V-shaped formation. Lheniva took point, and Jormon and I flanked her on both sides. If something went wrong, horribly wrong, we'd be the first line of defense.

A car ride would've taken half an hour with traffic, but the flight took less than five minutes. Far below, vehicles jammed up the road leading to the school's parking lot, and as we approached, I saw why. Military trucks staggered on both sides of the road, and soldiers operated a makeshift barricade as they inspected cars before letting them pass. No fewer than a hundred people gathered underneath the portico thrusting signs in the air. "Cursed Is The Man Who Integrates" in wild letters. "Keep Our Schools AMERICAN" in bold red. Others had more derogatory language. Their mouths twisted open in hideous hatred, no doubt shouting what their signs spelled out.

Lheniva pointed at the slab of concrete in the plot of grass between the parking lot and the road. The slab was red with the letter K etched in white, and the whole thing was outlined in blue. The school colors, I assumed.

We landed gently and snaked across the parking lot. The shouting became audible as we approached. By the time we cleared the last row of cars, it was so loud we couldn't hear each other.

"How are we going to get through that crowd?" I shouted. We scanned the mob, looking for a gap that we could squeeze through. In that moment, I wished I had brought a hooded jacket, or something with sleeves, at least.

"There! Right there!" Phae pointed at a pathway formed by metal barricades. Army National Guardsmen stood at several points along the thoroughfare. Were they there to protect us, or the protesters?

"It's way too narrow," I said. Waist-high barricades held the mob at bay, but they were set up like a cattle chute that got slimmer as it neared the door. We would be within arm's reach. If anyone wanted to, they could stab one of us easily.

"Lighten up, Little Brother," Jormon said with a grin, but his perfect smile had no effect on me. It was the smile that made people forget for a moment that we were Kaydan. But not today. The chaos was way too real.

"This is not the time for levity, Jormon. This is dangerous."

False motivation is better than no motivation at all. We have to be the example to Dirk, Taavi, and Phae. If you're scared, suck it up.

"Just walk straight through, eyes forward, and don't stop until you get to the door," instructed Lheniva.

The crowd shifted in our direction, and people who I didn't know, who I'd never met before, were shouting the filthiest things at us. Straight through, eyes forward, don't stop.

Jormon and Dirk walked ahead of me, and Phae and Taavi ahead of them. A large man in a red hat and olive drab coveralls leaned into the barricades and screamed insults inches away from Dirk's face. His bottom lip bulged from a soggy wad of chewing tobacco, and brown spit spattered as he shouted, punctuating his bigotry. Jormon, always the protector, grabbed Dirk's hand and squeezed it. As I passed the red-hatted man, something wet and odorous splashed the side of my face and shirt. It was piss, I knew. Cold, dated urine that he had saved for a moment like this. How long had he waited to do that to someone like me? Since integration? Since our arrival?

"Pack your shit and get the fuck out of here! We don't want your kind!" He leaned over the barricade and reached at my throat. His rough fingers sanded across my neck as I stepped back, but his fingers hooked my shirt collar. I couldn't shake him loose. He yanked me towards him, and his face was suddenly in mine.

"Let me go!" I grabbed his forearm, pulling it away from me as I tried to step back. His muscles flexed as his grip tightened. I didn't see the barricade fall, but a loud bang cut through the screaming and suddenly I was on my back and the man was on top of me. Every protective instinct in my body screamed for me to use my powers, to lift this fat fuck off me and send him flying. But that was the fastest way to get killed in Toombs County.

I looked towards the door briefly enough to see Taavi doubling back to help. When I looked at the man, a glob of brown spit hit me smack in the face.

Taavi's shoulder collided with the guy, and I was free to move.

"Get up! Get up! Let's go!" Taavi shouted.

I jumped to my feet and hauled ass into the building. Straight through, eyes forward, don't stop.

"You need to get these animals under control," Lheniva said. We were in the principal's office speaking to the man in charge, Mr. Alexander. Somewhere behind us, the white-haired receptionist sprayed Lysol in the air, maybe because I was a walking dumpster, or maybe she did that for everyone.

"Ma'am, let's keep this civil if we can. There's no need for name calling here."

"Do not lecture me on my use of words when we just walked through an active hate crime."

Mr. Alexander scratched at his graying eyebrows. "Ma'am, we have to be careful about how we use words like that."

"Can we put this all behind us?" I interjected. I wanted this to be over. I needed this to be. Lheniva had been yelling for ten minutes straight. Nothing makes an upset person angrier than being told to calm down, and Principal Alexander had told Lheniva twice. "I didn't really see who did it, and I don't want to go back out there to point them out."

"We will put this behind us when Mr. Alexander tells me what he's going to do to rectify this," Lheniva said. "This is a school, is it not? Teach these bastards a lesson."

"Ma'am, I'm sorry your son got a little wet, but we don't tolerate that sorta language on campus. We'll investigate as soon as we can."

"It wasn't my son who was assaulted. It was Prince Noan, son of King Rosh."

He didn't seem impressed.

"So not your kid, huh? Why are you here if these aren't your children?"

The question hit her like a slap in the face. "These three are my children."

The principal examined Dirk, Taavi, and Phae, searching for the family resemblance. "I didn't realize, Ma'am."

"If anything happens to them, you will realize I'm their mother."

"What do you mean by that?" Mr. Alexander stood as tall as he could, but he still wasn't as tall as Lheniva, and she didn't seem scared of him, not one bit.

"I will not be backed down, Mr. Alexander, and if you think I have a mouth on me now, wait until I start running it off to the king to tell him about everything I see going on here. Trust me, it would be better for everyone if my report of the problem is accompanied by a solution."

He knew he was beaten. The integration initiative had national attention, and when word got out that the king's son was assaulted, the problem would escalate beyond the principal's control.

"What do you want me to do, Miss Lheniva?"

"I want their names. All of them. The fat one, the black one, and every jackass who so much as shouted at the princes. Tell me who they are so we can deal with them accordingly."

"Ma'am, there's only so much I can do about them. They're not students. I don't have the authority to deal with them."

More words were exchanged in an attempt to mollify Lheniva, and a skinny kid sauntered in wearing khaki pants, a red shirt too hot for the weather, and a worn tan cap with a tarnished fishhook curled around the fraying brim. A blue T-shirt with the TCHS logo threaded in red draped across his shoulder, I assumed it was meant for me. "Sean, there you are," the principal said. "Your hat."

"Oh. Sorry, Coach." Sean removed his hat and tucked the brim into the back of his pants. He offered a timid wave.

"Everyone, this is Sean Cox. He's a good kid, I tell you. Sean, could you walk Noan to the boys' locker room so that he can wash up? Quickly." He asked it in the polite way adults tell kids to do things. Could you... Would you... *Let's just go*, I thought. Anything to be out of that office and away from attention.

"I'll go with him as well," Taavi said. He let go of Phae's hand and stepped between Sean and me.

"Stay with the rest of them," I said. The danger was over, as far as I could tell.

"Are you sure?" Taavi asked me, though his eyes never moved from Sean, who stood still and unbreathing.

"I'll be fine," I said. "Sean's a 'good kid.' The principal just said so."

"I don't care what the principal said. After what happened out there, you aren't going anywhere alone." Taavi leaned closer and whispered, "You can't trust these people."

He was right, but we didn't have a choice. "Stand down, Taavi. Good Kid Sean will guide me."

That was that. Taavi hesitated for a moment before stepping aside to let me join Sean and leave for the locker room.

A guide was hardly necessary. I'd studied the map in the welcome packet we received until I'd memorized every hall and classroom. The school comprised one main hallway and three halls that ran perpendicular to the main one, forming an irregular "E." Attached to the main hall was the gym and band room, their doors opposing each other, perhaps symbolizing the age-old dork vs. jock feud I'd read about.

Sean led the way to the locker room and waited on a wooden bench stretched between two rows of lockers. The air was damp and musty like I imaged a locker room would be, and the thought of my imaginings matching so closely to reality put me in a better mood.

"Are you always this quiet?" I asked.

"It's just a little awkward is all," Sean said, glancing at random things around the room.

"Is it because I'm naked? Or is it because I'm Kaydan?" I slid my underwear off and tossed my dirty shirt in the trash. I never wanted to see it again.

"A little of everything, I reckon. I don't spend much time around either sort."

"You don't have to stay if you don't want to. I can finish up here on my own and make my way back."

"I don't mind staying."

"Ah... Because I'm naked? Or because I'm covered in urine?" It was meant to be a joke, but he didn't laugh. "I'm trying to make it less awkward. You can lighten up anytime."

"I'll feel better once I get you out of here. I don't much care for locker rooms."

"I'll be quick, then."

"How are you okay? You were physically assaulted not ten minutes ago, but you're acting like it never happened. How come?"

"I'm used to people not liking me. It's a national pastime for humans." I walked over to the adjoining room with its blue and white tiled floors and shower heads spaced evenly along the walls. I turned one on and stood beneath the warm, hard water and let it wash away the morning. I closed my eyes and could see the man in the red hat so clearly. Thin build. Graying mustache. Retrieving a container from the inner pocket of his camouflage hunting jacket. Word would get back to Gray Flats that I was pissed on, and people would have yet another reason to not respect me. I could kill that man. I really think I could.

A bell rang, and the images faded from mind. Sean shouted from the bench that we'd be late. I shut off the water and rejoined him. "Is there a towel?"

"I didn't think about that. We don't really keep spares, but there are some paper towels in the box over there."

There was no way I was drying off with wads of off-brand paper towels. I asked, "Can I trust you?"

"Huh?"

"You look like the kind of person I can trust. Can I?"

"Of course. Most people think I'm a pretty good guy. What do you need?"

"Just your discretion."

"Huh?"

I extended my consciousness across my naked body until I distinguished the water from everything else. With little effort, I lifted the water from my body and molded it into a twisting stream that flowed into the shower drain.

"That was impressive. Won't you get in trouble for using powers on campus? It's on the list of 'Do Nots?'"

"That's why I need your discretion. Was I wrong to trust you?"

"I meant what I said."

By the time I finished dressing, another bell had rung. "Why are you doing this? Not that I mind the company, but people don't do things without a reason. And considering the way Kaydans are looked at, the way we are treated, you must want something in return."

"Or I could be doing it cause I'm a nice guy," Sean said. "Get to know me before you assume things. Ain't that what you're asking us to do?" We left the locker room and joined the streams of students flowing into the hallway. "You'll want to go to Mrs. Broadnax's class just down the hall. She's your Homeroom teacher. She should have your class schedule."

Jormon walked out of a classroom, and I assumed it was the one Sean had indicated. "Hey, Sean," I said as he walked away. He stopped and looked back. "Thanks for staying with me. I hope I see you around."

She seemed out of place in this ordinary school, Mrs. Broadnax did. Overly artsy, maybe. Or just flamboyant, pretending to be above it all. Dressed for a different time. She wore too many cloisonné bangles that matched her teal kaftan just so. Navy blue lines swirled around the midsection, complementing both her hoop earrings and her flat-heeled shoes.

As Jormon and the others streamed out of the classroom, she remained stationed by the door, a sentinel in the sea of departing students. Her lips pursed as I approached. She extended a hand holding folded sheets of printing paper, and her bangles clacked together like wind chimes. When she spoke, it was with an American accent I couldn't quite place. Not southern. Probably not even real. "I was made aware of your accident," Mrs. Broadnax said. "Tragic, I tell you. Just plain tragic. Still, you were absent from Homeroom. You'll receive a mark for that. Two more within the week and you'll have detention."

"What?" I asked. How could she do that? It wasn't my fault. She had to know some jerk assaulted me outside.

"Don't question my intentions, young man. That's another mark for you."

I hadn't stepped foot in a class yet and already I was in trouble. *The powers given to teachers*, I thought. One thing I was constantly learning is that, on Earth, powers of authority were all the powers people had achieved. Nothing special. Nothing permanent, even. And perhaps because the powers were so weak is why those with them were so often to abuse them.

Mrs. Broadnax continued, "Here, please, take this before my arm falls off." She shook the papers in my face, and her jewelry danced and jingled. "This is your schedule for the semester. If any of the classes prove too difficult, let me know and I'll drop you down to simpler subjects. I know little about your personal prowess, but I'm aware that certain types aren't that bright. The list of school rules is in there as well. Since you missed my review, I advise you to read them first. Now, run along and catch up with the rest of your kind. The bell will ring soon, and if I catch you in the hall when it does, that's strike three."

She waved me off with just her fingers, and her parted lips curled upward in a put-on smile.

Jormon and Dirk watched the exchange from down the hallway. Taavi scanned the crowd like a bouncer at a nightclub, and Phae stood next to him with her arms hugging her midsection. "What was that all about?" I asked once we were out of earshot.

"You missed a doozy," Jormon said. "She let everyone gawk at us as she laid down the law. Check this out?"

As Jormon searched his pockets and pulled out a list of rules, we passed a drinking fountain with a sign taped above it reading 'Humans Only.' The nerve of these people. With all the gadgets Taavi creates, maybe he could invent something that detects assholes.

"Rule Number One: The use or display of superhuman abilities is expressly prohibited on campus," Jormon read.

"We knew that one already. What's the next one say?"

"Rule Number Two: Kaydans must make all reasonable efforts to sit within the first three rows in class."

"So they can keep tabs on us. How is that supposed to work in Phys. Ed.?"

"Ah ha. Rule Number Three: Kaydans will be assigned 'buddies' during Physical Education to aid in their understanding of human contact."

"What does that even mean? How many rules are there?"

"Too many," Dirk said. "How are you feeling? What happened earlier was awful."

"I feel okay, I think." I wished Jormon would have stood by me instead of traipsing along with you, I wanted to say.

"Sorry about this morning, Your Highness," Taavi said "I didn't realize you were alone back there. I'll be there for you next time."

"Yeah, I'm sorry too," added Phae.

"Hopefully there is no 'next time.' Also, cut the formalities. None of these other brats will treat me like royalty, so your making it obvious will only put Jormon and me in danger."

I scanned my schedule to see if my locker number was written anywhere. It was. They'd placed us next to one another, and as we compared our schedules, we noticed it was the only consideration the administration had. "They did an exceptional job of splitting us up. Besides Homeroom, none of us share classes."

"We have the same lunch period," Jormon said. "First one there grabs a table for us all?"

The next two periods were comparatively uneventful, much to my delight. I managed to claim a seat in the front row in each class, allowing only the teacher an opportunity to look me in the face. I didn't want to know how many people were staring at me. It was also a delight that classes were relatively easy. Mrs. Wheeler's physics class was a cinch compared to Uncle's lectures on gravity manipulation. Making a bowling ball fall downward was easy. Making it fall upward took effort.

A series of bells rang every hour on the half-hour, rushing students through their day and, at last, when it seemed it would never come, the bell for lunch rang.

I spotted Jormon walking out of Mrs. Addleson's class with a short, slender blond at his side. She laughed at something he said—something that probably wasn't funny at all—and tossed her hair the way annoying girls do when they're trying to be attractive. "Oh, Jormon," I imagined her saying. "You're so funny and handsome." Hair toss, hair toss. "I want to be your queeeeen." Fat chance, lady.

I turned down a small hall that led towards the cafeteria, giving Jormon the chance to make new friends. I lost myself in the crowd funneling out of the double doors, the youth, like so many ants, marching towards the scent of food.

I made it through the line only to be told that I hadn't submitted the proper forms to receive lunch, and I watched as a bald man wearing a hair net dumped my tray into a large trash can.

There were no individual sitting areas, only seven or eight rows of rectangular tables stretching the length of the cafeteria. As was my wont, I found a seat at the farthest table from the crowd. There was a thin row of windows at the top of the wall—they, too, ran the length of the room—and I stared through them at the darkening sky.

Jormon walked into my field of vision, his head silhouetted against the framed sky.

"You look like you could use a friend," Jormon said as he sat in the vacant seat across from me. He only had an apple for a meal. Using his telekinesis, he split the apple into perfect halves, keeping one and giving me the other.

"You shouldn't do that. Not here. Someone could report us." He waved off my concerns and bit into his apple. "How are classes coming along?"

"It's only been first-day-of-school stuff. After Mrs. Broadnax's speech, I expected we'd hit the ground running. For the last two classes, all we managed were introduction exercises. 'Hi, my name is,' and 'Over the summer, I' type of stuff."

"Are you 'integrating?'" I asked. "I haven't gotten pissed on again, but I still feel like the outsider everywhere I am. Even when I'm alone."

"Most of these people have gone to school with each other for eleven years. Everyone who wasn't born here and hasn't gone to the same church with one another is bound to feel like an outsider. There are a few new students from Washington, D.C. Their parents are government officials here to manage some new project. They feel out of place as well, so I'm told."

"Is one of them the girl I saw you walking down the hall with?"

"Yeah, her name is Lindsey. Her and her mom moved into that big, yellow house on Canaday Street."

"Did she say what the project is? Do you think it has anything to do with this social experiment we're in now?"

"I didn't ask."

"You should have," I said, rolling my eyes. "The more we know, the better prepared we'll be. From what I could see, she was into you. Use that to your advantage. Flirt with her. Find out what she knows."

"I don't know how to flirt. And if I did, it wouldn't be with her. I'll tell her you said hello, though. Unless you've become a purist."

"Purism is for other people."

"Can you imagine what Dad would say if you brought a girl home? A human girl, at that."

"Probably the same thing he'd say when he finds out you and Dirk have been boning—Don't be so shocked. He passes by my window every night on his walk of shame."

Jormon fidgeted in his seat. "We haven't taken things that far."

"Oh, you've only been getting to know each other? How boring."

Looking down at his half-eaten apple, he leaned in and whispered, "I want to, you know, go that far."

108

"What's stopping you?"

"You know how—"

"Secrets don't make friends," came a voice, cutting directly into Jormon's sentence.

The voice belonged to Sean. He wore a brown, basic tunic that hung loosely over his thin frame and draped well past the waistline of his jeans. His brown boots made their way up his shins, and connected to his hip was a sheath with no sword.

"I'm Sean, remember? From earlier this morning? Mind if I sit?"

Before either of us could object, Sean had managed his way into a seat, being careful of the protruding sheath. "I don't usually dress like this, please don't think I'm weird. I have Drama right before lunch and I didn't have a chance to change."

"Welcome," Jormon said, sitting back and pretending we weren't just talking about his sex life.

"Well, ain't you a peach. I should be the one welcoming you," Sean returned, gregarious and nearly beaming, entirely different from who he was earlier. He wasn't kidding about how locker rooms affected his mood. "When I heard that some of you would be joining us in school this year, I gotta say, I was mighty excited. I've lived in this town my whole life and I ain't never met a Kaydan til this morning. And then all the pee throwing happened and it… Never mind. The shirt looks good on you, by the way. Go Bulldogs!" He pumped his fist in the air in mock cheer.

"There are thousands of us here," I said. "How is it possible to have never met one?"

"My dad never hired one to help around the house. He has a thing against em. I probably shouldn't've said that." He twisted the top off his orange juice and drank half the bottle in one gulp. "It's not like he's a bigot or anything. He just has a thing against—"

"Domestic help? Kaydans can be found in more places besides other people's bathrooms," I said.

"I don't know," Sean shrugged. "I mean, I ain't never seen a Jehovah's Witness either, and there are millions of 'em. Whenever they come round the house and knock on the door, my dad makes us duck down and shut up."

"That's a fair point," Jormon said before I could respond with anything defensive.

"You two should let me show you round campus. I can give you the rundown on how things work."

"I think I'm going to pass on that offer," Jormon said. "But take my brother with you. He loves people."

"Jormon, we were in the middle of a conversation."

"We can finish it another time."

"What about our meeting with the Cohort?" I reminded him.

"I can get the update from them. And if I need you for anything…" he pointed to his head and did a thing where he wiggled his fingers like signal waves. "Take care, you two." He placed his apple core on Sean's plate and walked out. More than a few heads turned in his direction, but he continued past the crowd, unfazed and undaunted by the attention.

"Your brother seems cool," Sean said. "Do you see the way people stare at him?"

"It's his charming personality," I said dully. "Or his dashing looks."

"Not that you're not cool too, or anything. Or dashing, I guess. I just meant that—"

"I know what you meant," I said. My stomach rumbled loudly. Sean must have heard it because he tore his rectangular slice of pizza down the middle and gave me half. "Thanks."

"Don't sweat it. About this morning—is that something that happens all the time? The screaming and hollering?"

"I don't leave the house often enough to know. People aren't usually so brazen from what I've experienced. Then again, someone has been sneaking onto our property and setting crosses on fire."

"I'm surprised it happens to you."

"Why not me?"

"Because you're… I'm sorry, but I just found out who you are, and I'm not sure if I'm supposed to know. You're Prince Noan!" he whispered excitedly, as if I didn't know who I was. "And that's Prince Jormon! Both of you! Here! In TCHS!"

It looked like he was going to flip, too.

After we'd finished eating, he led me to an area he referred to as the Senior Commons, which was a tiny court outside between second and third hall. A paved walkway divided two grassy stretches, both decorated with stone benches curved around circular tables. On the western side was a glass wall that looked into the main hall, but the eastern stretch opened up to an enormous field, and beyond that, tennis courts, and beyond that, a field of cotton in mid-bloom.

"There's also a track out there if you like to run," Sean pointed out. "If you get here early enough, you can find some shade under the oak trees over yonder."

We walked without a purpose, and every second or so, Sean pointed out random students he found worth mentioning. "The one rolling up her sleeves, that's Ashley Davis. She spent the summer in London two years ago, now she calls cookies 'biscuits.' Besides that, she's okay. That tall kid with the steam punk jacket is Daniel Caraway. We were friends in middle school 'til he became cool. Now he's the type of guy who wears jackets in the summer. Those two kissing by the tree, that's Jake Crowley and Shandrea Brown. We were friends in middle school, too."

"But not anymore?"

"Nope."

"And that kid over there, the one walking and reading. Who is he?"

"His name is David, but everybody calls him Homicidal Hutto after his dad disappeared a few years back."

"Did he kill him?"

"He's not in jail for murder, if that means anything."

"But did he do it?"

"I don't like to spread gossip. Do yourself a favor and stay away from that one, bless his heart."

The sky was ever darkening, and there was no need to search for shade. We found an empty space in the grass and took a seat.

"We only have a few minutes before we have to go back to class," Sean said. "Do you have questions about anything here? Anyone you want to get to know? I'm not the popular kid or anything, but everyone knows my dad—well, stepdad. Anyhow, they sorta give me a pass and speak to me, even when they don't want to."

What could possibly be so enigmatic that I would have questions? The school was the size of some post offices, despite the city having grown significantly over the years. And the people I'd encountered so far seemed as cookie cutter as gingerbread men. Every other girl had dyed blond hair growing from brown or brunette roots, and every other guy had hair gelled into forward points or upward peaks. There was no school uniform, but almost everyone was dressed the same. The guys: tan shorts, polo shirt, brown flip-flops of some brand or other. The girls: full-length shirts of acceptable patterns with jean shorts that reached just beyond the fingertips of their relaxed arms. Even the kids with foreign accents dressed like the locals.

Before I could say anything, something hard whacked against the back of my head. I winced and touched the spot where I'd been hit. No blood. Just a sharp pain that immediately began to throb. I turned around to find five people towering above me: three guys, two girls. I recognized the guys from earlier in the summer. The Bus Stop Bullies.

"Payback's a bitch, ain't it?" Brett said.

Without realizing it, I touched the spot on my chest where the leecher had sucked my powers. This guy was the reason for that.

I raised to one knee, and when I tried to stand up, Brett shoved me hard. "Stay down on your knees when you're in my presence, copper."

I tried to get back up. "What did you just call me?" He pushed me again, and his buddies egged him on.

Sean was on the ground beside me, kneeling where he had just been sitting. "Just stay down," he said to me.

"Yeah, copper. You'd best listen to your buddy. He's a smart one. He knows what a good ass whoopin feels like, ain't that right?" He winked at Sean and puckered his lips into a kiss. His buddies laughed, and Sean lowered his eyes. A small crowd had already formed and teemed around us like they were about to witness a cage fight. I would not let myself be cowered, not like this. Not on the first day of school. It was one thing to be disrespected by an ignorant adult who I'd likely never see again. It's another to bend to the will of some nobody jock.

I tried to stand again. When Brett reached out to shove me, I grabbed both arms and pulled him down instead. With his arms in my hands, I rolled backwards and used my feet to launch him over me. He landed on his back with a thud and groaned.

I shot to my feet and waited for him to stand. Bullies Two and Three slowly approached me. I couldn't take them both, not without using a *sahdr*, and I didn't stop to think about the consequences. There wasn't time. I raised my hands to conjure the wind. If I blew them back, maybe that would be the end of it. I didn't want to hurt them, but I would not stand by and be hurt instead.

Brett was on his feet again. "You know, you damn near broke my finger the other day with your little magic trick. That got me mad."

"Do you miss the feeling? Because you have nine more fingers I can 'damn near break,'" I mocked.

"Oh, you're tough now? Cause last time you ran like a bitch, and I couldn't catch your little faggot ass. I had to take my anger out on someone else, but I have you now."

"Someone else?" What was he talking about?

Blades of grass clung to the side of his mouth, and his cheeks were getting redder by the second. "I took it out on the copper bitch who cleans our house. Maybe you know her? Sandi Sumin-or-Other? I went home, dropped my drawers, and took a shit right there on the floor. Then I said to her, I told her 'Hey bitch, I'mma need you to clean this up, and I'm tired of coppers using powers around me, so do it with your hands. Your bare hands.' And you know what she said to me? She says to me, 'Yes, Sir.' So when you go home today and see a copper bitch walking around your little trailer park with shit-smelling hands, warn her that you've fucked up again, and that she's in store for something worse than last time." He winked and blew me a kiss.

"You crapped on the floor, yet humans think *we're* the uncivilized race," I returned, but my head was no longer in the argument. A rage that I'd never felt before filled me from within. Who was he to treat my people that way? I could hurt him for what he'd done, and I didn't care how many people were around to watch. They all heard what he said. They could testify that I was provoked.

I clinched my fist and focused on the wind. Just as the air in front of me swirled and thickened, a whistle rang out.

"What's going on over here?" shouted a voice from within the crowd. A few seconds later a man broke through the huddle. He was short, fit, and wore two tarnished whistles around his neck. "Did you do this?" He pointed to Brett, who still had grass on his face.

"No," I said. I was defiant in a way that would probably get me killed. I knew I should calm down, but I couldn't. "It's not what it looks like."

"Coach Stroud, I was just walking by, and this copper pushed me over," he lied. My face grew hotter. My fists clenched tighter. The breezed picked up again.

"Is this true?" Coach Stroud asked. The others of the Bus Stop Bullies nodded. Everyone else kept quiet. I couldn't believe it.

"Hey boy," Coach Stroud said, "we're not back in some trailer park on the other side of town. There are rules here, and we don't go around starting fights." He sounded more condescending than angry. Like he was talking to a child who was throwing food from his highchair.

"But I didn't start anything," I protested. I intended for it to be resolute and steadfast, but it came out all whiny and immature.

"I don't care who started it," he said. "I walk over to see one of my players sprawled out on the ground and you standing over him. I could have you expelled for that."

Sprawled? How long had this coach been watching? If it were long enough to see the kick flip, then he would've seen the rest. Regardless, I couldn't face expulsion. Uncle wouldn't like that at all. How could I explain I got kicked out of school on my very first day? Way to set the example. And if I weren't in school, no one would be here to look out for Jormon like I could. "I don't know what to say."

"You could start by apologizing," Coach Stroud said. He looked around for the nearest drone. Three of them circled overhead like buzzards waiting to nip at a rotting corpse. Coach Stroud removed his cap and waved it like a distress signal, and one of them abruptly broke formation and dropped closer into view.

"I'm sorry," I said. My tone was miles away from conciliatory, even still it pained me to say the words. My fingernails cut into my skin deep enough to draw blood.

"Not to *me*." He said it like I was a dog that had performed a trick wrong. "Apologize to Brett for attacking him."

I gritted my teeth. "I'm sorry, Brett." It hurt worse than the knee to the back of the head.

"That wasn't so bad now, was it?" Coach Stroud asked.

Again, I gritted my teeth. "No."

"'No' what?" he asked. I didn't understand the question, so I stayed silent. "Don't you mean 'No, Sir?' I see you haven't learned manners where you're from. But that's okay, I can teach them to you here, or in after school detention."

"Okay, Sir," I said. Again, another pain. Who was this guy to demand my respect? And why was I showing it to him? My anger was boiling inside, and I knew if things went any further, I would either fly away or explode with rage.

Coach Stroud blew into one of the whistles and the crowd, for the most part, dissipated. A few people stuck around in case the spectacle hadn't ended, but they all left once they saw Brett walk back inside with the coach.

"Thanks for your help back there. Your bravery outshines the morning sun."

"I'm sorry," Sean said. "Me and Brett have a lot of history. You wouldn't understand."

It was only lunch and I'd been knocked on the ground twice. I needed a better strategy if I wanted to survive high school. Being myself and trying to stay out of trouble wasn't the ticket.

"Hey Sean, could you show me where the nerds hang out?"

CHAPTER TEN
DIRK

I WAS THE FIRST ONE TO SHOW UP TO MY NEXT CLASS. I sat in the first row in the desk by the door. The bell rang. Mr. Dupree got up from behind his desk and stood by the door to perform his sentinel duties. Voices filled the halls, then the classrooms, then there was another bell. This was the rigmarole of school: students come to school to hang out with their friends, taking the occasional break to learn a thing or two, all the while being ushered by the bell. It was this school. It was my last school. It was every school.

The only difference was me. My *sheriaan* looped around my wrists in thick and thin lines of molten copper. The tips of the lines—the new growth—reached halfway to my elbow and was just turning a shade of green. As I walked the halls and sat through classes, I thought about Hester Prynne and the scarlet letter that marked her as a whore or whatever. These lines were my scarlet letter, and there was no hiding them.

I struggled for an hour during calculus and was completely burned out by the time the bell rang. I left the room heading towards my locker. The voices of students pouring into the hall were louder than before, more energetic. I fell in step behind two students and couldn't help but overhear their conversation.

"...but he *didn't* start it. That's what I heard," said the kid with an orange backpack. "He was minding his own business then, *wham*! Brett threw a rock at him."

"Wutn't no damn rock," said the other kid with a beige shoulder bag. "It was his knee. Brett kneed him in the head because he was checking out Patti during second period."

"Patti? Patti who?"

"*Patti* Patti. Patti with the stank breath, Patti. You know Patti."

"Patty Floyd?"

"Yeah, that Patti. Folks are saying he whistled at her or something."

"That's bull," said Red Backpack. "Brett just wanted to look cool in front of Darley and Hartley and them. To make the Riders proud, you know? Now Noan's gotta serve after school detention and Brett gets to keep strutting around like a goddam rooster."

"Hold up! You reckon Brett's a Rider?" asked Shoulder Bag.

"His dad is. I know that for sure. My momma told me. Oh, and the gay kid Noan was with. Sean, I think? The one who was outed at the Spring Fling last year. He just sat there like—"

They turned a corner down the main hall, and I lost their voices in the sea of sound. This Brett came off as the same Brett from the bus station when I first got to town. At least it sounded like it could be the same asshole. *Lord, forgive me.*

Another class. Two more bells rang, and school was out for the day. Everyone rushed to stash books in their lockers, but few left the building. It was pouring outside, but our time on campus was limited, rain or no.

Jormon was waiting underneath the portico, watching torrents of rain wash over the parking lot. A few parents were already lined up to pick up their kids. They sat in their vehicles safe from the storm, their wipers tossing the water this way and the other with hypnotic rhythm. The protesters must've washed away, too. If we were lucky, it would rain every day.

"Busy?" I asked as I approached him from behind. He didn't turn to face me. Rather, he stared intently at the rain as though he was trying to figure it out. "Worried?" I asked.

"No," he said, facing me at last. "Just preoccupied."

"Where's everyone else? We need to be off campus soon. Rule Number Eleven."

"They're on their way. We can wait a couple more minutes."

The rain showed no signs of letting up. "Phae spent hours on her hair. She won't like that we have to fly back in the rain."

"She'll like it more than she would being caught on campus after 3:45."

Just then, the rest of them showed up. Jormon took off in a cautious sprint, splashing buckets with every step. We followed closely behind.

We made it to the landing pad, and Taavi burst out laughing. He poked fun at how we looked jetting across the parking lot, running with raised knees like runaways being shot at. I'd never thought to joke like that before. The imagery was too powerful, and to joke about it disrespected the Kaydans who had lost their lives running away during the Hunts. Everyone else laughed as if they were in on the joke, and it made me feel out of place. I reminded myself that I was Kaydan, too, but I couldn't shake the feeling I didn't fully belong.

Lightning cracked in the distance. Then it cracked close enough to make the hair on my arms stand up.

"Don't be afraid of a little lightning," Jormon said. "Have you heard of the legend of the storm riders?"

I've been Kaydan for five minutes. I hadn't heard much.

"As the tale goes, there's a tribe of *mustediin* so powerful they can attach their spirit to a bolt of lightning and become one with the storm. They become the clouds and the rain, and their power can reach as far as the faintest tip of the farthest lightning bolt."

"Yeah, but I'm not one of them. I'm out here trying not to die. Can we go now?"

I changed into dry clothes and caught up on Taavi's day. He said something about football or tennis or something, but I wasn't paying much attention.

Minutes later, I was knocking on the front door of A705. Jormon let me in. He was wearing the same wet clothes he had on earlier. "No time to change?" I asked.

He gave a broad smile. "Not really. I never told you this, but I really like the rain. Anyway, come on in. Taavi and Phae didn't want to come?"

"I didn't think to invite them. I can go back and get them."

"It's okay. If I'm being honest, I much prefer your company. I'm exhausted and really don't feel like entertaining many people. You're the exception."

Without knowing it, I smiled. Was he trying to tell me something? I didn't want to be forward, not with the future king. "I don't understand."

"You know what it feels like to try to live up to other people's expectations. The fear that curtains pull back and everyone will see you for the person you really are. And that they won't like what they see. With you, it's like no matter how I feel or how I behave, you'll be okay with it."

We climbed the stairs slowly, or at least it felt slow to me. I was stuck between asking him what he meant and changing the subject altogether. *My, what crappy weather we're having today. Did you hear about Homicidal Hutto. I hope the rain doesn't set him off.*

I followed him to his room. "Could you shut the door? If Nana Lura sees the mess, she'll kick me out, I swear."

I did as asked. The window was open, and the rain whipped past relentlessly, but none of it blew in. "Nice manipulation," I said.

"It's something Noan taught me. I can teach it to you if you want." He took his shirt off and tossed it in the hamper. His chest was smooth, and he was more muscular than I remembered. Or did I remember? More muscular than I'd been imagining he was?

I turned away and stared at the wall. It was bare. I turned my gaze towards the ceiling and watched as *Heemrah* cast a final look at the world. I heard the undoing of a zipper, followed by a sloshing thud against the floor. I felt myself pressing against the inside of my jeans. "I think I should wait for you downstairs, if that's okay."

"Am I making you uncomfortable? You told me you were on the football team through middle and high school. Aren't there locker rooms involved? I figured you would have seen plenty of naked guys by now."

"It's not the same."

"Did they have two butt cheeks and a dick?"

"Yeah."

"Then it is the same."

Except it wasn't. None of those guys made me feel the way he did.

A drawer opened and closed, and I focused my thoughts on the furniture and not his body. When I thought he was dressed, I dared to look over. His butt was exposed, and he balanced on one foot as he struggled to slide on a pair of underwear. Water slicked down the hairs between his thighs. I looked back at the ceiling.

"Can I get you a towel?" I cleared my throat, hoping it would clear my head. If he said yes, I didn't think I'd be able to move.

"It's okay. I prefer to be a little wet these days."

There was a joke in there somewhere, but I couldn't think straight enough to put it together.

More sounds, more clothes. I looked over and he was mostly covered, but still shirtless.

"I don't know what I'm doing here, Jormon. Maybe I should wait downstairs."

"I—maybe I misread something. If you don't want to be up here, I can meet you in the parlor. Let me finish getting dressed. It'll be a couple more minutes."

"You didn't misread anything. I want to be here." That was the problem. I wanted to be there too much. It wasn't enough that I was in the same room. I wanted to be closer. Close enough to know how his skin smelled after the rain.

"Thank you. Your being here is keeping me from thinking about everything else."

I wanted to mention what I'd overheard, but it wasn't the right time. "I wouldn't want to be anywhere else."

"You're a good friend, Dirk." He walked over and hugged me. He felt it. He must've felt it because he cut the hug short and took a step back.

Then a step forward.

It was too much. His face was inches away from mine. His breath warmed my lips and nose as he exhaled in long, calming streams. I counted the drops of water racing from his wet hair. I looked into his hazel eyes and saw the world reflected back at me. I smelled his skin, so sweet like summer rain, so soft like a misty breeze. He smiled at me. I smiled back.

"Are we going to kiss? We're going to kiss, aren't we?" I couldn't tell if I was stammering or not.

"I'm waiting on you." The fruity hints of apple on his breath invited me nearer. He liked his apples, and I liked him.

"It has to be you. You have to start it."

"I can't start it. It would seem like I'm using my position to get what I want."

"I can't start it either. It would be crossing a line for me to assume I could up and kiss a prince. I don't know a lot about Kayda or Maerin or whatever, but I know that much. I have no right to."

"Is that all you need, the right? Okay, then. You have the right. I'm giving it to you."

"Then it's settled?"

"Yeah, it's settled."

CHAPTER ELEVEN
NOAN

THE FOLLOWING DAY WAS DISTURBINGLY SIMILAR to the one before. I took extra steps to pack a change of clothes, and I was extra vigilant when navigating the mob. The barricades stood closer together, and while no one doused me with anything, someone was able to latch onto my shirt collar and tear the elastic.

"I told you to stay close to me," Taavi said once we were inside. But it wasn't for him to protect me. The people don't protect the prince.

When he saw me approaching the locker room, Sean waved to me with the scrunched-up shirt held loosely in his fist. I pointed a thumb at my backpack, and he got the hint.

"Did you see who did it this time?"

Yeah, I did. "No. There was too much going on."

"You gon' be alright?"

No, probably not. "Always."

"See you at lunch?"

Don't bother. "Sure."

The bell rang just as I crossed the threshold into Mrs. Broadnax's class, and I swear I heard her curse under her breath. I smiled on the inside. I sauntered over to the desk between Jormon and Taavi and plopped down in a huff. A loud beep shot from the intercom speaker, and a pleasant voice began reading off the day's lunch menu, the football scrimmage schedule, and the humiliating list of rules. "So make it a great day. Or not," the voice concluded. "The choice is yours."

I tried not to hate the voice, but I couldn't help it. The amiability of her inside voice juxtaposed so closely in time to the vitriol just outside, it was a punch in the gut to those of us targeted by aggressors thronging the walkway to the school. It was hurtful, to say the least, but I couldn't live in that hurt and mind my surroundings all day so I shook the thought and tucked the feeling away to relive in private.

The rain came earlier in the day. And harder. Hard enough to wash the scum away again. "Is one of you doing this?" I asked. Instead of going to the Senior Commons after lunch, Taavi, Phae, and I huddled at a far table in the cafeteria and waited for the bell to ring.

"You'd know if it was me," Taavi said, picking over the scraps in his tray. "The sky would be lit up like the Fourth of July, and rain would fall in perfect symmetrical drops, like liquid crystals."

"Nah. We'd know because your face would be as red as *Heemrah* and veins would be popping from the strain of making a few drops fall," Phae joked.

"Like you could do better," Taavi shot back. "You'd be so scared to get your hair wet you'd probably cause a drought instead."

"It's called taking care of yourself, Mop Top. You should try it sometimes. Also, stop talking about my hair. You make me out to be some self-obsessed bimbo with nothing more to offer than her good looks (of which I have plenty). I've got skills, 'Bro.'" She threw a hardened fry at him and he caught it in his mouth. "You're gross. Noan, tell him he's gross."

He wasn't gross to me. He was comfortable being himself, as far as I could tell. Something I wished was true about me. But I wanted to fit in, so I played along. "You remind me a little of Sandi Nash's ratty-looking cats." They both laughed and Phae kept the joke running, but I was hung up on Sandi, our fellow Kaydan and Brett's housekeeper. I'd completely forgotten what Brett had done to her, and I was lost thinking how he may have targeted her after our spat yesterday.

124

"Noan, are you with us?" Taavi asked. I must've gone deadpan.

"Yeah, I was just thinking—There you are," I said. Jormon and Dirk walked briskly over and sat by Taavi. "Where were you two?"

"We've got something to tell you all," Jormon said.

"I've got something to say, too, but you go first."

Dirk updated us on what he'd overheard the day before, including the rumors about why the fight with Brett started, finishing up with something Coach Hardey and Coach Stroud said about deliberately trying to get them all kicked out of school.

"What do you think they meant by it?" I asked.

"That's what we tried to find out today." Jormon lowered his voice to just above a whisper. "We went into Coach Stroud's computer."

"Jormon, tell me you're kidding. Do you know what would happen if you got caught?"

"We weren't going to get caught," he said with too much confidence.

"It was too risky, Jormon. I don't like that you did that."

"But it was necessary, Noan. I thought you, of all people, would understand."

"Oh lord, Mommy and Daddy are fighting," Taavi said. I got the hint. So did Jormon.

I nodded for Jormon to go on. "We didn't find out much, but there was a note on his desktop about a meeting of the First People, whatever that means."

"It's a church," Sean said, scaring the shit out of everyone. He was standing over my shoulder, waiting to be invited to sit.

"Sean, now is not the time," I said. "Can we talk later?"

"Oh, yeah. I was gonna ask if you wanted to meet up after school. Maybe hang out for a bit?" A cheesy grin stretched across his face, and he leaned toward me expectantly.

"I can't. I have lessons after school." I gave him no further explanation.

"You should go," Jormon said. "We'll just go over old material."

Everyone would love that. Taavi and Phae would have an easy lesson, and Dirk and Jormon could keep running around being the Hardy boys while I entertained the notion of a friendship with a human.

"Fine. I'll go."

"Are you sure?" Taavi asked. "I mean, you don't have to hang out with this guy if you don't want to." Phae shot Taavi a look, and Taavi shrugged. "What? He hardly knows him."

"I can take care of myself," I said. Taavi glared at Sean, who pumped his fist as though he'd won a prize.

The bell rang, and the collective sliding of chairs as students stood to leave echoed off the walls, and it was too loud for me to even begin telling the Cohort what I'd learned about Sandi.

I met Sean by the lockers after the final period had ended. I told him I needed to be off campus as soon as possible, and he eagerly accommodated the request.

"Let's go to Tastee Freeze. I could use some coffee ice cream. Or just coffee. Or just ice cream." He closed his locker and checked to see if I agreed.

Students crowded the halls, and another gaggle stood blocking the main entrance. I followed Sean past them and through the band room and out a separate door that exited to the north side of the parking lot. It surprised me how cold the rain felt for a summer afternoon. It beat down on me in chilling pellets as we ran, and I wondered how the Cohort felt flying in crumby weather two days in a row.

A chirp and flashing headlights, and we were inside a silver SUV. It was the second vehicle I had ever been in, but I knew this one was nice by anyone's standards. Sean started the engine and warm streams of air erupted from the vents. "Sorry," he said, reaching to turn down the flow. He tilted his head to one side and squeezed down the length of his short-cut hair. Water dripped over the middle console, plinking off the shiny head of a short hammer tilted over in the cup holder.

126

"Why do you keep a hammer in your car?" I asked, picking it up and testing the weight in my hands.

"Guys at school used to put nails in my tires last year. I keep fix-a-flat in here somewhere. Hey, you wouldn't happen to know a spell that would dry my hair out, would you?"

"We don't call them spells, but yes, I can help you." I recalled the *sahdr*, it was an easy one. I released the energy and our water-darkened clothes lighted both in color and weight as the water separated from them, pooling in front of me in a growing sphere. "If you could let down the window, please." He did, and I hurled the water outside.

"That was awesome!" he exclaimed, patting himself down in disbelief at his dryness. "What else can you do?"

"I appreciate your curiosity, but I'm not here for your entertainment," I said. He sank back in his seat, and his smile faded little by little. "What I meant to say is that what you asked is not a polite question to ask a Kaydan you just met. But if it means anything, I'm better than a novice *mustedi*. Which means I can do a lot of unimportant things, like dry your clothes." I laughed, hoping he'd laugh with me. He did, and the mood relaxed.

It was a lie, but what good would it do to tell the truth? I had powers he did not, and I was skilled at wielding them. What would it serve to tell him—or any human—exactly how different we were? It was better to focus on how alike we could be. That was, after all, a pillar of integration.

"What's Brett's story?" I asked once we had made it out of the parking lot. "His reputation, from what I can see, is less than venerable, yet people still seem to like him. Especially the coaches."

"Ugh, that guy. Be careful with him. His folks are Riders. I was at his house a year back and went rifling through his daddy's office. We were looking for a key to the shotgun case."

"Shotgun case?"

"It was deer season."

"Ah, understood. Go on."

"Like I was saying, we were looking for the key to the shotgun case…"

He was really making me wait for the reveal. "And?"

"And we found a key, alright. But it didn't go to no shotgun case. It opened a locked closet in his dad's office, a closet where they keep their Rider clothes. You know the ones. They have the red hoods and blue sashes crisscrossing on the front."

"If that's true, I really have to warn Sandi to be careful."

"That boy has been bad news since the third grade. So have the rest of his crew, Alexander Darley and Kevin Summerset and all the rest of them."

"Yet you were close enough friends to go hunting together. I assume they've wronged you in some way?"

"That's one way to put it."

I told him of my encounter with Brett and what happened at the bus stop earlier in the summer, and how I sent Brett flying. Inadvertently, of course.

"He's gonna have it out for you for a while. That guy has more pride than a summer in San Francisco. If you embarrassed him in front of his posse, he's never gonna forget it.

By the time we pulled into the Tastee Freeze parking lot, the rain had become more intense. The parking lot itself was so flooded we could hardly distinguish parking spaces, so Sean stopped the car away from the few others that were already parked and shut off the engine.

"Do you have an umbrella in here?" I asked. Of course he didn't. In rapid succession, we exited the vehicle, ran through the rain, and dried off in the restaurant's vestibule.

It occurred to me I enjoyed using my powers with a purpose. Not for teaching or for practice, but for the sake of being good to someone else.

A school-aged girl stood behind the counter. "Welcome to Tastee Freeze. What can I get y'all?"

Of the variety of ice cream flavors tempting us from behind a glass partition, Sean chose coffee, and I picked butter pecan. "Whose grandma *are* you?" he joked. It was the first flavor Mrs. McCall let me sample. I liked it, so I kept getting it. I didn't have to explain myself.

The crowd was small. Most people sat across from empty plates, waiting for the weather to turn before venturing back out. We chose a table next to a foggy window and resumed our conversation.

"I want to go back to what happened this morning," Sean began. "Is that something that you grew up with? What was it like being a kid?"

"Destitute," I said, being honest with a near stranger for the first time. "Isolated. Even in my earliest memory, I was partially alone. Never fully alone, though. I always had Jormon and my uncle, Tobin. And Nana Lura, too."

"Your dad is the king of Kaydans. That must be nice."

"It's the opposite of nice," I said. "There's a lot of pressure to do well—to do *good*—when you're the son of the king. To everyone else, so nice and charming. But to me, he's not like that." I realized how close I was to airing my family's dirty laundry. Uncle wouldn't like that. Father would outright hate it. "What about you?"

"Life has been strange since y'all came to Earth, not that I have much pre-Kaydan time to compare it to. From what I can tell, y'all coming brought out the worst in people. Nowadays, anyone who isn't like *them* turns into targets." Them. The Riders. "You would think that aliens coming would push people to band together, that hatred for gays and blacks and cripple folk would end. It did, at first. Now, though…"

"The Riders turn on anyone. I get it." I tried to lock eyes with him and see what I could learn of his otherness, but he looked out the foggy window and became mesmerized by the falling rain.

After several minutes of silence, he snapped to and said, "What happened on your planet? If… If that's rude to ask, you don't have to answer."

ANDRE L. BRADLEY

How it all began. I'd never talked about that much, not that anyone ever asked me. Maybe people thought I didn't know. I was seven years old then and had a child's memory, but all that happened was quite unforgettable, even for a kid.

I remembered hunkering down in a small room back in our hometown, Maerin, on Kayda. It was in someone's house, I think. Maybe? It was small and plain, and there were chairs scattered around and a dead fireplace jammed into one of the walls. In the center of the room sat a wooden table no bigger than a footstool, and resting upon it was a black sphere with a yellow glow deep inside. Eight or so people—some of whom I recognized—sat around it like it was campfire and they were waiting their turn to tell a story, but that wasn't the vibe at all, *that* I remember clearly. The only thing they were waiting for was for my father to show up. "The king will be here soon," my mom kept saying. "We have to hurry."

Nana Lura had me on one knee. Jormon was on the other. He looked tired. I felt tired. It must have been late. Uncle became aware of something outside, and he rushed out the door. Minutes later, Momma left, too. I didn't ask her what was happening, although in retrospect I should have. I should have said something.

I remembered a voice echoing in my head, then my world seemed to shrink until I was the only one in it. The details of the room—the cushioned couch, the braided rug, and such—faded from focus until all I knew was the light from the sphere. And then there was nothing at all. No sounds, no sight, no sensations. My world had become a void. The rest of what happened, I only remember because I was told. There were explosions and hasty actions, and then chaos. Everything shook, and without warning, something ripped through the air, splattering a thick, golden streak across a flawless midday sky. The wind rushed upward in a strong pull, uprooting people from where they stood. Roofs peeled from houses and families were violently snatched from their homes and hurled toward the golden gap. As they catapulted through the air, they searched uselessly for something to grab onto, panicking as they vanished into the crack. Trees ripped from the ground and swept up into the void. Buildings splintered along their facades and broke apart, and their collapsing structures, like everything else in the vicinity, were caught in the updraft. I came to with my world topsy-turvy, my feet racing to the sky and the world growing smaller below me. I thought for sure it was the end for me.

Just beyond the crack, gravity reversed itself and everything fell, except it wasn't falling toward Kayda. The connecting portal dumped everything out miles above the ground here on Earth, raining down bodies and belongings and things of all sorts over southern Georgia from Vidalia to Valdosta. Those who could fly maneuvered through the falling masses, dodging what they could, casting whatever spells they knew to shield themselves from the tons of falling debris they couldn't escape that had become hundreds of deadly missiles. Most banded together to help others, shielding one another from entire houses raining down from the shrinking slit in the sky. The portal was open for less than two minutes, but in those two minutes, thousands of Kaydans—maybe a hundred thousand: no one has ever calculated a precise head count—suddenly became intruders in a strange, new world. A world full of people who hated us then, and hate us now.

"We came by accident," I said, afraid telling the story would upset me, or him, or both. "I should probably go home now."

"Already?" He glanced at his phone. "It's not even five o'clock yet."

"You can come back with me. I live in the trailer park down the road." I felt stupid as soon as I said it. Of course we live in the trailer park down the road. Who didn't know that?

It never occurred to me he would say no. It should have, though. He was human, I was Kaydan, and as a general rule, our species didn't socialize.

I was happy when he accepted the offer.

As we were walking out, the girl behind the counter called out to me. "You're Noan, right? I can tell from the tattoos. Aunt May

May wanted me to give you something." She left briefly, and when she returned, she carried a pie. "She told me to tell y'all it's too early in the season for sweet potato pies, but she made this one for y'all cause she thought you might need something sweet. And she asked if you could come by a couple weekends from now and help with the garden."

"Tell her thank you, and that I'll be there."

I had a friend over, and the reality delighted me in a most unexpected way. Sean oohed and aahed at the wonderment of the manor, and like any other host, I took secret pleasure in his admiration. I envisioned how it would be were life different. To be Prince Noan Phyrinot Ladoan of Maerin, hosting my people at a ball in honor of something grand. Or something trivial, for that matter. Watching them ooh and aah.

I left Sean in the sitting room and went upstairs to change. Jormon was home. I could sense him, and he could sense me, too. I didn't need him asking about my day or telling me I couldn't have human company. If he pulled rank and made me put Sean out, I'd be humiliated so I changed quickly and rejoined Sean.

Sweet tea, an assortment of canapés, and two apples, thinly sliced, all served on a second-hand pewter tray. We drank and nibbled, neither of us particularly hungry. Sean asked many questions, and I answered them as best I could. A downside to being a Kaydan refugee in America was that we did not receive formal, extensive study about where we came from. I had read a dozen books about America's rocky history and the rise of western civilization, and about Genghis Khan and the Silk Road. Of Kayda, however, I only knew what I was told. My family lived in Maerin, an island nation the size of Australia that anchored the Dragon Ridge archipelago to the main continent, Draelin, above it. Gaalind, the land of dragons, was positioned to the east, and Falsh, land of the *suhrat*, to the southwest.

"So, if it's possible to manipulate entire spaces, why didn't y'all just do that when you got here? Make your own Little Kayda out in the woods somewhere? The New War could've been shorter, and the Hunts wouldn't even have been a thing."

"But that wouldn't be any kind of life. To hide away like rats in a cupboard, only coming out to eat and returning to the darkness if someone sees you. It would only solidify the notion that we have no right to live in the open world. Not so much that we are other than, but that we are less than. No one should have to live that way."

The room warmed unexpectedly. I grabbed a small, blue cube the size of a die from a wooden box set atop the mantel. I tossed it in the fireplace and cold, blue flames crackled to life. "Frost fire," I explained. The room cooled immediately.

I wanted to change the subject, but there was no easy transition. "Something Brett said earlier has stuck with me, and I won't be satisfied until I know what he meant. Does he bully you? What did he mean when he said you've gotten your ass kicked before?"

Sean swirled what was left of his tea around in his glass. The silence was not long, but it was awkward, and there was nothing I could do to make it less so. The question was asked, and there was no going back. Finally, he said, "Everybody's got a past. You're new here, so you don't know mine. You don't want to know mine." He paused. "I try not to think about mine. It's how I stay so chipper."

"Did he hurt you?" My concern was genuine, but I probably came off as nosey. "Whatever he did to you, you didn't deserve it. I'm sure of that."

"You can't be sure of anything around these parts."

"I know you were nice to me when you didn't have to be. It wasn't that long ago that humans were sawing off our hands and preserving them in jars, thinking it would give them power."

"I guess I didn't do that, if that's where you're setting the bar."

I didn't understand his shift in attitude. I should have shut up then, but I could be stubborn and inconsiderate when I wanted to be.

"You don't have to be embarrassed. If it was anything like today, I can imagine what he did."

"Just let it go."

I wanted to let it go, but the notion nagged at me. The suppressed cough that makes your eyes water as you hold it in. "But I can help you. Isn't that why you're hanging around?"

"I don't want anything. I just… I don't want to go home right now."

"I don't get it."

"You don't have to get it, Noan. You just have to respect my wishes when I say I don't want to talk about it."

"Fine. I'll drop it for now. But if any of what you're hiding pertains to Brett, you owe it to me to tell me—I think owe is the wrong word. If you care to be my friend, and you know the history I have with Brett, it would be better for the sake of our own relationship that the secret is out in the open."

"In due time we'll be like two butt cheeks in the same pair of drawers, but until then, we both have family business we need to keep within the family, don't you agree."

"If that's all it is, then yeah, I agree."

We sat in silence for a few minutes, and it dawned on me yet again that I was the host, and as such, I was responsible for the flow of conversation.

"I hope I didn't ruin things between us. Could you stay a while longer?"

"You didn't ruin anything. I'm simply admiring the taste of this tea. For someone not from round here, you sure can make a good pitcher of tea."

I let him believe I made it. There was no reason to bring Nana Lura into the conversation.

"Let's go up to my room. I have an idea."

He sat himself at the foot of my bed, and it occurred to me I'd do well to get more furniture. A chair, maybe. Or one of those stupid, oversized beanbags I saw at Farmers' Furniture a few months back. I reached into my nightstand to retrieve a blank *sabej* in the shape of a ring.

"Are those snakes?" Sean asked, eying the handful of *soulfangs* tucked away in the back of the drawer. I'd been trying to analyze them to see why they caused me to smoke out at the Gaddalie Ball, but neither I nor Phea could figure out where their power came from.

"Never mind that," I said, closing the drawer. "I want to show you this." I held up the ring.

"Is that obsidian?" Sean said, quickly forgetting about what could be a wad of snakes hanging out in my nightstand for no good reason.

"You know your stones, I see. We call it a *sabej*. It can store energy indefinitely, until the energy has been used up."

"That's cool. Like that sphere on your nightstand. What's that?"

My eyes followed where he was pointing. Floating inches above my nightstand was a dark, translucent sphere the size of a ripe orange. Presently, it contained a storm inside. "It reflects the weather and light conditions of wherever you are. My uncle made that one for me when I was a kid." I waved a dismissive hand at it before a thought struck me. "Forget about the orb for a second. I've got an idea—I want to make something for you."

If it was protection he needed, I wanted to give it to him. Shield and protection manipulations came to me easily. They were of the first *sahdriin* Uncle taught us. With little effort, I used my energy to etch the corresponding runic shapes along the outer edges of the obsidian band. Dark purple specks flowed from my hands and raced along the ring like whimsical flock animals. Once all the figures were complete, I poured in raw energy. The ring glowed from the inside as it filled up, up, up.

"This is for protection." I handed the ring to Sean, who was still awestruck.

"What does it do? How does it work?"

"The runes—I think you call them runes—denote the intent of the *sabej*. I've carved shield runes to this one. Fire, projectiles, blunt force. That's all I could fit on this one. They're some of the same ones we used to protect ourselves during the New War. But the runes are useless if the *sabej* isn't imbued with power."

"Which is the last thing you just did, yeah?"

"Yeah. I probably put too much, but I haven't made one of these in a long time, and I wanted to make sure the protections are strong enough."

"Are they?"

"Hopefully you won't ever have to find out."

"But if I do need it, how does it work? Do I put my hand out like one of the planeteers and scream out?"

"Huh? No. As long as you're wearing the ring, you only have to think about self-preservation and the *sabej* will activate."

Sean slid the ring on his fourth finger; it wouldn't fit on any of the others. With his other hand, he spun the ring around until he had seen each symbol three or four times. "Well ain't you a peach," he said, perhaps understanding the power he now had to punish me if our acquaintance ever went sour.

"It's just a gift. Hopefully you never have to use it."

"It's more than a gift. It's an act of kindness. You're a good person. You're a helluva lot better than most people I know. Besides Jamilah. She's my best friend, and she would love to meet you. You'd think she was super cool, too."

"Does she go to our school?"

"Naw. She lives near Atlanta. We met while visiting our moms in Milledgeville."

That's where the psychiatric ward is. I heard of that place a lot over the years. People couldn't cope with our existence after we arrived, and some of them lost it.

136

"Oh," I said. If there was something else to follow up with, I couldn't find the words. Instead, we talked about something else, then something else after that.

CHAPTER TWELVE
JORMON

THE NEWS ABOUT NOAN'S INCIDENT WITH BRETT spread like a dragon's breath. On the third morning of school, the mob of protesters gathered in front was bigger, and the next day, even bigger still. By the end of the first week, the crowd was so massive it blocked part of the parking lot, and parents had to drop their kids off on the street. It was quite a show to put on for five people, but the size of the commotion suggested that, to them, even one of us was too many. I didn't care about any of it. I had my first kiss, then my second, and all I could think about was having more.

Inside the building, the reverse was happening. Fewer and fewer students showed up every day, and some who did show up in the morning were pulled out of school before lunch. By the end of August, nearly a third of the students had transferred to Vidalia High School. The protesters said it's because they were scared of us. It was more likely they were afraid of the protestors. During one eventful morning, the protest turned full on riot. A man ripped his poster-board sign from its wooden stake and threw it at us as we were walking past. It hit Phae in the arm, but she paid it no mind. That made it worse. Some of the others ripped their signs and threw their stakes too, as well as full cans of Coke. Most of the Cokes missed us and exploded on the concrete walkway, and by the time we made it inside, we were wet and sticky.

Homeroom remained crowded. Mrs. Broadnax ran her classroom with all the command of a military general, and the students, like soldiers, fell in line. Those who didn't, the ones who squirmed in their seats when she said an off comment about Phae's hairstyles or Kaydan tattoos, were removed from her roster and replaced with another student. Before we knew it, Brett Brantley, Kevin Summerset, Jake Crawley, Alexander Darley, and the Carroway twins had infiltrated the class. They filled the row immediately behind us and would occasionally lean forward and whisper insults. In early September, when Mrs. Broadnax had her back turned, Kevin Summerset pulled a marble-sized *sabej* from his backpack and flicked it at Taavi. It exploded in a noisy and bright display of crimson fireworks.

Mrs. Broadnax froze at the whiteboard. She was partway through writing a red, cursive sentence, and the tip of the dry-erase marker pressed into the "s" she was writing until the liquid bled down in a thin stream. "What was that?" she asked, still not looking over her shoulder.

Kevin and Alexander exchanged mischievous glances while Brett leaned forward, resting his chin on his folded hands, a smirk playing on his lips.

"No one has anything to say?" she asked, finally turning around. Her gaze locked first on Taavi, then down the line at Phae, then Noan, until, finally, they rested on me. "A loud bang erupts in *my* classroom, and no one knows a thing about it. Hmpf. I thought you people were supposed to be smart."

The school bell rang, signaling the end of the period, but Mrs. Broadnax motioned for everyone to stay seated. "Alright, class," she began, her voice dripping with feigned sweetness. "I've noticed a lot of... disruptions lately. I believe it is my duty as your educator to address any distractions that might hinder the learning process." She walked slowly over to Phae and reached a pudgy hand to touch her hair. The glass bangles she wore scraped across Phae's forehead as Mrs. Broadnax's fingers scratched across her braids. Phae shrank back in her seat. She turned her head to Noan and squinted her eyes as if asking what she should do, but Mrs. Broadnax dug her red-painted nails into her scalp and forced her head forward. "I'll start by reminding everyone about our school's dress code and personal grooming standards."

Phae's cheeks flushed, and she looked down to avoid Mrs. Broadnax's gaze. "You see," Mrs. Broadnax continued, looking directly at Phae, "There's a certain order to things. For example, wild, unruly hairstyles can be so... distracting, don't you think?" Phae's intricate braids fell loose from their clasp as Mrs. Broadnax's nails plucked at them and cascaded down her back. Beside her, Taavi tensed, and his Kaydan tattoos shimmered as though he was calling upon his power.

This isn't good, Noan said to me, noticing the same thing. Muffled chatter grew louder on the other side of the closed door as students passed by, oblivious to the scene unfolding in Mrs. Broadnax's classroom.

Brett chimed in, feigning innocence, "Yes, Mrs. Broadnax. And what about those tattoos? Aren't they against school policy to have them covered up like that?" He pointed at Phae's thin shawl, which draped over her shoulders and concealed her tattoos.

The room's atmosphere grew heavy. Silent stares were exchanged among students. The power play was evident, and Brett's smugness was palpable. Kevin and Alexander chuckled softly while other students looked away, uncomfortable. Mrs. Broadnax's eyes shifted quickly, most likely noting who didn't seem okay with what was happening. They'd be replaced by the end of the week.

Taavi's grip on his desk tightened. "It's cold in here," he said. "She didn't mean to break any rules."

Mrs. Broadnax raised an eyebrow. "Yet that's exactly what she did."

Noan, trying to defuse the situation, spoke calmly, "We mean no harm or disruption."

Mrs. Broadnax's eyes narrowed. "It's not about harm, Noan. It's about adhering to the societal norms of this institution."

My patience was wearing thin. "Our presence here isn't a threat to these 'norms' you speak of. We're here to get an education just like everyone else."

Alexander snickered, "Maybe there are other schools better suited for coppers."

The tension in the room was palpable, and I was really getting tired of Mrs. Broadnax, Brett, and all the rest of them. I looked over and caught Dirk staring at me. Shadows of uncertainty clouded his eyes, and every twitch of his expression screamed for this moment to end, and I was speaking before I even knew what I was saying. "If we didn't have to be in this shithole of a school, we wouldn't." The whole room breathed in audibly. "Kaydans have a fine institution where we study topics your feeble little brains couldn't begin to comprehend."

That's enough, Jormon, Noan said.

But it wasn't enough, not for me. "Do you think we want to be here in this school where the most interesting thing to happen before our arrival was the Future Farmers of America's greased pig contest, huh? Do you think we like walking through the crowd of idiots shouting at us in front of the school only to come inside and face more idiots lecturing us about standards and decorum?"

Jormon, cut it out. Now!

"I am the prince of our people. The crown prince, in fact, and I will one day be king. I'm the one person you don't want to piss off, so cut the crap and let us out of this classroom. We respect the school's rules, and we'll continue to do so. But we ask for the same respect in return."

Mrs. Broadnax stood at the head of the room, her posture rigid and commanding. The usually calm and collected demeanor she held had shattered. Her deep-set eyes filled with a blend of fury and disbelief, and her cheeks, typically a soft shade of peach, were now flushed crimson, contrasting starkly with the silver streaks in her tightly coiled hair. The room was thick with tension as every student awaited her next move, sensing the volcanic mix of anger and astonishment bubbling just beneath her surface. For a whole minute, no one said anything. The humming of the overhead fluorescent lights seemed to grow louder. The very air grew dense, as if the walls of the classroom had moved closer together, pressing everyone into a tighter space. Outside, the distant echoes of other classes, the shuffle of feet, and distant laughter stood in stark contrast to the stifling silence that now dominated our classroom.

Mrs. Broadnax pursed her lips, taking a deep breath. "Your daddy is the king, huh? Is that what's got you so uppity and smart mouthed? Well, let me tell you something. I don't care who your daddy is. This is my classroom, and in here, I'm the one in charge. For that little outburst of yours, three-day suspension."

"What?" I yelled, nearly rising from my seat. "You can't do that."

"Oh, yes I can. You and the rest of your lot can pack your things and head home, and if your daddy king asks who sent you packing, tell him it was me."

Noan's voice, soft yet firm, cut in before I could say what I thought about her and her stupid punishment. "Mrs. Broadnax, my brother didn't mean what he said. We really do want to fit in here."

But Mrs. Broadnax wasn't listening anymore. She was scribbling on a pink slip of paper and tilting her head from one side to the other. "Is that 'Royal Highness,'' capital R, capital H?" she asked. A wicked smile stretched across her face. "I've never suspended a king-to-be before. I have to tell you, it's pretty exciting. Almost as exciting as winning first place at a greased pig contest."

We were all on edge flying home from school. Someone from the school must've contacted Dad, because no sooner had we landed in the trailer park, Uncle Tobin met us at the front door with a message from him.

I'm not taking the blame for this, Noan said.

I didn't ask you to.

I'm just saying.

I shook my head and pushed past Uncle Tobin. There was no way Dad would leech me like he made me do to Noan. Would he?

That evening, the trailer park was a hubbub of whispered conversations from too many people finding excuses to be outside, all waiting on the king's arrival. Anxiety built in my chest like water at a dam, and I needed an outlet before I exploded. I needed to lose myself in the energy building up, and I made the mistake of gathering the Cohort for their *mustedi* lesson. In the end, I was too anxious to teach.

"I can't do it today, Noan. I just can't. You teach them, just this once." I was having trouble thinking. "It's the portal lesson, yeah?"

After three straight hours of struggling and being told how bad we were, Taavi snapped at Noan, who, for the first time in a long time, looked furious.

"Wait just a minute, *Sergeant* Noan. We're really trying. You yelling at us won't help us learn this any faster." The task for the evening was to create a portal. It was a *sahdr* none of us had ever seen before, but Noan pulled it off like he'd been doing it his entire life. He conjured a shadow, and it grew thicker and darker, like evaporated oil. It swirled in its own containment just in front of us. He poured energy into it, and it grew until it was roughly the size of a door. The blackness recoiled from the center and rolled itself around the edges, then we were looking at the tops of our heads. If this was the entrance, high above us was the exit. Noan stepped through the portal, then hovered slowly overhead. We'd tried for nearly an hour to conjure our own, and no one succeeded. Not even me.

"Don't get mad at me because you can't do it," Noan said.

"I'm not mad because I can't do it. I'm mad because…" Taavi turned his back and placed a balled fist over his mouth.

"Go on and say it," Noan said. "Everyone's always upset with me for some reason. What's yours?"

"Don't say anything, Taavi," Phae said, then turned to Noan. "He's just under a lot of pressure. We all are."

"I'm mad because you keep putting *them* over us," Taavi said, pointing in the darkness. Them. Humans.

"I'm not putting anyone over you guys. All I do is think about what's best for you," Noan said. Taavi rolled his eyes. "Wait. Please don't tell me this is about Sean." Noan stepped closer to Taavi.

"It's not about Sean," Phae said, but even I wasn't convinced.

"You don't have to defend me, Phae. It is about Sean, and about how Noan spends all his time having ice cream socials with that human." Taavi moved closer to Noan. "What do you see in him?"

"What's it to you?" Noan said. They were nearly shouting now and stood close enough that if one of them were to swing a fist at the other, it would connect.

"Whoa, guys," I shouted. "We're in training. This little lovers' quarrel can wait. Cut this crap out now. Taavi, take your position. Noan, resume training." No one moved. Taavi and Noan eyed each other with a passion I recognized but couldn't distinguish, and whether it was lust or hatred, I didn't care. "As your prince, I order you to move! Go! Noan, resume the damn training."

"Fine." Noan conjured a ball of light and tossed it. It became suspended in midair several feet over our heads. The light grew dense and flowed around itself in hot, liquid currents. Its harsh yellowness darkened into a molten orange and dripped onto the ground between Dirk and Taavi, boring a hole through the grass. The orb doubled in size, then tripled, and kept growing until it was as big as a bale of hay. Even from a distance, its heat was barely tolerable.

Whatever had been suspending it gave way, and it dropped. Without thinking, I extended my powers to levitate it, but it was too heavy. Taavi saw what I was doing—so did Dirk and Phae—and with our combined strength, we stopped it from falling. But it was still growing, and even with their help, it kept sinking.

I did what I knew how to do: I brought forth water from the ground and air. The water swirled in a thick river and pummeled Noan's makeshift sun. It was too hot. The entire stream turned to steam before it even got close.

"We can't keep this up," Dirk said. "I'm too tired."

"Of course you are," Noan shouted. Dirk's eyes met mine and I knew too well how he felt in that moment. Inadequate. Unfit for present company. Noan had a way of making others feel that way, but he had no right doing it to Dirk.

"We need to move it before it crushes us!" Taavi yelled over the swirling roar. The air had thickened with swells of heat as the growing nova spun and spat molten whips. Sweat ran down his face in torrents, and a hole had burned clean through his shirt.

"Can we toss it? Okay, over my shoulder on 'three'," I shouted. "One, two…"

We heaved it, but it barely went up, much less up and over my shoulder.

"Noan, stop this! I get what you're doing, but this is dangerous." The muscles in my arms twitched, and the ball of heat inched closer to our heads. Sweat stung my eyes and my vision blurred, but I could see Noan close by, walking slowly with his hands behind his back like Uncle Tobin.

"All you have to do is drop it in the lake." His nonchalance wore on me, and I wanted to throw this ball of hot shit in his face.

A shadow formed beneath the orb. A tiny speck in comparison to the hovering flame, but it quickly expanded until we could no longer see the light. The shadow peeled slowly back from the center. It was a portal, and through it we could see the moonlit surface of the lake.

"Which one of you is doing that?" Noan asked with astonishment.

"I am," Taavi shouted. "Drop it on the count of 'three.' One, two…"

We released. We exhaled. The fiery orb fell through the portal and into the lake. Steam shot back through the portal like a blow torch, and we all jumped back to avoid being burned.

"Good job. Class dismissed," Noan said.

In the seconds it took me to get off the ground, Noan had conjured another portal and stepped through it. I ran after him, but the portal had already begun shrinking. I could make it, maybe. I jumped headfirst and flew through just before the shadowy rim rolled closed. I landed hard at Noan's feet, which pissed me off even more.

We were outside the trailer, and Noan had his hand on the doorknob.

"Hey!" I shouted, and Noan turned in surprise. Before I knew it, my fist struck against his face. "That stunt you pulled back there was reckless. You were way out of line. Someone could've gotten hurt."

He cranked his jaw left and right and felt at the spot that was turning red. "Are you worried about them, or yourself?

"What's that supposed to mean?"

"It means that I had everything under control. The only thing that got hurt was your pride because you couldn't do the *sahdr*. And now my jaw. What the hell, Jormon. You never hit me. What was that for?"

"You deserved it."

He wriggled his chin left and right. "I was doing everyone a favor."

"By nearly burning the shit out of us? Some favor."

"Because of me, Taavi can create portals. If you're in trouble and I'm not around, Taavi can help you escape. If the cost of making this happen is a few burns and bruised egos, then so be it."

"If you hurt someone, Dad will do more than leech you."

"Lately, the only person hurting me is you."

The hand I punched him with was starting to swell. I flexed my fingers and pain shot up my arm. "Crap. I think it's broken."

"Do you want me to fix it?"

"I know the *sahdr*. Just get out of my face."

CHAPTER THIRTEEN
NOAN

ZEREQ WAS ALONE IN THE KAYDAN SKY. ITS SOFT blue light painted my bedroom in cool shades of cerulean and sapphire. Shadows crawled along the walls as clouds moved in and out of its light. It was my favorite sky of them all, but I couldn't enjoy it, not with the distant murmurs and muffled footsteps down the hall. Father would arrive soon, and Jormon would have some explaining to do. I braced myself for the possibility that Father would blast down my door and leech me, but I couldn't keep up that level of anxiety for long. I was exhausted from being constantly on guard. Plus, my jaw hurt like hell.

As I paced the room, Phae flew through my open window, scaring the crap out of me. We'd gotten closer since school started, but her flying through my window unannounced was something I'd yet to get used to. "I thought I told you to stop doing that," I said, placing my hand on my chest as I caught my breath.

"If I scared you, you deserved it. What was that crap you pulled back there? What's going on with you?"

It wasn't the first time Phae had worried about me recently. Hell, it wasn't even the first time this week. She happened to witness Brett elbow me in the gut before lunch a while back and ran over to make sure I was okay. I wasn't, and she knew it. She wasn't okay, either, I found out in the days that followed. I'd been so preoccupied with the notion I was the only one suffering, I hadn't even stopped to think of how lonely Phae was being one of the only *suhrat* in Gray Flats.

Phae snapped her fingers. "Hello? I'm talking to you. What's up?"

"It's everything, Phae. It's the humans, it's the school…it's my father." I didn't know if I could trust her, but what was said could not be unsaid.

Phae moved closer, and I caught the scent of lavender and sweat. "So, all that yelling and grandstanding and nearly getting us killed, that's supposed to make you feel better?"

I felt cornered, my frustrations coming to a head. "Can we just talk like friends? Please don't analyze me. We hardly know each other."

She moved from the window and sat on the bed. "I know we're in this together. I know you're always angry, and not just with your dad or the humans. You're angry with Jormon, too I can feel it when he's around. Something about you changes."

I shifted uncomfortably. The truth was like a stone lodged in my chest. "He's my brother. I love him. But sometimes…sometimes I just want to shout at him. Make him understand how I feel. Make him see what I see." And challenge him, I wanted to say, but I wasn't sure I meant it. In fact, I knew I didn't mean it.

"He gets all the attention. He's the golden child, and I'm just…there. I want to be seen. Truly seen. Not as Jormon's brother, but as Noan." I shook my head, gazing at the blue ceiling. "I see you, too," I said, eager to shift the conversation. "You're lonely. It's the first thing I noticed about you when we formally met at the Ball."

She looked taken aback, her eyes widening slightly. She pulled back just enough to meet my gaze, searching for any hint of jest or deceit. "Why do you think that?" she asked, her voice regaining its usual sass.

I hesitated, trying to find the right words. "There was this look in your eyes, like you felt…out of place. Like you were surrounded by people but still felt alone."

Phae looked down, her fingers tracing along the *sheriaan* on my arm. Where she touched, orange marigolds blossomed and died in a matter of seconds. "It's because I can do things like this and no one else can. If it makes me an outsider, so be it. I am who I am. And, yeah, being yourself can sometimes be lonely."

I nodded. "I get that. Truly. Look if I've ever made you feel less than or left out, I'm sorry. If there's anybody who gets what it's like to not feel wanted, it's me. I should've paid more attention."

She smiled, her face lighting up and her mood shifting altogether. "I'm glad to hear you say that because you should open your eyes to Taavi."

"Excuse me?"

"You're too smart to play dumb. Taavi likes you, Noan. Prince Noan. Poor, penniless Taavi has a gigantic crush on you. I'm not telling you this for you to act on it. I'm not trying to get in your business like that. I'm only saying it so that you don't hurt him by accident."

I raised an eyebrow. "I doubt I could hurt Taavi, but thanks for spelling that out."

Phae sighed, brushing a strand of hair behind her ear. "Taavi is a blazing fire, but you...you're the deep, calm waters. Both have their strengths, both can be protective or destructive. As fire, he can get you hot—and I mean that in a non-sexual way. But as water, you can extinguish his flame."

"Meaning?"

"I'm just saying, be careful with his heart."

I pondered her words, thinking about the contrasting natures of fire and water. "And what are you in this analogy?"

Phae walked over to the window, her eyes reflecting the silver sheen of the moon. "I think I'm the wind. Always changing, always moving. Sometimes gentle, sometimes fierce. But always free."

I nodded in agreement. "That suits you. The wind that sweeps across the vast landscapes, touching everything, leaving a mark, yet remaining untethered."

She looked back at me, her eyes softening. "Maybe that's why we get along so well. The wind over the water. It's a peaceful coexistence."

A sudden, insistent knocking swiftly erased any good feelings I had. Father must be here. The reckoning I'd been dreading for was waiting on the other side of the door. "Go," I whispered urgently. "You don't need to be here for this."

Phae nodded, taking a deep breath. With a swift movement, she moved to the window and climbed onto the ledge. She looked back at me one last time before pushing off and hovering to the ground.

"Come in," I said, and the door creaked open slowly.

Jormon stumbled in, clutching at his chest. His torn shirt revealed the angry, inflamed lines where the *rhualka* had struck, the skin raw and swollen. The cruel imprints stood in stark contrast to his beautiful skin, now tinted blue in the light of *Zereq*. A soft whimper escaped his lips, punctuating the thick silence of the room.

Every step he took was labored, the soles of his feet dragging against the worn carpeted floor. His normally vibrant eyes were glazed over, shrouded by a film of tears, their usual light extinguished by anguish. His powers were drained. I could smell the saltiness of his tears, the sharp metallic scent of blood, and the acrid stench of sweat, each telling a story of the agony he'd been through. That I had been through, too.

Gently lowering him onto my bed, I noticed his fingers trembling, leaving behind streaks of blood where they grazed the sheets. The rhythm of his heart, which I could feel through his battered chest, was frenzied, like the wings of a trapped bird, desperate to escape its cage.

"Why?" His voice cracked as he managed to utter the single word, his gaze fixed on mine, searching for answers I didn't have.

"Because he's Father." The air grew heavy with the weight of unspoken words, emotions too raw to be vocalized. "Am I next?"

Holding his hand, feeling the rapid pulse beneath his bruised skin, he whispered, "Yeah."

I gave a feeble nod. Of course, I was next. Punished, yet again, for Jormon's actions. It was the life I knew. My only hope was that Jormon would be there to comfort me.

I returned to my room after my leeching to find it empty. The weight of loneliness pressed down on my chest, making it hard to breathe. The bed, where just moments ago Jormon lay battered and bruised, was now a chilling reminder of the relentless cycle of suffering we were trapped in, a suffering I would have to contemplate alone. I slowly approached it, running my fingers over the still-warm sheets, stained with his blood. Each smudge was a testament to our shared pain.

The place where Jormon should have been—where a brother would be—was now just a haunting void. A cold wind blew in from the open window, ruffling the curtains and sending a shiver down my spine. I walked over to it, staring out into the vast expanse, hoping to catch a glimpse of Phae, but she was nowhere to be seen.

Instead, there stood Taavi, shirtless, opening and closing portals as his body glistened in the moonlight. As though sensing my watching him, he turned his head towards the window. Our eyes met for a second, but it was long enough to break his concentration. His portal slammed closed in a loud pop. He didn't seem to mind. He took a confident step towards my trailer.

I shook my head, warning him to stay back. I didn't need him seeing me in such a state, not again. I turned away from the window and walked back to my bed, Before I could sit, Taavi sailed gracefully through the open window, landing softly on the carpeted floor.

I wasn't startled, not like when Phae had surprised me earlier. Maybe a part of me had hoped he would come.

Taavi said nothing. He crossed the room in two strides and grabbed me in a hug. I didn't mind the sweat or the musk. I simply stood there, happy and sad at the same time, until my arms found their way around him too.

CHAPTER FOURTEEN
JORMON

LABOR DAY CAME AND WENT, AND NOAN AND I hadn't spoken more than two words at a time to each other since the leeching, and those words were usually "hey" and "no." It helped we were both busy in our own ways. There was school, of course, which improved a lot following our suspension. I don't know what Dad did, but the National Guard was called in to control the riots, resulting in a relative peace. Still, we used the portal *sahdr* Noan taught us to sneak through the back entrance, and the rioters grew tired of not having anyone to sling their hate at.

Without the hysteria, school was a pleasant break from real life. No learning to be king or being worried that I wouldn't live up to everyone's expectations. No sideways glances from Noan when he thought I was teaching the evening lessons wrong. School was great. Almost. Some seniors had already turned eighteen or were about to, and they wouldn't shut up about voting in the upcoming US presidential elections. Uncle Tobin referred to one candidate as a 'blow hard' earlier in the summer. It seemed like an exaggeration— what was it, almost three months ago? Now, nearly half the students sported some form of merchandise with his campaign's logo: a signature black background and three-pointed crown with the slogan, "To Glory." Glory Gear, the media called it. Two teens were suspended for spray painting the logo on the walkway outside the school's main door. That was a week ago. The sign was still there.

Days fell shorter, the air grew colder, and the lake was losing its summer heat. I was in my bedroom thinking of this when Noan walked in. "Oh, you're alone."

"Why wouldn't I be?" I stayed focused on my math homework, figuring he'd take the hint and leave. If it was an apology he wanted, I wouldn't give him one.

"You ask as if Dirk hasn't been here every day for the past two months. I assumed he'd be here now. I was going to ask you both if you wanted to go to the lake. Today is the last day of swimming season. It won't be accessible again until spring."

We hadn't gone all season, what with school all week and training all weekend. It was just what I needed. It's what we all needed. "Should I ask Dirk to come? And the rest of the Cohort?"

"Fine." His sudden gruffness made me think it wasn't, but I didn't care. "I guess I can invite Sean, too."

"I'm sure Taavi will love that."

"What's that supposed to mean?" Noan snapped, and I threw my hands up in surrender.

"It meant nothing. Invite Sean. He's a good guy. He's kinda cute, too." It was easy to fall back into a familiar routine with Noan, and it suddenly hit me how much I missed it when we weren't speaking to one another.

Noan blushed. It was the first time I'd ever seen him do so, and I bit my lips to keep from smiling.

"Never mind. He doesn't need to come."

"Dude, don't be like that. I'm only teasing you because you're acting like an idiot."

"Take that back," Noan said.

"I won't, not if you're being an idiot. You have two guys who like you and you're refusing to get close to either one. If I had that type of freedom, the freedom to openly choose who I want to be with, I'd…"

"You'd what?"

I'd actually be happy, I wanted to say, but then Noan would launch into his standard speech about how good I have it compared to him. I wasn't trying to hear that. "I would take advantage of it."

"Whatever. Can we go?"

"Invite Sean first."

So it was, then, that Noan, Sean, Phae, Taavi, Dirk, and I planned an outing at the lake. Nana Lura packed us a lunch, and we set out on foot.

"Through the woods?" Phae complained. She had walked through a spider web and was grasping at her face. "Y'all know this isn't the ticket. Not for me, huns. Not in this outfit." She was wearing a green bikini top with a matching bottom, covered by a thin, diaphanous sarong that fluttered lazily with each step.

"Here's a plot twist: pretty little Phae doesn't do well in the woods," Taavi joked.

"I'm in the woods every day with you guys, but usually I'm dressed for the occasion. Do you see this material? This is organza, honey. You have no idea how many side jobs I had to work to afford this. I'm warning you now, if it snags, one of you will be transmogrified."

"Don't witches live in the woods?" Sean asked.

"We're not maenads running around with bare feet and sticks in our hair," Phae snapped.

"Sor-ry," Sean said. "I didn't mean to offend you."

"And don't call her a witch," Taavi added, leaving Sean confused and afraid to say another word.

"Hey, Taavi. Can you go ahead with Sean and explain why she's not a witch?" Noan said. His directness made it clear this was not a request Taavi could refuse. Noan walked closer to Phae and asked her to linger behind with him. When I looked over my shoulder, Phae's head rested on Noan's arm. Noan said something and she laughed.

Since when are you two so close? I asked Noan.

She gets me, he said.

We made it far enough to see the lake through the woods, and everyone picked up the pace until we were in the clearing.

I had never seen the lake so busy, but then again, I hadn't gone since humans and Kaydans could swim together. From the tree line

154

to the water's southern bank, the lakeside was a patchwork of green grass and multi-colored blankets, most of them vacant, held down by shoes and shirts and other things. Bare-chested men, and women in fashionable bathing suits bobbed in the water like so many fishing corks. Inwardly, my heart began to race at the sight of so many humans who could drown us if they wanted to and were quick enough. On the outside, I exuded a calm, collected demeanor, relaxing my shoulders and putting on a practiced smile.

"This place looks lively," I commented, making my voice light and breezy.

We hopscotched along the bank looking for an empty plot of grass to claim. Several somebodies had brought portable speakers, and music ebbed and flowed as we made our way to a small clearing on the edge of the crowd.

"No one thought to bring a blanket or something to lie on?" Phae asked.

"Crap!" Sean said. "I left it in the truck."

"Another strike," Taavi mumbled, and Noan shot him a look. Taavi shrugged his shoulders and said, "Sor-ry."

The lake itself was typically Southern. The water was murky and green. Towards the east, a number of oak trees grew close to the water's edge, and most of them had thick ropes hanging from extended branches, some ending in rubber tires that were used as swings or ball hoops. On the western edge, rocks scattered across the coast in a mosaic of shapes and sizes, and off in the distance, where the water deepened past the nautical rope's warning, fishing boats dotted the horizon.

The water was warmer than the air, and we waded through the shallows eagerly until we were all chest deep. We splashed around and shared stories of the week's happenings. Sean was telling some story about a chicken he took on a fishing trip when a hand brushed against mine underneath the water's dark surface. Dirk smiled as his fingers wove between mine, and I couldn't help but to smile, too.

Are you two having sex? Noan's voice thundered in my head in a mental shout.

"For *Heemrah*'s sake, Noan!" I said before realizing I was speaking aloud.

"Huh?" Dirk said, his face contorted in confusion.

"Uh, nothing," I said, clearly shaken. "Noan was just reminding me of a game we used to play as kids." It was a stupid lie, but it was better than saying my twin brother is checking my virginity.

"Ooh. What game?" Sean asked.

"Follow me," I said, happy for the distraction. I swam parallel to the shore, and they followed.

You guys totally are, Noan said.

So? What if we are? I extended my arms and swam faster.

I think it's great if you are, but I wish you would talk to me about it instead of treating me like a stranger.

Can we talk about this later? Or not at all.

Do you love him?

Stop being ridiculous.

It's not a ridiculous question. Answer it.

I love my dad, our king. I love my people. I love my duty.

You can lie to yourself, but I know you.

"You don't know anything!" I shouted. I looked over and Noan was right beside me. I stopped swimming, and so did he. My fists clenched beneath the water, and I wanted nothing more than to punch him. More than I wanted to be king, more than I wanted to kiss Dirk, I wanted to punch my brother hard enough to make him regret getting in my business.

"Umm, is this part of the game?" Sean asked meekly.

The others stood shoulder to shoulder, panicked at the thought that Noan and I would get into an all-out brawl right then and there. I plastered a smile across my face. The practiced smile. The smile that fooled everyone into believing it was genuine. "Noan is trying to psych me out like he always does."

We waded westward through the lake until we arrived at a small rock formation. We clambered over the damp rocks until we found a spot housing a small inlet of rippling water. "Noan and I went through this phase where we were fascinated with the City of Atlantis," I said.

"As in *The Little Mermaid*?" Sean asked.

"As in Poseidon."

"Or King Triton."

"That's Atlantica," I corrected him.

"It's the same—"

"Sean, I swear, if you say one more word…"

Noan jumped in before Sean found himself receiving the blow that was meant for Noan. "As a lark, Uncle replicated it for us right here in the lake."

"No way!" Sean exclaimed. "Me and my brother have been swimming here since we were knee high to a tadpole and not once did we ever see anything like that."

"That's because you didn't know how to find it," Noan said. "Follow me. I think you'll enjoy this."

"Will we enjoy it like we enjoy our evening training?" Taavi asked.

"You'll get to see me struggle as much as you do, so…probably." He stepped onto a slanted rock that poked into the water. He lay flat on his stomach, grabbed ahold of rocks on either side of him, and propelled himself forward, disappearing beneath the water's surface.

"I've seen weirder things," Sean said, and followed behind Noan. They all slid in reluctantly until Dirk and I were alone.

"Could you hang back with me for a second? I want to tell you something." Water tickled down my neck in the afternoon sun. A cool breeze cut over the rocks, causing goosebumps to sprout down my back and arms.

"Sure," he said so easily. He kept a calm way about himself. Relaxed, perhaps. Removed, like he was neither here nor there. Like he was happy.

"Noan knows about us. He said so just now."

"Is that what that was all about? What did he say?"

He didn't need to hear everything, especially the part where I denied my feelings for him. "That he's my baby brother and wants what's best for me. Or something like that."

"How does that make you feel?"

I shrugged and fidgeted with the hem of my shorts. I wished I could be happy like Dirk, but Dad's words haunted me. He had my future spouse in mind, and I'm damn sure he wasn't considering Dirk from the next trailer over.

"Are you worried?"

"He's not going to tell Uncle Tobin. He wouldn't. And he and Dad don't even speak to each other."

"Would it be so bad if they knew?"

I shrugged. "I don't know, Dirk. I don't know anything."

"Let me get this straight," Sean said. "I'm Aquaman?"

"No," Noan replied.

"King Triton?"

"We've already established that. No."

"But I'm a mermaid, that's for sure. Look at this sick tail!"

It was true. Under the lake's surface, in the bluest water imaginable, we were merfolk.

"Why do I have seashells on my titties?" Phae asked. "I did not sign up for this."

"Welcome to Atlantis!" Noan said. He was radiant. Happy in a way that I hadn't seen in months. His smile broadened with each word, and his eyes narrowed in childish delight.

"Do I get a trident?" Sean asked.

"That's all a part of the game," I said. I extended my arm and tightened my fist, and a golden trident materialized.

"Even if I'm human?"

"The power is in the *sahdr*, not in the person. I mean, you already transformed into a mermaid."

Taavi flapped his tail and swam in backwards circles. "Water doesn't even get in your nose!"

We all went wild, swimming at impossible speeds and angles. After a few minutes, even Phae joined in the fun.

"Is this the game?" Phae asked. "Swimming around and singing 'Part of Your World?'"

She closed her eyes and slowly twirled, singing the song like I'd never heard it before. The beauty and richness her voice carried left us stunned.

"You never told me you could sing," Noan said.

"I can hold a note," Phae said with a smirk. We floated there waiting for Phae to sing more, and were disappointed when she didn't.

Meanwhile, Sean swam in loops and twirls with all the excitement of a caffeinated chihuahua. He raced between Dirk and me, knocking us apart like bowling pins, then raced between Taavi and Phae. "This game is a-MAZ-ing!" he shouted.

"This isn't the game," Noan said. He pointed his trident at the city below, the Grecian wonder that was Uncle's imagining of Atlantis. Most of the city was water-worn ruins, though spread throughout were unscathed homes and in-tact caverns. It was marvelous. "*That's* the game."

"What!"

"There's a treasure hidden in the city below, guarded by monstrous sea creatures," Noan said. His voice was deep and brassy in narration. "The goal of the game is to fight off the monsters while searching for the lost treasure. It's that simple."

"Monsters?" Phae questioned.

"Don't worry, they won't hurt you," I said. "I mean, they are scary, and they will fight you, but the pain is only temporary."

"How do I take this stuff off?" She wriggled her tail and pulled at her fins, but the manipulation was inescapable.

"I'm down," Sean said. "Do we break into teams?"

"Sure," Noan replied. "Oh, and there's one more catch. A timer starts once we reach the city's perimeter. If no one finds the treasure in the allotted time, the kraken comes out and sinks the city into the ground."

"This is gonna be so fun," Sean said. "Epic. Epically fun." He flexed until he manifested a trident, jabbed it forward, and maroon lightning streaked through the water. "Guys! Check me out!" He reminded me of the first time Noan and I came here and how magical it all seemed, even for us.

"I'll team with Jormon," Dirk said. I tried not to smile.

"Well the joke is on you," Noan said. "Jormon is terrible at this game."

"I'm not, Dirk. Don't let Noan put you off. He's just jealous because I always win."

"What's the treasure?" Taavi asked. "Please tell me it's money. I'm tired of cycling through the same five decent outfits every week. Even the poor kids are making fun of me, and I'm one of them."

"We never found it," I said. "But knowing Uncle Tobin, it's probably a library card."

Phae teamed up with Noan, and Sean flapped over to Taavi. It hit me how normal this felt. Noan and I getting on like the good old days, and with friends who want to be with us not for our rank and title, but for the enjoyment of our company. I wanted to remember this moment as the way things are supposed to be. The way I'd have them be when I take over from Dad.

"On your mark!" Noan yelled. Everyone flexed until their tridents were in hand.

"Get set!"

Dirk grabbed my hand and squeezed.

"Go!"

We took off together. Our tails kicked in contrapuntal arcs, creating a bubbling melody in our wake. I felt free. Capable.

Our bodies crashed through a thick curtain of water near the sunken city, and a bell tower came to life with a wave of ringing and chiming that rippled across our bodies. We were inside the perimeter.

Dirk gripped my hand tighter as we swam towards a pile of collapsed pillars stacked upon themselves like tree limbs after a storm.

"I'm excited," he said. "And also scared." His hair had grown longer over the summer, and it waved behind him like liquid fire. I wanted to reach into the mass and test if it felt like hot silk, but that could wait 'til later.

"The monsters aren't so bad. We fought them off as kids."

It didn't take long to encounter the first one, a leviathan the length of a funeral procession. It created a sucking vortex, and I lost Dirk somewhere in the fight. Still, I attacked and was relieved to see yellow lightning bolts hitting the leviathan all over its face as I jabbed at its softer underside. Dirk was okay,

The leviathan flicked its tail, and it caught me square in the chest. I spiraled out of control, regained my bearings, and rushed back into the fight with my trident held forward. I plunged into its body and let off a series of bolt blasts once I was deep inside, then pushed through to the other side. It writhed and roared as it fell to the city below, then dissipated in a lackluster cloud.

We celebrated our victory with a few spins and flips and moved on to the next creature, and the one after that.

The bell rang three times in rapid succession. The kraken would appear soon.

"Have we really been under that long?" Dirk asked.

"We should head back. There's no winning against the kraken."

"This is so fun, though. Can we please just check one more spot?"

How could I say no? And how could I deny myself a few more minutes of being alone with him, far away from anybody who could object to this good thing we had.

We swam towards an unprepossessing structure that was perhaps a peasant's home. A cement hut with cartoonish windows and a door carved into one side. We moved cautiously until we were near enough to touch it. I poked my head through one of the windows and was surprised to see a black box, barely visible, tucked away in the far corner.

"You don't think that's the treasure, do you?" Dirk asked.

"I wouldn't know. Maybe. See how it's not covered by sand at all. I'm wondering if that could mean something."

"A Hardy Boy through and through."

A smile stretched across my face.

I swam through the window and grabbed the box. It resisted my pull as though a magnet was drawing it back to the corner. "I don't think this is the treasure," I called over my shoulder.

The box slipped from my hand and snapped back to where I'd found it. I swam back to it. *Nuur.* A stream of light left my chest and circled the box, reflecting off the silver diacritical markings of *Maerinish* script covering the lid. The letters marched around the box like sentinels on patrol, and I had to twist it this way and that to read it.

"I don't think it has anything to do with the game at all—No, stay back. Don't come in here."

The ground began to buckle and shake, and a deep crack raced through the roof of the hut. "We should go," Dirk said.

"I don't want to leave it here. Let me try one more thing."

"Maybe you should let it alone. There's a reason it doesn't seem to want to come."

I pointed my hand at the box, squeezed hard, and watched blue bolts fly from my fingertips. The bolts struck the box, then the world crashed down around me.

CHAPTER FIFTEEN
DIRK

JORMON'S BLAST HIT THE BOX, AND WHATEVER WAS in it blasted back. The explosion carried his body in a rush of water and before I knew it, I was swept away, too.

I kicked my fins trying to reorient myself, but they were gone, replaced by legs and feet too untrained to swim against the raging water. In that moment, I realized I needed air. Nothing was stored in my lungs. Moments ago, I didn't need to breathe, now my breath was all I could think about.

Panic set in. I was spinning out of control and didn't know which way was up. I was going to die if I didn't do something. *Jesus, keep me near the cross.*

I needed a *sahdr* that could give me orientation or breath, or both. I couldn't think of one. I couldn't think of anything except finding my way out. And of Jormon. Jormon!

My chest was being squeezed by the weight of the water, and my head felt like it was about to explode. It would explode. Damn, my head was about to explode. Where was Jormon? Where was the surface? I needed air. I needed…

I picked a direction and swam, swam until my arms burned with exhaustion. I wouldn't make it. Sorry, Jormon. Sorry, Momma and Daddy. Sorry, Novi, my dear sister. I should've left y'all a note telling y'all where I was fixing to go. You shouldn't have to find out this way, if you found out at all.

My body jerked as I took in water. As my eyes closed, I saw a vision of Jesus, coming straight at me in a gurgling whirl. *Thank you, Lord.*

"Give them both some room. Now! All of you, back up!"

I opened my eyes to find Jesus leaning over me. Not Jesus, Tobin, with his long hair falling forward, nearly touching my face.

"Good, you're alive."

"Wh-where's Jormon?" I croaked. "He was at the bottom with me. Did he make it out?"

"Hush. Hush now. No, don't try to sit up. Jormon will be fine. You both will be fine."

"And everybody else?"

"They're fine. They were at the surface when the manipulation gave way."

I cocked my head around to see if he was telling the truth. Phae sat a few feet away. She had her knees balled up to her chest and her arms wrapped around her shins. Taavi was on his knees behind her, rubbing her shoulders to calm her down. I twisted my neck the other way and there was Jormon, stretched out like me, with his head resting on Noan's leg. Good, he was safe. We survived whatever that was.

"How did you make it so fast?" I asked Tobin.

He gave me a look suggesting how dare I ask him such a ridiculous question. "What caused this?" he asked.

"I'm not for sure. We found a box at the bottom of Atlantis. It wouldn't come when we pulled at it, so Jormon shot at it. Next thing I knew, I was spinning through the water."

"I'm happy you all are safe. All of you, listen to me," Tobin commanded. "You have got to be more careful. Someone could've drowned."

"I think someone *did* drown," Sean said. He rushed over from the berm separating us from everyone else. "Folks over there are huddled around somebody. Some of them are crying, but most of them ain't saying anything. I can't say for sure what's going on, but it looks like that's what it is."

"Noan, can you see what's happening?" Tobin asked.

Noan closed his eyes tight. "A little girl is lying on the ground. A human girl. I don't think she's breathing."

"What else?"

"People. I just see people. Some of them are crying. Some aren't saying anything, just like Sean said."

"Do you feel anything? Are they panicked or scared? Are they angry? What is it, son?"

It felt suddenly cold. The sun tucked itself away behind thick clouds, and everywhere was in shadows. The stubble underneath Tobin's chin that was so wavy and brown before now looked black, as did the hollow part below his eyes. Jormon shifted in the grass and curled up as tight as a honeybun. A breeze kicked up, and he curled even tighter.

"I don't know what you want me to say, Uncle. I don't know how they feel. I don't think I can, can I? How would that help us now when we should be doing something to help? Can we do something? Can we help them somehow? It might not be too late."

"Not without jeopardizing our own lives," Tobin responded. "Did anyone see you here?"

"They did," I said. "Our stuff is still over on the other side of the hill."

Noan kept his eyes shut. "They're looking for us. Two—no, three guys. And a woman…and a kid I recognize from school. Alexander something…. They're looking for us…and they're walking this way."

Tobin ran his hand through his hair. I used the opportunity to sit up straight. That was a mistake. My breath felt shallow. My tongue felt thick, and my mouth filled with spit. My stomach cramped like never before, and I felt the vomit rushing up. I turned in time to avoid puking in my lap.

"Noan, I need you get everyone out of here without being seen. Can you do that?"

Noan looked over at Tobin. He bit at his lower lip and nodded gently.

"I can see them just over the hill. They'll be here in a few seconds," Sean said.

My stomach clenched at the thought of what would happen if they found us.

"Don't worry, son. Follow Noan. All of you, get ready."

"Wait! I left my phone over yonder near my shoes," Sean said. "I need to get it."

"Forget your stupid phone," Taavi snapped. "If we go over there, there's no telling what they will do to us."

"But you don't know my dad. If I come home without that phone…"

"Go on your own. You're human. Don't drag us into your daddy issues," Taavi shot back.

"Now is not the time to argue. Sean, stay behind with me. Everyone else…" Tobin nodded towards Noan, who was whispering frantically. My body suddenly felt cool and empty. The breeze that had chilled my skin a second ago now passed right through me. I was fading. Or the world was fading. It was hard to tell. The landscape blurred all around me, and when things finally sharpened, I was back in the trailer park.

"Watch out, Phae," Taavi said from beside me. "Dirk's gonna puke again."

There were no clocks on the living room walls, so I didn't know how much time had passed. The sun was steadily falling behind the treetops, and even as it fell out of view, no one said anything. It was as though speculating about what was happening would make those thoughts come true, and no one wanted that. To think the worst was one thing, but to speak it was a whole 'nother thing entirely.

Ms. Lura came in and out, offering hot tea one time and iced tea the next. No one touched either. No one moved. And no one dared ask Noan to scry the lake. What could we do if we saw the worst? If Tobin—the most powerful of us all—couldn't handle it, what the fuck could I do? I glanced down at my *sheriaan*. They looked pretty enough crawling up my arms, and now it seemed like they were nothing more than decorations.

A flock of drones buzzed over the trees. They were watching us, most likely. I inched away from the window.

I recalled a story my sister told me about her time in Iraq, back when wars were between nations, not races. She joined the service right out of high school, and though she promised our folks that she wouldn't deploy because of her job, she was shipped off anyway. She made a big show of being excited about the opportunity so that Momma wouldn't worry, but I knew she must've been scared. Who wouldn't be? In the story, she was sleeping with her battle buddy in some dusty trailer when mortars starting flying in. One or two hit before the warning sirens even went off, so she and her buddy threw on their gear and hauled ass outside to wait in a bunker. It was half packed when they got there, and still a few more stragglers rushed in as they listened to the boom, boom, boom of mortars landing. They waited for nearly an hour for the all-clear, she said. When I asked her what they did that whole time, what they talked about, she told me as plain as she could: "Nothing."

I should've asked her what she thought about. I wondered if she kept her mind from leaning towards the worst, or if the worst seeping in was an inevitability. The rise of the sun in the morning. The muddy road after the rain. The collection basket passed from pew to pew on Sunday mornings.

I wondered if she worried about me, or if any of them did. There one day; gone the next: the story of Dirk Wilkes. If my disappearance made the news, it was only the Tuscaloosa local news.

I looked myself up on the computers at school. The only thing that popped up was video footage from my days as Wren Emerson High's star quarterback. Not one word of my leaving in the middle of the night. Not a headline. Not a foot note. Nothing.

Ms. Lura came in again, this time with a plate of sandwiches cut into squares. My stomach had been grumbling for some time, but I wasn't sure if it was from hunger, anxiety, or because I'd almost drowned. I took two squares out of politeness, though I couldn't imagine eating, hunger or no. Then I remembered what Momma used to say: 'Don't go off and die hungry, 'cause in heaven they don't give you nothing but milk and honey, and in hell, they don't give you shit.' I ate them both.

Phae bit at the corner of her lip. She started to speak, then she stopped, then started again. "It probably isn't my place to suggest this, but I think we should call the king. This mess involves the royal family, so it feels appropriate."

Noan and Jorman shared a look. Jormon said, "It's best at this point that we don't."

"Is anyone else cold?" Taavi asked. "I'm pretty cold. I can't be the only—"

"I can try to see what's happening," Noan said.

"Only if you feel up to it," Jormon said, lifting his head from Noan's lap. His hair had dried wildly, and he favored a wire-haired mutt.

Noan shut his eyes. He took in a deep breath and exhaled slowly. As he did, my vision blurred. Grass spouted through the maroon carpet, and the air smelled like tropical sunscreen. Suddenly, the walls faded, and we were all standing amongst the crowd at the lake.

"Is this real?" Taavi asked.

Phae answered, "It's a vision. I feel hollow, like the way I do when I walk the spirit plane. Look." She pressed her hand against a woman's shoulder, and it sunk right through.

"Is this happening in real time?" I asked.

"It's a vision of the present," Noan answered.

He led us between the crowd until he reached the front. A wave of nausea hit me, and I wondered if I puked in the vision, would it land here on the grass, or in my lap back in the trailer.

CHAPTER SIXTEEN
NOAN

THE GIRL WAS DEAD. HER LITTLE FACE WAS BLUE around the mouth and puffy all over. Her lips had turned a purplish brown like two earthworms resting atop clotted cream. Her head tilted back at an impossible angle, allowing her eyes to rest in a lifeless stare at the rock formation hiding the entrance to our underwater pastime. It was an accusation from beyond, if there was ever such a thing.

The crowd cared little about the dead girl. They looked just past her body at a man with a sandy blonde mullet, the two other men in swimming trunks standing at his side, my uncle on his knees in front of them, and at last, perhaps most intently, at the silver revolver jammed against my uncle's temple.

Uncle's face had yet to swell, but red indentations under his left eye and along his jawline told me he'd been struck hard by something, most likely the butt of the gun. His bottom lip was split clean in half, and blood ran from it and pooled in his rusty beard before dripping to the grass. Blood matted his hair to one side where it oozed from a thick gash. He stared past the crowd, stoic despite the undeniable pain he suffered.

"They're going to kill him," I said. It was as simple as that. My uncle was going to die for something we did. Something Jormon did. Another victim of the crown prince.

"Can you do something about it?" Jormon asked. "This is your vision. I don't know how our powers work here."

I held up my hand. I didn't know where to begin, what *sahdr* could save Uncle before a bullet plunged through his brain. My mind raced past everything I'd ever learned. Phasing would be too slow. A portal would be too obvious, and Uncle would have to get to it for it to be useful. Forming a shield so close to Uncle's head would slice off his ear in the best-case scenario or sever the man's hand, making things worse. Attacking the men would provoke a fight, and knowing southerners like I did, I'd bet they all had a gun or two in their cars. Maybe attacking was the only option. When backed into a corner, when left with choosing to kill or be killed, I had to think about my own survival. My people's survival.

I didn't know if it would work, but I had to try something. I focused my energy in my gut. If I let it build up and perform a massive release, everyone hit by the blast would go flying back. That was the move.

Just as I'd convinced myself it was the right thing to do, Uncle shifted his eyes, and they locked on mine.

"Hey guys, I think Uncle can see us. He's looking right at me."

Uncle shook his head, and I knew it meant to stand down.

The man with the gun to Uncle's head started talking. "We can't stand here all day, Pastor Lumley. You've said it all along that these coppers would be the death of us, that they'd be the death of us all. Now look at your little Heather. She ain't been in this world long and already her precious life has been taken from her. He took it." He pulled back the revolver and swung it down so that the handle thudded against Uncle's skull. He toppled over and fresh blood ran like a river down his forehead.

"I hear you, Mr. Darley, but now's not the place." Pastor Lumley's accent was thick and his voice high-pitched. He sounded like a chainsaw revving up. "My daughter didn't deserve this, but we oughta be smart about what happens next. We can't be like them. That's how they win, by dragging you down in the filthy gutter with them. We got the Lord on our side."

"And the law. They won't blame us if we ended him right here. Sheriff Kuss will know we was within our rights. Well within 'em." An unsynchronized murmuring of "amen" filled the silence, but only for moment. Like the lightning flash that, once gone, makes the darkness even more pronounced.

"And what about little Becky right there, nuzzled up in her momma's arms? How's she gonna feel about seeing you shoot somebody in the head?"

Mr. Darley looked over at little Becky in the arms of a heavyset woman in a two-piece bathing suit. "If her momma taught her right, she'd know it's doing the Lord's work. This is your daughter, for Christ's sake! You're a man of the cloth. You know it's the right thing."

"I'm also a man of faith. I trust the Lord has a plan for Heather, just as he has a plan for all of us."

Mr. Darley gripped Uncle by his bicep and snatched him back to his knees. He raised the gun again and swung it down even harder. As it cracked against Uncle's skull, he fell over once more. No one in the crowd gasped.

I ran to him, then a hand grabbed my arm and pulled me back. "Let me go." I turned quickly to pry the hand from around my shoulder. "Uncle?"

He stood glaring at me, then at his other self, still held captive by the Riders. His face lacked the bruises, the blood, and the scratches.

"You shouldn't see this, Noan. None of them should. Shut away this vision now." He was upset. Mad, even. I'd never heard him use this tone before.

"You didn't come back," I said. "We thought you might need help."

"Is what you're doing helping?" He waited, but I didn't have an answer. Police sirens wailed in the distance.

"Did we do that? Did we kill the little girl?" Jormon asked.

"There's more going on than what you know," Uncle answered.

Sirens closed in on us. Suddenly, Jormon and the rest disappeared, and I was left standing alone with Uncle in the center of a crowd who wanted him dead.

"How did you—"

"Never mind that for now. If you truly mean to help, there is one thing you can do for me."

"Tell me. Tell me and I'll do it."

"Many years ago, I hid a powerful item deep in what you call 'Atlantis.' It was never meant to be discovered, but I think Jormon just disturbed it without knowing what it was. People will come looking for it, people who will want to misuse it. I need you to find it first."

"What is it? What am I looking for?

"You'll know it when you see it. It'll call to you like it did before."

A pounding rocked me back into the moment, and I was no longer standing with Uncle at the lake. I was back in the sitting room. Taavi, Dirk, and Phae were positioned near the door, ready to attack.

"Where's Jormon?"

"He went out to check on what that was." Taavi answered.

Another pounding boomed through the hallway.

"What's taking him so long?" Phae asked.

"I don't know." Taavi moved closer to the door. "Everyone, stand back and brace yourselves."

Was this actually happening? My heart beat through my chest, and I was sure everyone could hear it. *Get your shit together, Noan. You got this.*

Dirk moved to beside Taavi and stared at the open door. "*Ilbareq*", he whispered, and sparks formed in his fist.

Footsteps sounded somewhere down the hall. Dirk tightened his fist and lightning seeped between his fingers. I was drained from holding everyone in my vision for so long, but I stood to help. I'd erected shields for so many years I could do it without much effort.

Taavi held a ball of fire, ready to hurl it like a baseball, and Phae covered the floor in a thick mist that rose past my knees.

In a few seconds, someone would step through the door. Dirk and Taavi locked eyes and nodded. Three. Two. One.

A vision of Jormon flashed in my head. It was him. I was certain.

"Everybody stop!" I shouted. I was too late.

Lightning cracked through the air and blasted a fist-sized hole in the door. Jormon conjured a swirling shield of water just in time to catch the fireball that followed, which might have burned the door down completely.

"Whoa!" Jormon said, looking around for the next attack.

Sean stepped in from behind him. His back was covered in sweat, and between heavy breaths he said, "It's me. There's a lot going on. Can I get a glass of water? And can somebody tell Ms. Lura I'm sorry? I meant no disrespect." He rubbed his wrists.

Sean gulped the cup of water before collapsing to the floor against the wall. "It's pretty bad. *Really* bad, actually. The little girl that washed up from the lake is dead. And what's worse, she's Jimmy Lumley's daughter, Heather."

"We know," Phae said. She filled him in on what we'd witnessed.

"If the sheriff was on his way, that's not good," Sean said. "Your uncle needs help. If he gets in that car, they won't take him to jail. They'll take him somewhere else."

"Where? How do you know this?" I asked.

"I can't say how I know, and what I do know, I'm not a hundred percent about it. I just know you can't trust the sheriff to do the proper thing."

No one could be trusted to do the proper thing, whatever the case was. There was a dead girl lying on the ground and no one covered her up. Her father ignored her body and instead focused on galvanizing hatred around my Uncle. None of it was proper at all.

"Jormon, can we talk for a second?"

I led him to the foyer where no one could overhear, then farther to the kitchen where I could grab a quick bite. For whatever happened next, I'd need strength, and a few crustless sandwiches and sugary tea wouldn't do.

"I need you to do something," I said, raiding the pantry for calories. "Uncle doesn't know how much trouble he's in. We have to help him."

"What can we do that he can't? If he's in trouble, he can get himself out without help from us."

"It's not that he can't help himself. It's that he won't. You saw how he took a blow to the head back there. Two blows, even. He won't fight back."

"If he wants to go and get himself killed, that's on him."

I closed the refrigerator and glared at him. "Seriously?"

"What?"

"This is actually all on you. You killed that girl."

"I didn't kill anybody—And keep your voice down. All I did was play a stupid game that Uncle Tobin invented. And he put that stupid thing down there, whatever it was that caused the lake to buckle. If it's anybody's fault, it's his."

"Just like helping Dirk at the bus station and getting leeched was mine?"

"For *Heemrah*'s sake, Noan, would you let that go already? I said I was sorry for that, and you said you forgave me. If you meant it, stop bringing it up."

"I'm bringing it up now because I'm seeing the pattern more clearly. Jormon does whatever he wants, and other people bear the consequences."

"That's not a fair assessment," he shot back.

"Fairness? What a childish word."

"Damn, you sound exactly like him. It's so irritating, you know?"

"If the only feeling you have today is irritation, then something inside of you is broken."

"Says the shadow child."

"What did you just say?" I stepped closer. This time, Jormon would be the one getting jaw-jabbed. "Say it again. I dare you."

"This conversation is going poorly, and I'm sorry I said that— Tell me, how can I help? Or did you call me back her to make me feel like crap?"

I needed him, but I couldn't stand to look at him, much less ask for his help. It would be a mistake not to push him to help Uncle, but his offer wasn't sincere. If he half-assed going to the lake to get this mysterious object, he'd get himself killed. If he botched helping Uncle, he'd likely get everyone killed.

"Never mind, Jormon. I don't need anything from you."

"Don't kid yourself, Noan. If it weren't for me, no one would even talk to you." He spun around and walked away, forgetting his contrition and leaving me to juggle a third option besides helping Uncle and respecting Uncle's request: kicking my brother's ass.

I dashed upstairs to change out of my swim trunks. I opened my door in a sprint, and a firm hand grabbed my shoulder. "Goddammit, Taavi! What do you want?" I threw on some khaki shorts and a long-sleeved shirt.

"I think you're making a mistake not taking Jormon's help," Taavi said.

"It would've taken longer to convince him, and I don't have that kind of time."

"He offered—"

"He didn't mean it. If you're not going to be helpful, leave me alone and go back to watching out for me. I don't have time for this conversation either."

"I'm coming with you. You'll need my help for what's about to happen." Taavi looked around the room for something he could fit. Already shirtless, he pulled off his swim trunks and walked his naked body over to my closet.

"There's, um…" It was the first time I'd seen another naked guy, besides Jormon. "I don't think much in there will fit you. Here, wear this." I handed him a pair of shorts with an elastic waistband and an old, worn shirt.

"Cool. I'm ready when you are," Taavi said.

"Are you sure? You don't have to do this."

"If you're waiting for me, you're waiting for the wrong one. I'm in this with you. Let's go save your uncle."

We jumped out the window and dashed over to Sandi Nash's back porch. The sun fell behind the woods, shining the last of its light on the dozen or more drones cruising low above the treetops as though they were scouting for suspects in a murder. Or *to* murder. It wouldn't be safe to fly direct.

I was still weak from my earlier efforts, but I did what needed to be done. A portal formed at my whispered words, opening to a spot beneath a heavy covering of branches at the edge of the woods. We flew through, landing softly at the other edge.

Two police cars rushed down from the lake. I pointed the cars out to Taavi. "He's in the second one. See? There's someone in the back seat."

"There are drones too. Listen." Mixed with the crunching of tires rolling over dirt and rocks came a buzzing overhead, getting ever closer as a few drones trailed behind the cop convoy.

Two patrol cars sped near, kicking up trails of dust so thick they clouded the strobing red and blue of the police lights. They followed the curving path and disappeared between rows of pines.

"So, what's the plan?" Taavi asked.

"We can stop them over there where the trees close in on both sides. The path bends back on itself, so if we hurry, we can cut through the trees and meet them on the other side. It's narrower over there, and far enough away from the crowd."

"Then let's move."

Three drones followed overhead in a scattered formation. *Think, Noan.*

We flew low to the ground between the trees until I was close enough to the woods' edge to see them coming. "Stay low," I told

Taavi. I rose to a thick branch high enough to put me at eye level to the coming drones. I only had one shot at this.

They came closer. I could see them head on, and I prayed they couldn't see me. Not yet, at least.

They sped closer, still. I took a deep breath. *"Retajaan!"*

Three oval-shaped shadows appeared a few feet in front of the drones, one for each of them. They hit the darkness head on, but they never reappeared on the other side. A portal without a destination. I didn't think it was possible, but just like that, they were gone. Disappeared. No longer a threat. I'd have to ask uncle about that, assuming I could save him.

It was a huge assumption, too, given the state of things. Every portal opened and every inch I flew depleted what energy I had. To assume I could save him was to assume I could douse the sun with a bucket of water when I was too weak to carry the bucket.

But it had to be done, strength or no. It was only one more thing, then another thing after that, right? Anybody could do one thing.

I jumped from the branch and soared through the trees, careful not to lose sight of them. Taavi caught up with me easily.

The cars banked and turned along the path, but instead of following it out to the paved road leading to the police station, they cut through a clearing of trees and crept through an overgrown field. The grass brushed across the door handles and knocked at the lower parts of their windows.

"We should make our move now. There's nowhere to hide the deeper in they go," Taavi said.

"It's too close to the road," I said, but the truth was I didn't have a plan, at least not one I could pull off without one of the officers turning to shoot Uncle in the face. "For now, hover low and keep our distance."

"Until?"

"Until they stop. They must have a hideout somewhere up ahead."

Silence cascaded into the space as the officers switched off their blaring sirens. Darkness rushed in as the officers killed the patrol lights, leaving only the faint yellow glow of headlights as the vehicles pressed through one clearing, then another, past a small, forgotten cemetery marked by broken headstones and effaced graves, until they eventually arrived at an abandoned church. Its brown shingles were worn through to its rubber underside, partially covering a roof punctuated by a hole so big you could drive a tractor through it. Sidings that used to be white were visibly green, and what parts weren't torn, rotted, or missing were covered in thick, green vines.

The churchyard was overgrown with weeds, but the cars slowly pushed through. I hovered around and landed on the dilapidated roof, being careful with my weight so I didn't fall through.

They stopped in front of the rundown building and killed the engines. We perched gently on the other side of the roof, and I braced myself on an exposed beam. For a while, nothing happened.

Just when I thought I couldn't wait any longer, three officers and Pastor Lumley got out and huddled in front of the headlight's beams. I couldn't make out what they were saying, but they seemed at ease. One of the cops spit and brown thickness spewed from his lips, he tilted his head back in laughter.

I needed to get closer, but there was nowhere else to hide.

"If you want to get your uncle, now might be your only chance," Taavi said.

"There's something else going on. If Uncle is in the backseat of that car and they're standing around chatting like four crackheads trying to score a hit, they either trust that Uncle won't escape, or they have something that would make escaping impossible." There was a third option, one that chilled me to think. He was already dead. "We need to find out."

Taavi placed his hands to his lips in thought. "I have an idea. *Taqaim qahwa.*" Around his hands, space rippled in throbbing waves, radiating outward. I looked over at the cops as the waves swept over them.

They didn't react.

"What was that?" I asked.

"I'm testing to see if anyone around has a Kaydan energy signature. I can sense your uncle's energy, but something is blocking it from getting out. Do you have any idea what could do that?"

"It's a mystery for another time. Is he alive, though?"

"Yes."

"Are you sure?" I looked him in the eyes, and he nodded. I exhaled slowly and let relief come to me, but only for a moment. "Can you use your powers to get him out? I'm feeling drained."

"Let me try."

I peered over the roof at the patrol car. The handle lifted, then fell back into place.

"I don't think I can open it without ripping the door off. It's like my powers are only somewhat effective, I need to really push to do anything."

Maybe that's what I was feeling, too. Drained from exertion but limited by something else as well. "Then I'll bust him out the old-fashioned way."

"Don't be hasty. Whatever is blocking him could also block you if you get too close. I'll go instead."

"No. You stay here. If things go south, you can pull Uncle out. I don't have the strength to do the same for you."

He didn't argue.

I slid down the opposite side of the building and landed in the tall grass. It occurred to me that snakes might have made this abandoned building their resting spot as the seasons changed. I crouched low and pushed through the grass as cautiously as I could. I didn't know how much time I had. The night was quiet, and every step I took rustled the grass like a sonic boom. Quickly. Quietly. Just do it.

Before long, I was close enough to touch the car. I reached to grab the handle, and another set of headlights swept over the church.

180

I snatched my arm back and laid flat on the ground as a truck pulled into the grass and drove straight towards me. I needed to move before it ran me over, but there wasn't time. As the truck neared, I tucked my legs into my chest and turned sideways. Grass brushed at my face as it bent under the tires. The truck rolled over me and stopped. Someone got out from either side of the truck. Brown boots snapped the dry grass with every slow step and disappeared in the overgrowth.

"You fellas picked a mighty fine place to meet." Male. Southern. Unremarkable.

"And you picked a mighty fine time to show up, Sheriff," came a voice I recognized. Pastor Lumley.

"I got held up back at the station. The governor had questions for the mayor, the mayor had questions for me. You know how it goes."

"Yeah, yeah, who cares? Can we use him or not?"

"Jimmy, shouldn't you be home grieving your daughter?"

"What's there to grieve? Her death was all a part of God's plan. It came a bit sooner than we expected, but the Lord works in mysterious ways."

"That's cold, even for you."

"Because if your boy drowned today, you'd be a ball of tears— Not you, Cee Kay, I'm talking about his other kid."

"He's my stepboy, and don't tell me how I'd feel."

"And I'm saying the same to you. Daughter, stepson, who gives a damn? I wanna know if we can use the Kaydan or not."

A pause.

"Officially, I have to take him in. He's too big a fish."

"Are you serious?"

"Between the lot of us, he tried to escape on the way to the station. Maybe he tried to flip the car. Maybe we had to stop him however we could."

As quickly as I could, I crawled from under the truck and reached for the handle again. The latch clicked, and the door swung out wide and banged against the truck. *Shit.* Uncle crashed down on top of me.

Shadows stirred. Handguns clicked. Shotguns pumped. We had to go.

I pulled Uncle to his feet and stooped behind the car door for cover.

"You never do as you're told, do you?" he said. "I knew I could count on you."

A shot rang out, and glass from the window rained down on us. Then came another shot, then too many to count. Bullets dented into the car door or whizzed by our heads. It wasn't safe to fly, not as often as folks around here hunted ducks. We'd be just as helpless, and just as dead.

We ran around the church building away from the cops' aim right as Taavi hovered down from the roof. He conjured a portal barely visible against the moonless night, and I pushed Uncle through. A cop rounded the corner, and I jumped through, hoping he didn't see my face. Taavi followed swiftly behind me.

The shadow-lined hole unfolded and dissipated in the darkness. It all worked out.

We were safe.

For the moment.

Uncle and I waited in the sitting room for the shit to hit the fan, but it never did, at least not in a way I could discern. Maybe being pedantic—maybe to keep my mind occupied—he showed me new ways to heal different types of wounds. There's a *sahdr* for gashes, and another one for scrapes. There are two different ones for broken bones, depending on how clean the break is.

Nana Lura checked in on us with the regularity of a shift nurse, sometimes with food, sometimes with a stern look at me and Uncle and the untouched platters of fondant potatoes or salmon croquets.

"I don't suspect the police will show up on our doorstep. You should get some rest," he said.

"I'm not tired," I lied. I felt as empty as I had after the leeching, but I wouldn't leave his side. I ran my hand over his arm, using dregs of energy to see if there were wounds we missed.

"This reminds me of when you were really young, except it was the other way around." He spoke with unopened eyes. His head tilted to one side, resting on the ornate cluster of upholstery tacks running near the creases of the chaise lounge.

"How so?"

"After you were born, your father didn't know how to treat you. He loved you, of course, but he was deeply conflicted between his duties to our people and his obligation to protect his own family—you know that story already. Anyhow, I stepped in where I could to make sure you felt the love he couldn't show you. I would visit you—you were a baby, so there's no way you'd remember any of this. You were so tiny, too. Every time I held you, I was so afraid I would break you I'd nearly suffer a panic attack. It was one of the few things that scared me back then. I'd put you on my chest and recline in a chair exactly like this one, even down to the fabric grommets on the cushions. You'd fall into a sleep so deep I wasn't sure if you were still breathing. I'd hold my breath for minutes at a time until I was sure I could feel your heartbeat against mine."

I tried not to think about life in Maerin, not that I remembered much, and what I did recall felt like planted memories. Stories told to me so often I could see myself in the moment. Memories of playing Dragons and Gusts were Nana Lura's memories, not mine, but I felt them as my own. This new memory of a tiny me resting on Uncle's chest, letting his heat warm me in a chilly servant's shack, struck me with a sadness I'd never known. A deep and pleasant sadness of love lost or love I never knew I had to begin with.

He paused for so long I thought he'd fallen asleep. "Look at you now. I'm proud of you. We've all endured so much but look at how you've turned out."

"Stubborn?" I said, trying to play off my feelings until I could relive them in private.

"Just like me."

"Don't let Father hear you say that. He'd hate to know I'm not following in his footsteps."

"You think too lowly of your father. Give him more credit than you do. He loves you, no matter whose footsteps you follow."

"Why do you defend him when he's been nothing but cruel to me and to you? You can easily take him if it came to that. I know you could."

"Because I can doesn't mean I should. You're too smart not to already know this."

"It's just—I'm so mad with Jormon right now. He killed a little girl, and he's walking around with no compunction. I mean zero. And when I asked him to help me rescue you, he refused. It's his duty as the crown prince to help other Kaydans, and he failed. I could do so much better."

"Take it easy on him. He's still your brother, and accidents do happen."

"Not like this they don't. And when they do, we should take responsibility for the part we play in them. You were the farthest person from all of this yet you received the worst consequences. I hate that. I hate that when the worst thing can happen, it tends to happen to me or you. It's never to them."

"It is my fault. I'm the one who hid the *miftah* there in the first place. I should've been more careful with something so powerful."

"Jormon should've been smarter. He never thinks about his actions. He never thinks about anything but himself." My hand moved to the spot on my chest where the *rhualka* struck me, then to the spot on my jaw where Jormon's hand had connected. He wasn't a good person. He wasn't a bad person, but he damn sure wasn't good.

"I don't like where this conversation is going. Please, let us talk about something else."

I knew better than to push back, yet I was too deep in my feelings to pivot quickly. We sat quietly, and I nibbled the food which had become cold and dry.

"I'm sorry I didn't listen to you," I said. "I should've gone after the *miftah* like you asked."

He waved me off. "I shouldn't have asked you to. It isn't important enough for you to risk your life. I'm not that important either, but I'm happy you saved me."

"About that," I began. "I created portals with no destination, and the drones went through. Where did they go?"

Uncle didn't miss a beat before answering. "They went into the shadow plane. They are still out there flying around, you just can't see them."

"Can they ever leave it?"

"If you bring them back."

"How? How do I do that?"

"I think that's quite enough for tonight. I'm afraid I must rest now."

"One last thing, Uncle. What did you mean when you said it would call to me like it did before? The *miftah*, I mean."

"You don't remember anything about how we got here?"

"Only exactly what I've been told." My implanted memories. "Will you tell me more."

He opened his eyes for the first time in a long time. "It's a story for another day. You have to get some rest, and I have to get ready."

"For what?"

"For company. Hargi is coming by to talk damage control."

"Then I'll stay, too."

"You'll do no such thing. To bed with you. Now."

As tired as I was, I couldn't rest. My mind flitted from one vivid thought to the next, like a hummingbird feeding in a vibrant garden. A girl was dead. Jormon took her life—albeit unknowingly—and seemed entirely unremorseful. I shouldn't judge him for that, but it was telling. The girl's father spoke like she was always meant to die.

He sounded almost like she was a planned sacrifice, an offering to his version of the greater good. The greater God.

Then there was the *miftah* and Uncle's evasiveness about what it had to do with my past. And how he held me when my father could not. Would not.

There was a time I would go for a run and take to the skies, but that time was beginning to feel like a lifetime ago. Instead, I laid in bed and let the cool light of *Zereq* wash over me. Purify me. Cleanse me of my thoughts and emotions so I could do it all again the next day.

CHAPTER SEVENTEEN
JORMON

THE NEWS RAN A STORY ABOUT A LIMNIC ERUPTION in the lake that resulted in the death of poor little Heather Lumley, who was caught in the undercurrent and drowned. I combed every paper I could find and there was no mention of what happened to Uncle Tobin, nor what happened when the police took him away. During the two nights that followed, someone hurled Molotov cocktails at the trailer park, burning down a couple of trailers closest to the street. The papers didn't mention that either.

People who saw what happened at the lake spread the word that some young Kaydans were there. They couldn't confirm it was us, but it didn't stop kids from shoving against us in the hall or throwing erasers at the backs of our heads in class. Small apples compared to what happened to Heather. What I did to Heather. For that, I deserved so much worse.

We were working on a group project in the school library the following week. Sean was the only one willing to pair with me. I didn't mind that at all. Brett and his gang posted up two tables down, but they chatted loud enough for me to hear. David Hutto and Ashley Davis huddled together at the table between us and shushed them on the librarian's behalf.

"Just ignore them. It's easier than you think," Sean said.

"I'm trying. You were saying something about a carnival earlier and I cut you off." I was as sick of Civics as I was of Brett's murmuring about Heather and wanted to talk about anything else.

"Festival," he stressed. "It's the Fall Festival. It really is a blast. There are games and rides and a cakewalk. They say this year there will even be some Kaydan rides, too."

"And you sure it won't be cancelled after all what's happened in the past few days?"

"The city wouldn't cancel it in a million years. It's not as big as Vidalia's Onion Festival, but it's the pride of Lyons every fall. And because this is an election year, the mayoral candidates will be there giving stump speeches. We still have a few more weeks before it kicks off, so there's plenty of time for folks to forget about the lake, as much as anybody could forget something like that." He paused for a minute to think, then shook his head slowly. "Naw, it's not getting cancelled."

"If it's a political event, it doesn't sound like much fun."

"You won't even notice the politics unless you try. There's so much noise and food. And the rides! You all should really come. You're allowed this year, you know?"

I knew, I just didn't care. Being allowed to go someplace doesn't mean you'll be welcomed when you get there. Like Pastor Lumley waiting at heaven's pearly gates, I thought, which made me chuckle. "Have you asked Noan? I'm sure he'll want to go with you. Take Taavi, too." Noan would say I was being messy, but oh well. He can figure out his own shit.

It was late October, my first autumn in the trailer park in many years. The young trees squeezed in between old trailers began to change, their leaves turning shades of red, orange, and yellow. They looked like they were catching fire.

Just as the air was turning crisp, so was the political climate. President Sunwarden and the opposition frontrunner Thorne Blackwell were tied in the polls with less than three weeks before the election. The stakes had never been higher. President

Sunwarden, with her constant push for Kaydan inclusion, continued to harp on her plan to expand school integration given the precarious success seen at TCHS. On the other hand, Thorne Blackwell had demonstrated time and time again his penchant for drastic and often divisive measures. To many Kaydans, a Blackwell victory symbolized a potential erosion of our rights. Whispers circulated that his hidden agendas were darker than most dared to imagine, and it stood to reason that whatever rumors there were, however bad they could be, were true given the Rider's endorsement of his campaign.

The weight on my shoulders felt immeasurable, a gravity only those entrusted with the protection and well-being of an entire people would understand. Every time Blackwell's face appeared on a screen or his voice echoed through a speaker, a cold dread tightened its grip on my chest. I could see his plans, the veiled threats hiding behind his words, and I knew—I just knew—his winning could mean reverting back to the days of the Hunts. It was too much to think about, and I needed a break from it all. The Fall Festival couldn't come soon enough.

In the end, it was Uncle Tobin who convinced Noan and the rest of them to go. Sean picked us up in his SUV early that evening. Noan sat up front and kept questioning Sean on whether he was really okay giving us all a ride. In the backseat where the rest of us squeezed in, Dirk rested his hand on my thigh. I didn't mind at all. It was the closest I'd ever felt to being a high school teenager.

We arrived at the fairground shortly after dark, and the makeshift parking lot was already full. The air was brisk and laden with deep-fried smells, and as we neared the entrance, the cacophony of fairground sounds began to separate into distinct melodies coming from concession booths and game stands. The parking lot was lit only by the moon, but inside the festival, there were lights of different sizes and colors, lending the walkers-by multiple, lively shadows that grew and shrank with every movement.

"What should we do first?" Phae asked.

"That's always the question. If you eat first, then you might puke on the rides. If you ride first, all the food lines will be longer than my daddy's belt by the time you want to eat, and if you play games first, you can't ride nor eat with a gigantic teddy bear in your arms."

"The rides might be fun, but I'm starving. Let's eat first," Taavi said.

"Says the guy with the iron gut," Phae said. "I say we stand in line for a ride and play this game I call 'Is he looking at me because he wants me or because he wants to strangle me?'"

"In my world, that's the same thing," Taavi said, at which point Phae swung her elbow into his ribcage.

"I can't with you."

"Yet you'd miss me if I weren't here." He blew her a kiss, and she rammed her elbow into him even harder. Taavi swooped her into his massive arms like she weighed nothing at all and spun her around.

"Boy, I swear before the Naked Mother, if you don't put me down…" She couldn't stop herself from laughing. I couldn't stop myself from smiling. A weight seemed to lift off my chest and I could breathe again. *Not like poor, sweet Heather.* If only I could focus on what was in front of me.

"We can split up," I suggested. "Dirk and I can go with Taavi to eat, and you three can start with rides?"

We walked from the corn dog stand to the popcorn vendor, then to Miss Jeneva's Prize Candy Apple pop-up hut.

"Will you share one with me?" Dirk asked. "I don't want to eat too much before I get on the rides."

Of course I would. Biting at the same piece of fruit would be the closest my lips have gotten to his since the lake, and I would take what I could get. Dad wasn't there to know.

We browsed the selection of caramel-coated, chocolate-covered, sprinkle-laden creations before he settled on a classic, red candy apple. "How do I eat this without cracking my teeth?" I asked.

"You have to lick it until it gets soft," Dirk said and chuckled.

"I don't think it works like that."

"Are you boys talking naughty?" Taavi asked, then made vulgar licking motions. "Prince Jormon, never forget: he slept with me first."

"He means in the same bed." Dirk punched him in the shoulder. Taavi picked him up and spun him around as he'd done with Phae. Dirk's foot barely missed the tower display of white chocolate-covered apples.

"We should get out of here," I suggested. People stared at us, though they couldn't tell we were Kaydan: our shirts covered our *sheriaan*. To them, we were idiot high schoolers, prone to destruction and accepted for it. It felt great to blend in, for once.

We took our time eating the apple, giggling immaturely every time we passed it to one another. We were finishing the last bites when Taavi said, "I can see what's going on here. I'm going to find the others."

"Tell everyone we'll meet back at the gate at eleven o'clock. We need to get home before curfew."

He saluted and lost himself in the crowd.

We rode three rides together. The last ride resembled a pirate's ship and swung back and forth until it finally began to loop over on itself. "I haven't felt this nauseous since my first flying lesson with you," Dirk said.

"Yeah, I think I'm done with carnival rides for a long time."

We walked closely enough for our hands to brush against one another's as we strolled through the lights and smells and crowd. It was peaceful, despite the raucousness of the fair.

"Are we a 'thing?'" I asked. "I feel like we're a thing."

"Tonight feels like a date, if that answers your question."

"I've never been on a date, so I wouldn't know. Have you ever?"

He shook his head. "I never had the courage."

"Oh? How so? You seem plenty brave to me."

His lips twisted up in thought. "Maybe I am now, but I wasn't always. This, what we're doing now, holding hands and giggling over a candy apple like two schoolboys flipping through a nudy magazine, I could never do this type of stuff back home."

"Is—is that why you left?" I thought carefully before asking, afraid it would turn the mood.

"It played a part."

We walked around the Ferris wheel and turned down a long row of carnival games.

"You don't have to say if you don't want."

"I want to. It's time for me to. Just—give me a minute."

And so we walked. Past the pockets of people listening to political hopefuls, past the line of kids waiting their turn for the *Kaydan, Take Flight* attraction, we walked. Minutes went by with his hand in mine, and still we walked.

Right when I'd stopped caring whether he told me or not, when I had contented in being with him in the moment, he spoke. "I used to be really religious. I mean *really* religious. Years ago, back in Alabama, I used to go to church all the time. Never missed a Sunday. Even after Dad left us and no one felt like thanking the Lord, there we were in the first pew, damn near sitting on the alter.

"My freshman year, I started having feelings for this guy who was also in my grade. His name was Jason, but everyone called him Kirk because he liked Star Trek way after it was the cool thing to do. Kirk Thomas, Hollywood Highschool Eagles football running back, player number twenty. We hung out all the time. Dirk and Kirk, Kirk and Dirk. He stayed the night one evening as he often did in the summer. We sat up in the living room watching scary movies. Really, I was watching him. He was so handsome. I mean he was something to see. Curly hair, deep dimples…all of that, and more.

"We used to fall asleep watching whatever was on TV, but on this particular night, I went into my bedroom, hoping he would follow me. He didn't, though. I stayed up half the night expecting my door to push open and for him to slide under the sheets beside me. Talk about anticipation and disappointment…

192

"The next morning, I woke up and Momma was sitting at the foot of my bed. She asked me if I felt strange around other boys my age or if I ever felt 'funny.' I didn't know what 'funny' was supposed to feel like, but by the way she asked it, I could tell she didn't want me to say yes to either of those questions. Instead, I said 'no.'

"A couple Sundays later, the three of us—me, Momma, and my sister, Novi—were in church as usual. The next thing I know, the pastor, this evangelical bitch, started going on about how she sensed that someone in the congregation was being controlled by a homosexual spirit and that whoever it was should stand up and walk to the altar to be cleansed. Momma must've spoken to her. I just knew it. And she wouldn't let up. She kept insisting that the person—me, I'm sure—should stand up and come to Jesus.

"I was so embarrassed. Even though I never stood up nor gave anyone the satisfaction of seeing the gay churchgoer sashay down the pews, I felt that they all knew it was me. And in that moment, I knew that Momma didn't want me to be gay. From then on, I tried not to be."

"Until you met me."

"Until I met you. And even now, it feels like it's not real. I keep thinking this will all be put aside like some teenage dalliance. You'll go on to marry Calinea or some other rich bitch, and I'll still be here, figuring out where I fit in."

"Wow. Calinea has you cursing like that? What happened to the goody-goody, 'Lord, forgive me' guy I fell for?"

"He learned that the Lord is unforgiving. That life is unforgiving. That guy doesn't exist anymore. Now I'm all, 'fuck you, man' and "kiss my ass, Coach.' Do you think you can fall for the new version of me?"

We stopped walking and leaned into one another, closed our eyes, and let our lips touch. I didn't remember a time before when I felt so satisfied. It was the first time in my life I had gotten exactly what I wanted, and I wasn't ashamed of having it. If Dad wanted the Matchmaker to set me up with anyone who wasn't this beautiful guy whose lips pressed against mine in as much desperation as mine did into his, I would fight against them both. This is where I wanted to be, and Dirk is who I wanted to be with. "I'm not going anywhere."

Dirk snatched away. "Do you hear that?"

"I don't hear anything." I turned to see if there was something I missed, and there stood Brett, Kevin, and Alexander, each one giggling like a witch with two brooms.

"A copper *and* a queer. This one here takes the cake!" Brett said. He held a half-eaten caramel apple, and with a swift movement, he hurled it at me. Dirk pushed me away, but he wasn't fast enough to protect himself. *Thunk!* The apple banged against the side of Dirk's head. "You should lick the caramel off his face. I bet he'd like that— Hey, give me yours!" Brett grabbed Alexander's apple and readied himself for another shot.

The apple left Brett's hand headed straight for me. It flew through the air, its shiny, red surface catching and throwing light as it raced toward me. It wasn't going to miss.

Then it was gone, disappearing in a puff of shadow. And I was okay. Noan walked up from behind me.

"Are you guys okay?" he asked. Dirk nodded. I grabbed his hand and squeezed. "Brett, when it could be so easy to be a nice guy, you go out of your way to make life harder for us. First it was the bus station, then the bullying at school. Tell me why? You owe us that much."

"I don't owe you a goddamn thing. We've already given you people enough. The next thing I give you, you ain't gonna like."

"If it's a whiff of your breath you're talking about, you're right. It got here five minutes before you did, and I've been gagging ever since."

Even his buddies laughed, despite the tension, and Brett stepped closer to my brother with his fists balled.

"I thought I taught you to stay out of my way," Brett said. He looked over at his friends and said, "Looks like this one needs another lesson."

"You don't scare me, Brett."

"Oh, this one's madder than a wet hen," he said, causing his posse to laugh and high-five. "I might not scare you, but I bet those drones up there do. I bet they scare the shit out of you. Use one of your little spells on me. I dare you! The Law will be on your ass like stink on shit."

"Noan, it's not worth it," I all but whispered, grabbing him by the shoulder. "Let's just go."

"No." Noan pushed my hand away. "I'm tired of idiots telling me what to do. Brett has no power over me, and frankly, neither do the authorities, not if I decided to fight back. Let the police come. This harassment ends tonight."

But he didn't fight with Brett, not that night. There wasn't time. No sooner had he made his address, the sky peeled open. First was the light. A few miles above the ground, rutilant streaks of light broke out of the darkness like radiant rust particles. After the light came a deep roar like a thousand dragons exhaling at once. I covered my ears, but it did nothing to block out the noise.

I'd never heard a sound like that in all my life, but the light—I had seen the light almost every day since I began living in Gray Flats, coming and going across the ceiling of every room in the trailer. It was the light of *Heemrah*.

PART THREE

TO MEND BROKEN THINGS AND TO BREAK THEM

CHAPTER EIGHTEEN
NOAN

MY BREATH CAUGHT IN THE CRISP NIGHT AIR AND trailed behind me in translucent streams as I moseyed down the path to Lheniva's. In the moonless night, the light from the rift tinted the gravel a deep red, just as it did the soft coating of snow along the ground and on the treetops. My boots crunched the frozen grass, and before I'd made it to the front porch, Lheniva opened the door and welcomed me in.

"Is Prince Jormon already here?" I asked. It still felt strange to revert to the use of honorifics, but it was necessary. In times of crises, when you're surrounded by uncertainty, you find comfort in structure.

"Yes, Your Highness. He's waiting with the others for the program to start. Would you like a word with him first?"

"No. Let him do whatever it is he's been doing these days." I caught my persistent attitude and corrected course. "Forget I said that. How is everyone holding up?"

"Everyone's confused. They don't know what happened or what to believe."

"About the rift opening up, or the election results?"

"Things certainly turned, didn't they? I've never seen a sitting president lose as badly as President Sunwarden, but there you have it."

"The rift opening up was all the opposition needed." I pointed toward the trailer door. "They think I had something to do with the rift opening?"

"Like I said, they don't know what to believe."

"I'm hoping Father's interview will calm down much of what's happening. Can I come in?"

As I approached the doorway, she stuck her arm out, blocking my way.

"Prince Noan, you're always welcomed in my house, but some people here won't treat you like you are."

"Thanks for the warning. I'll stand in the back of the room. It's in the lounge?" There was no need to put up a fight or throw my title around like a bludgeon. They knew who I was; they just didn't care.

I let my hoodie fall over my face and hid easily enough in the back of the dimly lit room. The few chairs she had were spaced apart up front near the television and were already occupied. Brown hair, red hair, styled hair: my brother, his beau, and Phae. The rest of the room was packed with Kaydans, all waiting for Father's interview. I never stopped to ponder what he might say. If he decided to toss me to the humans for the sake of maintaining peace between the races, it would be a long way to the door if everyone knew I was here, and knowing them, they'd gladly hold me hostage until Father showed up to give me the boot.

The television was already tuned to the proper channel, and an anchor was giving her rundown.

"Tonight, on Channel Eleven News, a man who was not armed is dead. Autopsy results provide a tale of devastating police force. The accused are four Toombs County police officers, all of them veterans on the force, and the victim a Kaydan man who, it turns out, had no weapon and committed no crime. The incident in Lyons heightened tensions between residents and Kaydans and led to weeks of protest surrounding one central question: Do Kaydans have the right to live?"

The room filled with the voices of a few hundred Kaydans dismissing the anchor as a bigoted quack, and by the time the chatter died down, she was on to something else.

"A month has passed since the rift appeared over the Georgian sky, leaving everyone wondering: What's next? It's been more than ten years since the similar occurrence which opened our minds—and our borders—to an alien race. The question then was whether they came in peace. Depending on who you ask, the answer has been in affirmation. The question now, considering all that has transpired since the New War and the Hunts, is whether they still want peace. So far, officials claim nothing has entered or exited the rift, though they have confirmed that the energy patterns are similar to those ten years ago. Those same officials admit it is odd the rift has lingered for so long since its predecessor came and left in less than an hour. This one, this scarlet streak on our nation, shows no signs of ever going away. When asked about what it means, our sources declined to comment."

More people packed into the lounge. I moved farther toward the corner. I didn't need them to see me. Tonight wasn't about me or if I had anything to do with the rift. Uncle found himself on the receiving end of accusations, too. If everyone kept facing forward towards Jormon or the television, I wouldn't have to care about that tonight.

Just as I'd thought it, a hand brushed my arm. I pulled away, but the hand grabbed me.

Taavi leaned over and whispered, "Prince Jormon knows you're here."

"I'm not hiding from him. If he wants to talk, we can talk."

"He doesn't want to talk. He wants you to leave."

Who was he to tell me what to do? I snatched my arm away. "I don't have to leave. I have as much right to be here and hear Father's interview as anyone else does. Why are you telling me this and not him? Or his new pal, Rughor? Did he send you thinking I wouldn't say no to my sweet, sweet friend, Taavi? I can say no to you as well as I can to anyone else. No. I won't leave."

"This is my home. I live with all—most—of these people. I hear what they say about the rift and about you. Prince Jormon isn't wrong for wanting you to leave."

Dammit, Taavi. Don't be right about this.

"I'll leave with you." His tone was soft, almost apologetic, yet his fingers were still gripping my bicep. He was stronger than I was, but I was more powerful if it came to that. I didn't want it to come to that.

I shook my head. "I'll go by myself. You should stay and hear what the king has to say."

"I don't too much care." He thought for a second. "If you want, we can find another place to watch it. Won't Sean have a TV?"

I'd never been to his house, but Sean would have a television, certainly.

I thought no one saw me enter, but there was no doubt everyone saw me leave. The moment I shifted towards the door, nearby conversations lowered to a hush as they all glanced awkwardly over their shoulders. Those looks made me glad to get away.

I said my goodbyes to Lheniva and waited in the cold for Taavi to get his jacket.

I hoped Sean was home. If not, maybe Taavi and I would portal to Washington, D.C. to see Father's interview live. That would be a real shock to everyone, especially the police. We'd likely get shot right there in the studio and become another blip on the nightly news.

I cleared my mind and searched for Sean. He was an easy find, but he wasn't at home. I expanded the field of vision.

He was sitting in a packed pew alongside several other people I recognized from school. Mrs. Broadnax sat two rows up with her hands cupped around the opposing wrists, twisting her bangles in what was perhaps her own form of therapy.

I did a quick spin to take in what was happening. I hardly recognized Coach Stroud without his whistles, though he, much like everyone else, was dressed more appropriately for a trip to Walmart than for church. He stood beside Coach Hardy, both with their backs pressed against the main doors. Ushers, no doubt. At the opposite end of the aisle, just past the ornate wooden alter, Pastor Lumley stood high in the pulpit.

"Phae insisted on coming," Taavi said. His voice sliced through my vision, and suddenly I could feel the cold again. Pews were replaced by single-wide trailers, the faded carpet faded further into snow, the yellow glow from overhead lights receded into the stars, and everything was yet again bathed in a bloody red hue from the rift. Phae stood shivering next to him, her breath misting in front of her in quick puffs, her shoulders hunched against the cold, her eyes darting anxiously about. "We have a problem. Sean is at church with Pastor Lumley," I said, my voice catching in the sudden wind.

"The pastor from the lake? Why would Sean be with him?" Phae asked.

"I don't know, but it's a full house. He could be there for any number of reasons."

"Then we should see what's going on. Especially if he's in trouble."

We flew back to my place. The cold air stung my face, and the feeling left my cheeks in the short distance to my bedroom window.

"Do you think Sean is a Rider?" Taavi asked once we were back inside.

I thought about Sean sitting in Pastor Lumley's congregation. All I knew is he was there. I didn't sense how he felt about being there, nor did I know if he came on his own. "There's no way. Sean is a friend."

"You mean to tell me you've never lost a friend before?"

I never had a friend before to lose, especially someone so close to me as Sean. I told Taavi as much, and he laughed.

"Has he ever invited you to his house? Have you ever hung out with him and any of his other friends?

"No. We always hang out here in the trailer park."

"There's your answer. You're his little secret. He's compartmentalizing the relationship so that no one knows you two are friends."

"That's not true. If anything, he's protecting me by keeping me away from the bigots in the school."

"If anything, I'm the one protecting you by telling you the truth, Prince Noan. The pressure Sean is under to fit in with his own people must be immense. In times like these, if you stand out, you get put out. You don't know what he'd do to belong to a community."

"You never liked him, and I'm having a hard time buying your theory" I said, finding myself more annoyed with Taavi than willing to believe Sean could be a Rider.

"Boys, can we just do this," Phae snapped.

I focused my energy on the church, recalling the details and letting them sharpen into focus. My energy slowly seeped from my body as my room morphed into the church's foyer.

"This feels too real. Are you sure this is just a vision, and we didn't phase?"

We walked to the set of doors, and each tried twisting a handle. Our hands passed right through, though I could feel the cold metal as it did. Taavi shrugged his satisfaction. I took a deep breath and stepped inside.

Pastor Lumley had just finished making a point, and everyone clapped.

We walked farther into the church. The usual suspects were there: the Brantleys, the Darleys, the Summersets. I recognized a lot of faces from school, the lake, or the protests, but many faces were new. The first set of pews nearest to the pulpit were filled with well-dressed men and women. Their suits and dresses fitted them perfectly, and by the way the light caught in the fabric, it was clear they were expensive. Their backdrop was the couple hundred of their peers drowning in sweaters or sweat suits or bubble coats, making it obvious these few guests were different. More important. Invited from elsewhere.

Past them and beyond the pastor and his pulpit, a row of three ornate chairs formed a dais along the side of the stage. Overhead spotlights shone down on their purple velvet cushions, expectant, perhaps, of guests of honor.

The clapping died down. Pastor Lumley closed his massive bible and stepped in front of the pulpit. "We all knew this was preordained. We knew…" he drew the word out so long I thought he was singing. "We knew that one day, more of them would try to invade our lands."

"Amen," the congregation returned in unison, like so many androids operating with a hive mind.

"Our communities!"

"Amen."

"Our homes!"

"Amen."

Pastor Lumley continued. "I wasn't the only one who knew this. You knew it. And you knew it. And you knew it." He pointed in different directions, and every admission was punctuated with an 'amen' from the congregation. "You know who else knew it? Our newly elected President."

The crowd went berserk. They applauded the pastor, but even more so, they applauded themselves. They reveled in the landslide victory of the guy running on the platform that Kaydans are an inherent evil.

Sean put on a half-hearted smile and clapped almost imperceptibly. He wasn't here because he wanted to be. But still, he was here. The guy beside him nudged him with his elbow, and Sean, seeming to wake up, applauded with vigorous, resounding enthusiasm.

"Our great President could not be here with us today, but I have it on good authority that he is proud of the work we have done, and of the work we will continue to do."

More sickening applause.

"Now, ladies and gentlemen, here representing your interests and President-elect Thorne Blackwell's is our new mayor, Mr. Fitzgerald Kuss."

They stood in applause as Mayor Kuss entered from the shadowy wing of stage right and walked past the pulpit. As he moved towards the lectern, an officer greeted him, and they embraced deeply.

"Dude, this is bad," Taavi said. I'd forgot he was with me. "They're all in this together."

Mayor Kuss let the crowd adore him for a century or so before he finally spoke. He thanked them for their support and touted his close and personal relationship with the President elect. He said, "I'd like to show special appreciation to my brother, Eric Kuss—who you all know as Sheriff Buck—and to his boy, Chris, and stepson, Sean. It's been a long, hard road to victory, and I couldn't have done it without the support of my family."

"Sean's uncle is the new mayor?" Taavi asked, his eyebrows raised in suspicion.

"I'm still stuck on Sean's dad being the sheriff? Did you know any of this before tonight?" Phae asked.

"I'm as confused as you are," I said.

Mayor Kuss spoke for another half hour. Every second that passed cost me more energy, but I couldn't leave the vision until I knew how this played out. Every time Sean fidgeted in his seat, like a toddler on a road trip, the brunette guy beside him, his stepbrother, Chris, would lean in and whisper something to make him stop.

Mayor Kuss carried on with his oration. "We deserve answers. They've ripped another hole in our beautiful, God-given sky, and now they're denying they did it. Here's the scary part, folks. If they didn't do it here, then some of their kind did it from the other side."

The room went eerily quiet. The narrative had been thrown around since the rift opened, but the congregation heard it tonight like they were hearing it for the first time.

Mayor Kuss let them sit in their discomfort. He paced from side to side, scratching at the blond stubble on his chin.

"I'm not ashamed to admit: I was afraid. I was afraid that more of them would come soaring through the crack like last time. Maybe the first bunch was the scouting party, and next time, millions more would be ready to come in and claim what's rightfully ours. Like you, I was afraid. But I'm not afraid anymore."

The side door opened again. Three Riders in full regalia strutted in, dragging behind them a woman whose hands and feet were shackled in thick iron chains. Copper lines ran halfway up to her elbows on both arms.

"That's Sandi Nash!" Phae said. "She cleans for the Brantley family."

I recalled what Brett told me about how they treat her, and a shiver worked its way down my spine. I was on the verge of exhaustion, but I couldn't let up, not even for a second. One of the Riders handed Mayor Kuss a briefcase. He clicked it open and pulled out a revolver and a flat piece of obsidian the size of a drink coaster.

Taavi squinted at the *sabej*. "That looks like something I made. I sold a handful of those to buy the shirt I wore to the Fall Festival."

"What does it do?"

"It's a detector. You put your finger right in the center and the rim lights up in the direction of where someone—well, some Kaydan—is located."

"Why would the mayor of Lyons have one of your *sabejaan*?"

"Maybe he shops at Issek's like everyone else," Taavi said, biting at his lip as he watched Sandi shuffle across the stage.

Mayor Kuss signaled, and the riders unshackled Sandi. She looked around the room, confused. She took one look at the revolver in the mayor's hand and sprinted away. She leaped from the dais and flew high into the vaulted ceiling.

The congregation gasped and shifted in their seats, craning their necks to see where she'd gone.

"Prince Noan, can we help her?" Phae asked.

"I don't think so. By the time we make it there, it'll be too late." And I was already too tired to be useful, even if I could make it in time.

"Maybe if she heads for the window up there—"

Without warning, Sandi fell wildly to the floor, a vertiginous star, all limbs and angles, screaming all the way down. She landed in the aisle on both feet, and her bones crunched under her weight.

"What. Just. Happened, Taavi? What the hell just happened?" I asked.

"I don't know."

Mayor Kuss walked slowly down the aisle, giving reassuring touches to the shoulders of the men and women he passed. Sandi scooted on her backside towards the door, but she would never make it, and if she did, the coaches were standing guard. Still, she kept moving. Soon, she was near enough to me to see the white bone jutting out the side of each leg.

Mayor Kuss followed the twin trails of blood with slow, deliberate steps. "There was a time when I was afraid of them."

He cocked the revolver's hammer and shot Sandi. Even in pain, she conjured a shield. The bullet sucked into the shield and fell to the floor. The gunfire startled the crowd, but they didn't move.

"There was a time I was afraid of what they could do."

He shot again, and the shield held.

"Afraid of what they could do to me."

Another shot, and the shield still held. Pain and fear etched across Sandi's face, and her eyes pleaded with him to stop.

"Ladies and gentlemen, I'm not afraid of them anymore."

Mayor Kuss pressed his thumb into the *sabej*, and Sandi's shield dissipated. Her pain was replaced by panic as she tried to conjure another one. She flexed her wrists and pressed her hand out like she was feeling for a wall that just wasn't there. Her powers weren't working. Her defenses were completely down.

Mayor Kuss cocked the hammer, pointed the muzzle at her head, and squeezed the trigger.

I let the vision fade, but it still felt like Sandi's blood was on me. I patted my legs just to be sure. My ears pounded as blood rushed through my body.

Taavi paced between the window and the door, cursing to himself. "You don't have to say it. I really fucked up this time. Please don't be mad at me." He paced faster, and I worried he would jump out the window and crash land on the ground, just like Sandi. "It wasn't supposed to do that. Someone must've tampered with it."

"Taavi." I didn't know what to say next. He'd created something humans could use against us in the worst way. Poor Sandi. The snapping of her bones as she crashed down from the ceiling played on repeat. "Are you sure? There's no way you could've gotten the *sahdr* wrong when you made it. Or used the wrong runes?"

"I'm absolutely sure. Dirk and I share a room and I only have so much privacy. I use that thing all the time to make sure I knew when he's nearby. That's what I made it for. Especially since school has been suspended because of the rift. Everyone's around all the time and there's never any privacy."

Phae slumped in the corner. Her fingers clenched and unclenched as she undoubtedly replayed the horrifying scene in her mind. Her gaze was distant as if she were trying to dissect every frame of the incident. Occasionally she'd mutter to herself, trying to piece together the unfolding chaos, clearly struggling to make sense of it all.

Father's interview was still going on, meaning I couldn't disturb Uncle with this. I had no choice but to talk to Jormon.

Jormon, I need to see you. It's really important, I said, hoping my brother could drop his anti-Noan act long enough to be useful.

We waited in silence for nearly an hour, but Jormon never came. An hour after that and he still didn't show.

"Are you sure he got your message?"

"Yeah, he definitely got it." He's just too busy trying to be a Prince, or whatever. "It's almost midnight. You can sleep here tonight if you don't want to be alone. You shouldn't be alone, not tonight."

"It's okay. I have a shift at the Factory."

"Come here after your shift. I might need you to corroborate the story when I tell Uncle in the morning."

The time ticked by and Jormon didn't show up. Phae walked over to the window, gazing at the snow falling on the early November night.

"You think they've done this before? Used one of Taavi's *sabejaan* to help them kill someone?" she asked, her voice barely more than a whisper.

"I... I don't know."

Taavi didn't come back the next morning, nor in the evening, when Uncle returned from D.C. Uncle barely made it into the foyer before I bombarded him with my account of what happened to Sandi.

"And you're sure it was the new mayor?" he asked.

"Absolutely. I looked through the newspaper this morning to confirm for myself."

It hurt me to discuss Taavi's role in this, but he had to know. After thinking it over, he said, "They must have somehow merged the *sabej* with the technology they used to bind my powers in the police car. It's the only explanation I have at the moment. I'll think it over after I've gotten some sleep."

210

"Wait. Before you go, tell me about the interview. Did Father convince everyone?"

"You know how charming your King Rosh is. He did a remarkable job."

"Does Father still think I had something to do with the rift?"

"He never thought you were behind it. If he suspects anyone, it would be me. But we've gotten to the bottom of it, and that mystery is partially solved."

"Who did it? Was it the Red Cloaks? Or someone still on Kayda who opened it?"

"I'm only telling you this because I know you're discreet," Uncle said, casting a scrutinizing gaze.

"I won't tell anyone, Uncle. I swear."

"It was the Americans who opened the rift."

"What? How is that possible? You've always said it took the collective power of many great *mustediin* to open the rift ten years ago."

"I don't recall ever saying they were great, but that's beside the point. One of our own has been teaching humans how to interact with our technology and manipulate our energy. I think they've found a way to open the rift, but they haven't discovered how to go through it."

I thought about it, and it came to me. "The artifact in the lake. I was supposed to get it, but I followed you instead. If that's what they used to open the rift, then it's my fault."

"Don't beat yourself up so eagerly. When there are plenty of people out there ready to bash you, why bash yourself? Besides, they never retrieved the artifact. They looked for it, certainly, but it was already gone."

"You were able to get it. That's what you meant by talking damage control with Hargi that night."

"Partially."

"Where is it now? Does Hargi have it?"

"He wanted to hold it, but I didn't think it wise. I've hidden it away again, in a place where no one can accidentally trigger it like before."

"Is that what happened at the lake? Did we trigger it?" Did Jormon trigger it, I should've asked.

"Something like that. We can talk more when I've recovered. It's been a grueling week."

"Recovered from what? What happened in D.C.?"

"Preparing for the future, Prince Noan. That's all I can say until I've rested."

"I'll hold you to that, Uncle."

"As is your right." He placed a hand on my shoulder. We'd been talking in the warm parlor for nearly an hour, yet his fingers were like ice cubes, chilling my skin through my wool sweater. It was only then, with his face so near to mine, that I noticed how pale he was. Blue veins ran beneath his skin like secret rivers, and the sudden sight of it sent chills down my spine.

"Uncle—"

"Not now, Prince Noan. I know you want to talk, but it'll have to wait."

Upstairs in my room, Jormon stood before the frosted window, watching the snow sprinkle the adjacent rooftops. I plopped down on the bed and stared up at the ceiling. *Heemrah* loomed in the far corner, setting just as *Zereq* rose in the opposite side of the room, their combined lights painting the room in the rare, perfect shade of purple Kaydans call the Purple Peace. I closed my eyes and let the color set in my memory.

I felt Jormon's gaze on me. "If you're going to say something, say it. Otherwise, get out."

"Chill with the attitude. I caught the first half of your conversation with Uncle Tobin, and I wanted to see if you're okay. If it makes you feel any better, I don't think Sean is a Rider."

I let out a deep breath and pressed my fingertips against my temples. "You go for days treating me like a fucking pariah, and now you want to make sure I'm okay? Get out. I mean it, Jormon. Go!"

The floor creaked as Jormon walked closer to the bed. "Look, I know I could've handled the rift thing a little better, but you have to see it from my side. People look up to me. I needed to show them I understand their feelings. If I went too far by pushing you away, I'm sorry."

I lay there with my eyes closed, waiting for the sound of his footsteps.

"You're not going to say anything? Wow. So much for meeting me halfway. I hope you give Sean more credit for being a decent person than you're giving me."

Finally, the footsteps sounded, the bedroom door slammed closed, and I was alone. Rest did not come easy. I had the notion to scry Sean's location, but the idea I'd find him wearing a dumbass hunting jacket toasting Sandi's death with his asshole father and his redneck brother made my stomach churn. No, I decided. I'd rather keep my distance and stay ignorant. Perhaps not knowing was better.

CHAPTER NINTEEN
JORMON

DESPITE LOCAL AND FEDERAL MANDATES THAT Gray Flats remain open to humans, Dad convinced Uncle Tobin to perform a *sahdr* sealing off the trailer park. The barrier was largely symbolic, given the Riders' use of magical blockers, but it succeeded in keeping Sean away from Noan. Not that Sean didn't try. Over the past week, I'd spotted him pacing the perimeter, searching in vain for a way past the *sahdr*. Meanwhile, Noan moped around the trailer, dodging me ever since our argument. When I mentioned seeing Sean lurking outside, Noan dismissed it coldly. "He's probably checking our defenses for weaknesses," he said before telling me to get out of his room.

During the first week of his attempts to visit, Sean had come by every day. Eventually, his visits had slowed down, and after not seeing him for a week, it seemed he'd finally gotten the message that Noan didn't want to see him.

One morning, a neighbor came by with a note addressed to Noan. She'd found it weighed down by a rock near the trailer park's entrance. It was addressed to Noan in Sean's handwriting. I debated whether to open it or not, but curiosity got the better of me.

"Please, tell me what I've done," it read and had a drawing of a ring underneath the sentence.

The letter had gotten to me. Sean seemed genuinely hurt by Noan icing him out, and I seriously had my doubts that Sean was a Rider. When I tried to show Noan the letter, he set it on fire while it was still in my hand.

"I get that you're pissed, Noan, but you need to get over it."

His little stunt burning the letter had me pissed, too. I left the trailer without grabbing a jacket, and I immediately regretted it. The December snow slammed against my too-thin shirt, and by the time I reached Dirk's place, I'd lost all feeling in my torso.

As I reached the front door to Lheniva's trailer, Dirk opened it, visibly startled. "I was just about to head to your place."

"Yours is better. I don't want to be around Noan right now." We made it to his room, and I stopped him before entering. "I don't care to talk to anyone but you right now, and that's if we talk at all."

He kissed me on the mouth, and I loved him for it. He opened the door, and the instant warmth from the heaters inside was so stark against the biting cold outside it made my skin tingle painfully.

The smell of cinnamon and apples wafted from a nearby pot. Candles, with gentle flames, danced in the dimly lit living room, casting silhouettes against the wall.

"You look like you've seen a ghost," Dirk commented as we entered his room. He took off his shoes and placed them neatly by the door.

I tried to laugh it off, but my voice came out shaky. "I just… I wasn't expecting any of this. We spend so much time at my place, I… I guess I didn't know what to expect."

Dirk moved closer, his eyes searching mine, trying to read my what was going through my mind. He gently placed his hands on my shoulders, grounding me. "Is it to your liking, Prince Jormon?"

"You know I'm not fancy."

"Good, 'cause I don't want to be alone right now. Taavi is beating himself up over Sandi Nash, and Phae is with the Spirit Matron trying to find Sandi's spirit floating around somewhere."

I smirked. "Is that your way of saying we won't be disturbed?"

"Maybe." We sat on the edge of the bed, the worn springs creaking under our weight. I leaned my head against Dirk's shoulder, feeling the warmth of his skin through his shirt. The rhythm of his heartbeat was steady and calming, and I soon had to spread my legs to make myself more comfortable. Dirk's hand brushed against my cheek, gently lifting my chin so our eyes met. There was an unspoken question in his gaze, one that made my heart race faster. Our faces inched closer, the space between us rapidly disappearing.

Our lips met in a soft, lingering kiss. The world outside and the tensions of the evening faded, leaving only the two of us, connected by more than just a shared moment.

Pulling back slightly, Dirk's eyes sparkled with a hint of mischief. "To be clear, Taavi won't be back for a while," he whispered.

I leaned in and let my lips lock on Dirk's again. Taavi could watch, for all I cared. I needed this. I needed Dirk, right then and there, to let me know life could be a happy thing, not just something to endure.

For the rest of the night, we lay in each other's arms, the warmth of the room and each other's company erasing the icy chill of my brother's cold shoulder.

CHAPTER TWENTY
NOAN

WE WERE IN MID-DECEMBER FACING THE COLDEST winter ever, and still, the rift loomed overhead. During the day, it was easy to forget it was there. Sunlight drowned out the revolving shades of blues, purples, and reds and made the rift look, if anything, like a scar—sometimes crimson and fresh, other times green and gangrenous—on the dull sky. Red nights were good nights. The light painted the snow like blood, which spooked Riders into saying home. Blue night's meant trouble might happen. Purple nights meant trouble was definitely going to happen. On those nights, we watched and waited, breaths baited with an ear out for Riders driving by with mischief on their minds.

And still, there was high school. Once it became clear the open rift didn't mean imminent death to the humans, classes resumed, and our father told us in no uncertain terms we were to return without delay. We missed all of November, which meant twice the homework and triple the hate in December.

Though President-elect Blackwell hadn't been sworn into office yet, his pending power gave life to his supporters, and Glory Gear practically became the new school uniform. The increased hate we felt was the only thing keeping us together. Sean continued to make subtle attempts to speak to me, but Taavi ran more interference than a wide receiver, according to Dirk. When I asked him what that meant, he laughed.

Needless to say, I'd never been so happy to take a test as the end-of-semester exams meant the holiday recess was waiting. The

Cohort turned in our books, aced our exams, and flew the fuck out of Dodge.

I was in my room when Jormon knocked on my door and pushed in before I could tell him to go away.

"Good morning, Little Brother." He was unusually chipper. We had come to a tenuous peace given our common goal of surviving the semester, but we still weren't on proper speaking terms.

"You need help with a *mustedi* lesson or something?"

"Don't be that way, Little Bro."

"Bro? Did you pick that up from Rughor? I figured with him being pseudo-British, he'd be more of a 'mate' sort of guy." Rughor was clever. The moment Jormon distanced himself from me, Rughor swooped faster than a crack whore running to the crack store and, lately, Jormon was everyone's drug of choice. With Father busy in D.C strategizing to preserve Kaydan rights ahead of the Presidential Inauguration Day, and Uncle here in Gray Flats seeking justice for Sandi Nash, Jormon quickly became the person everyone turned to for guidance. Drac had even given him an office in Craux Hall, one of the social appendages of the Academy usually reserved for faculty meetings, like he was a full-on goddamn professor. I wasn't the least bit jealous.

"Never mind where I picked it up. Do you know what today is?" he asked.

"It's Saturday."

"And?"

"And it's December—December twenty-third." I didn't realize. There was so much going on, I hadn't bothered to think about myself. "It's our birthday."

"Ding, ding, ding!"

"Jormon, please, get out of my room. I've gotten used to not having you around, and now you're standing in my doorway 'dinging' like a goddamn bell. I'm not in the pretending mood." With a whispered word, the door swung closed, but Jormon jammed his foot in the way just before it shut.

"Noan, hear me out," he grunted, shoving against the door.

"Let me guess: Dirk and Rughor want to do something, and Dirk asked you to ask me to join so Rughor wouldn't be a third wheel?"

"You think you're so smart, don't you?" He whispered something, and the door flew open. The doorknob banged into the wall and went right through. "Sorry."

It wouldn't be the first thing you ruined, I wanted to say.

"You're wrong, though," he continued. "Dirk has something small planned, and he insisted I invite you, seeing as it's your birthday too."

"Well, ain't he a sweetheart," I said, mocking Dirk's Southern drawl.

Jormon gave me a sharp look. "Don't do that," he snapped. "Dirk's a great friend, and he wants to do something nice."

"Boyfriend."

"Huh?" Jormon's face twisted in confusion.

"I think the word you're looking for is 'boyfriend,' isn't it?"

Jormon's composed demeanor unraveled, and he shifted his eyes to avoid my gaze. "He's just a good friend, and I like spending time with him."

"That's bull crap. These walls are thinner than you think. I hear you two moaning and groaning when he comes over, and I know damn well you're not doing Pilates at midnight." Jormon's face turned as red as *Heemrah*, no doubt wondering if Nana Lura had heard his late-night passions as well. "I've already told you I'm happy for you. Don't try and walk back the relationship just because you're becoming some big shot with your own office."

"And I've already told you Dad has plans for my future, plans that won't include Dirk, so can we just drop it and do some birthday shit? Please? And no, Rughor's not coming. It'll just be the three of us. Taavi is pulling double shifts at the Factory and Phae is with the Spirit Matron in New Orleans dealing with a leg pie."

"Huh? Oh, you mean Papa Legba." It made sense. The Spirit Matron working with spirit witches in Louisiana seemed normal to me.

"Whatever. I want you to join us. If you're so pressed about us drifting apart, let this be the way we come back together. Besides, if you don't join in, it will dampen the whole day. Please, Little Brother. Come celebrate with me. You can bring Sean along as well."

My face hardened. "You know I'm not talking to Sean."

"You've got to give him a chance to explain himself."

I didn't have to give anyone anything.

"You know he likes you. He wouldn't do anything to hurt you."

"I wonder if you actually hear yourself sometimes, or of you just say shit just to say it."

"Oh, Your Highness! You have a foul mouth, which I will ignore because it's your birthday. And it's my birthday. And I'm tired of this conversation already and just want everyone to be friends. So please… Pretty please… I'll do your laundry for a week, please… Talk to Sean. Invite him over. Tell him we're doing this new thing all the kids are doing called 'getting along.'"

"Fine," I told him. "You are so annoying."

"Awesome! Dirk's already downstairs cooking. If we're not having fun before it's over, we can raid Uncle Tobin's bourbon and drink until we are."

I thought about Sean, and as it often was when I thought about people, his life came into view. He was sitting on the edge of his bed, staring at the floor-length mirror affixed to the closet door across from him. Maybe he was debating whether to get up and join his own family for breakfast. Maybe he was contemplating smashing the mirror and using one of the broken shards to slit his own wrists for betraying me.

I walked to the kitchen to show Dirk my enthusiastic smile, which was as put on as Jormon's. Dirk was balancing a glass mixing bowl and a whisk in one hand when the bowl slipped from his grip and shattered on the floor. He smiled back at me all the same, adding a playful apology for the broken bowl.

I stepped outside into the thick snow and conjured a portal directly into Sean's room.

He was gone. The mirror was still intact. Frigid air blew in through the open window, circulating scents of cedar and dirty laundry.

As I was examining the room, the door opened, and a startled Sean walked through. He wore plain red pajamas with flecks of silver trimming along the sleeves and down the pant legs, giving him an exaggerated boyish appearance. "Christ!" he exclaimed.

"Noan, actually. It's nice to see you, too." I leaned over the desk mirror and examined a photo of him and a light-skinned girl with braces, hugging outside of a hospital. "I'm realizing only now that you've never invited me to visit, though I'm pretty sure I know why. I think I like your room much better than my own. It feels more...more lived in. More adolescent."

He closed the door behind him. "How did you know where I lived? How did you get here? You shouldn't invade other people's privacy. I could've been doing anything in here."

He picked up a crusty sock lying beside his bed and tossed it in the hamper in a far corner, then took to tidying up his unmade bed and the mess of dishes on his desk.

"Are you upset with me for coming? I heard you've been asking about me and I came to see what you wanted." It was glib at best, confrontational at worst, but I was there, he was there, and we were talking.

"Please be quiet," he whispered. He connected his phone to a pair of desk speakers and pressed play on a random song. "Chris is in the other room, and my folks are downstairs."

"Your parents? Is your mother here? Did she break free from her cell in Milledgeville?" Not so glib, definitely confrontational.

"Dad gets her and brings her home for the holidays. Why are you being an asshole? You don't talk to me for a month, then you pop up out of nowhere—literally—and crack jokes about my mom. That's not cool."

"Neither is pretending to be my friend while also enjoying the chilling entertainment at Rider meetings."

His eyes widened and he stopped breathing. "You…Wait, were you there? Is that why you've been avoiding me this whole time? I can explain, Noan, just not here. Please, you have to leave before someone comes. I'll go with you, and we can talk, but you aren't safe here."

"Because your dad is Sheriff Kick Ass? When I told you about breaking my uncle free from the cops, you gave a vague, half-assed warning. You could've told me then that your dad is a Rider, too. Which explains why I've never met him. He doesn't know we're friends." Unless he did know, and Sean has been spying on us since the first day of school. The moment I thought it, fresh anger washed over me.

"He wasn't always a Rider. He blames Kaydans for ruining our family, sure. Then Pastor Lumley came along and tapped into something awful in him. Noan, I'm not like my dad. I'm your friend. You have to believe me. I'd never do anything to hurt you. Let's go. We can talk about it more somewhere else."

I was still fuming, but I wanted to hear what else he had to say. "Fine."

"Can I get changed at your place?" he asked, and I agreed. He rushed around the room grabbing things to wear, then he picked up a packaged wrapped in purple and black with a silver bow affixed to it. "Happy birthday. I wasn't sure if I'd get the chance to see you today, but I got it for you just in case."

His kindness put me off guard, like the bear that mauls an entire family but lets the kids escape, or the boss who yells at you all day, then buys your baby a onesie. I wanted to be furious with him, but instead I stood there confused, waiting to see if there would be another turn in his actions, something to put me back where I started.

I created a portal to the trailer park. There was snow on the ground, and he wasn't wearing shoes.

"Be quick about it. I'm right behind you."

We dashed in tandem, stepping out of the warm room and into the snowy outside, then into the foyer of our trailer.

He showered and changed, and I filled in Jormon and Dirk as quickly as I could, which was easy considering he hadn't told me anything yet. He was on the way to join the three of us when I stopped him in the doorway of the kitchen. Water dripped from his hair, and I dried it for him as I had done the first week we met. He smiled an unfamiliar smile, something sad and shameful.

"Do they know about the meeting?"

"They do. Your uncle killed one of our neighbors. I had to tell them."

He wiped his face with both hands, rubbing at his cheeks until they were as red as cherries. "I wish you knew how sorry I was for everything. I didn't want to be there, and I definitely didn't want anything like that to happen."

"I need more than that, Sean. We all do, but especially me."

"There's not much more to say. Chris—my stepbrother—surprised me after school. He said Dad wanted us to meet him at the church. I couldn't say no, so I went along with it. That's it, I swear."

"And the rest of it? Keeping me a secret from your family?"

"You've seen my dad and what he gets into. I'm not like them, and I was afraid if you knew where I came from, you'd think I was and wouldn't want anything to do with me."

He was telling the truth. I'd seen him rehearse his lines for Sky in the school's rendition of *Guys and Dolls*, and I knew from that he couldn't act. He was being genuine, which was sweet and awkward.

Suddenly I missed him. With everything I was going through, he'd be the one person I could talk to about it. I should have known he wouldn't betray me deliberately. We were too similar in the way that all abused children are, bound by scars unseen, etched not only on the skin, but on the soul.

I felt foolish for keeping him away for so long. I pulled him close and hugged him, and I felt something in our embrace, some feeling I couldn't quite identify. "I'm sorry I pushed you away. I didn't realize you probably needed me around as much as I needed you. Listen, you don't have to be someone you don't want to be. You should've come to me. I would've protected you."

It wasn't that I was attracted to Sean. Or maybe, on some level, I was. But the longer I stood with my arms around him, the more I felt I was where I wanted to be. His heartbeat against mine. It felt so good I could cry. I moved my head slightly, and my lips brushed against his cheek.

He backed away. He wasn't upset, but he didn't look happy. "Don't do that. It doesn't mean the same thing to you as it does to me. I see you're trying to do something nice, but this isn't it."

"I'm sorry," I said, shaking my head in confusion.

"Don't be. I enjoyed it for what it was, but I'd rather it not happen again." He smiled, and it was genuine and reassuring. I knew we were okay.

Jormon and Dirk had already made a mess of things. The countertops were dusted with flour, and two eggs had fallen to the floor. One of the egg yolks ran from the broken shell to the recess underneath the refrigerator. I used a *sahdr* to clean it up before Nana Lura could swoop in and put a stop to the breakfast experiment.

"Looks like I arrived just in time," Sean said.

"That, you did," Dirk said. "Okay, Jormon and Noan: out! This breakfast is our treat to you on your royal birthday. It might not be fit for a king—or a couple of princes—but it will come from a place of profound love, trust, and respect."

They shooed us to the sitting room where we kept to ourselves until they returned half an hour later with a breakfast charcuterie that defied my expectations. Prosciutto, bresaola, foie de volaille, and rillettes de canard paired with chèvre and brie, all served with

224

grape clusters, an assortment of jams, and baguette cut into miniature medallions.

"I thought we were having pancakes," Jormon said, at which point Dirk removed a green grape from its cluster and hurled it at him. "None of this screams southern breakfast. Where are the grits? Where's the plate of scrambled eggs?"

"The southern stuff comes next," Dirk said. "This just kinda showed up with a note from Mr. Tobin saying 'Start with this,' so we started with this—Why isn't he here? Or your daddy? Shouldn't they be planning a party for you? Shouldn't everyone? You're royalty."

"We've skipped our birthdays ever since we landed on Earth," Jormon said. "Celebrating would just throw a spotlight on why we're here in the first place."

"Oh."

As we ate, we found it difficult to find trivial things to talk about. Everything that came to my mind was about murder and inequality, neither of which was fitting for a birthday celebration. Jormon wanted to talk politics, Dirk brought up religion, and Sean brought up school. In the end, we settled on gossip. We talked about the irony of Chastity Barfield's teen pregnancy and Sean mentioned Shandrea got caught cheating on a calculus exam right before school was suspended.

We picked at the breakfast spread until all that remained were the damaged grapes, then took the party to the dining room and devoured the tower of pancakes Dirk and Sean prepared. Conversation slowed and then dropped off altogether, leaving us to sit in a prickly silence.

Drawing a deep breath, Jormon finally said, "Uh, Dirk and I are gonna check something out in my room."

I quickly interjected, my voice slightly higher than usual, "Or we can go for a walk?" The thought of being left alone with Sean was both intriguing and nerve-wracking, and I wasn't ready to confront whatever this thing was I felt for him. Besides, Jormon had invited me to this birthday celebration, and now, he was stuck with me.

Jormon's eyes narrowed slightly, studying my face. I met his gaze head-on, a silent challenge passing between us. He glanced briefly at Dirk, who raised his eyebrows in a silent question, then looked back at me. Finally, with a dramatic sigh, Jormon relented. "Fine," he said, not bothering to hide his annoyance. "Let's go freeze our asses off."

An armada of dark, foreboding clouds dominated the horizon. The wind which barely stirred earlier that morning now blew so hard it unraveled our scarves from around our necks. Gusts pushed at the trailers, and their tin siding bucked and bowed, sounding like an erratic chorus of snare drums. The trees ahead groaned and creaked as they danced drunkenly and off-beat to their own music. I looked up at the rift. Light blue going on teal.

We traveled in a gaggle, not exactly huddled together, but not in a line abreast, either. Sean walked close to me, but when his arm accidentally swung into mine, he walked farther and faster away. Had I fucked things up between us? I replayed the scene in my mind, doing my best to recall every detail: the way Sean rubbed his face, the genuine desperation in his voice as he apologized, the way his face felt against mine, and the sound of our heartbeats colliding when we embraced.

I'd been so sure I didn't have feelings for Sean, that my friendship was just that: friendship. How could I have been so dismissive? My stomach churned at the thought of having to offer another apology, this time to Taavi; one was plenty enough. Also, I couldn't like Sean. His dad was a Rider, for *Zereq*'s sake!

I quickened my pace, my boots sinking deeper into the snow, until I was side by side with Sean. He looked over, eyebrows raised.

"I've been thinking," I began, the cold air making my words come out in stuttered puffs. "About what happened back there. About us."

Sean looked straight ahead, his face unreadable. "I meant what I said, Noan. You can't toy with people's feelings."

I winced, the truth in his words sharper than the wind's bite. "I know, and I'm truly sorry." Damn. Another apology. That wasn't so bad. "Here's the thing, though. Forget I said anything. Forget I did anything. Just…forget it all."

"What?"

Dirk and Jormon, sensing the tension, walked on ahead, giving us space. The forest's ambiance was eerily silent, save for the whistle of the wind and the rustling of trees.

Sean finally turned to face me. Snowflakes clung to his eyelashes, and it took everything I had not to get close to him and brush the snow away. It took me a few seconds to collect myself. "I just want to know we're still friends, right?"

"I'm here, ain't I?"

"Yes, you are. So…we *are* friends, yeah? Just friends."

Without any warning, a shot rang out, stopping everyone in their tracks. Then another. Dirk whipped his hand to his stomach, leaned into Jormon and collapsed in the snow.

"Get down!" I shouted, but Jormon was already down, leaning over Dirk's body. Blood leaked from underneath his puffy coat. Something had pierced his abdomen.

"Wh-what was that?" Dirk sputtered, and blood bubbled from his lips. Footsteps sounded nearby, running towards us. I hunkered down in defense, my arms extended and at the ready to do whatever *sahdr* came to me in the moment. Seconds later, two men emerged from the trees. They wore winter camouflage draped in fluorescent orange mesh, and both were carrying rifles. I recognized one of them. Alexander Darley.

Alexander dropped the rifle as he approached. His hands shook, and his shallow, rapid breaths created tiny puffs of condensed air that lingered around him like steam. "It was an accident," he managed. "We were hunting... I didn't see him... I thought he was a deer."

"A deer!" Jormon shouted over Dirk's body. "An animal! How stupid are you!"

"I swear it was an accident!"

Alexander had begun to cry when Jormon stood up and said in a voice I had never heard him use, "There's no fucking way that was an accident." Dirk's body lay motionless in the snow. Sean kneeled beside him, tapping at his cheeks and patting around his body, searching for the wound.

Please don't be dead.

For a moment, Alexander stopped breathing. He backed slowly toward the other man. "Dad..." He was panicked and didn't know what to do. He stood with his mouth agape, looking to his father, then at Dirk, then back again.

"Look, son," the man said to Jormon. "It was an accident, just as sure. We didn't see you boys, is all." His country accent made him sound condescending.

"You know me! I would never do anything like this. Sean, tell them! Tell them it was an accident!" Alexander pleaded, but there was no telling Jormon anything.

The wind, so erratic just moments before, swirled around us in a controlled roar. Alexander was shouting his apology, but the air was too loud, too commanding, not that Jormon would hear him anyway. His eyes clouded in a nocturnal blue radiance. His energy, raw and unbridled, filled his body with want of somewhere else to go, needing to escape more than anyone ever needed anything. He screamed, and the world shook, and pure energy exploded from his body.

The wave rushed towards me, and my defenses were up instinctively. A translucent wall went up around me and covered me from the blast. But Sean was on the other side of Jormon, bent over Dirk with his ear close to his mouth listening to know if he was still

228

breathing. He must've caught the wave from the corner of his eye, but there was nothing he could do. I tried to extend my shield to cover him, but it all happened so fast, and I was too slow. He threw his body across Dirk's as the wave rushed at them.

Mr. Darley was already placing himself between Jormon and Alexander when the blast shot out. The blue hit him, and it was instant death. It was snow falling into a volcano. It was spitting on the sun. One moment his body was there, alive, protecting his son, and in the next moment it was gone. So absolutely gone. No blood. No body. No blown-away hunting cap. Nothing.

Mr. Darley's body caught the brunt of the blast, but the sheer energy still hit Alexander, and he flew back several feet. Jormon fell to his knees. He was spent. The havoc had been wreaked, and he had nothing left. He kneeled there as empty as if he'd been leeched.

The blast melted the snow for yards around, leaving the trees as clear as they were in the fall, and the ground just as devoid, save for the three bodies stretched around Jormon's kneeling figure. The wind had stopped almost entirely, and off in the distance came the familiar humming of drone propellers. Eight drones, I knew, and they would arrive in minutes.

"Jormon!" I yelled. He had moved over to Dirk's body. Dirk's body! Sean's body, too! The blast didn't erase them. I ran over and examined Sean. I placed two fingers on the side of his neck, just below the chin. I didn't realize, but I was holding my breath. It was there, his pulse, but how?

The ring! It hit me so fast I nearly screamed. I forgot about the ring I gave him to protect himself.

"Jormon, he's alive—Jormon, I need you to snap out of it! *Jormon, can you hear me?*" I projected. He turned to face me. "We need to get everyone to Uncle. Do you have the strength to carry them? Jormon, focus! Can you carry them?" Useless, as always. Fuck!

With a thought, a smoky portal materialized beside the bodies of Sean and Dirk, and with a whispered word, I lifted the bodies and moved them through. Blood pooled where Dirk had lain. Too much of it. "I can get them to our front door, but no farther." As the portal shrank to a close, the front door opened, and Uncle stepped out. What happened next wasn't for me to worry about.

I walked over to Jormon and helped him to his feet. "What have I done?" he asked, looking at the blood covering the grass. "I've ruined everything. They'll never accept us now. They'll kill us. It's going to be the Hunts all over again."

"It's okay, Big Brother. You didn't ruin anything, nothing at all. Everything is going to be just fine. For now, we need to focus on getting out of here." The drones were closer, almost overhead.

"They'll hate me for this. Everyone will. Our people. The humans. Everyone."

"It's not as bad as all of that. If we get out of here now, they won't even know we were here."

"That's not enough. If there's even the smallest chance someone could find out I lost control, they'd never trust me. You know it's true. Dad will kill me."

I'd never seen Jormon cry before, but there he stood with tears filling his eyes, staring at me, waiting for me to save him.

"What are you saying?" I asked, though I knew well what it was.

"Noan, I wouldn't ask you this if there was any other way."

"What are you saying?"

"If there was any way to take the blame off me."

"Jormon, what the fuck are you saying?" I needed him to say it so he'd know what it felt like to ask what he intended for me to do.

"Say you did it." It was a statement, not a plea.

"I can't."

"It's the only way."

I shook my head. "They'll hate me."

"They already do. Noan, I'm your brother and the crown prince. I can make sure nothing happens to you. Do this for me. Please."

He was asking the world of me. He was asking me to risk everything. But he was right. He was the next one to lead us. He needed to come out of this with clean hands.

I hated that he was right.

"I'll do it," I said. "It's the last thing I'll do for you. It's the last thing I can do for you. You realize that, don't you?"

"I know what I'm asking, and I'm sorry I had to ask it. Thank you, Little Brother." He hugged me with the most sincerity he's shown me since the rift opened. "How do we pull this off?"

I created a portal to our backyard. "You're pale. Go through the back door. Eat something before you see anyone, else they'll know you were somehow involved. If anyone asks, say that Riders attacked, and I fought them off."

"Aren't you coming with me?" His face was a mix of panic and confusion, and his voice… I'd never seen him so boyish, even as a child.

Tears warmed my face. I wanted to hug him. I wanted to fight him. I wanted to never see him again. My big, stupid brother didn't get it. To everyone else, I would be a murderer. There would be no place for me in the light of day. From then on, mine would be a life lived in the shadows. For the fourth time that day, I apologized. "No, Jormon." I pushed him through the portal and closed it quickly. There was no time for final goodbyes.

The drones drifted down, finding their way through the higher branches.

My thoughts shifted to Homicidal Hutto, and I wondered if he actually killed his father. It didn't matter, I supposed. If enough people think you killed somebody, it's almost the same as actually doing it.

I opened another portal, and a salty breeze from somewhere over the Atlantic Ocean whipped through. Using more energy, I ripped up the ground and hurled every bloody rock and root and blade of grass into the ocean. The drones hummed ever louder as they closed in on me.

As I spun around to make sure I'd gotten everything, Alexander sat up and coughed until he vomited. Something else I'd have to clean up.

"Hey," he coughed. "I'm sorry—Where's my dad? Where is everyone?"

It was unexpected but welcomed. I could use him to sell the story. "I'm sorry, Alexander. I lost control. Your dad…he's gone, and it's my fault."

He shook his head so vigorously it looked like it would snap off. "It wasn't you, it was the other one. He was standing right there, and blue light swelled up in him. I remember that much."

"That was me, Alexander. I was upset and I couldn't control myself." I didn't have time for this conversation. A few more seconds and the drones would be right on me.

"Naw," he stood slowly and stumbled until he reached a tree to lean against. "He had on a different coat. It was the other one."

No one would know what jackets we wore today, but if the word spread that the light was blue and not the nocturnal purple signature to me, the lie would be over. They'd know it was Jormon, and that, we could not have.

With a thought, a shadow-lined portal widened, and the ocean stretched before us with more clarity. The salty breeze was strong, but the water was so still it could have been frozen. "Alexander, I wish you hadn't said that."

CHAPTER TWENTY-ONE
DIRK

PAIN BURNED THROUGH MY BODY, AND I WATCHED with blurred vision as a figure approached. It was sideways, walking on white, crunchy walls. No, I was sideways, not the figure. I was sprawled in the snow in front of a trailer. Was it mine? Where was Lheniva? Or Taavi? Or Phae? Where was Jormon?

The air grew dense with a coppery scent, and I rolled my head around, searching for the source.

Blood soaked through my jacket and pooled along my midsection. I was shot. Someone shot me. My heart pumped through my ribs and my breath came and went in shallow puffs. Someone shot me.

"What happened?" I recognized the voice as Tobin's. He was the figure now crouching on the wall—I meant ground. His hand waved over my body and a weight lifted from my chest. My jacket was gone, as was my shirt, and I watched helplessly as blood gushed from an unseen wound. "Where are my boys?" Tobin asked.

I tried to answer, but another voice cut in before I could form words. "Still in the woods. They're coming soon, I think."

Sean. I turned my head in search of him, then everything went dark.

"...much more that I can do. How long has he been like this?" It was a lady's voice. I opened my eyes and found they had moved me inside, but inside of where, I didn't know. A woman with short, yellowish hair leaned over me. Her breath smelled of chocolate and mint, and when she spoke, it made me think I was in a candy shop. It was quite disorienting. I opened my mouth to tell her to stop talking, then everything went dark.

I woke up in the same room, but it was empty this time. Moonlight shone through the lone window just above my bed, allowing me to take in my surroundings. A plain, wooden chair, an ornate coat rack with a caryatid on each of its four legs, a mahogany chiffonier holding up a tidied stack of books and a lamp with no lampshade, and at the foot of my bed, my mother. Her face, though half in shadow, wore deep lines I didn't remember, and the tendrils of her black hair seemed to have more streaks of gray. She'd put on weight since I last saw her, twenty pounds at least. It wasn't just her presence that startled me but the quiet intensity in her eyes. For a moment, time seemed to stop.

"Momma?" My voice wavered, betraying my unease. Six months has passed since I left home in the dead of night, leaving the fractured remains of our family behind. And yet, here she was. The room seemed to close in on me, as a weighty silence settled.

She shifted uncomfortably, clutching her purse tighter, her knuckles white. I could feel the unspoken questions, the tension hanging between us like an impenetrable fog.

"How...?" I began, my eyes darting around the room, searching for some hidden clue that could explain what this lady, this woman who had been so good and so bad to me, was doing here. Her gaze didn't waver, but the subtle tightening around her eyes told me this wasn't a joyous reunion.

"So, you don' came all the way to Georgia just to get yourself shot, huh?" She dug in her pocketbook. For a second, I thought she was going to pull out a gun and shoot me again. Instead, she pulled out her phone and began reading, putting on the fake proper accent she used when talking to bill collectors, "'Mrs. Wilkes, I don't wish to alarm you, but Dirk has been involved in an incident. So as not to cause panic, I will withhold the details of what happened, though I can thankfully share he is presently okay. As I've done before, I urge you to reach out—' I'mma skip that part. Da, da, da…da, da, da. Anyway—'If you will allow it, I will retrieve you from your home or other location of your choosing. I do hope you allow it.'" She tucked her phone back in her purse and clutched it near her stomach as though she were afraid I'd lunge at her and steal it.

"Who sent that?"

"That Tobin fella. He reached out to me shortly after you skipped town. I figured you'd be home directly, but he said he was fine wicha stayin' and all. Said you was set up nice in a trailer park, and boy, didn't that tickle me. You know we didn't raise you to live like that. After he said it, I figured it wouldn't take long for you to come to your senses, but you always was a stubborn one. You 'member that time I caught you in my makeup kit, and I told you, 'Boy, if you don't put down my 'spensive Chanel lipstick, I'm gon' make you wear it?' You 'member that? Just as stubborn as you wanted to be."

"Yeah, I remember," I said bitterly. "I didn't put it down fast enough, then you made me put it on and wear it to the grocery store."

"Ah, boy. Don't be like that. It was funny."

Not to me, it wasn't, and I didn't want to talk about it anymore. I had fresh wounds to worry about, there was no need to reopen old ones.

"Momma, why didn't you tell me I wasn't human?" I wanted the question to put her off balance. She was at fault here, and it was time she owned up to it. "You let me go my whole life thinking I was something I wasn't. Do you know what that feels like? To be lied to for so long?"

She slid a chair close to the bed, the legs scraping against the worn linoleum in a grating noise that drew a sharp breath from me. She brushed the back of her long skirt flush against her legs and let gravity pull her down, grunting as her butt hit the seat. A sudden rush of air carried the familiar aroma of her usual perfume, and for a second, just a second, I was disarmed. "My knees ain't what they used to be," she said. She looked up, her brown eyes searching mine, looking for something. Pity? Understanding? I couldn't quite tell. "Now look,' she began, her tone firming up, "whatever you think I did wrong don't justify you up and leaving my house without a word said. You know I was worried sick. Sick, I tell you. And hell, what was I supposed to say to you?"

"How about the truth?" I shot back, my voice full of frustration.

"Hey, don't be sassin' me. I am still yo momma. I'm the one who raised you. Me. Me and your daddy, not them."

"You're getting so mad when all you have to do is tell me the truth," I pressed, my voice more controlled but dripping with desperation.

"The truth ain't easy."

"I bet it's easier than holding a lie for seventeen years."

Her face went cold, then sad. In the silence, the room seemed to chill, as if it were our words alone warming the air. When I thought I couldn't take it anymore, she spoke. "It wasn't s'posed to happen the way it did. None of it was. Your sister joined the Army right out of high school. Nothing about fightin' or patriotism or nothing like that. She wanted to be a Chinese linguist is what she said, and I thought that was so silly. What she look like speaking Chinese? Anyhow, she graduated that May and shipped off to boot camp in June. That was the summer the sky opened up the first time. The Army had other plans for Novi, and she wasn't gon' be no Chinese linguist.

"The war kicked off soon after the aliens arrived. Aliens, Kaydans—you know what I mean. They were powerful, and we lost a lot of good folks. The Army cancelled Novi's orders to Fort

Rucker and assigned her to the Third Infantry Division in Hinesville, Georgia, just a few miles up the road from here, really. She didn't want to go. You know your sister; she doesn't have a violent bone in her body. But wasn't nothing she could do about it. No mo' Chinese. No mo' big plans. Just Novi and the war nobody saw coming. Anyhow, there she went, right on. Eighteen-year-old Novi, strapped with a rifle and a few grenades, off to fight the good fight. Your daddy was so proud. He never said a word, but it showed in his face any time somebody would ask about her.

"Kaydans attacked, we attacked back. They attacked, we attacked. It was a bloody cycle, at least that's how the news described it. Anyway, Novi called us one day. Said she'd made a big mistake. She told us she was clearing houses or something when she shot a woman on accident. As the woman laid there dying, the most beautiful boy with the reddest hair she'd ever seen came running from out the closet. He fell on top of the woman and hugged her as she laid there dying."

Momma paused long enough to wipe her nose on a tissue she fished out of her pocketbook.

"She couldn't leave you there. Everybody else in the house was dead. She was afraid to tell her platoon sergeant you were alive cause she thought he might kill you, or worse, ask her to do it. So she asked if we could do her the biggest favor she would ever ask of us. She told us where the house was—said she told you to stay put and someone would be there to help you. She didn't know if you understood what she was saying or if you even understood English at all, but you stayed. We hauled tail to get there—in Claxon, it was. Claxton, Georgia: the fruit cake capitol of the world, or so it used to be. Anyhow, when we found you the next day, you were still sitting there next to the dead woman. You didn't want to leave. We tried to drag you out, and you fought us, tooth and nail. See this scar on my forehead? Ooh, you had some kinda fight in you."

I pictured a little version of me draped over a woman's dead body while she slowly decayed. In my head, she was my mother. I was wearing a green and white shirt with blue jeans. She was wearing a sundress and had red hair like me. In the end, though, it was just a picture. I shook the thought before it became imprinted in my memory.

"How did you get me to go?"

"We didn't. We sat there with you. You were so precious. So helpless. There were bodies rotting in every room of that broken down house, and we knew we wasn't gonna leave you there. I woke up one morning, and you'd come and laid your head on my lap. That was that. It was like you'd decided you were ready. We left that same day, and you'd been with us ever since."

She looked like I felt: pained and exhausted. She'd probably been waiting a lifetime to get that off her chest. The dark secret of the church lady with the stolen kid.

"Does Novi know who the woman was, or anything about her? Did she ever say her name?"

"Honey, nobody knows. I'm so sorry it happened that way, but you have been such a blessing to us, praise the Lord."

I cringed. The Lord had nothing to do with the death and destruction serving as the backdrop to my life, and if He did, it was all the more reason for not wanting anything to do with Him.

"Did I ever show signs, you know, of being Kaydan?"

"All the time. Every time the weather turned, and lightning struck, your hair would stand up on end and your eyes would go from green to bright gold."

"That's why you never let me go to school during bad weather."

She nodded. "It stopped happening right 'round the time you turned 'leven. You probably don't remember it used to happen."

I didn't. I remember how Daddy kept the Weather Channel going all day. This explained why. "You remember finding me on the side of the road that Friday night? And I told you I'd done magic? Why didn't you tell me then? Instead, you made me feel crazy."

"I remember you was out drinking with your little friends, and they 'bandoned you in the woods."

"That's not what happened at all. Like I told you, I was riding my bike home from a football game that Friday evening. It was late and dark, and my bicycle light fizzed out. I was already on the dirt road by then, and I started thinking about snakes and how I wouldn't know if a rattlesnake or something was right in front of me. I panicked. Suddenly—lightning fast, I mean—these glowing dots poured out of my chest and hovered above me, shining my way down the lane. I fainted, right there on the spot. I was scared, Momma. I didn't know what to do."

"I remember finding you. I could swear you'd been out drinking. It didn't make any sense that you'd be in a ditch for no reason."

"Yeah, I remember you laying into me when we got home. I also remember you saw these." I pulled up my sleeves. "They weren't this long that night, but I know you saw them. The way you looked at me and left the room. It reminded me of when Kirk stayed the night."

"It wasn't like that, Dirk. 'Sides, I just spent the past hour 'pologizing for my past. Let's just let it be and go home. Novi and your daddy back there worried 'bout sick to death."

"Momma, this is my home now. I'm not going back to Alabama."

"After I don' came all this way, I bet you are. You were just shot. It's too dangerous here."

"It's dangerous for my people everywhere."

"I'm your people, now don't go getting brand new on me."

"I'm not going back. I don't belong there, especially now. You will always be my momma, but these people here in Gray Flats are my family."

She shook her head violently, her resolve and determination evident in her every movement. "All they're saying on the news is war, war, war, and I don't blame them. This Prince Noan fella killed that poor family in cold blood, and ain't nobody heard from him since. Is that who you're calling family now?"

"If you're talking about Alexander, I think he's the one who shot me."

"The news ain't saying nothing about that. What they say is a dad and his son were out hunting, and no one has seen them since. Even if this boy is the fella who shot you, the law is still the law, murder is still murder, last I checked, and people have the right to due process."

I blinked back tears, feeling the raw sting of both my wound and her words. "You traveled miles to see me, yet you're so far from understanding who I've become. It's like you still hear my words but don't truly listen. I'm lying up with a hole in my gut and you're siding with everyone but me. For my own healing, Momma, I need space. You should go."

"I came all this way, Dirk. I'm not leaving without you. I didn't do it then, and I won't do it now."

"Things are different now. Everything has changed, including me. And if there's a war brewing, I don't think we're on the same side."

Her voice quavered, and it broke my heart. "Abraham Isiah Wilks, don't you say stuff like that," she said, using my full real name. "I'm always on your side."

"You think you are, Momma, but you're not. If you don't understand what I'm saying, I can't explain it to you."

"I don't believe you mean that. I believe we can work through all of this mess. Come home with me and we can talk it over at the house."

Closing my eyes against the rush of emotions, I whispered, "Just go, Momma. Please. Just go."

CHAPTER TWENTY-TWO
JORMON

"GOOD MORNING TO ALL YOU VIEWERS OUT THERE, and welcome back to Morning Tea. Today in Hot Sips, we continue our conversation about the missing teen and his father, who both disappeared while hiking through Gordonia Park two days before Christmas. The prime suspect: the Kaydan king's very own son, Noan Ladoan. I'd call him a prince, but in a New Year's Eve interview, his father stripped him of his title and offered Kaydan support in the search for this rogue fugitive. But it's been more than a month, Todd, and authorities have no leads. How is that possible?"

The blond host contorted her face to show mock concern, but the question was as loaded as the rifle Alexander used to blow a hole in Dirk's gut. Her co-host, Todd Evans, played his role with equal talent. "Isn't it obvious? They're hiding him in Gray Flats. The Toombs Country Sheriff's Office is being blocked at every attempt to search the home of the prime suspect in a possible double homicide investigation. They've even gone so far as to put up a magical barrier to stop humans from entering the trailer park. Last I checked, that was illegal. They are still on American soil, are they not? If they don't want to follow our rules, they should just go back where they came from."

"That's total bullshit," Taavi said. "The barrier is there to stop them from burning the place to the ground. The common room was empty, save for Rughor, Taavi, Phae, Dirk, and me, but Taavi shouted like he was addressing all of Gray Flats.

"But let's go back to the missing teen and his father, both wholesome members of the community…"

I grew sick of listening to sob stories about the Darleys. They had what was coming to them, even if it was all one giant fuck up on everybody's part. Yes, I'd lost it. Yes, they'd done wrong. But the heart of it: Noan. He just had to go for that damn walk. He couldn't stand to see Dirk and me content, so he dragged us into a situation that spiraled beyond our control. Now look at him. Look at all of us.

Todd and Jennifer droned on while pictures flashed across the screen. Alexander as freshman posing in his clean baseball uniform. Alexander as a senior wearing his red, white and blue letterman jacket. Alexander and his dad holding up a string of white perch after a fishing trip.

"Turn it off," I said, my voice quiet, yet commanding.

"They're about to talk about the Presidential Inauguration later today. Shouldn't we—"

"I said turn it off." My voice came out as a growl.

"Jormon, I think—"

"*Baadu!*" The room seemed to vibrate with my fury as the flatscreen hurtled across the room, shattering against the wall. My voice, cold and sharp, sliced through the silence, "It's Prince Jormon. Commit that to memory, Taavi. All of you." My eyes landed on Dirk, whose face held a blend of fear and disbelief.

"Of course, Your Highness," Rughor said, almost eagerly.

"The King and I are leading the search for Noan. Rughor, I want you to join me."

"I can come too," said Dirk in a feeble attempt to recover from his shock.

"No. Stay here and clean up this mess. I'm sure one of you knows a *sahdr* to fix a broken TV."

Winter storms had already crippled most of Georgia and South Carolina, and the cold was racing up the eastern coast like an arctic storm. The forecast called for freezing rain all day, but the Presidential Inauguration wouldn't be postponed for any reason. Neither would our search for Noan. I recalled Uncle Tobin's words: We must punish our own so that humans don't have to. Even if that was morally correct, Noan was innocent. Mostly, I mean. He did kill the Darley boy, but the asshole had it coming.

I flew abreast with Dad over the dull acreage of the Okefenokee Swamp, zigzagging like a flock of birds that couldn't decide where to go for winter. Rughor and a few others followed far behind to catch anything we may have missed. It had been hours, and no one spotted a thing.

My cheeks burned from the cold, and the hair that fell loose from my cap froze against my ears, which were numb and probably as red as a *Heemrah*. The wind picked up, forcing us down until we were flying so low the treetops scraped my baggy coat as we passed. We came upon a campsite, and Dad took it as a chance to group and re-strategize.

"He was supposed to be here. The Spirit Matron said she felt his soul in this swamp," Dad said.

"Somebody was here," Rughor added, picking up a warm ember and rubbing it between his fingers. "Maybe he knew we were coming and took off."

"Jormon?" It was an accusation as much as it was a question.

"Dad, I would never undermine you. Even for my brother." I couldn't tell if I was telling the truth or lying through my teeth.

"What do you see?" he asked.

I dug through the past, a talent I'd always possessed and the one *sahdr* I could perform better than Noan, and suddenly, it was like I was watching a movie. Noan sat by a fire reading a book. He looks up at the sky, then shifts his gaze and looks me right in my eyes. I don't know how, but it's like he sees me scanning the memory. Then he disappears.

"He was here. I don't know where he is now, but he was here less than an hour ago."

Dad's face darkened with resolve. "When I find him, I'm going to kill him. Nevermind serving him up to the President, I'm going to kill him myself. You're all free to leave. We'll resume the search tomorrow. Jormon, stay behind with me, will you?" It wasn't a question.

The others left without much ceremony, leaving an oppressive silence in their wake.

Noan, where are you? It doesn't have to be this way. It was a dumb thing to say. He would know as well as I did I had no power to stop what would happen to him if he showed up. I was glad he kept evading us, especially if it meant my brother would still be alive.

Dad extended his arms to the side, and the world went white. My nose flooded with scents of burnt wood and fishy water, but I couldn't see anything. The white nothingness rippled, and there on the log sat a shadowy figure. Its form flickered in and out like a beat up TV losing its antenna signal, but it was clearly Noan.

"He's here," Dad said. "He's hidden in the shadows, but he's here. We can say what we want about Noan, but no one can deny he's clever."

"Can we get him?" Please say no. I made efforts to still my pounding heart, afraid of what would happen if we actually caught him.

"We can't reach him where he's at. But he can't stay there forever."

The world snapped back into color. In the short time we were in Dad's blinding light, snow had begun to fall again.

"What do we do now? Do we wait here?"

"There's no point in it. He can move in the shadow plane and exit from anywhere, and we'll never see him. Besides, I have to get back to D.C. for the inauguration. It's a big day and I don't want to be late.

"Dad, don't you think it might be too dangerous? If what Noan said about the Riders is true, if they really can disarm us, you'd be defenseless if something happened."

"As Head of State for our people, I don't have much of a choice, do I?"

"You can send Uncle Tobin as your representative?"

"It saddens me to say it, but I no longer have confidence in your uncle. I haven't for a while now."

"What did he do? If this is about Noan and the shooting, that wasn't Uncle Tobin's fault."

"It's something he did a long time ago. I've pushed it out of mind over the years because we had to work together for a shared future. Now, I don't think we share the same vision of the future that we used to."

"You've said that much, but that's the same as not saying anything at all. What did he do?"

"Are you sure you want to know? Once I say this, there's no going back."

"I'm eighteen now. I can handle it."

Dad took a seat on the overturned log, right beside where Noan's shadow was. He held out his hand, and the fire roared to life.

"We were never supposed to be here, you and I."

"You told me that already. Tobin was supposed to take Noan and leave, but he messed up and dragged the rest of us here." I was shocked at first when Dad confided in me, but I never let the truth slip.

"The story we told everyone wasn't the full truth. Sit with me a moment." He brushed the thin coating of snow off the log right beside him. It was the exact spot where Noan existed in the shadow plane. It felt odd to sit there, to overlay my physical presence where I knew his shadow to be. Dad caught my hesitation, and he patted the spot ever so gently. I sat, and he continued.

"When Noan was born, your mother insisted he live, despite Maerin's history with shadow children and the laws that were established way before my time to prevent such evil from thriving. We made a compromise for the sake of our family: you would be raised as our only son and heir to the crown, and Tobin would raise Noan as the illegitimate child of a whore, or something like that. The problem was your mother. She couldn't part with him. Instead of letting them live far away from the castle, she insisted they stay close. And it worked, for a while.

"When King Ahthril of Draelin discovered Noan's existence and spread the word as far as he could, it shook my kingdom. The only way to keep our people from fighting each other and from turning against the family was to do to Noan what had been done to every shadow child since King Leander."

"You were going to kill Noan."

"I was. I really was. It would've broken your mother's heart, but it would have repaired what was broken in the kingdom. But your uncle wouldn't let it happen. He ran off with Noan, and we had no choice but to hunt them down. I led the party that found them. I'd been on the hunt for days when we received a tip on their whereabouts. Imagine my surprise when I showed up to blast down the door of some little hut and your mother answered. She was so defiant, so determined to have her way."

"What happened to her?" I could feel my heart quickening, each beat like the echo of a drum in a hollow room.

"My men took her back to the castle to wait for my return. Everything that happened next happened in a flash. I entered the house. You were sitting on Nana Lura's lap, and Noan was picking up an artifact. You know the rest."

I did. We were all sucked into the rift, and everyone lived happily ever after. What I didn't know was that it genuinely was Noan's fault. Not because he was a shadow child but because he meddled with things he had no business touching.

This was never meant to be my life. Knowing that I was taken from him, that my mother and uncle planned to steal me away from my life, was a punch in the gut. Dad and I could still be in Kayda where we wouldn't be hunted. Where we'd have rights. I was here by accident because my mother couldn't do the right thing. This was her fault as much as it was Uncle Tobin's, and now only *Heemrah* knows where she is, if she's even still alive. Why would they do that to the family?

"That's not the end of your mother's story. The rest of it--the full truth about what happened to her—is why we stayed on Earth."

Everything in that moment felt suspended. Even the snow itself seemed to stop falling. Dad was about to unearth a long-buried secret. He was going to trust me with it. A mixture of anticipation and apprehension welled up inside me, tying my stomach in knots. Taking a deep, shuddering breath, I braced myself, ready to face whatever truth was about to unravel before me.

"Dad, I still don't think you should go to the inauguration."

We were back in the parlor, warming up from the hunt. Uncle Tobin came in to greet us, and my body tensed up. I consciously relaxed my fists and let my shoulders fall back into place. He was still my uncle. What I just learned shouldn't change anything. We were all in this together.

"Your son is wise, Rosh. You should listen to him."

Dad responded without the least bit of anger, "I'll be careful, Tobin. You worry too much."

I realized in that moment how practiced Dad was at concealing his feelings from everyone else. It's a lesson I hoped to learn someday.

"Scouts report that the Church of the First People—the one led by Pastor Lumley—has been busy for days. Even on Saturdays."

"A packed church worries you? Tobin, we've faced worse than the Riders. Besides, Hargi will patrol the crowd along with my usual security detail." Dad looked down at his watch. "I should get a move on. Tobin, would you see me out?"

When Uncle Tobin returned, he asked about the search for Noan. Suddenly, I was seeing him through different eyes. He'd never cared for me. To him, it was all about Noan. I didn't want to be alone with him. I answered his questions and excused myself to go to Lheniva's. When I arrived, the common area was already filled with people watching the media coverage of the inauguration. Dirk and Phae sat in the front next to Rughor and Calinea. As I approached, an elderly gentleman next to them relinquished his seat.

"What did I miss?" I asked.

Dirk began speaking, but Rughor cut in, "It's almost noon. The President is about to take the oath of office. King Rosh took his seat a couple of minutes ago. You can see him there, just off to the other side of the Second Lady."

"The new Second Lady?" Dirk asked, searching the screen.

"The Vice President's wife. Idiot," Rughor said.

I wanted to say something in Dirk's defense, but I couldn't bring myself to challenge Rughor, at least not in front of everyone. I needed to keep him on my side. He hadn't been through everything the Cohort had. He also didn't care much for Noan, which meant I didn't have to try so hard to convince him I was the good twin.

I patted Dirk's thigh. I'd reassure him later.

Noon came and went, and President-elect Blackwell still hadn't arrived. On one side of the television screen, they rotated live footage of the famous and influential attendees, and on the other side, the anchor reviewed what she'd heard about the President's upcoming address.

"I have a bad feeling about this," I said.

"King Rosh knows what he's doing," Dirk said, but it wasn't reassuring.

"Noan, where are you? Can you hear me?" If there was one thing that would reassure me, it would be having my brother near me.

The Chief Justice swore in the Vice President, and a B-list musician sang a cover of some patriotic song. The camera switched focus from the singer to Dad, then back again, and I noticed Hargi wasn't anywhere in the frame.

At about twelve-thirty, the President arrived, and everyone stood in ovation. Even Dad. Some representative introduced the President, and he was sworn in. He was now in charge.

Sleet pelted the window as the wind picked up outside, and it hit me that the weather was nice in D.C., despite the forecast. Dad must have arranged for someone to manipulate the atmosphere, maybe as a subtle offering to the new President.

"Are they ever going to stop clapping?" Phae asked. "It's been going on for nearly ten minutes."

"People really wanted this person in office," Dirk said. "I'm just waiting on the speech to start and the Rider hoods to come out."

"Don't say that," I said. "I know you mean it as a joke, but something doesn't feel right. Where are the drones? Look at the sky behind the President? There's security all around, but there aren't any drones flying. If you wanted to spot a threat, wouldn't you want drones."

"Unless you don't want a recording of an attack," Phae said. "Without evidence, there's no one to hold accountable."

"This assumes King Rosh is the target. If Riders wanted him dead, they would do it somewhere less public than an inauguration."

Noan, I really mean it. I need you.

"Maybe it's because of the weather," Calinea said. "If they thought there would be too much wind to fly in, they wouldn't have scheduled them."

"That's not it. They had to know the area around the Capitol Building would be climate controlled," Rughor said. The pit in my stomach plunged deeper. "Can we do anything about it?"

"We can try to warn him, but it would have to be from a distance. If the secret service sees a bunch of Kaydans approaching, they'd assumed we were a threat."

"I can go," Phae said. "I can stand on a rooftop and send a message on the wind. I do it all the time when the Spirit Matron and I are separated on our walks."

"We need something more reliable than witch magic," Rughor said.

"First off, don't call me a witch; and second, the magic I use can't be blocked."

"You don't know that," Rughor said dismissively.

Phae narrowed her eyes at him. "Except I do, smart ass. *Suhrat* draw magic from nature *and* the spirit plane. Our stuff can't be tampered with by some weak ass power blockers."

"But you don't know that for sure," Rughor said. "And I'm not risking having you come only to be a liability."

"Don't stand there and tell me what I do and don't know about my own magic. The Spirit Matron and I have tested this—" she stopped abruptly. "You know what: I don't have to explain myself to you. I'm going with you guys, and I know I can help." She flipped her braid over her shoulder and strode past Rughor without waiting for an answer.

"Dirk, did you ever learn that scry thing Noan tried to teach us?" I asked.

"Yeah, but I'm not good at it. Sorry."

"Sorry is right," Rughor said. "What good is your power if you can't even use it."

"Kiss my ass, Rughor."

"You'd like that, wouldn't you?"

"Both of you, knock it off," I said. The last thing I wanted now was for my new friend and my boyfriend—if I could call him that— to come to blows. "We need to focus on King Rosh. Has anyone been to D.C. and knows of a building we can portal to?"

"I've been there several times with my father," Rughor said. "The buildings in D.C. aren't that tall."

"Okay. What's tall enough?"

"The Washington Monument," Calinea suggested. "You can get there without being spotted, but they'll have security inside the observation deck, I assume."

"Phae and I can go. The fewer we are, the better chance we have of not being seen."

"Your Highness, I'm not letting you go alone," Rughor said. "The three of us can go." Dirk looked like he wanted to say something, but he shrank back instead.

"Fine, but we need to go now. The President is about to start speaking."

I ran out so fast I forgot my coat. Dirk brought it out to me before I stepped off the porch.

"Jormon, please be careful. If it's as dangerous as you think it is—"

"I'll be careful. Hey, don't take what Rughor says to heart. He wants to get closer to me. Can you blame him?" I flexed a muscle. Dirk smiled and pushed it away.

"As long as he doesn't try to get too close. Can I get a kiss before you go?"

"And when I come back." Our lips touched, and it warmed me from the inside out.

"Your Highness, we should go."

It took everything I had not to run back into Dirk's arms again.

"I'll portal us up to the very tip of the Washington Monument," I said, frantically waving my hands as the portal opened. "We'll be over 600 feet in the air at the pyramidion."

"So, we're flying through," said Rughor. "Got it."

I nodded. The vantage point will give us a clear view of the Capitol Building while keeping us out of sight from the ground…mostly."

Rughor was the first one through, followed by Phae. They fell out of view before levitating back up to the sloped tip of the Monument. I looked back once more at Dirk before jumping headfirst and letting the portal whoosh shut behind me.

I quickly took account of my surroundings. Loud cheers reached up from the other side of the Monument, but the National Mall was empty where we hovered.

"Phae, be quick about it. Let him know to be vigilant. Tell him about the lack of drones." Even though we were inches apart, I had to shout to be heard over the zealous crowd.

She whispered into the stillness of the day, and the air swirled around her, echoing her soft words. She whispered faster, and the voices swirled and flowed until her whisper became a melody, and the melody drifted out of earshot. Suddenly, she stopped.

"Did he get it?"

"I don't know," she shouted.

"Did he say anything back?" I asked.

She shook her head. "I kept the channel open long enough for him to say something, even in a whisper."

"I told you her dollar store magic wouldn't work," Rughor said.

"It's working, idiot!" Phae said.

"Maybe he can't," I said, my voice barely a whisper.

"Huh?"

"Maybe he heard you, but he can't respond," I shouted.

"This isn't good, Your Highness. If the manipulation for the atmosphere holds but the message from within is being blocked, it means something near the king is blocking it."

"They're blocking his powers. He probably doesn't know it. We need to get to him."

Noan, if you can hear me. I'm sorry. For everything. Just help me.

"I agree, Your Highness. What's the plan?"

"We can't get close to him. We'll have to do something big from over here. Something that will disrupt the President. Something—"

Screaming. Everyone screaming. Collective screams ripping through the air. I peeked around the tip of the monument. The crowd running away from the President's platform like it was on fire.

"I don't know what's happening, but we have to get to Dad."

Without thinking, I flew in a rush. The crowd below was a scattering of color that bled from the green grass and white chairs onto the sidewalks and away from whatever I was heading into.

I fell.

My powers were being blocked, and I couldn't fly anymore. The ground rushed up at me. From this height, I would surely die. The line of white chairs came into focus as I fell faster and faster. I had to warn the others.

I spun around. Phae was still in the air but was falling fast like me. I led them into this, and now we would all die. Wind whipped past my ears, drowning out the shouting mass I was falling towards. I flailed my arms trying to right myself, but there was no right way to fall and survive this. I had failed. In my rush to be a hero, I had failed them all, now good people were going to die.

Above me, Phae rushed down and grabbed Rughor's arm. With her other hand, she shot a beam of green light at me. It passed through me and struck the row of white plastic chairs positioned on the lawn. Vines shot up though the grass and caught me, carrying me slowly to the ground.

I didn't have time to thank her. I needed to get to my dad.

I sprinted as fast as I could, jumping over felled chairs and the bodies of people too scared to run away. I ran until my lungs burned through my throat, until my legs threatened to quit on me.

The President's podium was cleared. All the leaders and famous guests were gone. The only one that remained was my father. His body slumped backwards in his chair.

"Dad!" I yelled, but he was beyond hearing me.

I ran faster.

ANDRE L. BRADLEY

The clear blue skies over D.C. suddenly darkened as the *sahdr* granting the Inauguration its nice weather was disrupted. Ominous black clouds rolled in, releasing torrential freezing rain. The smell hit me first. The metallic scent of blood permeated the air as hard raindrops splashed my dad's blood across the concrete platform.

I grabbed my father's head and my fingers squished through the massive hole in the back of his head. His mouth hung open, his eyes rested lifelessly. The king was dead.

CHAPTER TWENTY-THREE
NOAN

I SPRINTED AS FAST AS I COULD TOWARD MY FATHER'S slumped body. He couldn't be dead. There's no way my father, this man who had been such a constant fixture in my life, could be gone, felled by something as simple as a bullet. This was the same man who once commanded an entire kingdom, whose number one job was to protect our people. It couldn't end like this. It just couldn't. Where were his guards? Where were any of our people?

I fought against the pounding rain, cursing the throngs of panicked people as I pushed past them. The blockers must've moved out of range, because my powers returned to me in a tidal wave that crashed into me and dropped me to my knees. It warmed me from the freezing rain. It fed my hunger to get to my brother and father.

Voices blurred together into a cacophony of chaos, screams and cries mixing with the pounding rain. I jostled and shoved, fighting through the crowd of panicking spectators. A heavyset guy wearing Glory Gear fell into me and sent me flying toward the ground. I maneuvered quickly, twisting my body and jetting upward in flight before he landed on me with his full weight.

"Jormon!" I shouted, but the rain and commotion drowned out my voice. My heart raced faster as I flew over the crowd. The distance between us felt like miles, even though they were only meters away. Phae and Rughor stood a few feet behind Jormon, all shrouded in a cloud of sadness and disbelief as hordes of humans sprinted in every direction, running from a shooter who had already hit its only intended target.

When I finally reached the platform, I stumbled, slipping in the wetness, my own tears mixing with the rain. I came to kneel beside Jormon, placing a trembling hand on his shoulder.

"We have to move," I said, fighting the lump in my throat. "It's not safe." The sight of my dead father filled me with fantastic terrors. His fallibility revealed in the most indecorous way. The hole in his head from which his blood flowed like a river haunted me then and would probably haunt me for the rest of my life. In this darkest hour, Nana Lura's words from long ago came to me: surrender to the Celestial Sovereigns, *Heemrah* and *Zereq*, and they shall wipe your slate clean. I remained frozen for whoever knows how long, looking into my father's empty eyes. The screams and freezing rain receded to the furthest parts of my consciousness, and it was only me and Dad. Daddy. Father. This man who was so familiar to me, but who was also the most enigmatic person I knew.

Jormon shook my hand off his shoulder, pulling me out of my trance. His anguished eyes met mine, and in that moment, amidst all the chaos, something transformed in him. His eyes went dark, clouded by a deep blue light. "Where were you? I reached out to you for help, and you ignored me! How dare you show up now when it's too late?"

His words shook me. Was he blaming me for this? "You sent me into hiding and expected me to come running to you when you call? You can't have it both ways." I wouldn't say more, with Rughor and Phae present.

Jormon balled his fist and swung it toward my jaw. I saw it coming, and I caught his fist in my hand. His eyes narrowed, and the deep blue light flashed bright as he pooled his power to blast me. "*Dura*," I yelled, and a shield of energy surrounded me, protecting me from his blast. The distant sounds of sirens grew louder as emergency vehicles approached, but Jormon didn't relent. He rushed toward me ready to do whoever knows what when a pale green light slammed to the ground between us. Suddenly, I couldn't hear his shouts, or hear his pounding at the glowing wall of light. I looked over, and Phae was moving her hands in a way that looked like she was weaving the air.

On the other side of the wall, Rughor grabbed Jormon's arms and shouted something. Jormon snatched away, and Rughor pointed in the direction of the Washington Monument. Red and blue lights sped toward us, still, Jormon turned his back to Rughor, mouthed something inaudible to me, and a steam of fire rushed at my face. Phae's protective enchantment held.

"He can't be reasoned with," Phae said. "If you want him to leave, to get to safety, you must leave first."

"I need him to know I'm here for him!" I shouted. We'd both just lost a father. We needed to be comforting one another, not fighting.

"Give him time to cool off."

I nodded, all the while staring at my brother, who was so filled with rage.

"Go!"

I nodded again.

I opened a portal and stepped through it. Phae dropped her shield. The last thing I saw before my portal closed was the bright red glow of a fireball aimed at my head.

PART FOUR

TO FIND ONE'S BEGINNING

CHAPTER TWENTY-FOUR
DIRK

THE MORNING SUN CUT THROUGH THE TREES AND melted the snow, lending the morning an unspeakable serenity. Water beat down on frozen leaves in unrhythmic plunking, and gurgled together in the flow of dirty water that fed the roots and the grass during winter as the smell of chilled pine announced itself with every breeze. It all reminded me of being in a candle store. Even the view favored the woodland picture stuck to the side of the jar.

When Grandma Re died, we held the funeral at the family church, a different church from the one my parents attended. The sobbing was loud, and the music was somber, and the church smelled like the food brought over and stored in the back for after the ceremony. That was a funeral. This pine-scented escape, I didn't know what this was.

Besides the watery band, it was quiet. The Spirit Matron stood with her back to us. She moved her arms this way and that, as though she were conducting an unseen orchestra. The silver trimming on her white gown ebbed and flowed like the ocean with each movement. King Rosh's body hovered in front of her, captured in a glowing aura that matched the white of his death robes.

"Is anyone else coming?" Jormon asked. Of the thousands of Kaydans still remaining on Earth, fewer than a hundred were gathered, deep in the woods where the trees were thickest.

"People are afraid to leave their homes," Tobin said. "Some think the funeral might be the target of a secondary attack. This is it. This is all of us."

Jormon didn't care about the rest of them coming, I knew. His thoughts were elsewhere, far deep in the shadows, thinking about, hoping for, above all else, Noan's arrival at their dad's funeral. Despite their last encounter, Noan still held a big place in his heart. I had to believe that was true, because if it wasn't, if Jormon could dismiss family so easily, what chance did I stand?

Shadows filled the hollows beneath Jormon's eyes, the lone marks of bereavement on an otherwise beautiful face. He licked his pale red lips, waited a moment, and said, "Let the Spirit Matron know she can proceed."

Phae approached the Spirit Matron at a crawling pace. She gripped in both hands a silver whip covered in thorns. It wrapped around her bare arms, but the care she took with each deliberate step saved her from being scratched. The Spirit Matron chanted a song, and Phae sang the lines back to her. I thought back on the deacon in my old church and how he'd use his deep baritone voice to move the congregation in devotion. *Jesus knows our every weakness; take it to the lord in prayer.*

As they chanted and sang, they wrapped the whip around King Rosh's body so delicately. When they were done, they took a step back and clasped hands, finding a new melody. Upon the first note, two apertures on the handle filled with an endless darkness as the whip came to life, clenching the King's body. Squeezing it. Breaking it. And all the while, it sang the most beautiful song I'd ever heard.

Jormon's hand found mine, and he looked on as the whip changed from silver to teal as it filled with the king's energy, then with the king himself. Barely audible under the complex melodies, the crunching of bones and tearing of skin played out, until the king was gone. It was gruesome; it was beautiful, and it was done.

The whip's slender form continued to shift. It twisted and curled until the thorns became feet and wings and scales. When it was done, it resembled the dragon Bamuut, Jormon's favorite.

The dragon puffed its metallic chest and blew colorful flames at the Spirit Matron. The fire burned her gown, but her skin, unfazed by the flames, glowed with the king's energy.

When the dragon was done, it collapsed back into its original form. Phae dressed the Spirit Matron in a plain, white frock, and the service was over.

"That was beautiful," I told Phae.

"Thanks. It's not complete, though. Now the Spirit Matron has to deliver the king to the Lake of Spirits."

"I've never heard of that. Is that where all spirits go?"

"That's where all spirits *should* go. In a proper ceremony like this one, it's easy enough to collect the spirit and deliver it. Otherwise, you have to call the spirit to you, which takes a lot of work. That's one of the things I've been training to do under the Spirit Matron."

A chill ran through me at the unnerving thought of spirits floating around aimlessly, and I wondered what my momma would say to that.

"You've been calling the spirits of Kaydans who died in the war?"

"You're curious about your mother, aren't you?"

"I am. Have you seen her? Her spirit, I mean. Ever since my momma—my other momma—told me about my birth mom, I've been curious. I have this weird image of a woman without a face, and it leaves me unsettled."

"I'm sorry, Dirk. I wouldn't know if I had or not. We've called hundreds of spirits. If one of them belonged to your mother, I wouldn't know it from anyone else."

"Is there a way I can check?"

"Maybe. You'd have to go to the Lake of Spirits. If your mother's spirit is there and she recognizes you, she might come to you."

Lake of Spirits? My mind shifted back to the lake in Gordonia Park and the dead girl who washed up the last time I was there. I blinked away the image, and it was replaced by another, one with a faceless corpse lying where the little girl lay. I blinked that one away, too.

"You okay?" Phae placed a hand on my shoulder. Her face flooded with confusion and concern.

"Huh? Yeah, I'm good."

The woods were especially cold at night, and I regretted not bringing a thicker jacket. The frigid air pierced my skin, and every inhale was like swallowing shards of ice. I shivered, then, afraid of making any unnecessary noise, I willed myself to stop. I assumed my mission wouldn't take that long, but Sean was late. If he got caught, or worse, if someone followed him, I'd have to fight my way out of something bad. I hoped that wasn't the case.

As minutes turned to hours, I began to pace, each footstep making a muted crunch against the frost-touched ground, my breath forming small clouds of vapor. The gnarled trees cast eerie shadows in the glow of the rift, their bare branches trembling slightly in the breeze, and I thought of Sean and whether he was safe. When he finally emerged from the shadowy depths over an hour later, his cheeks rosy from the cold, the relief was palpable. "Sorry, I had to wait until everybody was asleep." He hugged me. "Your hair has grown. I like it."

I dared a laugh, eying his tousled locks. "Yours, too. You look so handsome."

He ran his fingers through it casually. "How's everyone?"

"Everyone is scared, as you can imagine."

"King Rosh's death changed everything. Sorry to hear about that."

"It's President Blackwell who changed everything. Any word on who was behind it? Don't look at me like that, Sean. Your dad or brother hasn't said anything?"

He shook his head. "I'm out of the loop. I swear. Any word on Noan?"

It was my turn to be clueless. "None."

"The Rider's won't stop looking for him."

"Can you believe they blamed the killing of the king as an assassination attempt gone wrong? That the bullet missed it's intended target: the President? What a load of crap."

"You're preaching to the choir."

"I know, sorry. I'm just frustrated. All of these executive orders rolled out and they are really hurting us. We are running out of food, but we can't go to stores. The city cut off our water and our electricity. It's inhumane."

"It's all provocation. Don't do anything stupid."

"It's not my call. I'm subject to Kaydan leadership like everyone else in Gray Flats."

"Are you and Jormon still a thing?"

"Yes. I think so. We'll see what happens after his coronation." No sooner had I said it, a flurry of doubts consumed me. Becoming king wasn't just about wearing a crown. Jormon would be watched, every decision and choice under the microscope. And where would that leave me, the stray without any legacy or place, suddenly thrust into the glaring spotlight of royalty. How could I ever belong there? And in the midst of it all, the stark reality was that we were all just trying to survive. Our love—if it was a shared love—felt like a delicate bloom in a raging storm.

"Wow. To be a king at such a young age," Sean said, brining me back to the present.

"We grow up fast. We have to. Anyway, you said you wanted to see me."

"Right." He dug in his pocket and handed me a folded note. "It's a list of Kaydan-friendly folk in the area. If you're ever out and need a place to hide, go to one of them. If you guys need food, ask one of them. So far, it's not against the law to help you guys."

"Yeah, so far. If it ever gets that far, promise you'll do the right thing and protect yourself."

He shook his head. "Yeah, I'll do the right thing, Dirk. You can count on that."

CHAPTER TWENTY-FIVE
JORMON

I SAT BESIDE UNCLE TOBIN. ISSEK SAT DIRECTLY across from us, Hargi beside him, and Drac, the only other person I readily recognized, was at the head of the table. Everyone else at the table I had met before, multiple times even, but I couldn't recall their names. I blamed it on grief, but really, I was never good with names. Dad always upbraided me for it, and it was only then that I understood the importance of what he was trying to teach me. These were my people, and by not knowing who they were, it was as if I didn't know who we were.

There were no pleasantries exchanged, and everyone handled the discomforting silence in their own way. Issek curled and uncurled his fingers in front of himself like he was testing his grip. The woman to his left leaned her head from side to side occasionally, and the man to her left grabbed at his elbow and massaged it momentarily before switching to the next. I was continuing around the table when Drac suddenly spoke out.

"Good evening, everyone, and thank you for your attendance in the emergency conclave. We have decisions to make, so let me begin by outlining the facts. More than four months ago, a tunnel to Kayda emerged and has lingered over us in an inexplicably dormant state. As far as anyone knows, nothing has come out nor gone in, despite no lack of trying for the latter. Governments around the world want to know what is happening and what to expect. They are getting restless, as are their people.

"We don't know what caused the reopening, though speculation follows two paths. The first is that the Americans have found a way to tunnel into Kayda. We know they've been trying to harness our powers ever since we landed. It's possible they have found the missing *miftah* or created one of their own."

Miftah. The artifact I accidentally uncovered in the lake.

"If they possessed a *miftah*, they would be able to enter the portal," Uncle Tobin said. "In fact, it would be the only way to enter. I will comfortably posit that the reason they have not entered is because they don't have one."

"The alternative, as frightening as it may be, is that the portal was initiated from the other side, and we do not know by whom," continued Drac, but I was still hung up on how the portal could open without a *miftah* to begin with. Noan would know.

"If it's more refugees, then it would add to our numbers here. We'd have a stronger fight for equality," said the lady who tilted her neck, pulling me from my thoughts.

"Fight is right," Issek said. "Any additional Kaydans that come falling from that crack will be seen as hostile. The humans will think we were the torch party sent in advance to prepare for a broader conflict. An invasion, if you will. It won't be a fight for equality, rest assured. It'll be a fight for survival."

"Can't you make a *miftah*, Tobin?" Hargi said. "You did it before. That's how we all got in this mess in the first place. We should use this opportunity to pack up and leave. They want us to go back to where we came from, and I say we do just that."

"We came here for a reason, Hargi. We don't know what's become of Maerin in King Rosh's absence. There's a reason my late brother decided we should make the best of life on Earth."

"Then tell us. I'm dying to know. We're all dying, in fact, your late brother being the most recent of us."

"Focus, everyone. I have more to say." The chatter simmered down and Drac continued, "This morning, the President tightened the curfew from nine o'clock in the evening to six o'clock, effective immediately. Multiple Kaydans who still hold jobs in human spaces notified us that without the use of powers, they won't make it home before the curfew sets in."

"That's the second curfew shift this month," someone murmured.

"What else?" I asked.

"The burnings," Drac said. "The Church of the First People has increased the frequency of their attacks and the variety of their targets. The latest attempt was to burn the Blue Marquee, which we all know houses Issek's Mystical *Mitjer*. We believe the *Mitjer* was the intended target."

"And the damage?" Neck Tilter asked.

"None," Issek said. "I was in the store that evening and I was able to stop it."

"That's very fortunate." Drac quickly dismissed the subject. "Now, on to the reason we are here. We need to establish unitary leadership amongst the Kaydans. We need a new king."

The room fell silent, and it was my turn to fidget with my elbows. It was what everyone knew but didn't want to talk about.

"Given the state of things, I strongly believe the choice of king should be unanimous. We need a unified front, especially if things go so far as to lead to war," Drac said.

"We are already at war," Elbows said. "Have you not seen it out there? Kaydans are getting murdered where they stand. Without anything coming from the rift, we need to think about how to deal with the problem at hand."

"They problem at hand is that these young Kaydans don't know how to behave within the confines of our situation," Issek said. "If they would just do what the police say, there would be no need for them to get shot. It's as simple as that."

A woman in a green blouse spoke next, challenging him. "Issek, it would be you to think this way. Just because you're the richest among us doesn't exempt you from mistreatment. Do you think the police can see your wallet when they're aiming at your head?"

"All I'm saying is that if you do what the police say, you'll be safe. I tell Calinea this all the time."

"Enough of this," Drac interjected. "Whether or not they deserve it can be debated later. More urgently, we must deal with the fact it's happening."

"And we need unified leadership to do that?" asked Neck Tilter.

"Orira, it is my belief that we need to unify our fighting forces for whatever possibility we may face," Drac said.

"It sounds like you're talking about a King's Army," Elbows said.

"Yes, Cetus, if it gets there. I'm suggesting a trained fighting force comprising the best among us, serving all Kaydans. We can't confront what's coming with a handful of ragtag fighters."

"If King Rosh wanted an army, he would have established one."

"King Rosh wanted peace. We're beyond that now."

"We'll only be beyond that if we establish a military presence," Issek said.

"People, please. We're getting off topic. First let's discuss the king," Drac said.

"It's all on topic. We need a king that will know the delicacy of war and peace."

"Is that your way of suggesting yourself? Tobin, you've been quiet over there. What do you have to say to this?"

"You know how I feel about it. Prince Jormon is the crown prince and next in line to be king. It's his birthright."

Bodies turned in their seats, and all eyes were on me. My first instinct was to find Noan's hand and squeeze it, but he wasn't here.

"Him? You can't be serious." Issek pushed back from the table and stood up. "He's just a kid. And more than that, his brother is a murderer. Think of the message that will send to our people. To the Americans! For either of them to lead would be a slap in the face to us all."

"He's not a kid," Uncle Tobin said, pulling everyone's attention, "nor is he his brother's keeper."

"I believe he knows where Noan is, and he's been keeping it a secret," Issek said, and at this, Uncle Tobin stood.

"I will not lose my temper with you, Issek. But if you say one more word about my nephews, I'll——"

"Yes, yes, Tobin. Wise Tobin. The Wisest of Us All, Tobin. I'm not fool enough to challenge you." He threw up his hand in exaggerated surrender.

"Can I say something?" asserted Hargi, who until then had sat observing the discourse. "I don't say this to diminish Prince Jormon's capabilities, but more as a procedural highlight. Prince Jormon would be graced the king's title were it given to him by he or she who holds the position. In this case, King Rosh, may his soul rest, died before formally relinquishing the title. Meaning——"

"——the title is not inherently mine," I said, almost in a whisper. My head spun. I'd lost so much in the past few months with Noan's disappearance and Dad's death, now I was at risk of losing my future and everything I'd always thought would one day be mine.

"Anyone can lead, but our people won't fall behind just anyone," Drac said. "The Ladoan name has meaning."

"I'd say," Issek retorted.

"Most of us know them as well as we knew King Rosh. Most of us here aided them in their first years in Maerin. There's logic in the choice, regardless of how either of you two feel." With that, Drac sat down, as did Uncle Tobin and Issek.

The room was silent for longer than it should've been. Eventually, Issek said, "Let's say we follow your logic. Is Prince Jormon ready?"

"None of us are ready for what is coming," Green Blouse said. "At least Prince Jormon has experience."

"Knowledge and experience are disparate things," Issek said. "Being the son of the king gives one as much experience in leadership as being a tooth gives you experience at being a dentist. The boy was just along for the ride."

"Excuse me?" I asked. I sat straighter in my seat, which I noticed for the first time was too wide, fitting for a bigger man. "Be mindful of how you refer to me."

"Oh, yes, your Highness. My mind has been on you for quite some time."

"Can we just get the vote started already? It's getting late, and we don't want to get caught in transit," Green Blouse said.

"Thank you, Ayida," began Drac. "Are there any other suggestions? Issek, Cetus, Hargi?"

"If we're asking for suggestions from amongst our children, I propose my son, Rughor. He's as skilled as Prince Jormon, if not more so," Hargi said.

"Does anyone second the nomination?"

"I do," Issek said. He sported an expression I couldn't quite place, like he was deliberately trying to avoid looking pleased.

Other names were mentioned and seconded, but my head was whirling. It felt like a rug was being pulled from under me. I always assumed I was next in line, but these worthless people were suggesting I wasn't.

"Of the twelve of us in this room, nine represent the districts where Kaydans reside, Tobin is Regent, and Issek is the fiduciary," Drac said. "Our votes are all it takes to make it happen. After the selection, any other person has the right to challenge the king for authority, following proper procedures, of course. The coronation will be held in a small ceremony tomorrow here at the Academy. We must be swift in this decision, and we will not leave tonight until we have a king."

"What about me?" I asked, finally daring to speak. "Do I have a say?"

"Prince Jormon, you are here as a formality and in respect for your late father, who was unable to pass on authority to you. You are here to witness the transparency of the process in case it does not go in your favor. Forgive my bluntness, but you are not a voting member. Okay, everyone. Let's vote."

The conclave went through two rounds of votes, but no candidate achieved a true majority. Each time, I held my breath, and even in the cool air, sweat formed around my neck, my hands were so wet I couldn't place them on the table without being ashamed. Before the third round, names were removed until the only two remaining were mine and Rughor's.

"Two candidates and eleven votes to cast. The one who receives six votes has the majority. Tobin, we will start with you," Drac said.

"Jormon."

"Well, that was simple enough. Now I suppose on to Hargi representing District Nine."

"Rughor."

"Issek, who will you be giving your money to?"

"Rughor."

"I'll speak for District One: Jormon," Drac said. "Ayida of District Two, what say you?"

"Jormon."

"Orira, District Three."

"Rughor."

"Cetus, District Four."

"Jormon."

"District Five, what say you?" She thought for longer than a minute. I wished Rughor were here to see this too, so that he could sweat as bad as I was.

"Rughor."

"District Six, what say you?"

"Rughor."

I rubbed my hands against my pants. Rughor had five votes to my four. He needed only one more and he'd be the next king, and I'll be reduced to being the ousted brother of the shadow child. I wasn't sure if I could live with myself if that were to pass. I reflected, and not for the first time, on what Dad would say.

"District Seven, what say you?

"If Noan tries to come, don't let him in," I said. If he couldn't bother to attend Dad's funeral, then he doesn't get to see me take his place.

Rughor pulled at the back of my jacket and straightened my pants so that my belt was centered with the buttons on my blouse. He didn't show it, but he must've known I'd beaten him to keep my spot as the leader of the Kaydan people.

"Rughor, I feel like we need to clear the air. Did you befriend me hoping that you'd eventually replace me?"

"King Jormon, that's ridiculous. I would've had to know King Rosh would be assassinated or otherwise unable to pass on the crown. If you're going to accuse me of the first thing, you have to accuse me of both."

He was so matter of fact about it. He tucked three blue, button-shaped stones in the diagonal pockets that ran from shoulder to waist.

"You're right. I'm sorry to have asserted that." I checked myself out in the mirror. I'd always looked more like my mother, but there, in full regalia, I was unmistakably my father's son. "Thanks, Rughor. You've been a good friend to me over the past few months, and I don't know what kind of friend I've been to you. I know you didn't have anything to do with my father's death."

"No need to apologize. These are dark times, and you have to be careful with who you trust."

"No hard feelings?"

"None at all, Your Highness."

"Please, call me Jormon."

"You'd like that, wouldn't you?" He winked, and we both laughed. I didn't know he was a little flirt.

The door opened and Dirk walked in.

"You look handsome," he said. "Hello, Rughor."

274

I kissed him without hesitation and was struck with an unexpected guilt. I flashed a smile to hide it. "You look handsome, too. What's it look like over there?"

"You'll be impressed with the room. Pretty good turnout, too. I think almost everyone from Gray Flats came out to see this. That's a good sign. They want to support you."

"Even with the teal sky?" I asked, walking over to the window to catch a view of the rift.

"I should leave you two alone. Jormon, summon me if you need anything."

The door closed behind him, and I was alone with Dirk for the first time since Dad's funeral.

"How do you feel about all of this, really?" Dirk asked.

"I'll admit this only to you: I'm nervous. I told Rughor to kick Noan out if he sees him—which he probably won't—but really, I just want my brother here. I want the gang to be together, and for things to be like they used to."

"That's the same thing my mom said."

"Oh yeah? You haven't said much about her visit."

"You had a lot going on with the search for Noan and your dad's funeral. There was never a good time."

"I've learned some things as well about people I love, and I don't know how to process it. We can talk tonight after the ceremony."

The ceremony took place in the Academy, using the room normally set aside for graduation ceremonies. Uncle Tobin had done fine *sahdr* work to fashion it into a reception hall so grand it would make the residents of Buckingham Palace shit themselves. But that was the extent of the extravagance. The coronation lasted just a few minutes. If times were normal, if we were able to sleep through the night without the threat of attack, the ceremony would've gone on for an hour or more. But times weren't normal.

Uncle Tobin presented me with Dad's bangle and matching black headpiece. He said a few words, Drac said a few words, then it was official. I gazed at the faces painted with a mix of joy and apprehension. It was only the next thing; after that I had to lead.

If the ceremony was simple, the reception was even simpler. With food supplies limited, it seemed wasteful to have a traditional smorgasbord. Everyone understood, and they settled for the floating platters of cheese and apple slices without complaint.

What the event lacked in food, it made up for it in entertainment. The music was lively and unending. I danced when I could and made conversation with everyone who wanted my attention. I wished my dad could see me. He would've been proud of how I handled myself, and happy to see how others received me. I could picture him with a furrowed brow saying, "If you're worried about me, you're worrying about the wrong thing. What you need to be worrying about is…" I couldn't think like him, and I didn't know how to finish the thought. I laughed to myself to stop from crying, but it had the opposite effect. Just when tears formed in my eyes, Dirk grabbed me and dragged me into a waltz.

"I didn't know you could formally dance. Did they teach you this at football practice?"

"You should know by now I keep plenty of tricks up my sleeve."

We danced together, and I danced with Calinea. Even Rughor asked for a dance. I was over the moon. The only thing that would make the night better would be to have Noan with me. I shook the thought away before I felt the urge to reach out to him. It's because of our distance people were happy with the choice. If he were here, he'd probably go up in smoke like he did at the last classy function or do something else equally frightening.

My mind had eased into one of those rare moments of stillness when a shift in the ambiance snagged my attention. The great door flew open and slammed into the wall. The bang cut through the music, and everyone turned to see what the commotion was about. The distant clamor of alarmed voices grew louder as the wave of panic washed through the crowd. Uncle Tobin was at my side before the news hit.

276

"Fire! The trailer park is on fire!" a woman shouted.

The woman ran up to me, and Rughor grabbed her before she got too close. Her clothes were stained black and reeked of smoke. "What's happening?" I asked. I was trying to keep my cool, but failing at it. I was painfully aware my voice had risen several octaves. I was also aware of everyone's eyes on me.

"The Riders," she said through shallow breaths. "We're. Surrounded."

"Can somebody get this woman some water!" I shouted. Her rushed breathing aggravated my senses and muddled my thoughts. As I hesitated, I felt the scalding gaze of Issek, doubt clouding his eyes, while Tobin remained curiously mute. If I didn't act now, this is how everyone would remember me. The king who lost the kingdom his first day on the throne. The ground seemed to tremble beneath my feet, and I closed my eyes to still myself. A hand touched my shoulder and squeezed, and it was though my mind had found clarity in all the chaos. I opened my eyes, but there was no hand there, just the feel of five fingers relaxing my mind and body to deal with the matter at hand.

Swallowing the boulder of apprehension in my throat, I signaled to Drac, Hargi, Orira, and Ayida. "Rally anyone you know who can put out fires. Find where the fire is worst and start there." I turned to Dirk, who held a glass of water for the poor woman to drink. "Dirk, take Rughor and protect our trailer. Find Taavi and have him put a shield around your trailer as well."

"But who's gonna—" Rughor started, but I cut him off.

"Go! I'll be fine." I looked over at Issek. His eyes radiated a combination of excitement and fear. "Uncle Tobin, find out how they were able to get past the barrier." Something didn't feel right.

As I turned to search for Phae, I could swear a smile etched across his face.

Phae needed no instructions, nor was she difficult to find. Her body hovered high overhead in the middle of the room. Pale white streams of light flowed from her as smoke does from a candle. One of those whisps of light flowed toward me, wrapping around my wrist and setting my *sheriaan* aglow. "I have Taavi, Dirk, and Mr. Tobin on comms," she said. She was far enough away I barely saw her lips move, but her voice was clear and audible. What's more, I could see the whole room as she saw it. Countless heads searching in different directions for answers that weren't there. Toppled trays of food and drinks. I saw myself, standing alone among the crowd.

Before I could praise Phae's quick thinking, Uncle Tobin spoke. "The Riders have surrounded Gray Flats from the south. Fires are pushing in from the east and west. If we need to evacuate, it'll have to be through the woods."

At the sound of his voice, his experiences flooded my vision in blinding blurs of red and yellow flames. Smoke trailed up to meet the starless night sky. Something in the woods drew Uncle's attention, but it was too dark to tell what it was. More danger, most likely.

"Any sign as to how they bypassed the barriers?" I asked.

"Through the woods," Uncle Tobin said. "The *sabejaan* I'd hidden there have been destroyed. With even a few stones missing—"

"It would've been enough to break the barrier." Well damn. Something definitely wasn't right. "Can everyone still use their powers?" I asked.

The collective response came to me as a powerful image pieced together from everyone's vantage. My eyes weren't my own; they shifted, fluttered, and danced between perspectives. From Dirk's viewpoint, the looming silhouettes of Riders crept through the trailer park. Their grim expressions were cast in the eerie light of torches which, one by one, were hurled towards the trailers below. The darkness was pierced with an orange fury as flames began to lap at row after row of mobile homes.

As my consciousness melded into Uncle Tobin's sight, the scene became even more grim. The heart of the trailer park was quickly succumbing to the flames. I could feel the heat just as he could, and it felt as if the very air was being sucked dry. The wood and metal of the trailers sizzled and popped, sending sparks skyward. Twisting, writhing smoke climbed upward, painting a thick veil of despair across the starry night. Through Uncle Tobin's experienced eyes, I could also pick out desperate families dragging belongings and loved ones away from the engulfing fire, their faces reflecting terror as they ran from the flames.

But it was through Taavi's gaze that the true horror was realized. From his angle, directly above the inferno, I could see the trailer park's layout in its entirety, like a miniature town being consumed by a ravenous beast. The flames, once isolated to a few trailers, now connected in a deadly dance, jumping from one home to another in a choreographed wave of destruction.

The combined terror and heartache from Dirk, Uncle Tobin, Taavi, and Phae amplified my own emotions. This wasn't just an attack. This was a declaration, a vicious statement that even in our safe spaces, we weren't safe anymore.

The trailer park's smoky haze thickened, curling around the remnants of once-cherished homes and memories, now fuel for the advancing inferno. The faces of those around me who showed up to celebrate my crowning now canvases of sadness. At the center of this maelstrom there was me, and every eye in the room seemed to turn to me at once, waiting, watching, demanding.

"Stop them," I ordered, my voice unwavering. But even as the words left my lips, I knew it wasn't enough. The solutions weren't simple, and every path forward seemed fraught with consequence.

Dirk's face was grim as he pointed towards the burgeoning fires. "We should focus on the fires. Without intervention, the whole park will be gone by dawn."

"We need to get the people to safety," Taavi interjected, his eyes scanning the area for a clear route. "The outer perimeters are still untouched. We can guide them there."

Rughor, his usual calm demeanor slightly ruffled, said, "We have to stop the Riders from advancing, or there won't be anything left to save."

I could feel the weight of every gaze, the burden of every expectation. Every suggestion seemed valid, every choice urgent. As I wrestled with the barrage of opinions, Issek, ever the opportunist, slithered in with his own proposition.

"Why not negotiate with the Riders? We can offer them something. It's not like we haven't dealt with them before," he suggested. He wasn't tethered to Phae and couldn't experience the destruction in the same way I could. If he did, maybe he wouldn't think that. He continued, "Maybe we need to understand what they want. Perhaps there's a compromise in there. Are you sure attacking is the right idea?"

Taking a deep breath, I centered myself. As new king, indecision wasn't a luxury I could afford. "Dirk, I already sent people out to deal with the fires. Lead them in the effort. Tell them their king placed you in charge. Taavi, work with Tobin to lead the evacuations to the outer perimeters. Rughor, set up a defensive line against the Riders. If they get too close, turn it into an *offensive* line. Those are my orders."

I shook away Phae's connection. I needed to be present in the room. People huddled together in small clusters, comforting one another in their overwhelming sense of uncertainty. They turned to me as I levitated overhead, and I stared down at their expectant faces.

Words failed me.

I looked them over, each person frightened and unsure. What could I say to ease their minds? All of a sudden, I was just a kid again. Not the leader that everyone needed, but a boy looking for his dad, or his uncle, or for anyone who could help.

The doubt I'd shaken off moments ago returned with a vengeance and I began to panic. Just as I contemplated lowering to the floor and getting lost in the crowd, he spoke to me, my dear brother, as though he'd never left my side. *Just tell them it'll be okay.*

CHAPTER TWENTY-SIX
JORMON

THEY PUSHED THROUGH THE DOOR IN A RUSH. Calinea and Dirk staggered in carrying a third person who couldn't stand on her own. Blood ran from somewhere—from everywhere—pooling at their feet and spreading quickly until it hugged the walls and oozed into the corner. How many people had bled here, I wondered. How many more will bleed? Through the window, the fires were dimming, and the distant shouts of the Riders grew quieter as some of them retreated, but the fight was far from over.

I hurried over and felt for a pulse.

"Your Highness, you shouldn't be the one doing this," Rughor said.

"I'm the king now. It's my responsibility."

Her pulse was faint, but it was there. She had a chance.

I extended my consciousness across her body. Seven bullet holes, four from entry, three from exit. The bullet still inside her is… There it is. Now I just have to…

She screamed. Screams meant she was still alive.

The bullet floated out, and I let it fall to the floor.

"Hold her tight. Tighter than that." They put her on the floor and leaned their weight on her arms. Rughor held her legs down with a *sahdr*. "This part will hurt the worst."

Her screams tore through the Academy halls, but everyone was used to screams at that point. I patched her up as quickly as I could.

Finish fast, rest up, and be ready for the next person that comes in bleeding.

"What's happening out there?" I asked.

"They're everywhere," Dirk said. "It's like the whole damn town decided to become Riders overnight. We waited in the woods behind Mrs. Mayola's house until the coast was clear. As soon as we made it to the back door, they were on us. I don't know how they're doing it. It was a bloodbath after that. We ran in the house to hide and—I'm sorry to say this, but Mrs. Mayola was sprawled on the living room floor with her throat slit. So was Mr. McCall."

Not Aunt May May. I pushed back tears, telling myself they were always closer to Noan, not me. I hadn't shelled peas. I never got pies. I was his plus one in their friendship.

"How did you escape?"

Dirk and Calinea looked at each other. Calinea said, "You said fight. We fought."

"Dirk?" I reached to wipe a streak of blood from his neck, and he pushed my hand away.

"We didn't have a choice." He couldn't even look at me.

"You were able to use your powers?" I asked.

"Yeah, at first. Then it's like someone turned a switch and shut our powers off." Dirk said.

"That's when Phae blinded the fuck out of them with some witch spell, and we ran," Calinea said. "Even blinded, they shot at us as we escaped. They got Elly pretty good."

"What about the food? Supplies?"

Dirk shook his head, and a knot tightened in my stomach. I had no idea how long we'd be barricaded in here, and feeding everyone was at the top of my list of things a king should worry about.

"King Jormon, I don't think we can trust that list Sean gave us of Kaydan-friendly folks in the area anymore," Rughor said.

"He's right. By now it's either outdated or the people are being watched," Dirk said.

"Can you reach out to Sean and find out what's going on? Maybe get a new list while you're at it?"

"Of course."

"Calinea, find a bunk for Elly and get someone to clean up this mess. Then find Taavi, Phae and Tobin and have them meet me in Tobin's study. Rughor, tell Lheniva I appreciate what's she's doing to turn her trailer into a medical bay. Let her know I'll have supplies for her as soon as we get them."

After Rughor and Calinea scattered, Dirk said, "You need to rest. You've been going hard since the attack two days ago, and you can barely keep your eyes open. Find someone else to stand in."

"There is no one else, Dirk. Look around. Half the people in here are too old or too young to be useful. Uncle Tobin is fortifying the space as best he can and providing defense on food runs, Drac is keeping everyone calm. Everyone has a job, and as king, my job is to protect everyone. If that means I have bags under my eyes, so be it."

His eyes searched mine, heavy with emotion. "I'm only looking out for you, Jormon."

"And I'm looking out for everyone. Now can we just drop this? I have a strategy meeting to attend."

I should've kissed him. With times being what they were, who knew if I would get another chance. I should've done anything to let him know he's still my guy, and that I'm afraid for him every time he's out of my sight. But the moment had passed. He went one way, I went the other, both of us going somewhere important. Uncle Tobin and Taavi were already waiting in the study as I entered. Phae showed up minutes later, followed by Rughor, who came to say that Elly had gotten situated at Lheniva's.

"Rughor, you should stay and hear this as well," I said.

Uncle Tobin conjured a round table with enough chairs for all of us. He discretely rubbed at his chest like he was massaging a sore spot, and I wondered for the first time if he was pushing through exhaustion, too. Our fight for survival had barely begun, and already we looked as though we'd lost.

"We need a plan," I said. "Uncle Tobin, do you think you can get the barrier back up and running? The food run was a bust, and if we're going to be hungry, we should at least feel safe."

"I've asked Issek to to help with that."

"Don't," I said, perhaps too quickly. Everyone's glares shifted as they waited for me to say more. "I want to keep my circle tight. If you can, Uncle, do it alone." He nodded weakly. "Taavi, how much food do we have in storage?"

Taavi shrugged. "We raided every pantry still intact. There's maybe a thousand of us, give or take. We can probably eat for a week, and that's if we cut back to one meal a day."

"Some of them won't survive on one meal a day," Phae said. "Lheniva is doing what she can to tend to the old and broken, but these people have to eat."

"We all have to eat," Rughor said. "If we starve ourselves, the Riders won't need power blockers. They can just walk in and shoot us in the head as we sit around, weak and defenseless. If anyone needs food, it's those of us who are protecting the others."

"If we don't feed them, there will be no one to protect," Uncle Tobin said.

"Say that to me without drooping over," Rughor replied.

Uncle Tobin realized he was slouching and sat up straight. "I'll be fine with less. Someone else can have my meal."

"It's about more than food," I broke in. "It's about our survival. We can't stay held up here forever. Notice how there are no drones in the sky? No emergency support? We're on our own here. Our survival depends on what we do next."

"What are you suggesting?" asked Uncle Tobin.

"An attack. I say we strike back. We pick a target and hit them hard."

"We can't do that. It goes against our own interests."

"He's right," Taavi said. "When word gets out what's going on here, we need to come off as the victims. If we come off as aggressive, we lose the world's support."

"It's better we lose their support than lose our lives," Rughor said.

"We hit the church," I said. "It may as well be their headquarters."

"It'll definitely send a message."

"Do you hear yourselves? You're talking about attacking a church. In South Georgia. That'll worsen everything. Church is sacred here, you know that," Uncle Tobin said. He'd lost all slouch and was fully engaged.

"We need a move that will slow them down. If we remove their leader, they'll scramble for a new one. We can use that time to build up our defenses. And to eat, for *Heemrah*'s sake," Rughor said. "I say we target Pastor Lumley."

"We should do both," said Phae, who had been uncharacteristically quiet. "I'm not a fan of murder, but have any of you actually been to the med bay at Lheniva's?"

"King Jormon, don't listen to this. It's a temporary solution with a permanent outcome. They will retaliate," Uncle Tobin said.

"Maybe so. Then again, if we do this right, it could scare them off for a while. We can prove our own strength."

"It'll give us leverage to negotiate with higher leadership," Rughor said.

"And it will give higher leadership cause to deploy the military. We don't want a war like the last one," Uncle Tobin said.

"Look around, Tobin. We are already at war, and we are losing," Rughor said.

"King Jormon. Think about your people. They aren't ready for war. What would your father say to this? He worked so hard to make us part of the same community. Think of how he would feel knowing your actions work against all he has done," Uncle Tobin pleaded.

His words flipped a switch in me, and all of the grief and anger I'd bottled up inside stirred. "My father is dead. They killed him. They're killing all of us! And you want to stand there and talk peace? We don't have time for peace. We don't even have time for this conversation. They are *killing* us while we stand here talking about not getting killed. I'm done. No more talking. We're taking that church tonight."

Taavi pushed back from the table. "I can't participate in something like that. I won't."

"You can, and you will," I said. "If not, you'll find out what I do to traitors."

Rughor stood erect with his chest puffed out. "Then it's settled?"

"Yeah," I said. "It's settled."

CHAPTER TWENTY-SEVEN
NOAN

I SAT AT THE EDGE OF THE TENT I STOLE FROM Walmart. The sun was setting, bringing in the harshness of another cold winter night. I shivered, nestling deeper into the tattered sleeping bag that separated me from the frozen ground below. I dug into the canister I kept beside me and pulled out an orange and black cube that sparked shadow fire, which was good for heat, but not for light. I tossed it onto yesterday's dead ashes, and the fire came to life as hot as a phoenix and as black as a raven.

The nocturnal animals were waking up with creaks and screeches. Somewhere in the night, a feline roared, warning other animals to stay clear.

I pulled out the stack of books I'd been slowly raiding from Uncle's study. I settled on "Energy Transformation in the Modern Age." I don't know how long ago it was written, but I was sure the modern age it referenced was long gone.

I've tried every *sahdr* in these books. For locating an item: didn't work. For locating an energy source: didn't work. For locating energy imbedded in an object: didn't work. *What am I missing?*

Uncle Tobin said the artifact would call to me. I was listening; nothing was calling.

Suddenly, a rustling behind made me freeze in place. I resisted the urge to ask who's there. I flew into the air and spun around just as someone slung themselves against a tree. *"Nared."*

I guided the cluster of light overhead until I could see who was approaching. "Taavi?"

"Help," he croaked.

His body slumped forward, and as he thrust a wet and bloody hand out to catch himself, I moved to grab him, but he hit the ground, and the wind left his body in a rush. He sucked frantically for breath. I watched, horrified, as he reached up to me for support. My own hands were frozen in a mix of shock and fear.

My heart raced, every fiber of my being focused on the figure sprawled before me, wheezing and gasping. My voice took on a desperate edge, "Calm down, Taavi. Focus. Breathe." It was like telling a drowning man to just swim.

My voice became an urgent whisper, the cold wind carrying it away, "Taavi, focus on me. I need you to sit up. Can you do that for me?" Fear and pain reflected in his eyes, but he nodded and strained to sit upright.

"That's it. Now, inhale slowly through your mouth. Feel your stomach expand," I urged. The rhythmic sound of his breath began to interweave with the whooshing of my own as I demonstrated what to do. "Exhale. Suck that stomach in. We need to keep your lungs moving." His shallow breaths started to deepen, his chest rising and falling more assuredly.

The moonlight glinted off his face, making the beads of sweat on his forehead glisten. With trembling hands, he pulled his shirt over his head, revealing a gruesome sight. The wound on his chest pulsed with every heartbeat, bubbling blood with every breath he took. His voice, laced with vulnerability and shock, barely carried above a whisper, "Am I... Am I going to die?"

Fuck yeah, you are. Unless I could save him.

"I fell out of a tree when I was a kid and got the wind knocked out of me." I dug through the stack of books again. "What you're experiencing—hey man, stay with me. I'm not an expert, but I'm going to try a few things." I flipped through the pages until I found something on healing deep wounds.

"Do whatever." He coughed up blood and wiped it with the back of his arm.

I did whatever. I found the bullet in his body and dragged it out of its entry wound. He screamed in pain as it raked past his insides, touching places nothing was ever supposed to touch. "This next part is going to hurt."

"That first part hurt," he said, breathing quick, shallow breaths through clenched teeth.

As I pressed the wound together with my hands, blood oozed between my fingers, making them slide off course.

"Shit!" Taavi screamed.

"Hold on. That's not the painful part." I invoked the *sahdr* to start fires, and the bit of Taavi's skin held between my fingertips burnt, cauterizing the wound. Taavi gripped my forearm so hard I thought the bone might snap. I stopped the burning, but he held on until the pain subsided.

"Better?" I asked.

"I'm not dead," he replied. He tried to sit up and winced as the pain hit him again. I helped him into the tent, and he gingerly lowered himself onto my stolen sleeping bag, lying down with a sigh of relief.

"What happened?" I asked, beating myself up from not keeping a closer eye on things.

"Trying to save your stupid boyfriend is what happened," he grunted through gritted teeth.

Oh shit. Sean. Jormon must've done something stupid. My heart clenched. "Sean? Where is he? Is he…" I couldn't finish the sentence. My mind raced through every possible scenario, starting with the worst.

Taavi coughed, the pain evident in his eyes. "It all happened so fast. He… he was at the church when we got there."

"He told me he's not part of the Ri—"

"He's not," Taavi interjected. "He was there to warn us that the Riders knew we were coming. Next thing you know, Jormon and Rughor are up in the air hurling fire at the church, the Riders are inside shooting out the window. That's when Sean ran back in, I'm guessing to get his people to run away instead of fight back. I ran in behind him."

"Why would you do that?" My voice quivered with fear and confusion. "You could've been killed."

Taavi's gaze softened, and for a moment, the pain seemed to fade into the background.

"Because you care about him," he whispered, a hint of sadness underlying his voice. "And maybe, just maybe, I care about you."

The weight of his confession hung in the air, heavy and undeniable. My mind raced, guilt and gratitude swirling together. "Taavi... I... I don't know what to say."

He managed a weak smile. "Don't say anything. Just find Sean and make sure he's okay."

A wave of realization crashed over me, and the implications of his actions and words started to take root. Taavi had risked everything, not just for Sean, but for me as well.

"Look," Taavi continued, trying to lighten the mood despite his pain, "I'd rather not have a hero moment and then find out the guy I saved and the guy I did it for end up together without me getting at least a thank you."

I chuckled, tears forming at the edge of my eyes, a cocktail of emotions. "Thank you, Taavi. You're more special than you know."

As I gazed down at Taavi, I felt an unfamiliar warmth towards him, feelings I hadn't given myself the time to explore. Yet, the urgency of the situation pulled my focus. I had to find Sean and ensure he was safe.

Taavi's hand reached out, brushing against mine for a brief moment. "Go find him. And if you bring him back here and have sex in this tent, make sure I'm dead first."

I laughed. I couldn't help myself.

I walked over to the edge of the trees, hoping I had enough power for whatever was to come.

Opening shadow portals had become as effortless to me as breathing—no more fumbling with the edges of space like trying to find the start of a tape roll.

With a sweeping gesture, I carved an arc in the air before me. Dark tendrils of smoke, thick and alive, weaved together to form a hazy border.

Focusing on Sean, I let the sensations flood in: his brown hair, like so much chocolate; the feel of his skin against mine, the sadness that hides behind his eyes. The image in the shadow portal sharpened, and the fiery spectacle therein blinded me amidst the dark forest. The intense heat from the burning church immediately hit me, and the sound of flames devouring polished pews tore through the portal and echoed through the woods around me.

There stood Sean, huddled with Sherriff Kuss and a guy who looked not much older than him. They both held rifles aimed at something I couldn't see without stepping through the portal. The hairs on my neck stood on end. I was sure it was my brother they were aiming at and, if not him, then someone else I knew. The repercussions of my choices weighed heavily. Betray my kind, and I lose any chance of ever returning to my people. Aid my brother and risk losing Sean forever.

A groaning sound echoed, followed by the shrill cry of splintering wood. A massive beam, dislodged by the flames, came crashing down towards them.

"No!" I screamed, my voice loud enough to overpower the roaring fire.

Using the full force of my power, I shoved Sean and his family just as the burning wood crashed on the ground. A dense curtain of smoke and ash covered everything and, panic set in as I waited for Sean to pop up. Five seconds passed. Then ten. My eyes darted frantically, searching for signs of life. Thirty seconds. "Sean?"

A full minute passed.

"What's happening?" Taavi yelled from inside the tent.

"I don't know. I think—"

A small break in the plumes of smoke lasted just enough to see Sean standing over the sheriff. Sheriff Kuss's leg was pinned under the fallen debris, and the other guy, probably Sean's brother, strained to pull him free.

"Sean! You have to get out of there!" I screamed.

He looked around to see where the shout was coming from. He spotted me, and a silent understanding passed between us. Sean motioned to his brother, gesturing towards the portal. His brother shoved him away. Their mouths were moving but I couldn't hear a word over the raging fire.

Sean reached down to remove the wood trapping the sheriff's leg. It must've been too hot, because he quickly snatched his hands away and patted them on his thighs.

Fuck. I'm gonna have to free this mother fucker, I thought.

I extended my consciousness until I felt the weight of the beam in my mind and I lifted it enough for the brother to pull Sheriff Kuss from under it. Sean helped the sheriff to his feet and with his brother on the other side, they carried him toward the portal.

Then the sheriff saw me and his eyes went dark. His face transformed as he forgot he was in pain, and he searched around for the rifle. It was on the floor next to a burning row of pews. He bent to get it, but Sean held him up. Sheriff Kuss pushed Sean away. Sean's arms flew over his head and he yelled something to his father. I didn't need to hear him to know what was going on. It was a plea for reason. His father would rather shoot me and die than to have a Kaydan help him survive.

Sean shook his head and ran toward the portal. Toward me. When he was nearly there, he stopped. He looked down at his hand, eyeing the ring, then doubled back to his brother and gave it to him. As he raced back toward me, the entire roof collapsed, raining a cascade of ash and cinders around him.

CHAPTER TWENTY-EIGHT
JORMON

IN THE DAYS FOLLOWING OUR ATTACK ON THE church, we cobbled together a network of underground tunnels connecting the remaining trailers, all of it stemming from a crude fallout shelter hidden deep below Uncle Tobin's trailer. It was our last line of defense against total annihilation, which was a real possibility considering the swell of Riders that flocked to the area. Uncle Tobin's once cherished study now bore the marks of a war room, its stacks of books pushed against the walls to make room for a replica of the Lyons, Georgia, which, if anything, was a battlefield. Hovering a few feet above the map was a chilling census: glowing indicators revealing human numbers in the tens of thousands within a ten-mile perimeter. Not all of them were Riders, of course, but it was safe to assume that the few thousand newcomers were. As for us Kaydans, a mere count of five hundred twenty-five, a figure that seemed to lessen with each passing hour as someone died from inflicted wounds.

"We just have to risk it," I said to Uncle Tobin, who sat next to me during most of our strategy sessions, but who now paced around the floating image of the city, deep in thought. My eyes followed him as he paced easily behind Rughor, then Phae, then Dirk, and stopped at Hargi, who insisted he join the latest strategy huddle.

"Hargi, tell him what your scouting mission revealed." Uncle Tobin said.

He pulled a folded newspaper from his waistband and held up the front page for all to see.

"Read it to me," I said, annoyed I had to ask.

"The Localized Ionic Grid Hindering Telekinesis (L.I.G.H.T) device is a sleek, palm-sized contraption, effortlessly blending functionality with modern design. Crafted from a matte black alloy, it fits snugly in the hand, its weight substantial enough to feel its presence, but light enough that it doesn't become burdensome.

"The top surface features a soft touch-sensitive button with an embedded LED indicator, which emits a soft blue glow when activated. This blue light indicates the device is working, generating the Localized Ionic Grid that hinders Kaydan telekinesis.

"With its understated elegance and powerful functionality, the L.I.G.H.T. device has quickly become an essential accessory for those wary of Kaydan abilities, embodying modern humanity's resilience and resourcefulness in the face of a new world order."

"New world order? They've made a device using *our* powers and are using it against us. It's like they're okay with powers, as long as *we* don't have them."

"If I may, Your Highness, these things are everywhere, like they were mass-produced overnight. They're giving them away for free at the National Guard Armory, and the line for them is longer than anything I've ever seen."

"So if we teleport into a grocery store, chances are someone will have one on them, and there's no way to get back."

"Even during the day," Hargi added. "Every place that sells food has a Rider guarding the door."

"Even in Atlanta? D.C.? Hell, London?"

"We don't have the resources to scout everywhere," Hargi said, folding the newspaper and tucking it back in his waistband.

Noan could check it out, I thought. He could scry from right here and know exactly what was happening. But I couldn't call on him. I wouldn't.

"If I may, Your Highness," Hargi said, and I motioned for him to continue. "We've taken big steps to attack the locals, but we still have a chance to implore forgiveness from President Blackwell. I'd go so far as to suppose he'd be willing to pardon anyone who surrendered themselves."

I couldn't believe what he was saying. In what world would I turn myself—my people—over to someone I believe had a hand in my father's death? The audacity of the thought made my skin crawl. Why would Hargi even ask that, unless…

Memories came crashing into me like a wave. Hargi returned from his overseas assignment earlier than expected. It could've been in anticipation of Rughor joining the Cohort, but I saw him at Issek's shop, and Calinea lied about it. And what did Calinea say about those fucking love serpents or whatever? The Matchmaker ordered them from Issek? He could've easily tampered with them to cause a violent reaction in Noan. They knew Dad would have to keep Noan at bay, that people would fear him. Now Noan is fully out of the picture, and who shows up? Hargi's eager-as-fuck son, who then becomes a contender for the throne.

Whispers of doubt intertwined with my thoughts, causing them to spiral uncontrollably. It was as if I was trying to piece together a shattered mirror, the shards reflecting twisted versions of the truth. "Thanks for your input, Hargi, but you can go now. You too, Rughor," I said.

Confusion flashed across Rughor's face as he stood and took leave behind his father.

"What's going on?" Dirk asked.

I paced the room for a moment, stopping briefly to look out the window where the blackness of Gray Flats clashed with the snowy backdrop of the woods beyond. "It's the pattern of things," I said, still unsure whether I was succumbing to conspiracy theories of my own creation. "Why does is seem like the Riders are expecting us at every turn? We've gone to school with some of them; they're not that smart."

"There's a mole," Phae said, never the one to miss a beat. "You think it's Hargi."

"Close. I'm guessing it's Issek."

"But you're not sure," Phae said, raising an eyebrow. "If you are gonna accuse him of something as big as this, you have to be sure."

"There's a way to be sure. To know for certain what's going through his head," I said.

"Are you talking about mind manipulation? That's forbidden," Uncle Tobin said.

With a forceful stride, I closed the gap between us, my face inches from his. "According to who?" I challenged.

Uncle Tobin met my gaze. "According to doctrine. According to all wisdom found beneath *Heemrah*'s gaze and *Zereq*'s shadow."

Feeling the intensity of the room's gaze, I backed away, looking around at the familiar faces. "Right now, we're under *my* gaze, and I see betrayal. Dirk, you're looking like you want to say something."

Dirk shifted uneasily, his gaze met mine. "I might not've been Kaydan long—in a manner of speaking—but this doesn't seem right. If Tobin thinks we shouldn't, we probably shouldn't."

My mind flashed back to the conversation I had had with Dad and what he told me about Uncle Tobin's betrayal. Everything that happened to me could be linked back to that moment when Uncle Tobin chose to run off with Noan instead of letting the law prevail. He wasn't spouting about Heermah's gaze back then. No, doctrine be damned, he did whatever pleased him, and now we are stuck on Earth in yet another bloody battle. How dare he act so self-righteous.

"Dirk, you don't know everything. My uncle is a big fat liar with a history of disobedience," I said, and watched as Uncle Tobin's jaw dropped open. "He knows what I'm talking about. Regardless, Tobin, I need you to do this for me. I don't know the *sahdr*, and I know you do, being so wise and all."

"I won't do it," Uncle Tobin said. His refusal stung more than I'd cared to admit, and I hated him for it. I hated that he was superior to me in this way, even though I wore the crown.

"*Rhialqaraq*," I whispered, and it materialized in my hands. At first glance, it looked like a snake coiled tightly around itself, silver with thick, ornate scales. I held one end and let the other fall to the floor. That's when they saw it for what it was: a whip, thin as a razor at the tip and completely covered in dull, rusty thorns up to the handle. With a fluid motion, I brought the whip crashing down onto Uncle Tobin. Its eerie cry as it made contact echoed through the trailer, and the very walls seemed to shudder.

Phae's eyes grew as big as the moon, "What the hell, man?" she screamed as she backed away from the *rhualka's* reach. Dirk ran over and grabbed Uncle Tobin, who had already begun to slouch after just one strike.

Dirk looked up at me, afraid and confused. "You don't have to do this," he said.

"You're right; I don't. And if my uncle does what I ask, I won't have to."

"Really? You're beating your own people now? Is this who you've become?"

Uncle Tobin's words came back to me. We punish our own so they don't have to. I laughed, taking it all in. "This is who I have to be," I whispered.

In the end, it didn't matter that I wanted to use a forbidden *sahdr* to plunge into Issek's memories. He was nowhere to be found. Neither was Hargi. I found Rughor alone in his room. His red eyes and damp face told me he'd been crying. He shook his head slowly as I walked in. "I'm sorry," he said, finding the courage to look me in the eyes. "I didn't know."

"And they just left you here?"

He shook his head vigorously. "I chose to stay. Whatever plans they had, I didn't want any part of it."

"Did they say anything before they left?"

"Only that it's best I leave with them." He stood up and took his shirt off, then pointed at the *rhualka* coiled around my hand. "I'm prepared for any punishment you deem fit."

"Oh yeah? What if I told you to leave Gray Flats and never return? I can't trust you, which means you're no good to me."

"You are my king. If that's what you truly wish, I'll go."

His bicep bulged as he tossed the shirt across his shoulder, and I realized I'd never seen Rughor shirtless. His chest, broad and firm, heaved slightly with each breath as he grabbed a black duffle from the corner and stuffed it with clothes. The room's dim light reflected off the copper lines swirling around his muscular forearms, every twist and loop telling stories of challenges he'd overcome. It caught me off guard. It wasn't so much his physique that did it, but the raw humanity it represented. In that brief moment, I could so clearly see he was the product of his father, who'd no doubt told him exactly what he could do and who he should strive to become. We were a lot the same, Rughor and I, except my dad was dead.

"Stop packing," I said. "For now. Tomorrow, start earning my trust, yeah?"

"Blinded by *Heemrah*, guided by *Zereq*," he whispered, taking a knee and extending an arm toward my feet. His *sheriaan* shimmered three shades of brown as his essence poured over my feet.

I was tired. Exhausted, really. The sun was setting, and there was nothing to do about Issek and Hargi, at least not without putting someone in danger.

I passed the study on the way to my room and flinched. Uncle Tobin had likely gone to bed already, but the last image I had of him lingered: shirt torn, hair wild, chest bloody, pale, and weak.

Dirk stood in front of the bedroom window, looking out at the glow from the rift, now purple. I walked up behind him and wrapped my arms around his waist. He wriggled out of my embrace and wiped his face with both hands. "Don't touch me right now," he said.

Not this shit, I thought. "Because of what happened back there? Uncle Tobin will be fine in a day or two. Besides, I didn't mean for it to go that far."

"You pushed it that far. You had every opportunity to reel it back in, but... I don't know. It's like you liked having that much power. I don't get it."

"I'm sure you don't," I said. I didn't mean it, but I was too tired to put in the effort.

He took a deep breath, raking his fingers through his hair. The weight of his gaze felt heavy on me. "Talk to me, Jormon. Make me understand. Because what I saw today wasn't the man I fell for. It was someone...darker."

I moved closer to him, and he walked to the other side of the room. The purple light washed over my face, and I was momentarily distracted by its beauty. "When you're king, when the safety of everyone rests on your shoulders, hesitation is a luxury you can't afford. Every decision carries a weight. Every action, a consequence."

Silence stretched between us, disturbed only by the soft whistling of air seeping through a crack in the window. Dirk's voice came softly, "But it's not just about the weight of decisions. It's about how you make them, Jormon."

My fingers clenched, my nails digging into my palms. I could feel the heat of his gaze on my back, but I couldn't bring myself to turn around. "I have to be unyielding," I began, my voice low, "because hesitation is seen as weakness. Weakness invites chaos."

He scoffed. "Being a king doesn't mean you resort to violence and fear. There's a difference between being firm and being cruel."

Spinning around, I met his eyes. "Do you think I enjoyed what I did to Uncle Tobin? It was a necessity! I needed to assert dominance. To show that I won't be taken for granted or manipulated."

Dirk took a step towards me, his voice tinged with desperation. "But at what cost, Jormon?"

My heart pounded loudly, each beat echoing the turmoil within. "Do you think I wanted this? This crown, this...burden? I'm eighteen, Dirk. This was supposed to happen years from now! But now that it's mine, I have to bear it. And sometimes it means making choices I hate, that will keep me up at night."

He paused, studying my face, searching for the Jormon he once knew. "I just miss the old you," he whispered, his voice breaking.

The pang in my chest was sharp, immediate. "I miss him too," I admitted. "But this situation we're in, our people need a king who's willing to make the hard choices. Even if it means becoming someone else."

Dirk's eyes grew misty, and he took a shuddering breath. "And what about us? What happens to us if you continue down this path?"

"It doesn't change how I feel about you," I said, my voice raw with emotion. "I love you, Dirk. But you need to understand, this is bigger than just us." Shit. I said it. I told Dirk I loved him on this day of all fucked up days. My face flushed. It wasn't supposed to come out like that.

He pulled me close, holding me tightly. I could feel his heartbeat, steady against mine. "I've waited a long time to hear anybody say that to me."

"And? Are you going to say it back?" I whispered, holding onto him as if he were my anchor.

Dirk pulled back slightly, holding me at arm's length. His gaze, previously soft and concerned, hardened. "Do you remember what Noan used to say?"

I stiffened. "Why bring him into this?"

"Because Noan," Dirk replied, his voice laden with emotion, "he balanced you. You probably couldn't see it the way we could, but it's true. He would have been heartbroken to see what you did to Mr. Tobin."

I felt the sting of Dirk's words. "You think I don't know that? Do you think I want to be this person? This king who's ready to harm his own family? But Noan... He was never truly tested. He never had to bear the weight of the crown. Maybe if he had, he'd understand the choices I have to make."

Dirk's hands dropped to his sides, his face a mask of anguish. "You don't give him enough credit. He faced challenges in his own way. And he always led with his heart."

A bitter laugh escaped my lips. "And where did that get him?" Dirk took yet another step back, and I felt a surge of regret. "I didn't mean it that way. It's just... I'm so scared of losing myself. There's a rage inside me, Dirk. An anger that's always been there but now... now it feels magnified. With each act of violence, with each betrayal, with every time I have to exert my authority, it grows. I fear that one day I won't recognize the man in the mirror."

The corners of Dirk's lips twitched into a gentle smile. "I remember the first time I met you. You were so different from anyone I'd ever met. So calm and brave, at least that's what I thought back then."

"And now?" I asked.

He took his time answering. "Now we are at war."

We got in bed without washing. He closed his eyes, and I admired his face. Tears collected in the corner of his eyes, but they never fell. They sat like little mirrors, distorting my reflection as I stared into them.

I don't remember falling asleep. I don't remember dreaming. I woke up and Dirk was gone. The spot where he lay was still warm. I pressed my nose into the place where his head was. It smelled of smoke. And of him. I smiled.

It was the light that caught my attention, the distant glow of little fires overhead as mortars connected with the shields protecting Gray Flats, then came the thunderous sound as those shields gave way.

CHAPTER TWENTY-NINE
DIRK

"WHAT WAS THAT?" I ASKED. MR. TOBIN CURLED UP IN a single bed, beads of sweat pooling on his head and dampening his pillow. He gagged into the bedside trashcan I'd just emptied into the commode, and paused as a series of faint thuds sounded overhead. His eyes, already big, grew bigger.

He fumbled a hand, and I took the hint and hoisted him up. Just as we made it to the window, a bomb exploded in the yard directly in front of us. The force sent us flying against the far wall, and shards of glass stung my face as window fragments shot at us like daggers. The impact left me with a deafening ringing in my ears. In the suddenness of it all, I forgot every *sahdr* I had ever learned.

"Get me to my study," he said. I got to my feet, and another explosion shook the trailer so badly my legs bucked from under me. Panic set in. The metallic tang of blood filled my nostrils, and I could feel wetness on my face. It was a moment before I realized it was my own blood mixing with Mr. Tobin's. The distant cries and shouts of others in Gray Flights rose above the din of destruction.

"We need to move, now!" Mr. Tobin's voice was weaker than I'd ever heard, but there was an urgency that spurred me into action.

Debris from the room scattered around the floor, and we shuffled slowly through it. Mr. Tobin's arm was slung over my shoulder, and he was using every ounce of his strength to keep pace. Every step was an agony of effort.

The hallway was littered with broken glass. I maneuvered us around it, doing my best to protect him. Each time the ground shuddered under another explosion, Mr. Tobin's grip tightened around my shoulder.

As we neared the study, another explosion and a piercing scream echoed through the corridor. "Lura," Tobin said. He pointed to the closed door across from the study.

I paused, torn. Every second mattered, but I couldn't just leave them. "Hang on!" I shouted, adjusting Mr. Tobin so he could lean against the wall for a moment.

I pushed open her bedroom door and was met with a powerful wave of heat, carrying with it the stench of burning flesh. I couldn't bear to look, but I had to. I stepped inside the room. A large hole was blown into the ceiling. Ms. Lura lay sprawled on the floor, her clothes and skin blackened. A gaping, seared cavity had been torn through her abdomen, edges curled back to reveal organs and seared flesh within. Blood pooled underneath her, coagulating from the intense heat. My stomach turned, and I puked against the wall. As I left the room, I saw the door to the study had already been opened. Mr. Tobin stood beside the replica of the city hovering in the middle of the room. Flashing above it in dark red lights read the count of Kaydans remaining. 501… 496… Another explosion rocked the trailer. 477.

"We need to stop this," I said.

"I'm not good to anybody in this state," Mr. Tobin said. "You go. Go, now! Save everyone you can."

"And what are you gonna do?"

He closed his eyes briefly, as if gathering strength, then met my gaze with an intensity that froze me in place. "I need you to get a message to Noan for me. Remember it well, because it's for you too: Phae will guide you to the answers you seek."

"I don't get it. Huh?"

"Never mind. Go. Find Jormon. Save who you can."

I couldn't leave him. He'd die for sure if I didn't do something.

"Go!" he screamed, and a strong force sent me crashing into the hallway. Mr. Tobin collapsed into the ground just as the door slammed in my face. I pounded on it, but it was sealed shut.

I had to keep moving. I dashed down the stairs and found Jormon, Rughor, and Phae huddled near the front door.

"…I can do it," Phae insisted.

"What are we talking about?" I asked.

"Dirk!" Jormon shouted. He sprinted to me and grabbed me in a tight hug. "I didn't know where you were." When he pulled back, his face was wet with tears.

"I'm okay. Where is everyone?"

"Everyone is everywhere," Jormon said. "Drac is taking the old folk down to the bunker. Lheniva's staying with the injured. Everyone who can shield is spread out in the trailers. As for firepower, we lost a lot of that when Hargi left. How's Uncle Tobin and Nana Lura?"

"Upstairs," I said. "Safe." There was no need to tell him the truth, not when he had so much to worry about.

"As I was saying," Phae began, "we need to see what we're up against. I can go. My powers won't be blocked if they're carrying L.I.G.H.T.s—Lights, whatever."

"No," Jormon said. "I need you here. If all else fails, you are our last protector."

"I can go," Rughor said. "This is probably my dad's fault. I owe it to everyone, even if it means the end for me."

"Ugh. Don't be so dramatic," Phae said. "Fly high. I'll provide cover."

"Witch's magic is as reliable as a flashlight in a horror movie," Rughor quipped, but his sad eyes betrayed the half smile he gave.

"Well, if you find yourself up there suddenly exposed, blame it on my shoddy magic and not on my deep hope that you die," Phae said with a wink. Their eyes met, and an unspoken understanding passed between them.

Outside, the sky grew angry. Rain poured as fiercely as the mortars, and lightning seemed close enough to touch. My skin itched from the inside.

"Go," Phae said to Rughor. "I'll have you on comms." She tilted her head and opened her mouth, and white smoke escaped. It swirled overhead and separated into thin wisps that lashed out in all directions. Latched onto us.

Rughor pushed open the door. A distant boom caused him to freeze with his hand still on the knob. Finding the courage, he launched into the air. Immediately, his eyes became our eyes; his ears became our ears. What he saw and heard stopped my breath.

A massive hoard of Riders, more than I'd ever seen before in my life, maneuvered around the fringes of the trailer park. Their armor gleamed menacingly in the flashes of lightning, and the pounding rain reflected off their helmets, making them appear as a tumultuous sea threatening to drown us all. Behind the main force, several Riders loaded and fired mortars, each explosive rising in a trail of smoke and crashing in a blossom of fire.

Phae's storm whipped through the park, turning debris and remnants of destroyed homes into projectiles. It howled and moaned, creating a symphony of despair that meshed with the Riders' war cries.

"We have to do something," I murmured, more to myself than to anyone else. The realization that we were vastly outnumbered, and out powered sunk in, but retreat wasn't an option. We had to defend ourselves. It wasn't enough that we hunkered down and shielded ourselves. We had to strike back.

The tingling in my skin grew more intense, ebbing like a wave in sync with the rhythm of the storm outside. It felt as if my body was resonating with the very energy of the atmosphere. A memory flashed in my mind, a conversation I had with Jormon about the Storm Riders—the *mustediin* who could attach their essence to lightning and traverse the skies. Could that be? Could I be a—

"Dirk?" Jormon's voice broke through my trance, snapping me back to the present. "What are you thinking?"

As I looked out into the stormy abyss, an audacious idea began to form. "I think... I think I can help."

"Dirk, you can't go out there. Look at them. They're everywhere!" Phae protested, but I could see the hint of hope in her eyes, the possibility that I might have a plan.

Without a word, I took off towards the door. The wind howled in protest, battering against the fragile shelter, but the pull from the storm was too powerful. I needed to be out there, amidst the chaos.

"DIRK!" Jormon's voice echoed in desperation, but it felt distant, drowned out by the howling wind and roaring enemy.

I stepped outside and felt the full force of the storm. Rain drenched me within seconds, and the wind threatened to knock me off my feet. My heart raced in tandem with the flashing lightning and thunderous roars above.

Taking a deep breath, I jumped. As my feet left the ground, a brilliant bolt of lightning struck. Instead of the pain and finality I expected, I felt an exhilarating rush. I was no longer a spectator of the storm; I was a part of it.

My senses expanded, and the energy of the storm coursed through every fiber of my being. I was one with the lightning, a conduit of its immense power. The landscape below was a patchwork of fire and destruction, but from this vantage point, it was stunningly beautiful. I got lost in the feeling, and I barely registered the danger as the sea of Riders pulled out their rifles and fired into the trailer park.

CHAPTER THIRTY
NOAN

THEY'RE IN TROUBLE. THE THOUGHT FILLED MY brain the way a train's horn fills your ears.

"Taavi, wake up. They need our help. Taavi, get up!"

"What's happening?" He wiped his eyes slowly.

I was already out of the tent, staring into the distance at the dark clouds swirling over Gray Flats.

"Holy shit, Batman!" Taavi's eyes squinted in confusion.

"There's a feeling I get when Jormon is afraid, and I'm telling you, he's scared shitless right now."

Sean crawled out of the tent and joined us. "Damn," he whispered, taking in the chaotic panorama.

"He's in trouble, we can't stand here doing nothing."

"And you're sure we'd be welcome back? I mean, the last time I saw him, I was flying into the building *he* was attacking to save the people who are now attacking him."

"My brother's an ass, but he's not stupid. He needs our help."

"What's the plan?" Sean asked.

"I say we open up a portal into the trailer and have everyone escape," Taavi said.

"You can't—"

"Yeah, yeah. Can't open a portal into a manipulated space. I forgot. Sorry. What about the serpent's thingy Tobin did to get us all to D.C. that time?"

"I can't do that, but you gave me an idea. Did our trailer survive the attack the other day?"

"Yeah, why?"

"I have a plan. I think I know how to help everyone."

"Care to enlighten us?" Taavi asked.

"We head in. You provide the shields. I'll do the rest."

"What about me?" Sean asked.

"I can't ask you to help my brother." Worse, I couldn't ask him to fight against his own people. If his dad and brother somehow survived the church fire, they'd likely be in the front lines looking to settle the score with Jormon.

"I'm not going to stand here and do nothing. Let me go. I can fight. I will fight for you."

"Hey Sean, nothing against you, bro, but sit this one out," Taavi said.

I opened a portal to the front porch of our trailer. As it opened, the sound of gunfire rang in my ears. Taavi stepped through first, and I followed quickly behind. All around us, tempestuous winds swirled. Flashes of light burst in the darkest pockets of the storm, revealing the ranks of men closing in on the trailer park. But then something changed—their advance halted, some clutching burnt rifles in disbelief. Above them, lightning danced through the sky, a brilliant display of nature's fury. *Phae?* I thought as each bolt leapt from cloud to cloud before striking down with surgical precision.

I flexed my arm and fire came to life in my fist. *My powers still work from here. That's good.*

The barrage of bullets drew my attention to the east. Riders had their weapons pointed at a figure in the sky, a figure surrounded by an iridescent tan shield. Whose colors were those?

"Taavi, go up and help whoever that is. Not sure how long the shield can hold. *Dura meed. Dura nur.*" I stacked a metal shield around the base of the trailer and surrounded it with a shield of swirling, raging fire. Steam rose up in rapid waves as the rain met the undying flames. "If you see this fire go out, that means the power blockers have stopped us. It means—"

"I know what it means," he said. The look on his face matched mine. Anxiety. Fear. Sadness.

"If it goes out, go high and far. Stay out of range so you don't fall."

"Or get shot. Got it."

I placed a hand on the side of his face. The rain made his skin slick and smooth and masked his tears just so. "We'll make it out of this. Now go!"

Two mortars bent towards us. I cast them in shadow, and they were gone. Gone into the shadow plane to explode in the vast nothingness.

With a final nod, Taavi lept into the air and flew up and out of sight. I tried the door handle. It was locked. I banged with my fist coated in an orb of pure energy, and the door exploded inward. Jormon stood at the end of the foyer. Blue flames circled his body, and as I stepped through the door, he shot the fire directly at me. "*Dura maai,*" I whispered, and an orb of water formed around me, catching the heat of Jormon's attack."

"Noan!" he cried. He ran to me and grabbed me in the deepest hug he'd given me in my life.

"It's good to see you too, Big Brother. It's good to see you, too." For a while, we just held each other. His fear poured into me, and all I could do was cry. The overwhelming sense of responsibility pressed against my chest until I couldn't breathe, and still, I held him. His worry became mine, the gnawing fear he wouldn't be king in the wake of our father's death. That feeling morphed into the self-doubt Jormon felt during the first attack on Gray Flats. The suffocating uncertainty, the questions that plagued his mind, the 'what-ifs' and 'if-onlys.' A swirl of emotions, all tinted with a shade of helpless vulnerability. Then there was rage like a blazing inferno. I could see the church, its spires high and mighty, as he set it alight, feeling a twisted sense of satisfaction as it crumbled and turned to ash. A dark, vengeful force that threatened to consume him. Finally, the swirl of sadness, anger, and betrayal as he leeched Uncle Tobin. Jormon's desperation, the battle within him as he grappled with choosing between duty and love, and ultimately making a choice that would haunt him.

Jormon, what did you do?

Tears streamed down both our faces as we pulled away. "I didn't want any of this," he whispered, voice cracked and broken.

A flood of memories rushed through my mind. All the moments Jormon had stood a little taller, eyes alight with the unspoken belief that he was born to lead, that he had the answers. I recalled the countless times he'd challenged Uncle's decisions, sure of his own wisdom. It was always there, this drive in him, barely contained and now breaking free. "Jormon…this is all you ever wanted," I said, wiping my tears. "But that's a conversation for another time. Where is everyone?"

Jormon filled me in quickly as bullets pinged against the shields surrounding the trailer.

"I saw the lightning outside, but I thought it was Phae. You're telling me Dirk jumped into the storm? Like a Storm Rider?"

"I couldn't believe it either."

That certainly changed things for the better. "I have a plan, but I'm not sure if it'll work. If it does, promise me you'll get everyone out. Don't try to fight them, just leave, leave as fast as you can."

"Noan, what are you gonna do?"

"Just promise me!"

"Okay, okay. I promise."

"Good. If Dirk's what you think he is, he can hold the Riders back as long as Phae keeps the storm going."

Phae caught my eye from over Jormon's shoulder, and I was struck by the transformation. The girl who once seemed quietly lonely and indifferent to fitting in had vanished. In her place stood a radiant woman, commanding the elements as if she were a maestro at the helm of a grand orchestra. Her body was enveloped in an ethereal glow of raw energy, each movement she made akin to the stroke of a conductor's baton, directing a forceful symphony of wind and rain. I'd never seen her so vital, so utterly alive.

The room grew darker. I whipped around to face the door, only to find the fire shield extinguished. My pulse quickened. Blockers were in range, suppressing our defenses. The Riders were zeroing in. Dirk and Phae, valiant though they were, could only do so much against the incoming swarm of enemies.

"Get everyone out!" I shouted, dashing up the stairs, which flattened and disappeared with every step as the *sahdr* manipulating the trailer waned and gave out. The blues and red of *Zereq* and *Heemrah* faded, leaving behind the white stipple ceiling. I needed to get to my room before the two-story trailer collapsed into a single-wide heap of junk.

I sprinted as fast as I could as the floor disappeared beneath my feet. The walls faded, and through them I could see into Uncle's study as rows of books rained down from their vanishing stacks. The fading digits "369" caught my eye, dissolving into thin air. Only then did I spot it—Uncle Tobin's lifeless body sprawled on the floor below. My breath caught and I stumbled, nearly falling. I pushed through the door to my room just as it disappeared and lunged for my nightstand. I snatched the drawer open, and there they were. A handful of *soulfangs*. They came alive at my touch, snapping at my arm as my bedroom floor vanished, and I fell through the air. The *soulfangs* latched onto both my wrists. Just as I hit the floor of the room below, the darkness from within me hissed out. I didn't panic like before. I embraced the pain and let the world around me go darker and darker until I couldn't see or feel anything.

Lightning flashed all around me, but even the powerful bolts didn't cut through the darkness like they should have, the darkness spilling out of me and empowering my people. Still, Dirk guided each bolt with precision, and everywhere it struck, a yell sliced through the roar of Phae's storm, and a body collapsed to the ground. Nearby, muffled by the winds and the sounds of battle, I faintly heard my brother's voice yelling, "Through the portal, now!" My darkness had given them the time and power they needed. They were escaping.

And then, as footsteps pounded toward me, it all went black. I had drained myself to the last drop, and as my consciousness faded, I hoped my sacrifice was enough.

CHAPTER THIRTY-ONE
JORMON

THE WOODS SPREAD OUT AROUND ME, A TRANQUIL patchwork of shadows and beams of sunlight. My breath plumed in the chill air, merging with the mist rising from the snow. I found a spot on the edge of camp to sit and catch my breath. We'd saved as many as we could, but still, our numbers were eerily low. Even the thought of it caused my heart to sink. *This is what extinction feels like.*

We had no home. Gray Flats was little more than a graveyard, piled with the bodies of hundreds of Kaydans and thousands of humans. Drones hadn't patrolled the trailer park since Mayor Kuss took office, but they were back now, buzzing overhead. So many lives had been lost on my watch. I closed my eyes and let the tears fall. Would things have gone differently were Noan in charge? Was attacking Riders the wrong thing to do? I'd never know, and the best I could do to keep my people safe was to stay the course. The Riders—the world—needed to know that Kaydans would no longer stand by and become victims of a system that was never meant to serve them.

"Jormon?" Dirk's words interrupted my thoughts, and I wiped my tears away. "You told me to get you when Noan woke up."

"Oh. Thanks."

I walked over to the cheap tent. Sean sat at the entrance as though he was Noan's bodyguard. I nodded my appreciation, and he stood and walked over to the fire. I approached cautiously, each step crunching the frozen terrain beneath my boots. Kneeling beside him, I gently brushed a hand across his brow. His face bore the weight of my decisions, of our battles, of our losses. For a moment, I allowed myself to be drawn into the peaceful allure of his countenance. It was a rare sight seeing Noan so vulnerable.

A sharp pang of guilt pierced through me. He'd always been there, standing by my side, supporting every decision, even the ones he didn't agree with. And now, all these months later, as I stared down at him, I wondered if perhaps he'd done too much for me.

Softly, I whispered, "Noan, what did you do?"

His eyes fluttered slowly open. "It's good to see you too, Big Brother." He attempted to sit up and reached a hand to me for support.

"I'm serious, Noan. What happened back there?"

"I had a theory. Remember back at the Ball when the *soulfang* bit me and the room filled with smoke?" I nodded. "Afterwards, when Taavi came to help me, he told me he'd never felt so powerful. It got me to thinking that whatever was seeping out of me enhanced his powers. I figured, maybe, just maybe, it would be enough to out power the blockers. I was counting on it, actually."

"It definitely helped. I was completely powerless until the shadow hit me. It felt like I'd been jolted back to life. Rughor and I were able to start shooting flames again, Dirk's lighting picked up tenfold, and Taavi portaled everyone out. That was good thinking, Noan. Without it, we'd all be dead." As if our minds were perfectly in sync, we drew a collective breath. Uncle Tobin was dead, and it was my fault. Nana Lura was dead, and it was the Riders' fault. Whoever was to blame, it didn't make them any less dead, and it didn't make it any less sad. I—we—didn't get to have a farewell moment. There were no words of pre-parting forgiveness. Nana Lura died, and the last thing I did for her was treat her like the help. Uncle Tobin died, and the last thing I did for him was...

Noan placed his hand on mine. "Did he get everyone out?"

I nodded. "He even managed to find you in the darkness."

The air seemed to hang in a weighted silence, each awkward second ticking by like an hour. My eyes met Noan's, then quickly darted away. He wouldn't like what I had to say next, but I had to say it all the same. I took a deep breath and remembered I was his king, too. "You might not agree with me on this, but we need to attack the Riders."

"For *Zereq*'s sake, Jormon. Haven't we been through enough?" He stood slowly, cautiously and left the tent. Outside, Dirk and Sean waited. "Running away, leaving this place, it's our best shot."

"There was a time, long ago, when I might've agreed. But now? After everything we've lost? They need to pay."

Sean's posture grew rigid. Dirk stepped forward and said, "Mr. Tobin told me something before he…before he died."

Dirk shared Uncle Tobin's final words with us. Noan's eyes sparked with enlightenment. I was still in the dark. "What does that mean?" I asked.

"It means we actually have a way out of here. A way back to Kayda. We don't have to attack anyone, Jormon. We can just leave."

"We can't leave," I insisted. "Not now. Not after everything we've been through."

"The humans won't stand for it. These were Riders who attacked us this time. What if it's the whole damn U.S. military who comes to retaliate."

"We'll be ready for them," I said. And I meant it.

"Why are you telling me this? It looks like you've already made up your mind."

"I need your help. I'm not asking you to fight, but I need you to find them."

"I don't have the strength, Jormon." He held up his arms, showing me the tiny bite marks on both wrists.

"Find the strength. The Riders will regroup. We need to stop them now."

"If I do this for you, if I help you commit mass murder, I don't think I could ever talk to you again."

"I'll find a way to be okay with that."

It was Dirk who spoke next. "Jormon, do you hear yourself? This is your brother. He's all you have left. Don't do this."

"I'm doing this for him. I'm doing this for you, too. I'm doing this for all of us."

He shook his head as he slowly backed away, his boots leaving deep imprints in the snow. "You're doing this for yourself." And then, with a turn of his heel, he was off.

As I chased him, I brushed past Rughor, Phae, and Taavi in my haste, their shocked expressions a blur. "Go to Noan," I managed to yell back, my voice heavy with emotion. "Let him fill you in."

I found Dirk leaning against a tree. The silent forest seemed to hold its breath as we locked eyes. I tried to speak, but he raised a hand, silencing me. "Jormon, I love you, you know I do. But this isn't the way." His voice broke, the pain evident. "I can't do this. I'm not a soldier."

"But you're a survivor, Dirk. Look at where you are. Look at where you started. I just watched you ride a lightning bolt and zap our enemies by the dozens. You're so powerful now. You're fulfilling your destiny."

"Is that what you think this is? Destiny? How can I know my destiny when I have no clue who I am?"

My voice caught in my throat as I tried to find the right words. "You're Dirk. You're a storm rider! You're the love of my life."

His next words were almost drowned out by the sorrowful sigh of the wind. He swiped at his eyes, wiping away the tears that threatened to spill. "I've never cried this much in my life, and I'm so tired of it. You think I'm strong, but I'm not. Not yet, at least. You go off and be the big, bad king who demolishes the enemy and saves the townspeople, but I need to find out who I am before I'm… Before all I am is 'the love of your life.' I need to know myself."

A chill ran down my spine, one that had nothing to do with the snow around us. "What are you saying?"

His gaze bore into mine, a storm of emotions swirling within. "I'm saying that we need a break, Jormon. You need to find out who you are as king, and I need to find out who I am as Dirk, the storm rider."

For a moment, all I could do was stare at him, willing him to change his mind, to take back those words. But deep down, I knew he was right. The paths we were on had diverged, and perhaps it was time to face that truth.

Slowly, I closed the distance between us, reaching out to gently cup his face in my hands. His skin was cold from the frosty air, but beneath my touch, I could feel the familiar warmth, the heartbeat that had once resonated with mine. We locked eyes, both of us searching for something, some reassurance, some semblance of the bond that had once been unbreakable.

"Promise me this isn't the end," I said, my voice breaking.

Dirk placed his hand over mine, squeezing it gently. "You're the best man I've ever known. You're my PJ, and I will always love you for what you've done for me."

I looked up, meeting his eyes but feeling a wave of confusion wash over me. "PJ?" I asked, my eyebrows knitting together as I tried to decipher the unfamiliar term. "What does that mean?" Then it hit me. Prince Jormon. PJ. The nickname he never told me the first night we spent together. Simple and cute, and it used to be mine, all mine. As King Jormon, I'd lost both the name and the boy who gave it to me.

CHAPTER THIRTY-TWO
DIRK

IT TOOK A WHILE TO COLLECT MYSELF, AND BY THE time I made it back to the campsite, Jormon, Rughor, and Taavi were already gone. Phae searched the survivors to see if the Spirt Matron was among them, and Noan, drained from having to exert himself, rested in the tent with Sean as his dutiful guard. A small fire warmed the area near the tent entrance, but as I peeked my head inside to see Noan, I felt a chill in the air.

Noan slept with his lips parted and his arm thrown over his forehead. He looked so much like Jormon it scared me. He was thinner, though, maybe from living in the wild all this time. I let my eyes drift up and down his lean body, searching for what made them physically different. Sean misinterpreted my actions and said, "Getting wandering eyes? Jormon's not gonna like that."

"Huh?" I said before catching his meaning. "Oh, Noan? Never. He's like the brother I always wanted. Besides, I'm pretty sure he has a thing for you."

"What?" Sean sat up straight. "Noan isn't like that. He kissed me once, but it was for selfish reasons."

"Taavi said he saved you from being burned alive. Was that for selfish reasons, too?"

"That was different. That was life or death. I'm grateful that he did, but I don't want to look into it as anything more than what it was."

"And if he kissed you again after all of this, what would you say?" Sean paused for too long. I smiled a knowing smile and hoped that some good might come from us all having survived in this life so far. "Can I ask you something?"

Sean held his hands close to the fire. "Sure."

"You left your family behind to join us, and we might not last that much longer. Was it worth it?"

Sean went uncharacteristically quiet. "I could ask you the same thing, yeah?"

He had a point. Somewhere out there, my momma, daddy, and sister were probably seeing images of a burned down Gray Flats, scared I didn't make it out alive. It's probably for the best they think I died. It was too dangerous for Momma to show up again like she did after I got shot. Besides, I knew something about myself that I didn't know before. I was a storm rider, and though I didn't know anything about what that meant, it was a lead that would get me closer to finding out who I was, and that's what I came to Gray Flats to do.

"'Phae will guide you to the answers you seek.' Those were his exact words?" Phae asked. Noan wasn't back to full strength, but he was well enough to walk. Phae insisted we get away from the crowd. "The only place I know that neither of you do is... I shouldn't say. I'm not supposed to say."

"Phae, if you know something that can help us get answers, you have to tell us. It's what Mr. Tobin wanted."

She bit her lip. "Have either of you ever been to the Lake of Spirits?" she asked. Her eyes darted back and forth between Noan and me as we shook our heads. "It's the only place I know, but it can be dangerous if you're not careful."

It couldn't be more dangerous than getting killed in a trailer park raid, could it?

We walked for over an hour, and though I had traveled every inch of these woods sneaking around with Jormon, I didn't recognize where we were. The path began to wind clockwise, but no matter how far we walked, it didn't double back on itself. It bent tightly around, a spiral, perhaps, and just when I thought I might get dizzy from the turns, the trail ended at a puddle the size of a sewer hole cover. We leaned over it. Our dirt-tinted reflections stared back at us from the still, brown water.

"It's through there," Phae said.

It reminded me of the entrance to little Atlantis, and a sudden pang hit me as I reflected on times gone by.

"Are you sure it's safe?" I asked.

"It's safe enough."

I looked into the puddle, took a deep breath, and jumped feet first into the unknown.

I sank quickly through a dark vastness. There was brown all around, then blue, then I was on the other side, falling upward from the ground until I was on my feet at last.

I looked down at a turquoise puddle, the cleaner image of the one I'd just jumped through. I was alone in woods dissimilar from the ones I left behind. The trees were thicker by meters. The constant greens and browns of the Georgia pine trees were replaced with something far more colorful. A sea of green and blue Festuca grass covered the ground from here to infinity, curving around trees, broken only by their roots, some of which were so tall I couldn't see beyond them. The sun shone brighter, yet it was far cooler than before.

The sudden change was so disorienting I had to close my eyes to settle myself.

I stood there beside the puddle, eyes shut, waiting on the world to make sense. Moments into this, my breathing evened out, and I noticed the air smelled of petrichor. I loved the smell. Rain washed away the past, especially harsh rains.

"Hey, are you okay?" Phae asked. Noan stood next to me with the same sick look on his face.

"Yeah, I'm okay. Lead the way, would you?"

We walked more. Where the roots were too massive to go around, I helped Noan over. After a while, the autumnal air thickened until it was as dense as cake batter.

"Are we getting close?" I asked, breathing in thick, wet flows of air.

"It feels about right."

And so we walked more. And more, until the giant trees blocked the sun, and the only light came from the colorful, almost magical glow of the flowers sprouting in thick beds all around us. Our steps got shorter, as did our breath, and just when I thought I would need a break, Phae said, "It's just over there." She pointed in the distance, where the glow was brightest. "You have to go the rest of the way on your own, and guys, please be careful."

"How does it work?" Noan asked.

"Is my mother's spirt in there?" I followed.

Phae shrugged and shook her head slowly. "I can't tell you that." She pointed again, and I knew we'd get nothing else out of her.

We approached the glow, careful not to stamp out the lights of the flowers. The ground sloped until it dropped off completely, and down below in the floral canyon sat the most beautiful lake I'd ever seen. The waters churned and swirled, and Noan walked slowly into them.

My skin warmed against the chilly air, and I removed my shirt. I leapt from the grassy plateau and hung in the dense air, moving slowly closer to the water's edge. My feet touched down softly at the place where water met land. I took my shoes off and waded in the warm water. I stopped when the water was up to my neck. What next? *Momma, if you're here, please come to me.*

Nothing happened.

I walked farther, until my chin, then my nose, then the fiery tips of my hair were submerged. *Find me.* I released my energy into the lake, and the gold and silver particles shoaled this way and that like so many fish.

The water bubbled and churned, and a man's figure appeared in a yellow glow.

"Do you know who I am?" I asked.

"I know you don't belong here. This is the place where spirits go to rest."

"I'm looking for someone. For my mother. I hoped she would come to me if I called. I hoped she'd know that I need her now."

"Her spirit isn't here."

"How do you know? Who are you?"

"If she were here, she would have come when you called, just like I did."

"I didn't call you. Why are you here?"

"I'm here because we share the same blood."

"Are you my father?"

"No, son. I'm no one's father. I'm a warrior. A hunter. An uncle."

"I don't understand."

"I was sent to Maerin to find my nephew, the stolen child of Ormr and Qila. If I heard your call, then you are their child."

"Where are they? Are they on Earth? Are they alive?"

"Your real parents were never on Earth. They never left Gaalind."

My real parents were never here. My head swirled. They were never sucked through the rift. The people I thought were my Kaydan parents stole me from them. But why?

My chest burned from the news. No, not from the news. I'd been holding my breath this whole time. I just had a few more questions.

"Sir, tell me about my parents. What were they like?"

"You can't stay here. You don't belong here."

"Here in the lake? Here on Earth? What do you mean?"

"You must go now."

"Wait! I have more questions."

The yellow glow dulled until all could see was lake.

"Come back." I waited until my chest burned and I couldn't stand it any longer.

I swam to the surface and filled my lungs, then plunged back in. I called and called, but he never came back.

I don't know how I made it back to the surface, much less onto the thick grass near the water. When I came to, I was supine in the flower bed. Noan lay beside me, and Phae was on top of him, pinning his arms down.

"What happened?" he asked.

"You happened," she said, more calmly than I imagined she would. "That thing happened. You were in a trance."

My eyes moved up from Noan's face to his outstretched hand. It was round and black and covered in glyphs, and it looked as heavy as a cast iron skillet.

"I thought the lake was calling to me. I thought it was Father," Noan said.

"When I found you, you were at the bottom of the lake holding that thing. There's no telling how long you'd been down there. I was waiting for you at the top but you never showed up."

Noan lay there, catching his breath. "Do you know what this means? It means we're free."

"I don't understand," Phae said.

"This is our ticket home. We can leave Earth!"

CHAPTER THIRTY-THREE
NOAN

THE NEWS THAT I HAD FOUND THE *MIFTAH*—THE key to leaving Earth—was met with mixed emotions. While some were eager to return home, to know what had become of Maerin after our sudden departure, others looked anxiously toward King Jormon for guidance. Nonetheless, the air was tinged with a sense of change, and we united in celebration. That night, people danced in the open air, unbothered by the threat of another attack. Happy to be alive.

I don't know when the music began, but it played on, switching beats so seamlessly at the hands of an unseen DJ. I watched from my perch on a high branch of a nearby tree as their bodies moved slowly this way and that. And they laughed—oh, did they laugh. The beautiful sound reached me and beyond. The music was great. It was the laughter that hurt. The thing that reminded me they were a community, and I was an outsider. An other. The one to blame when all other excuses fail. It didn't matter that I'd risked my life to save theirs. Nothing I could do would ever be enough.

Jormon joined me when the gathering was at its liveliest. He sat so close that his leg touched mine as we let our feet dangle off the limb.

"Do you remember the time before we could fly, when we climbed that one tree in Gordonia Park, and you fell and broke your arm?" Jormon asked.

"I remember you pushing me off the branch."

Jormon shot me a sideways glance. "I didn't push you. I lost my balance and tried to grab onto you."

"And I fell because of that, didn't I?"

"Yeah. I didn't mean to, though."

"I don't think you ever mean to hurt me, yet I always wind up getting hurt."

He sighed. "It does happen that way, doesn't it?"

"I don't hold it against you, not all of it. I've played a part in setting myself up to get hurt."

"But our relationship is more than just pain, Noan. Tell me you see that."

"I do. It's love, and love can be pain. It was like that from the beginning."

"What do you mean?"

"My earliest memories are of us as kids. I'd wait around the hut with Uncle until Nana Lura brought you by the gardens. He'd see you coming from through the rows of flowers, and I'd tell him to comb my hair to look like yours. I wanted to look as much like you as possible. I figured that if you saw yourself in me, you'd want me to stay with you."

"I never did," he said, looking down at the ground below.

"Not once. You'd wave goodbye like you were ending a playdate, and I'd go back inside and cry."

"Every time?"

"Every single time."

We sat for a while in silence, listening to the music being carried by the breeze. "What about now? I'm asking you now, Noan: stay with me. I need you now more than I've ever needed you before. Please, don't go."

I shook my head. "It's probably not obvious to you, seeing how we are strolling down memory lane, but I hate you, Jormon."

Concern flashed across his face as he said, "You don't mean that."

"But I do. Because of you, Uncle is gone. Nana Lura is gone. I love you because I have no one else to love. But I hate you, too.

The only reason I'm not screaming at you now is because, come tomorrow, I'll be gone as well."

He inhaled deeply, hiding the sting of my words, if he felt it at all. "Just know that you're always welcome in my kingdom, however tattered it may be."

"You can leave, too, you know?"

"I can't go back there, Noan. All my life I thought that's what I wanted, to go back to Maerin and grow to be king there, but that's not for me anymore. I want to finish what Dad started here, except I want to try things my way."

"The violent way? Your Malcolm X to his Martin Luther King Jr.?"

"I wouldn't put it that way, but yeah, maybe. Dad saw something in our belonging here. If humans come to accept us, we'd be a great contribution to life here."

"They've always seen us as a threat. Attacking them won't change that idea."

"They've seen us as a lesser race as a way to dismiss our greatness. I want to show them we're great."

"At what cost? What if you get everyone killed? Do they know what following behind you means?"

"I'm not asking them to do anything they don't want to do."

"What happens if they refuse to obey your orders?"

"I'm still king."

Whatever that means.

The lively music changed to something slower. People were now sitting cross-legged in the grass as bubbles of fire floated just overhead.

"I heard you were a real terror out there," I said.

"I wouldn't put it like that," he said casually.

"After I came back with the *miftah,* I overheard Rughor telling someone that you all burned the whole city to the ground. Even the high school."

Jormon shrugged. "Eh. That sounds about right. I need the world to take us seriously. Now they know what kind of leader I'll be."

I shook my head. "They won't let this stand, you know. Where do you go from here?"

"Toombs County is now ours. Ayida is working on a way to shield ourselves from outside attacks. Where do you go from here? Will you stand with me? We could use the help as we rebuild."

I didn't know where I would go from here. I didn't know what awaited me on the other side of the rift. How had Maerin changed after thousands of people got swept up in the middle of the night?

Jormon looked at me for the first time, waiting for my answer.

"For so long, I wanted to be by your side. If you had asked me this question last year, I would have pledged my life to you. Now I have to pledge my life to me, and I can't do that here." I looked past the survivors down below, enjoying their victory and living life to the fullest before the next challenge comes. They'd never want me the way I needed them to, so it was better not to need them.

"It feels weird to stand around like this, like it's the first day of school all over again and we're waiting on Lheniva to give us a pep talk," Phae said. Except it was different to that. None of us were the same people we were back then.

"I half expect her to show up with a cigarette dangling from her lips as she says 'children…you look beautiful,'" Taavi said.

"You all do look beautiful," I said, looking out at the dozen or so people who decided to hop the ride back to Kayda. "It's a shame she's not coming with us."

"I thought there'd be more," Phae said.

"It probably would be if someone else was leading them," I replied.

Sean pushed through the small crowd. "Wait!"

"We already said our goodbyes. Did you come to see me off, too?" I asked.

"No. I'm coming with y'all."

"I don't think that's a good idea. Go home, Sean. Your house is right where you left it."

"I don't belong out there. I won't belong out there until things are made right. As long as there's warring between Kaydans and humans, I'll be torn down the middle."

"This is a big decision, Sean. What if the rift closes when we go through, and you can't get back?"

"Then I'd be okay, as long as I'm with you. You've always made me feel like I belong."

"And you've always made me feel comfortable being myself. Sean, when I hugged you before, you said it didn't mean the same thing to me as it did to you."

"I remember that. On your birthday."

I put my hand on the back of his neck and let our eyes meet. I wanted him to see inside me, to see enough to know I meant what I was about to do.

His lips were cold, but the kiss warmed me all the same.

"You were right when you said it then, but things have changed. I have changed."

"We get it," Taavi said. "We've all changed. Can we get this show on the road?"

"Not until—here they come."

Jormon and Dirk held hands as they slowly walked over. Their eyes were as red as cranberries. "Dirk, really? You're gonna miss me that much?" Taavi joked.

"No, he's going to miss me," Jormon said.

"Nooooo. Why would you? I don't get it."

"I need to find where I belong. I can't do that here." Whatever he and Jormon needed to say had already been said. Dirk kissed him one last time and let free his hand.

"Jormon—King Jormon. My big brother. Are you sure you don't want to come with us? Please, let's go together. Let's take this next step as a family. We can dislike each other when we get where we're going, but at least we'll all be safe."

"I'm not here to change your mind, Prince Noan. Please, don't try to change mine."

But I've never been without you, not entirely, I said to him.

He mussed his hair, then he did the same to mine. *So that I'll recognize you when I see you again.*

The sadness swelled like a heavy breath, but I didn't let it show. I held on to the feeling in case I never got the chance to feel it again.

"It's time to go," Taavi said.

Time to go. Time to move on. Time to move onward.

The rain fell beautifully on that cold February day. Taavi grabbed onto Sean and made a comment I pretended not to hear. Together, they rose into the air, followed by Phae and Dirk. Jormon's eyes streamed warm tears as Dirk's feet left the ground. With a nod, I was off, too. We flew up, up, up toward the light of *Heemrah*, and still, the rain fell beautifully.

I didn't look down at the world I was leaving. I knew that world, and I wouldn't miss it. As the rain drenched my hair and patted my face, I looked up to the sky and thought about something Uncle told me a long time ago when looking down was all I'd ever done. *Look up into rain that falls and see a different beautiful sky. A beauty we miss looking at the ground to shield our eyes.*

Acknowledgements

So it comes to this, the "thank you to all" and "appreciation for everything," and I couldn't be happier.

The first two people I want to acknowledge were alive when I first started *Trailer Park Prince* but who I lost along the way. The first of them, Adam Posadas, was a brilliant writer whose flame died out too soon. He was my sounding board and constant battle buddy. If you ever meet me, ask me what he meant to me as a friend and fellow author. More than my husband, more than my mother, Adam would be the most excited to see what has become of this book. The other, Wesley Sims, was a lovable idiot who I spent countless hours trying to convince to pick up a book. I know for certain he'd be a fan of *Trailer Park Prince*.

This story has gone all over the world with me. I wrote my very first words at a Green Beans café in Afghanistan, sweating over my keyboard until an alarm sounded, warning us a rocket attack was imminent. I continued writing upon my return to Washington, D.C., sometimes at Politics and Prose while sipping on a London Fog, and other times at Kramerbooks & Afterwords waiting on my then-boyfriend-now-husband, Tal Rosner, to finish a shift waiting tables. I shelved it for a while, ultimately picking it back up during my years living in Mexico City, Mexico, sometime between COVID-19 and the adoption of our son, Shai Bradley Rosner. This is where more thanks enter the scene.

Thanks to my husband, who graciously picked up the slack when my writing kept me up in the late hours of the night. For the diapers changed (Shai's, not mine), solo walks he took while I finished writing a scene, and all the ways he gave me the liberty to write when we were unsure if this book would ever see the light of day, I give many, many thanks.

Thanks to my son, Shai, who is, if nothing else, a constant motivator. I think back on all the times he saw me typing away and wanted to join in. It's impossible to write good prose when a one-year-old is sharing your keyboard, so I had to write quickly and be done with it. I will remind him of that for the rest of his life.

To my mother, who shines through many characters in this book, thanks for always encouraging me to keep at it. To Stephen Savioli and Jeff Vance, thanks for sharing your opinion when I needed it the most. To Rickey Adderly, my best friend, former roommate, and the most voracious reader I know, thanks for your guidance and rapid reviews when it came time for me to pitch this book.

I must also give thanks to Scott Dewey, who did an amazing job with the cover. We met in the online lobby of a video game back in…2015? He is a talented artist, and I'm grateful he was able to take on this project alongside his other work. I'd like to give a special thanks to Monica Odom of Odom Media Management. She was the first person in the industry to make me think I could actually do this.

This brings me to Joshua Perry, who saw all the good in *Trailer Park Prince* and made it better. He also saw all the soft spots and firmed them up just so. It was amazing to find someone as invested in the lives of Noan, Jormon, Dirk, Taavi, and Phae as I was, and through that mutual investment, we worked hard to give the reader the full Trailer Park experience. I'm extremely happy with the resulting story, and I couldn't be more grateful for Tiny Ghost Press.

If you're reading this, it's with thanks to Reuben Davies-Hoare, who was responsible for getting the book out to the public, and to Lewis Hughes for marketing this book from Toombs County to Kayda. Thank you both. And thanks to Tim Frost for his diligent copy editing. I gave you the cleanest version I could manage, and like any professional, you found the dirt and dust and wiped it all away. Thank you to Thomas Shah and Jeremy Gibson, the editorial assistants who provided support throughout the process. The Tiny Ghost team is a mighty beast, and I owe so much to them.

More than anything, thank you, dear reader, for diving into this story. Now that you've made it off the ride, I hope you feel you know a little more about me. This story has been a part of me for so long that it's inevitable I would have left parts of me on every page. I do hope you enjoyed it.

About the Author

Andre Bradley is the author of adult and young adult fantasy fiction. He began his writing journey in 2006 as a young soldier serving in Iraq, and he has been creating people, places, and things ever since. Andre is from Vidalia, Georgia—home of the sweet onion—and though he has lived all over the world, he currently resides in Rockville, Maryland with his husband, son, and two dire wolves (ahem, regular dogs), where he works as a U.S. Diplomat.

Learn more at andrelbradley.com or by following @drebrad on Twitter (or whatever it's called now), or @billysgoatgruff on Instagram.

A ROMANCE TO HOWL HOME ABOUT

BOOKS ONE AND TWO IN THE BESTSELLIN

THE ALPHA'S SON

SERIES ARE NOW AVAILABLE!

AVAILABLE IN PRINT, EBOOK & AUDIOBOOK

WWW.TINYGHOSTPRESS.COM
@TINYGHOSTPRESS

www.ingramcontent.com/pod-product-compliance
Lightning Source LLC
Chambersburg PA
CBHW011602210726
48287CB00012BC/2680